FREEFALL

A HIGH RISK NOVEL

FREEFALL

A HIGH RISK NOVEL

JoAnn Ross

A SIGNET BOOK

SIGNET
Published by New American Library, a division of
Penguin Group (USA) Inc., 375 Hudson Street,
New York, New York 10014, USA
Penguin Group (Canada), 90 Eglinton Avenue East, Suite 700, Toronto,
Ontario M4P 2Y3, Canada (a division of Pearson Penguin Canada Inc.)
Penguin Books Ltd., 80 Strand, London WC2R 0RL, England
Penguin Ireland, 25 St. Stephen's Green, Dublin 2,
Ireland (a division of Penguin Books Ltd.)
Penguin Group (Australia), 250 Camberwell Road, Camberwell, Victoria 3124,
Australia (a division of Pearson Australia Group Pty. Ltd.)
Penguin Books India Pvt. Ltd., 11 Community Centre, Panchsheel Park,
New Delhi - 110 017, India
Penguin Group (NZ), 67 Apollo Drive, Rosedale, North Shore 0632,
New Zealand (a division of Pearson New Zealand Ltd.)
Penguin Books (South Africa) (Pty.) Ltd., 24 Sturdee Avenue,
Rosebank, Johannesburg 2196, South Africa

Penguin Books Ltd., Registered Offices:
80 Strand, London WC2R 0RL, England

First published by Signet, an imprint of New American Library,
a division of Penguin Group (USA) Inc.

REGISTERED TRADEMARK—MARCA REGISTRADA

Printed in the United States of America

PUBLISHER'S NOTE
This is a work of fiction. Names, characters, places, and incidents either are
the product of the author's imagination or are used fictitiously, and any resemblance to actual persons, living or dead, business establishments, events, or
locales is entirely coincidental.

The publisher does not have any control over and does not assume any
responsibility for author or third-party Web sites or their content.

ISBN: 978-0-7394-9274-1

To the military men and women who stand in harm's way around the world, and to the families who stand by these sons, daughters, brothers, sisters, husbands, wives, fathers, and mothers, awaiting their return home. Those of us who enjoy our country's blessings owe you all a debt of gratitude for your service.

And to Jay—cheerleader, best friend, supplier of chocolate, and the forever-after grand love of my life.

Acknowledgments

Heartfelt thanks to Robin Rue, matchmaker agent extraordinaire and empress of lunches.

A huge thank-you to the wonderful people at NAL, who made writing this first of my High Risk books so much fun: Leslie Gelbman; Kara Welsh; Claire Zion (who rescued my first manuscript from the slush pile so many years ago); my super editor, Laura Cifelli; Rachel Granfield; and Oceana Gottlieb and Anthony Ramondo, whose talented art department created a cover guaranteed to heat up frigid February nights! Thanks also to Rick Pascocello and Craig Burke for the enthusiastic welcome.

With gratitude to the always fabulous Iris Johansen, who took time from her own writing to read *Freefall*.

Thanks to FBI Special Agent Gary L. Kidder for answering my questions.

And last, but certainly not least, a special thank-you to all my readers, who've made it possible for me to live my dream these past twenty-five years.

We few, we happy few, we band of brothers;
For he to-day that sheds his blood with me
Shall be my brother.

—WILLIAM SHAKESPEARE, *Henry V*

1

Swann Island, South Carolina

In her dreams, Hallie Conroy was married to a hottie heart surgeon who could have graced the cover of any of the romance novels she devoured like Godiva truffles. Together they lived with a pretty four-year-old princess who looked like her, a six-year-old ball of energy whose dazzling smile—an echo of his father's—could make her forgive his youthful transgressions, and a shaggy English sheepdog named Nana straight out of Peter Pan.

Her suburban home was tastefully furnished with pieces handed down through the generations of her family. A family that, like so many others on Swann Island, traced its roots back to the American Revolution.

In her dreams, Hallie's life was blissful. Beyond perfect.

In her dreams, Hallie wasn't in a cage.

She heard the crunch of tires on gravel. The sound of a car engine cutting off. One door shut. Then a second.

Her heart sank.

Closing her eyes, she leaned her head back against the steel bars. Although it had been a very long time since she'd believed in that hell-and-brimstone vengeful God she'd been taught to fear as a child, Hallie prayed to survive this night.

2

Chief Petty Officer Zachariah Tremayne had been shivering in the bite of a lingering Afghan winter for three hours. Not that Zach minded being cold. Or waiting. Being uncomfortable and forced to wait was part of a SEAL's job description. He'd known that going in, from stories his old man told about the long, wet hours hunkered down in the swampy waters of the Mekong Delta, waiting for Charlie to show up.

But in this case, for every minute that passed, the closer they were to the mission going south.

Which damn well wasn't an option.

Bad enough that the moon was riding across the sky like a gazillion-candlepower spotlight.

Worse that the sky, which had been clear as crystal only five minutes ago, had begun spitting wet snow.

Worse yet that they were only three hours and fifty-eight minutes from sunrise, and if there was one thing that would be more dangerous for his team than humping up the side of the damn Kush mountain beneath a full moon, it would be climbing it in daylight, when they'd be silhouetted against the white snow and gray sky.

It was rotten luck that the first helo had burned up an engine, requiring a replacement to be flown in from

Bagram. Then they had to wait for the newly arrived bird to be refueled.

And just as they'd finally climbed aboard the Chinook, damned if the delayed timeline hadn't gone crashing into a B-52 bombing raid on nearby mountains that lit up the sky in a psychedelic pink, yellow, orange, and purple northern lights–type display.

As cool as it was to watch, the demonstration of American firepower was one more thing eating up the clock. It was vital for the planners to get their collective ass in gear.

Now.

While last week's earthquake may have shaken things up, the mountainous land in the lawless area along the Afghan/Pakistani border had already become destabilized as various factions struggled for supremacy.

Recently one al-Qaeda leader dubbed Rambo—due to his tendency of going off on his own tangents rather than sticking with any united terrorist program—had begun a move to control the entire region. Making matters worse were his taunting videos, which had put him in U.S. military crosshairs.

According to the latest intel, Rambo was holed up in one of the many subterranean tunnels. Zach's SEAL team had been tasked with finding the ratlines supplying him, locating the "bat cave," then calling in massive amounts of ordnance on it.

Having shared his take on the situation with enough brass to start their own Afghan marching band, Zach was cooling his heels with three other members of the team, breathing in the sweet airfield scent of jet fuel and oil, when Lieutenant Mike Roberts came out of the command post.

"We've got two choices," Roberts said as he spread out a map on the metal floor of the Chinook. "Since there's no way we're going to be able to reach the LZ in time to make the climb in the dark, choice number one is to abort and delay until tomorrow."

"I vote for bumping twenty-four hours."

Studying the map, Zach already knew what was behind door number two. And it wasn't pretty.

"That's what I advised command. But given that they've been getting a lot of pressure from Washington, I was instructed to 'seriously rethink' choice number one."

"Meaning there *is* no choice number two." *Shit.*

"This mission is also getting bigger."

"How big?" Zach asked suspiciously.

"We've taken on some non-operatives. A couple of CIA guys."

"Not surprising." There were probably as many spooks in these mountains as locals.

"And the Marines want to play."

Of course they did.

"How substantial a contingent?"

"A security unit of nine. Ten with the captain."

Zach thought about that for a minute. Bringing in the Marines could create some command and control problems. But then again, with the jarheads taking care of security issues, including holding sniper positions, Zach's team would be able to concentrate more fully on their mission.

"I suppose we can always use a few more guns," he said.

"That's what I told them. Which is why I went along with the army throwing in some Rangers."

"Hell, next we'll all be wearing party hats and breaking out the piñata."

"There's more."

"Of course there is." Given events so far, Zach should have expected nothing less

"Sorry." Roberts ran his hand through hair that he, along with the other members of the team, kept long to blend into the general population when the team went undercover. "Mach-11 swept the area for any activity and cleared us to go in. But they've been called off to assist troops in combat and won't be able to cover us."

"Screw that."

SEALs routinely pushed the envelope. More than pushed. They tore through it on a regular basis.

But there was risk.

And then there was reckless.

Wading into a full-bore hot zone without gunship coverage was flat-out reckless.

Zach dragged a gloved hand down his face. "We're going to be sitting ducks slogging up that hill."

"That's why we're changing the LZ to the top."

Yet another choice that wasn't a choice.

Landing on the top of the mountain would be like putting flashing red lights and sirens on their helmets, jumping up and down and shouting, *Hey, here we are, all you insanely armed radical insurgent terrorists! Shoot us!*

Then again, if you looked up "flexibility" in the dictionary, you'd find it under "Special Operations Warfare techniques."

"If they want someone who needs the risk reduced to zero, they might as well send in some Girl Scouts," Zach muttered.

It was the lieutenant's job, as ranking officer, to define the mission. Zach's job was to figure out how to get it accomplished.

The difficult his team could do immediately.

Impossible took a little longer.

The good news was that their pilot, Shane Garrett— a member of the army's elite SOAR Night Stalkers— was the best copter jockey in the business. He'd shuttled the team on so many successful missions over the past nine months, they'd come to think of him as their lucky charm.

Minutes later the ungainly-looking Chinook finally lifted off, carrying Zach's team along with the Rangers, the Marines, and the two CIA agents, one of whom Zach

recognized from their days hunting Saddam in Iraq.
Team members flipped their night vision goggles—
which, along with providing an advantage over the
enemy, added to their badass reputation—down over
their eyes.

A cloud moved across the silver-dollar moon, plunging
the inside of the copter into pitch-black darkness. But
Zach could see Quinn McKade—who'd been in BUD/S
training with him before becoming the team sniper—
seated next to his spotter, Sax Douchett, a Cajun from
south Louisiana who was moving to whatever jazz was
coming through the earbuds of his iPod.

Lucas Chaffee, a medic trained by the navy, was doing
a last-minute check of his "Mike" bag. Chaffee, a guy
who followed the old axiom Hope for the best, prepare
for the worst, was loaded for bear with a vest pack,
backpack, supply bags hanging from both the vest and
the backpack.

A heavy loaded Mike bag ran around twenty-six
pounds. Knowing that Lucas always added more stuff
that he'd collected from sources around the world, Zach
guessed he was carrying thirty pounds of supplies. He
hoped to hell the medic wouldn't get the chance to use
any of them.

The scene below, illuminated in an eerie green by his
NVGs, showed mud walls separating acres of hardscrabble farmland covered in snow.

The helo was flying without lights, but the binocular
goggles transformed the night into a bright landscape.
Zach could see the outline of each of the mud rocks
making up the walls, could count the trail of dual foot-
prints in the snow to one field, where, despite the isola-
tion and the hour, two men stood.

Dressed in long tunics and billowy pants, they looked
up as the Chinook passed overhead.

They could be harmless. Probably were. After all,
these mountains had been home to Afghan goatherds
for centuries. How they managed to live and work at

fourteen thousand feet was something Zach—who'd grown up at sea level on Swann Island, off the lowland South Carolina coast—couldn't begin to fathom.

Or they could be the enemy and were even now calling ahead on some damn cell phone, warning of the American helicopter.

As the Chinook flared to land, its huge tandem rotors churned furiously in the thin mountain air, kicking up clouds of ice and snow around the windows and ramp. The team silently gathered at the open ramp hinge as they'd done hundreds of times before.

Sticking to their motto, Rangers lead the way, the army guys insisted on being the first off the bird. The Marines would follow and set up a defensive perimeter.

The lieutenant would be next. Then McKade, then Douchett, then Chaffee. Zach would be right behind them.

The Chinook was still hovering when Garrett shouted, "RPG!" from the cockpit.

The rocket's fiery glare was blinding as it hurtled toward the left side gunner's door.

As machine-gun fire began raking the Chinook, the rocket-propelled grenade slammed through the side, rocking the huge bird like a roundhouse punch. It sliced through hoses, spraying hydraulic fluid all over the team before blowing McKade's M4 to pieces.

Then all hell broke loose.

3

Florence, Italy

Something was very, very wrong. Sabrina Swann should have felt on top of the world.

Well, perhaps not exactly the *world*.

But certainly her little corner of it.

After graduating high school at sixteen, then racing through college in two and a half years, she'd scaled the hospitality corporate ladder and now, two months before her twenty-seventh birthday, she'd been appointed manager of the Paradiso Angeli Hotel in one of the most beautiful, romantic cities on the planet.

It was a dream come true. No, better than a dream. It was a shining fantasy that had dwelt in both her heart and her mind for years.

Although the hotel was part of the worldwide Wingate Palace hotel chain, there was nothing "chain" about it. On the contrary, it combined all the conveniences of a five-star American hotel with the refinements and idiosyncrasies that had once made the City of Flowers the center of the artistic world.

Rather than having to endure the overwrought gilt, crystal, and heavy satin that made so many luxury European hotels appear to have been decorated by Marie Antoinette, visitors to Paradiso Angeli came away with a deepened appreciation of everything the Renaissance taught about perspective and harmony. The hotel was a former monastery built atop the ruins of a first-century Roman temple, and, Sabrina suspected, its past residents would have appreciated the fact that every room had been named for a saint and was under his or her protection. She also wondered if the lush sensuality of the rooms might have more than a few monks spinning in their tombs.

But as much as she valued Florence's splendorous history, Sabrina had never been one to dwell on the past. She'd always prided herself on looking forward to the future. And her future was looking downright rosy.

"So, what the hell's the matter with you?"

Oddly and uncharacteristically depressed, she poured a self-congratulatory glass of champagne from the bottle that had been sent up—along with a single crystal flute, which looked a bit lonely—on a silver tray from room service. In contrast to her strangely subdued mood, the wine sparkled like sunshine on water.

Sure, she was tired. Okay, perhaps, if she were to be perfectly honest, she was exhausted. For the past six months, she'd been averaging four hours' sleep a night in order to keep the hotel running like a Swiss watch. The pampered, jet-setter guests at Paradiso Angeli had come to Italy to bask in La Dolce Vita, and they were accustomed to receiving exactly what they wanted. When they wanted it.

Those sleepless nights had paid off, as her promotion proved.

Surely it would get a little easier now that her probationary period was over and she no longer had the chain's New Orleans–based home office second-guessing every decision she made—from the color of the damask napkins in the newly redecorated banquet hall, to the uniforms of the bellmen, to the hiring of a tennis pro to go along with the new red clay courts that had been built behind the formal gardens.

She swiveled her hips across a tile floor that was the rich earthen hue of a Tuscan vineyard. Then, although no one was around to witness her sorry attempt at a happy dance, she still felt unreasonably foolish.

"So, you're dancing on the inside." Wasn't that what her grandmother Lucie had always said about her?

The thought of her grandmother put a touch of tarnish on her day.

Sabrina sighed as she took her champagne out the French doors to the wrought-iron balcony, where the view spread out beneath her like a Renaissance painting.

In the distance, ancient stone hills the color of flax were touched with gold by the setting sun. The vineyards and olive groves reminded her of the Swann family's tea plantation, which, in turn, caused a little pang of homesickness.

She'd only spent summers on Swann Island, yet since she had grown up in boarding schools and hotel rooms, her grandmother's house was the closest thing to a home she'd ever known.

"I should've gone back. Before it was too late."

You didn't know she was sick, a pragmatic voice of reason in the back of her mind assured her, just as it had when she'd first learned of Lucie Somersett Swann's fatal heart attack.

It hadn't eased her guilt then.

It didn't now.

Sabrina blew out a breath. Took another sip. Directly below, the fabulous Neptune Fountain harked back to a time when Cosimo de' Medici was building his fleet of galleys, determined to make his city a world naval power. It was here that the strict social critic Savonarola had convinced Florentines to light the bonfire of the vanities and burn their ornate clothing, jewelry, and tragically, even much of the city's most exquisite art.

Those same citizens, chafing beneath laws banning gambling, vice, and frivolity, subsequently burned Savonarola in another, final bonfire.

Shoppers thronged the Ponte Vecchio. Back in the

fourteenth century, the shops on the bridge had sold fruits and vegetables to locals, but these days they sold silver and gold jewelry to tourists, who remained blissfully unaware of any ancient edicts against adornments.

Across the cobblestone Piazza della Signoria, on a balcony where a lazy cat lay curled among crowded clay pots of flowers, a young Sophia Loren look-alike braided the hair of a small girl whose perfectly oval face belonged on a cameo, while a blind man sat on the stone steps of the Palazzo Vecchio, at the feet of a copy of Michelangelo's *David*, singing plaintively about a lost love. The liquid, weeping sound of an unseen violin picked up the melody from some open window.

Despite having nearly half a million citizens crammed together in a small area, Florence, known as the jewel in the Renaissance crown of Italy, lacked the hustle and bustle of Rome, partly because it was such a pedestrian city, with many of the streets and squares closed to cars. The slower-paced life reminded Sabrina of the American South. Of Swann Island, in particular.

She'd promised her grandmother she would be home for Christmas. But then the assistant manager's wife had given birth to twins, and the concierge had eloped to Venice with the sous-chef, and, well, Sabrina couldn't leave the hotel without a guiding hand over the holidays.

Right on the heels of New Year's came La Fiera del Cioccolato Artigianale. The annual chocolate festival always brought in tourists.

February was out of the question. While Carnival might not be quite the spectacle it was in Venice or Rome, the hotel was filled to capacity and the staff, encouraged to dress in costume, could, if not carefully managed, get caught up in carnival fever and allow the Paradiso Angeli's standards to slip.

Lent was usually a slow time, the only festival being the popular Festa della Donna celebrating women, which was why the home office had chosen that month to repaint both inside and out and replace the lobby carpeting before the horde of summer tourists arrived. It had, needless to say, fallen to Sabrina to oversee the work.

And hadn't her grandmother claimed to totally understand the impossibility of coming home for Easter? Not only was this a hugely important time in such a Catholic country, but people came from all over the world to attend the first major folk festival of the year: the Scoppio del Carro, or Explosion of the Cart.

Every Easter morning, going back centuries, a cart loaded with fireworks, drawn by two white oxen and accompanied by costumed revelers and various city officials, entered the Piazza del Duomo and stopped in front of the cathedral.

With much fanfare, a mechanical white dove flew down a wire and ignited the cart, setting off a well-choreographed sequence of flashes and explosions. According to legend, if all went according to plan, the people of Florence would be guaranteed good harvests and a prosperous year.

So, one thing had led to another, and now it was June, her grandmother was dead, buried in the family cemetery without fanfare, as her will had instructed. But that hadn't stopped the flood of legal papers from Lucie's attorney regarding her inheritance. Also, the mayor kept e-mailing her about a planned memorial service to celebrate Lucie Swann's incredible life.

And still Sabrina hadn't returned.

"Soon. Maybe for the service," she murmured, knowing it was a lie.

No way was she going to be able to get away now that she had achieved her goal.

Lucie would've hated everyone making a fuss, that little voice piped up again. *You're only respecting her wishes by not having any part of the public circus.*

Sabrina wished she could believe that.

A newly married couple, the woman dressed in a beaded white fairytale gown, riding in one of the carriages so popular with tourists, passed beneath her balcony, the horse's hooves clip-clopping on the cobblestones. The groom's arm was wrapped around his bride's shoulder; their faces were close together. Obviously enraptured with each other, neither was paying any attention to the scenery.

When the bride closed the distance, lifting her smiling lips to her husband's, Sabrina experienced an odd little twinge of envy.

How long had it been since she'd had a man's arms around her? A man's lips on hers? A lover whispering sexy words in her ear as the groom in the carriage was openly doing?

Much too long to remember.

Well, that was another thing that was going to change. Now that she'd won her promotion, it was time for a new goal. How hard could it be to find herself a lover? Florence was, after all, a city overflowing with gorgeous men who tossed out seductive compliments like confetti on New Year's Eve.

And while she lacked the smoldering dark looks and voluptuous curves so popular in this country, males seemed to find her long blond hair and green eyes an intriguing change from the women they'd grown up with.

Of course, those very same males, from what she'd been able to tell, were not the most monogamous of creatures. Which would prove a problem only if she were looking for happily-ever-afters.

Which she definitely wasn't.

After all, as much as she loved the country, the city, and the people, as beautiful as the Paradiso Angeli was, Sabrina figured she had two years, maybe three, before she was transferred again. The worldwide hotel business did not lend itself to long-term relationships.

Determined to enjoy this moment, she was thinking how little had changed since Michelangelo had passed through Florence, when a fish vendor's truck appeared on the street below.

"That's odd," she murmured.

Deliveries always occurred early in the morning. Usually before dawn. And certainly never now, when hotel guests were enjoying the end of the day in the courtyard garden with bottles of local Chianti.

Damn. Wasn't this all she needed on her first day? A fishmonger wheeling his crates of smelly iced mullet between the umbrella-topped tables?

She might no longer be on probation, but the trio who'd arrived from Louisiana to announce her promotion wasn't due to leave until morning. In fact, leaning over the railing, Sabrina could see them seated at one of the tables, dipping chunks of crusty Tuscan bread into the olive oil she bought from a local orchard.

She had turned to run back downstairs to forestall the problem when a blinding fireball exploded. Her eyes burned, as if she'd looked directly into the sun.

The balcony beneath her feet swayed. The world shook.

Screams filled air that only moments before had been floating with violin and song.

Sabrina felt herself falling.

Then mercifully, everything went black.

4

Zach had been in hot zones before. But damn, not this hot.

The enemy was peppering the sky with tracers, smoke was pouring in from overhead, flames were shooting from the hydraulics, and a big chunk of metal, which he guessed to be part of the back rotor, flew past the open ramp.

The Chinook began to spin. Not a single man in the back of the bird needed to be instructed what to do. Standing up on a deck slick with hydraulic fluid was asking for more trouble than even a Special Ops guy relished. Sitting down without back protection during a hard hit could crush a spine.

Zach hit the deck spread-eagle on his stomach—the better to distribute the impact throughout his body when they crash-landed.

A moment later they hit with a jolt. Rocked hard to the left. Then settled.

In a big empty field of snow.

A huge dark helicopter, sitting broken, on white snow beneath a full moon. Could they make a bigger target? Zach didn't think so.

They'd landed in an effing shooting gallery.

And they were the goddamn sitting ducks.

The fusillade of machine-gun fire being poured down on them was cutting holes into the metal sides of the bird. Quinn braced himself at the ramp, spraying return fire while trying not to slip on the oil that had turned the floor into an ice-skating rink.

Another RPG hit an oxygen tank hanging on the wall, sending sparks flying. One of those sparks started a small fire.

Grabbing an extinguisher from the bulkhead, Zach sprayed the fire with foam. Which got rid of the flames, at least for now, but filled the cabin with acrid black smoke.

With the final scene from *Butch Cassidy and the Sundance Kid* running through his head, Zach instructed the Rangers to hit the ground running.

The first guy got hit with a bullet in the back, right below his rear bulletproof plate. When he went sprawling, two Rangers grabbed him and dragged him behind the ramp, while a third started firing his M4 in the direction of the enemy fire.

Even knowing that this could turn out to be as bad as when their grandfathers had landed on Omaha Beach back on D-day, with shouted hoo-ahs, the remaining Rangers stormed off the Chinook, peeling to the left and right.

Although there'd been no hesitation, Zach couldn't see that any of them had a whole lot of choices. As the Marines stormed into the breach, he turned to the LT, who would be the first of the SEAL team to evacuate.

Shit. Roberts had gotten hit by shrapnel. His face was the color of wax. His eyes were open, but glazed. His chest wasn't moving, at least from what Zach could tell.

He pressed his fingers against the LT's throat. The barely-there pulse was thready.

With the LT out of commission, Quinn was the first SEAL to dive off the ramp. A bullet pinged off his helmet. He didn't seem to notice.

Zach had just lifted the unconscious Roberts onto his shoulders to get him off the copter, when he realized that he hadn't heard or seen either Shane or his copilot leave the cockpit. Which didn't make any sense, since there was no way this helo was going to fly again. He tried calling forward on the communication system, but either one of those wildly ricocheting bullets had hit a vital wire or the pilot was incapable of answering.

This was not the first time Zach had been shot at. If he survived this experience, it probably wouldn't be the last. But the idea of losing any team member, even one who wasn't technically a SEAL, made his gut clench.

Yelling at the two CIA guys—who were looking as if they wished they could have Scotty beam them back to their nice comfortable desks in Langley—to evacuate, he lowered the LT to the floor.

Then, staying low and trying to keep out of the way of the bullets whizzing over his head, with shot-up ceiling insulation falling on him like pink snowflakes, Zach crawled on his belly, arms stretched in front of him, toward the companionway at the front of the Chinook.

5

It was dark. Dark as midnight. Or a tomb. Or death.
Was that what had happened? Had she died?

Sabrina lifted her right hand, and although she was
holding it right in front of her face, she couldn't see it.
Something above her shifted with an earsplitting screech
of stone on stone. As she tried to wipe the thick, chalky
dust from her eyes, nose, and mouth, she began to cough.

Pressing her uninjured hand against her chest, she
took a few shallow breaths. It felt as if she were breathing live flames.

Over the distracting ringing in her ears, she heard the
frantic wail of sirens.

Acrid smoke, tasting of chemicals and melted plastic,
began to slip into her small space between the stones.

Although she dearly hoped it was her imagination,
Sabrina thought she felt the rocks getting hotter.
Whether they were or not, she feared that if she didn't
escape soon, she'd die.

Marshaling every bit of strength she possessed, and
using her right arm as leverage, she managed to push
herself up into a semi-upright position.

And slammed her forehead into the low stone ceiling.
Stars swam in front of her burning eyes. Her stomach
roiled again.

She fell back, hitting her head with a nasty thud.

And was instantly thrown into the void.

6

On those rare occasions when she allowed herself to think about it, Hallie would wonder how she'd gotten herself into this situation.

One thing she was sure of was that it had all been her snake of a husband's fault.

Jake Conroy hadn't been anything like the polite Southern boys she'd usually dated. Boys who would address her career military father as "sir" and remember to bring flowers to her mama.

Which had been precisely the point.

Jake had been exciting. Hot. A bad boy in black leather who actually owned a Harley, he hadn't been the least bit impressed with her straight-A average, but had told her, that first night they'd met, that the way her tits looked in her tight red cheerleader's sweater made his cock throb.

No boy had ever used such graphic language in her presence. And while her typical dates were not above trying to cop a feel while watching a movie in the back row of the Magnolia multiplex, never in all her sixteen years had she ever felt like such a sexual being.

She'd known, as a fever began to burn beneath her skin, that the bad boy known as Jake the Snake knew things. Wicked, dangerous, thrilling things. Things she wanted to know. Things she ached to experience.

Unfortunately, she'd been wrong. Jake turned out to

be far too selfish and concerned with getting off himself
to ever think about giving a girl pleasure.

Bad enough that she'd run off to Savannah and married him two weeks after they'd met, setting up
housekeeping in a tacky trailer park, which had experienced yet another meth bust last month.

When Jake turned out to be incapable of holding
down a job, she was forced to struggle to support them
both on what she made selling kitschy knickknacks in
the Swann Island village during the day and working as
a cocktail waitress across the harbor at the Somersett
Wingate Palace hotel six nights a week.

They'd been married a month the first time he stayed
out all night.

Which was when she should've left.

But to go crawling home to her mama and daddy in
shame, admitting she'd been so wrong, hadn't seemed
like an option at the time. Besides, hadn't Jake apolo-
gized? And come home with that filmy red baby doll
nightie from Wal-Mart?

He'd declared their makeup sex the best ever.

Not wanting to drive him away by being a nagging
wife, Hallie lied and agreed. And forgave him.

Until the night she'd stopped to toss a load of dirty
clothes into the washer before leaving for the hotel and
found lipstick on the front of his tighty whiteys. Which
she sure as hell hadn't put there. A subsequent search
of his jeans pocket revealed a credit card receipt from a
motel in Somersett. Not only was he a cheating snake,
he was a stupid one.

Putting two and two together, Hallie knew as well as
she knew her own name that his story about going deep-
sea fishing with the guys this weekend was a bald-
faced lie.

After her shift at the hotel was over, she drove to that
same no-tell motel, where she found him fucking some
bottle-blond bimbo.

She yelled.

Screamed.

Cursed like a drunken sailor on shore leave.

She snatched a lamp from the table and threw it at his lying, cheating head. She would've thrown the TV, too, but it was bolted to the damn dresser.

Meanwhile, the slut leaped out of the bed and raced for the bathroom. Hallie grabbed her hair, intending to pull every damn strand out by its bleached roots, but Jake caught her around the middle and lifted her off her feet.

Kicking ineffectually, she informed him that if his things weren't out of the trailer by this time tomorrow, she was going to burn them. She had a lot more she wanted—needed —to say, but when a voice yelled from the neighboring room that they were calling the cops, she decided the time had come to leave while she still had a bit of dignity intact.

She spent the next hour driving around aimlessly, unwilling to go home and face that wedding picture she'd had enlarged and framed, which was currently hanging on the wall behind their bed.

Capping off the shittiest night of her life, shortly after she drove off the ferry and onto the island, her right front tire began thumping on the road. Immediately afterward, the rear one started making the same ominous sound.

Damn. Bad enough she'd gotten one flat. But two?

She kicked the second tire and felt the sting of her toes hitting hard rubber all the way up her leg.

As she stomped down the dark, deserted road in the pouring rain, alternately sobbing and cursing the man she'd been foolish enough to marry, Hallie decided to cut her losses and divorce the snake.

Before things got even worse.

Before she ended up pregnant and stuck with a kid to take care of.

"I hope they both get a fucking incurable STD," she fumed.

The idea of Jake's prick being covered with oozing

red blisters was bringing a bit of comfort when she heard a car slowing down behind her.

She may have made a fool of herself over Jake the Snake, but that didn't mean she was a total idiot. She had, after all, been an honor roll student before she'd fucked up her life.

Hallie kept walking, her strides longer, her pace faster, the spike heels she wore to earn extra tips in the hotel's bar clattering on the uneven pavement.

"You're a long way from home," a male voice said.

Although the low-hanging clouds had covered the moon, turning the night as dark as a tomb, Hallie thought she recognized the voice bouncing around in the fog swirling all around her.

The car crept along beside her. "I passed your vehicle back there a ways on the road," the driver said when she didn't immediately respond. "Swann Island isn't the big city, but it's still not safe for a woman to be out so late, on a deserted road. And you're soaking wet. Why don't you at least let me drive you home, Hallie? And you can call the auto club in the morning."

Okay. He knew her name. Then again, everybody pretty much knew everybody around here. Wasn't that what made the place so damn boring?

And, she admitted secretly, wasn't that partly what had once made Jake, the outsider from the big city of Miami, so exciting?

Hallie heard the click of a lock. Then the passenger door opened. It would only be much, much later that she'd realize the interior light hadn't come on.

During her imprisonment, she'd come to fear him. And hate him.

It didn't take a degree in psychology to understand how auctioning her off like some nineteenth-century chattel last week had given him a sort of sick pleasure. His excitement had been palpable, rolling off him in hot waves as he buckled the black leather cuffs around her wrists, then raised her arms over her head, chaining her to the steel suspension bar hanging from the ceiling.

Displaying her in the most degrading ways, he moved his hands all over her body, turning her to show off the letter *S* he'd burned into her flesh.

The stranger's laugh had been rough with lust as he accepted the invitation to strike her on that brand.

Once.

Twice.

A third time.

The slaps stung, but things were about to get worse. Much, much worse.

The man, the *monster*, she'd made the mistake of trusting, had jacked off while watching her submit to another man's lash, being taken in ways most men only dared imagine in their darkest, most private fantasies.

Afterward, when he slit the man's throat—to keep him from ever talking about what he'd seen, what he'd done—Hallie threw up.

Which had only earned a second, more brutal beating that still had her peeing blood.

She heard the all-too-familiar crunch of tires on gravel. The sound of a car engine cutting off. A door opening and closing.

When the key rasped in the padlock, Hallie tensed, her heart pounding painfully against her ribs, unaware that this would be the night her desperate prayers to stay alive would be in vain.

7

The shouts of the rescue team as they cut through the heavy stone, tunneling their way toward Sabrina, sounded like a chorus of archangels.

It was going to be all right.

She was going to be all right.

"Ciao!" a deep male voice called out.

"Sono qui!" she shouted back. *I'm here.*

There was an earsplitting sound of stone scraping against stone as the barricade between her and freedom was pushed away, and then she felt herself being lifted into a pair of strong arms.

Into a nightmare.

A huge black cloud rose over a scene that could have burst up from Dante's lowest circle of hell. The moon, barely visible through the acrid smoke and dust, was bloodred. Chaos reined as wails rent air usually perfumed with the fragrance of flowers. Now it was scorched with the stench of cordite and burning flesh.

Body parts and shredded clothing were everywhere—lying on the cobblestones, hanging from tree limbs, floating in the fouled waters of the Neptune Fountain.

The hotel appeared to have simply collapsed in on itself, floor atop floor. The steel beams that had been added to strengthen the building over the centuries were twisted together like a snarl of snakes. Hundreds, thousands, of pieces of paper had been thrown high into the air and floated down like falling snow. Or confetti.

Two men in bloodied white coats rushed over, took one look at her, instructed her rescuer to put her on a stretcher, and began running.

As they fought their way through the crowd, Sabrina wondered if she was going to die.

8

Zach found both Shane and his copilot still seated in the cockpit. Like the LT, the copilot was dead.

"I tried kicking out the door," Shane told him as another round of fire hit the smoking instrument panel. "But nothing happened. I figured my flight suit had gotten caught up on something." He glanced down at his leg. "Guess I was wrong."

"I guess so." Talk about your friggin' understatements! The leg in question was spurting blood like Old Faithful. The material of Shane's flight suit had been blasted away, revealing flesh that was glowing green through Zach's NVGs.

"Shit." Zach ripped off a glove. "You're hit."

"It appears so," the helo pilot said mildly as he stared down at his smoking flesh.

"You've caught a tracer round." Zach dove into the wound with his bare hand.

Shane hissed through clenched teeth, proving, not for the first time, that an army flyboy could be as tough as a SEAL.

"How bad is it?" he asked.

"Hell, even for a Winnebago jockey, you don't rate a yellow tag," Zach lied. He pocketed the tracer, then took the lanyard off his 9 mm and using it as a tourniquet, tied it around Shane's bloody leg, right below the knee. "Maybe a green."

A green tag was triage talk for "walking wounded"—
injuries that needed treatment but were unlikely to dete-
riorate over a few days. A yellow was any injury that was
potentially life-threatening, a wound that would require
extensive treatment.

Which, although neither man was prepared to admit
it, was probably what they were talking about here. If
the pilot was lucky.

"Okay," Zack said as he handed Shane back his M4.
They both ducked as another round of machine-gun fire
tore through the cockpit. He unfastened the copilot's
seat belt and put him on his back. "Let's go get the LT.
Then we're out of here."

Pulling himself forward by his arms and one leg, dragging the other behind him, Shane followed Zach as they
crawled through the companionway to the back of the
bird.

Which was even more of a mess than the cockpit.

It was also on fire.

Again.

Not a good thing, given that they'd topped off the fuel
tank before leaving Gardez.

Anyone who'd ever watched *ER* would immediately
have recognized that Lieutenant Michael Roberts was
definitely a black tag.

Something the medic on the scene confirmed. "He's
gone," Chaffee said.

Roberts's eyes were open but glazed. His chest
wasn't moving.

Zach pressed his bare fingers, bloodied from having
gone spelunking in his best friend's leg, against the LT's
throat. Then shook his head.

He exchanged a look with the other two men and
knew they were all thinking the same thing.

It didn't matter that dragging two corpses through the
snow during a firefight would be time-consuming, ex-
tremely complicated, and meant a low chance of their

own survival. All that mattered was the code that all Special Ops forces, no matter their service affiliation, would, if necessary, follow to their own death.

Leave no man behind.

"Okay," Shane said, as wires jumped and sparked around them, bullets pinged as if they were inside a giant pinball machine, and this second fire, even more dangerous than the first, began greedily eating its way up the side of the bird. "Let's go show those tangos who's in charge of this show."

"Fuck!"

Yanking on the steering wheel of the pickup, Zach pulled over to the side of the oystershell road and slammed on the brakes.

Reaching into the console between the seats, he pulled out a yellow plastic lemon. His hands were—dammit!—trembling as he unscrewed the cap and shot a stream of the concentrated lemon juice onto his tongue.

Thank you, Jesus, it worked. The tart acid taste jerked him from what had turned out to be a slaughter in the Afghan mountains back to Swann Island.

He'd been stateside six months. After experiencing a flashback that had him pulling a gun on his dad, who'd stopped by the house to drag Zach out of the bottle he'd been trying to drown himself in, he'd reluctantly admitted he might, just maybe, have a small problem.

So he'd gone in for counseling, and while he figured it would be a long time before he got the images of that mountain battle out of his head—how about never?—at least he was able to fake being a reasonably normal person.

Most of the time.

He'd tried the antidepressants Doc Honeycutt had pushed on him, but they hadn't done anything for the nightmares, and had left him feeling flat. Empty. Which he supposed some people might consider an improvement over the flashbacks of battle.

Zach wasn't one of them.

Besides, he wasn't stupid. Nor was he ignorant about PTSD. Hadn't he seen enough cases of it up close and personal? He knew damn well he wasn't the first veteran to deal with post-traumatic stress.

And unfortunately he wouldn't be the last.

"One day at a time."

The military shrink at the VA hospital he'd gone to in Somersett when the flashbacks started getting out of hand had suggested he try talking to himself out loud, to remind himself that he was back home in South Carolina, not in a war zone.

Sometimes that helped.

Other times it didn't.

Which was why he'd locked his weapons away.

He'd lied when he promised to get rid of them. But hey, if there was anything he'd learned during his years in the military, it was that bad guys could show up when you least expected them to.

Better to be ready than sorry.

Which was why he'd kept his guns.

Just in case.

He'd also, on the shrink's advice, quit watching the nightly news. Which hadn't proven hard at all, given that most of it was flat-out depressing. Zach wasn't positive, but he thought the nightmares had lessened somewhat once he'd gone cold turkey on those twenty-four-hour cable marathons that he'd stayed up all night watching while trying to drink the state dry.

He was working on being more social again, too, like the shrink advised. Not isolate himself so much. Which was why he'd forced himself to drive into town and spend a couple hours at The Stewed Clam on the waterfront, nursing a non-alcoholic beer and knocking brightly colored pool balls into pockets.

And why he'd taken his dad up on the offer to do some construction work out at Swannsea Plantation. Although he was in better shape than the average guy, twelve hours of swinging a hammer had proven a lot tougher than he'd remembered from all those summer vacations working for his old man.

Most nights he went home and crashed. Which at least allowed for a few hours' sleep before the ghosts returned.

It had been two weeks since he'd last been ambushed by a flashback.

Three weeks since his last full-fledged panic attack.

"Which is an improvement," Zach reassured himself as he turned the key in the ignition and pulled back onto the road.

Plan for the worst, hope for the best, accept whatever happens. The SEAL saying was meant to be applied to combat situations, but since Zach was discovering day-to-day life could be a battle, he figured it applied.

He could do this.

Or he could let the ghosts win, sink deeper into the void, and end up one of those burnout cases who'd pop the first pill before getting out of bed, then spend the day hiding from the world in the dim light of a bar, lying to themselves about there not being anything wrong with tossing back bourbon and branch water for breakfast.

Which occasionally didn't seem like such a bad idea. If you spent your day buzzed out on booze and drugs, well, hell, you couldn't be expected to be responsible for anyone.

Which let you off the hook.

Until the day you climbed a tower or walked into a fast-food restaurant with an automatic rifle and let the demons hiding inside you escape.

Wasn't that a rosy fucking scenario?

Zach tensed at the flash of headlights in his rearview mirror.

"Just some civilian, driving home after a night on the town."

Maybe a couple who'd been out to dinner and a movie and were now headed home for some hot monkey sex.

Those were ordinary, everyday headlights. Not tracer bullets. Not the enemy.

He wasn't undercover in Afghanistan, or Iraq, or Russia, or some godforsaken, mosquito-infested Central American jungle. He was in the good old U.S. of A., in one of the most serene, molasses-slow-moving towns in the universe.

There was absolutely no reason for anyone to be following him.

To think otherwise was sliding back into Paranoiaville.

"You can absofuckinglutely do this," he assured himself for the gazillionth time as he pulled up in front of his rental house.

He *had* to do it.

Because the alternative was not an option.

One day at a time.

He waited in the truck until the car that had not been tailing him passed by. A late-model Volvo, which, last time Zach looked, was not exactly the choice of terrorists. He'd bet dollars to Krispy Kremes that there was a kid's car seat strapped into the backseat.

Taking a deep breath, he climbed out of the truck and, carrying his toolbox with him, walked up the steps to the front porch. The front door had three locks, which admittedly might be overkill, but Zach was going to fight his demons one day at a time, and triple locks sure as hell weren't hurting anyone.

He was beat, but wired from that flashback of what he hoped would be the most horrific day of his life. Because if things could get any worse, he wasn't certain he wanted to stick around to witness them.

He carried the metal box over to the kitchen table, spread out his tools, got some oil and a cloth, and began cleaning them.

After a mission, every SEAL put all the things he

might be aching for—food, sleep, a shower, a cold beer—on hold until his weapon was broken down, cleaned, and put back together. Because you never knew when you'd need it.

Okay, so the hammer and screwdrivers and chisels might not need cleaning. The thing was, Zach found routine soothing.

And these days a guy had to take his comfort wherever he could find it.

9

Three weeks later

Although the sun had long ago set, the air remained hot and dripping with humidity. Just another summer night in the Deep South. The salt-tinged breeze coming off the ocean lifted the hair off the back of Sabrina's neck, creating a bit of welcome natural air-conditioning.

A full moon floated across the sky, turning the water of Somersett Harbor to beaten silver. Gulls squawked, whirled, and dove for fish churned up by the wake of the ferry. Sabrina stood at the railing as they left the dock, passing by the towering statue of Admiral James Somersett, the privateer who'd settled the coastal southern city.

The crescent beach where she used to go beachcombing for shells, and where she'd often witnessed dolphins hunting schools of fish by driving them onto the sand, began on the south side of the island, then wrapped around the eastern coast that faced out to the Atlantic.

A panorama of wheat-colored marsh made up the west and north coasts and between them, on a long peninsula, Swannsea stood like a beacon, gleaming alabaster in the moonlight.

Sabrina hitched in a breath at the sight of the Swann family home. For a moment she pictured her grandmother, standing on the upper veranda, her hand shielding her eyes as she looked toward the mainland, awaiting Sabrina's arrival.

The image in her mind was so clear, so vivid, it was hard to believe Lucie wasn't standing there. Sabrina blinked. Then looked again.

Both verandas were empty.

As empty as she felt.

She tried, as she'd been doing for weeks, to console herself with the idea that no one could've expected Lucie Swann to die before her sixty-fifth birthday. Her grandmother had, after all, made the Energizer Bunny look like a slacker. Sabrina had traveled the world, met a lot of important, powerful people. Yet she'd never met anyone who possessed half the energy of her grandmother.

"Okay." She shook off the depression that always seemed to be lurking nearby lately. "You can do this." She took a deep breath before heading back to the parked car she'd rented at the Somersett airport. "One day at a time."

Things hadn't changed.

Sabrina hadn't expected them to.

That, after all, was the appeal of Swann Island. Once a home base for pirates, including the infamous Blackbeard—whose feud with fellow privateer James Somersett had filled the pages of dozens of books and was celebrated annually during Buccaneer Days with a mock battle in the harbor—the island had become known for both its bred-in-the-bone resistance to change and, even more than its neighbor on the mainland, its parties.

It was at such a party, the story went, that Margaret Mitchell had impulsively decided to use Swannsea as a model for Tara, in what would become her blockbuster novel. Of course, Lucie Swann had always been quick to point out when tourists would mention the similarity, there were more homeowners all over the South making the same claim than you could shake a hickory stick at. So who was to know, really?

What Lucie did remember was her own mama telling
her that the beautiful, vibrant Margaret, who could've
been a role model for her rebellious fictional Scarlett,
had cut quite a figure with her scandalous Apache
Dance, had enjoyed her Madeira, and had entered into
a flirtation—and, it was rumored, a sizzling affair—with
Junior Honeycutt, the island's dashing, and twice-
married, physician.

Sabrina opened the sunroof as she drove off the ferry.
The heat flooded in, turning the rental car into a sub-
tropical terrarium, but ever since the terrorist bombing
of the hotel, when she was buried alive, she'd been
claustrophobic.

Even with the Xanax her Italian doctor had pre-
scribed, the flight back to the States had proven horribly
nerve-racking.

Now, she felt a bit of tension release as she followed
the white shell road ribboning through the marsh.

After Eve Bouvier, CEO of the Wingate chain, had
encouraged her to take all the time she needed to get
back to full strength, it had only made sense to come
back to the island.

Not for any permanent move. Just long enough to
work out the kinks, get her sea legs back, toughen up,
and get back on that horse she'd been blown off of.

"Got any more raggedy old metaphors you want to
toss in there?" she asked herself as she turned onto the
narrow, winding road leading to Swannsea.

She'd also made the right decision to buy coffee, milk,
yogurt, and fruit at the Somersett Piggly Wiggly before
continuing on to the ferry terminal. She'd always been
a bit of a curiosity—Miss Lucie's Yankee granddaughter
from New York City—but now, after the bombing, she
suspected the whispers and murmurs she'd grown up accustomed to hearing would become a deafening clamor
of questions.

Questions she was reluctantly prepared to answer.

"But not tonight."

Tonight she wanted to settle in.

Driving through the mile-long tunnel of towering oaks, Sabrina thought back to the first time she'd seen the ethereal Spanish moss dripping from the broad tree limbs. She'd just finished reading *Gone with the Wind*, and to her vivid imagination, the moss had reminded her of feathery boas discarded by Southern belles.

Years later, it still did.

As she turned the last corner to the house, her headlights flashed on the ancient scar on the bark of one of the oaks. According to family lore, twenty-year-old Jedidiah Swann had been racing off to join the Confederate army when his horse, spooked by a nest of copperheads in a pile of rotting leaves at the roots of the tree, threw him, dragging him to his death and leaving his bride of two weeks a grieving widow.

The wound to the tree, the story went, had been created by the saber he'd strapped on to take into battle against the Yankees. The same saber his granddaddy Thomas had wielded against the British in the War of 1812.

Unbeknownst to either of the newlyweds, he'd left Anne Swann with child, thus ensuring that the Swann lineage would continue. Because their funds, earned from their lucrative tea trading business, had remained tied up in English banks during the War Between the States, the family had escaped ending up as impoverished as most of their neighbors once Lee surrendered his sword to Grant at Appomattox Court House.

That was the good news.

The sad news was that Anne never married again.

"Yet more proof that Swann women are unlucky in marriage," Sabrina said as she reached the magnificent house.

Not only had her grandfather deserted Lucie, but her own parents had married and divorced each other five times before their BMW roadster had gone over that seaside cliff in Monaco. Afterward, witnesses at a Monte

Carlo café had reported that they were shouting at each other as they drove away.

As tragic as their death had been, Sabrina had often thought her jet-setting mother would have at least enjoyed the idea of dying in the exact same place where Princess Grace had lost her life.

A single yellow light gleamed a warm welcome from an upstairs window.

Lucie's former housekeeper, who'd been with her since Lucie came to the house as a bride, had moved to Savannah to live with her daughter, but when Sabrina had called Lincoln Davis, who had taken over the day-to-day operation of the farm from his father, to let him know she was arriving early, he'd told her he would leave the lights on.

She hadn't realized he meant that literally.

The old carriage house had been turned into a garage in the nineteen thirties; the doors opened with a rusty, unused squeak. Sabrina parked her rental car next to her grandmother's battleship-sized, purple-finned Cadillac.

She would have to sell the car. Which, unless all those Elvis-conspiracy folks were right and the King turned out to be not only alive but hiding out on Swann Island, probably wasn't going to be all that easy.

One good thing about having her life blown up from beneath her was that she was traveling light. Even after she bought a few basic pieces of clothing and some cosmetics, everything she owned fit into two overnight cases.

Although she suspected the bouquet of perky purple heliotrope in a white teapot in the center of the kitchen table was another of Linc's welcome-home gestures, the familiar summer flowers made it seem as if Lucie would come walking into the room at any minute.

Not that her grandmother had ever merely walked anywhere. She always swept through life, like those cruise ships that were always steaming out of Somersett Harbor on their way to grand adventures.

Sabrina's eyes filled.

"Dammit, Gram. This wasn't the way things were supposed to happen."

Sabrina would be the first to admit that she was a control freak. Lucie, who had tried to loosen her up during her visits to the island, said that it was an understandable reaction to growing up with a father whose picture would no doubt be in the dictionary next to "Peter Pan" and a mother too wrapped up in her art gallery to even notice that she'd given birth to a daughter.

With Sabrina's parents traveling the world, Lucie had been the only real family she had ever known. And now, proving yet again that control was merely an illusion, her grandmother, like her parents, was gone.

Swiping at hot tears, Sabrina managed to put the yogurt and milk in the refrigerator before the jet lag that had been chasing her since she'd boarded her flight in Milan finally caught up, crashing down like a four-hundred-year-old oak.

She left the bag of coffee on a counter cluttered with a collection of antique teapots and dragged herself—and her overnight case—up the curving staircase and down the hall.

She paused in front of her grandmother's room—which was where the welcoming light had been coming from. It looked just the same—as if a crate of grapes had exploded in a overcluttered antique shop.

Everything, from the walls sprigged with lilacs to the fluffy violet satin comforter, matching drapes, and array of crystal perfume bottles in various shades of purple from palest lavender to plum, was just as she'd last seen it. The scent of lavender potpourri caused another flood of emotions as a mental picture of sitting out on the veranda with Lucie, stuffing dried purple flowers into pillows, flashed through Sabrina's mind.

She realized that along with selling the Caddy that the

locals had always called Miss Lucie's Grapemobile, she
was also going to have to do something with the rest of
her grandmother's belongings.

However, like Scarlett, Lucie's all-time favorite heroine, Sabrina decided she would think about that
tomorrow.

Her old bedroom also hadn't changed since that summer her grandmother had it redone as a surprise for her
sixteenth birthday.

The walls were still what the paint chip had called
ballet-slipper pink, while the canopy arching over the
bed was the darker pink of a peony.

Photos pinned to a white-framed bulletin board shared
space with a *Titanic* movie poster. One strip of photos
taken in a harborside booth during Somersett Buccaneer
Days made her smile. She and her best friend were sticking their tongues out at the camera, and two fingers appeared to be coming out of her head.

Although Sabrina and Titania Davis, Linc's sister, had
kept up with occasional e-mails and phone calls, they
hadn't gotten together for . . . what?

Six years?

Too long.

But she'd been so busy. At least that was what Sabrina
kept telling herself over all those days and months and
years.

Too busy for family.

Too busy for friends.

She'd never been all that introspective. But fatigue
and jet lag seemed to have tumbled emotional barricades
already lowered by the bombing. Although only three
weeks ago she would have vehemently argued against
the idea, it now occurred to Sabrina that perhaps she'd
grown up to be more like her parents than she could
ever have imagined.

She wasn't one to whine about being disadvantaged—
she'd certainly always had a roof over her head (even if

the roof in question belonged to either a hotel or a
boarding school), and she'd been granted anything material she'd ever asked for.

Gifts, she'd learned early, came easily for her parents.
So long as they were the material kind you could buy
in a store. Or, better yet, have a personal assistant pick
up on a lunch hour.

But it had been Lucie who had always given Sabrina
the gift of time.

As she stripped off her clothes and pulled the oversized La Fiorentina football jersey she used as a nightshirt over her head, guilt returned to weigh heavily on
her shoulders, like a wet wool blanket.

Going into the adjoining pink and white bathroom,
she brushed her teeth and washed the travel grunge off
her face, then returned to the bedroom, where she
opened the plantation shutters and threw up the window sash.

Night dampness and salt air, perfumed by the scent
of Confederate jasmine trailing up the trellis below the
window, rushed into the room, stirring the lacy white
curtains.

Sabrina didn't take the time to remove the menagerie
of stuffed animals she'd left behind before she collapsed
on the mattress. After too many hours alone in the dark,
she'd taken to leaving a bedside lamp on.

Nevertheless, every muscle in her body suddenly tightened as she heard a faint scraping sound from the attic
over the four-poster bed.

Instantly, every woman-in-jeopardy-alone-in-a-scary-
old-house slasher movie she'd ever seen flashed through
her mind.

It's only mice, she assured herself, attempting to shake
off the odd, tense feeling. Or, more likely, it was her jet-
lagged mind playing tricks on her.

Whichever. Although she'd always hated even stepping on a spider, she would have to buy some traps when
she went into the village in the morning.

Just in case.

The strange scratching sound ceased, and all she could hear was the familiar island music of the sea and the buzz of summer cicadas outside the open window.

It was only your imagination, she assured herself. *Only Swannsea settling for the night. The way all old houses do.*

She took several slow, deep breaths, as one of the counselors who had rushed to Florence after the bombing had taught her. Coaxed her body to relax.

As a waning sliver of moon continued its journey across a cloud-scudded sky, beneath the benevolent gazes of Kate Winslet and Leonardo DiCaprio, Sabrina passed a long, restless night chasing sleep.

10

"Jesus." Twenty-year-old Randy Beaudine lay sprawled on the backseat of the pimped-out Mazda. "Are we still alive?"

"For now." Madison Fraiser managed to get a hand between their sweat-slick bodies and pressed it against his bare chest. "But I'm at risk of suffocating to death if you don't get up so I can breathe." She pushed harder. "Besides, I'm not about to risk that condom leaking."

"Spoilsport."

It was what she always said. Not that Randy could blame her. To hear her tell it, she'd had her career mapped out by the time she was seven years old, back when she'd been designing clothes for her Barbie doll.

By age ten she was sewing for her mother and sisters. By eighteen, she'd saved up enough money to attend the Savannah College of Art and Design by creating knock-offs of pop celebrities' outfits for her high school classmates back home in Chicago.

She was the most driven girl—person—he'd ever met, which occasionally made him feel guilty about his parents' not only footing his tuition bill but also springing for a three-room apartment in Savannah's historic district.

Although there wasn't anywhere else he'd rather be at the moment, Randy sat up, grabbed a paper napkin from the take-out bag on the floor and cleaned up.

"Besides, unless I lost my memory when you blew the

top of my head off, sugar," he said, "it seems you're the one who talked me into stopping for a quickie."

They'd made the trip out to Swann Island today so he could finish up a portfolio for his Villa and Garden class. The professor had already covered the Hanging Gardens of Babylon, the Alhambra, Versailles, Monticello, and Fallingwater as examples of locations where art and nature coexisted in ideal harmony.

But Randy considered Swannsea Plantation, with its green fields of tea plants, peach orchards, acres of holly trees, kitchen gardens, and gleaming white antebellum house dating back to when cotton was king, to be right up there with those more-famous sites.

"Like getting you to stop took any convincing." Her voice was muffled by the sundress she was pulling back over her head. "And I'm not even going to let myself wonder how you knew about this place."

"I used to gig frogs in this pond when I was a kid." It wasn't actually a pond—more a wide spot in the marsh.

"Ooh, ick." She was searching on the floor for her sandals. "Is that what it sounds like?"

The sandals were white, with pink flowers that she'd hot-glued to the leather. He found one under his jeans, which were still in a heap on the floor.

"Pretty much. Some folks like to use a gun, but—"

"A gun? For frogs?" She took the sandal he held out toward her and slipped it onto a tanned bare foot tipped in nails the color of a ripe peach. "Wouldn't that pretty much blow them away?"

"Not if you use a .22 loaded with snakeshot."

"You country boys have the strangest ways of amusing yourselves."

He wisely didn't point out that some of the kinky things she'd thought up to do in bed sure as hell topped any amusements he'd ever known.

"When you're a kid, nothin' beats staying up past midnight to slither around in muddy water, playing with a flashlight and hunting bullfrogs."

"It sounds delightful." Her dry tone said otherwise.

"It may be a guy thing. But it was a helluva lot of fun. And unlike for a lot of sports, you don't need to go out and buy a bunch of equipment. All you need is a gig, an old broom handle, a flashlight, and a sack to put the frogs in."

"Eeeww." She shuddered dramatically. Randy often thought that if she weren't dead-set on a career designing clothes for the rich and famous, she could make a good actress. "Disgusting."

"Hey, aren't you always going on and on about all those French designers you get off on—Christian Lacroix, Valentino, and who's the other one, John Paul Jones, or something like that?"

"Jean Paul Gaultier." She corrected him on a lift of her cute pointed chin.

Which he knew, since she was always quoting the guy like he was the Bible or something. Randy liked teasing her because, although he had enough sense never to tell her, she was as cute as a speckled bluetick pup when she got on her Yankee high horse.

"And for your information," she said, "Valentino's not French. He's Italian."

"Still, I'll bet old Jean Paul has eaten himself a few frog legs in his day."

"You may be right." She tossed her blond hair. "But I'll bet he didn't gig them himself."

"Probably had servants to do it for him," Randy replied.

"You're impossible." She blew out a long breath. "I've got to pee."

That was no big surprise. She always peed right after sex.

"Let's go."

He grabbed the flashlight from inside the center console.

"You're not coming with me!" She sounded more

FREEFALL 45

shocked by that idea than she'd been by the idea of him gigging amphibians.

"You wander off the road on your own, darlin', and you could end up in the swamp. Which, unless you've always wanted to experience an up-close-and-personal meeting with a gator, isn't something I'd recommend."

"An alligator?"

"You're in the Lowcountry, sugar." He stroked her blond hair. "Where do you think those fancy shoes and purses you like so much come from?"

"I suppose it's a lot like what they say about making sausage. It's best not to think what goes into it."

But she was thinking about it. He could tell by another shudder that perversely made him want to take a nip of her smooth bare shoulder.

"You don't have to worry, cupcake." He nuzzled her neck, drinking in the scent of gardenias. "You'll be safe with me."

"That's what you said that first night you showed up at my apartment with a pizza. If I remember correctly, it took you exactly ten minutes to get my panties off."

And hadn't she been more than willing to help? Hell, the way she'd attacked the zipper on his jeans, he'd worried she might cost him the opportunity of fathering the next generation of Beaudines.

"I can't control myself around you, darlin'," he drawled. "You set my poor male head to spinning."

She folded her arms. "I suppose you think that good old Southern boy so-called charm works on me?"

"I was hoping it would."

She laughed in feminine resignation. Randy had always liked girls, and fortunately for him, they'd always liked him right back

"Well, you're right. It does."

He might not be as wise as he would have liked when it came to the mysterious ways of women, but he was smart enough not to gloat. Instead, he leaned over and opened the door.

She frowned as he climbed out of the car behind her. "There's no way I'm going to let you stand here and watch me pee," she complained. "I need my privacy."

Personally, he thought it was a little late for modesty, after she'd had his cock in her luscious mouth and he'd been deep inside her, but he didn't want to ruin the lingering sexual afterglow with an argument.

"Okay. Why don't you stay right here by the car, then." There was enough moonlight he figured she'd manage not to fall into the pond without the flashlight. "I'll walk a bit down the road and give you that privacy."

"You're going to leave me alone? On a deserted road? In the dark?"

Jesus. Stay. Go. He couldn't win. "I'll only be a few feet away."

"Don't listen."

Resisting a mighty urge to roll his eyes, Randy lifted his right hand. "I promise." He began walking away. "You give a holler when you're ready for me to come on back."

It felt good stretching his legs after having had them folded into pretzels. He figured some people might consider making love in the backseat of a car on a deserted Southern lane romantic. When you were six-foot-four, it proved more than a little cramped.

Not that he'd been complaining. Although they'd been together for nearly a year, they still couldn't keep their hands off each other. Which suited Randy just fine.

It was also surprising, since usually by now things would've cooled off. At least on his part. Hell, what women insisted on calling their "relationship" had never lasted more than a couple months before. Which had him wondering, on occasion, if maybe he and the sexy little dress designer had stumbled into something that might prove permanent.

However, his mama hadn't raised a dummy, and since

Madison had told him right off the bat, that first night
when they'd shared a pepperoni pizza and a marathon
of hot sex, that she wasn't looking for happily-ever-
afters, he'd wisely kept those thoughts to himself.

Still, they were about to graduate. Go off into the big
wide world. And selfish as he knew it would be, he would
like to get some sort of commitment before she took off
to New York City, or Paris, or London, or wherever the
hell her yellow brick road to fame and fortune took her.

He hoped she would let him tag along. Nice thing
about coming from money was he didn't need to work
for wages. Which allowed him to indulge his interests.
Which, for the past four years, had been architectural
history. Fortunately, all those famous fashion centers
she'd starred on that world map tacked up over her desk
had lots of both architecture *and* history.

The twisting narrow road followed a bend in the pond.
Moonlight shimmered on the tobacco-dark water, turning
it a burnished copper. The air, thick with the scent of salt,
rotting wood, and decaying spartina grass, dripped with
moisture. Across the pond, a stand of tupelo, draped with
ghostly moss, created an impenetrable black wall.

A chorus of deep *jug-uh-room, jug-uh-room* bellowed
from somewhere in the dark. A lone barred owl
hooted questions.

As he scanned the weed mats, lily pads, and fallen trees
with the flashlight, looking for the shimmering yellow eyes
of a bullfrog, Randy could understand how a Northern city
girl might not be able to appreciate being twelve years old
and getting to go out on the jonboat with his dad.

But given time, Randy figured, she might come to appreciate the almost primeval beauty of the Lowcountry.
Maybe even learn to love it as much as he always had.

He was indulging in a fantasy of someday bringing his
own son out here in the swamp to initiate him into the
rites of Southern manhood when a bloodcurdling shriek
shattered the night.

11

Nate Spencer had come face-to-face with death before. During his years in the Marines, the enemy had done their best to kill him, just as he'd killed some of them. He would have preferred not to take those lives, but that's the way it was in war, and until all the world leaders stood hand in hand on some mountaintop and sang "Kumbaya" and the Coca-Cola song, Nate figured things wouldn't be changing anytime soon.

But, damn, the civilian world was supposed to be different. Especially this little hidden corner of it. The last murder on Swann Island had been sixteen years ago, back when he was still in high school, and even that hadn't been premeditated.

As well as he could remember, Kenny Bonner and Pete Sullivan had gotten liquored up down at The Stewed Clam and gotten into an argument over which was the best Vietnam war movie ever made.

When Kenny had insisted it was, hands down, *Apocalypse Now,* Pete had reluctantly allowed that it could have been a fair enough movie if Coppola hadn't cast Martin Sheen in the part of Willard. Like anyone could buy a pansy Hollywood liberal as a Special Forces officer?

Hell, no. According to witnesses who'd been in the waterfront bar at the time, he'd banged his bottle of Bud on the bar to emphasize his point.

The best flick, hands fuckin' down, was *The Deer*

Hunter. Because it depicted real life. And De Niro was more of a real man than Sheen could be in his faggiest wet dreams.

As if to make his point, Pete had pulled out a Colt revolver and dared Kenny to prove he wasn't as limp-wristed as his movie star hero by reenacting *The Deer Hunter*'s Russian roulette scene.

Kenny, who may have been drunk, but not as stupid as Pete, declined to play.

Which was when Pete spun the cylinder, dumped out the bullets, and before the bartender could grab the gun from his hand, placed the barrel against his best friend's temple and pulled the trigger.

At his sentencing, Peter Stonewall Sullivan was still insisting he'd honestly believed the gun wasn't loaded.

Nate's dad, who'd been sheriff at the time, had believed him.

Unfortunately, both men had been too drunk to notice that only five bullets had landed on the scarred wooden bar. A sixth, which had lodged in the cylinder, blew that hole through Kenny's alcohol-sodden brain.

Pete pleaded guilty, served three years of a five-year term, and although dried out, the former alcoholic left prison a shattered man. Not wanting to see him end up on the street, Nate Senior had given him a job doing janitorial work around the station. A job Nate had continued to fund when he'd been sworn into office.

That death had been reckless, stupid, and avoidable.

This death was flat-out ugly. On all counts.

"Oh, God, oh, God, oh, God." The young girl was sitting in the front seat of his cruiser, slender white arms wrapped around her body, as if trying to hold herself together.

The girl's companion, who looked pale as paper himself and smelled of vomit, sweat, and, Nate couldn't help noticing, sex, was leaning against the fender of the black-and-white, trying to focus on the questions.

"I told you," he repeated, "I don't know what time

we got out here." He raked a wildly trembling hand
through his shoulder-length hair. "We'd been out to the
plantation. I wanted to take some shots for my senior
portfolio."

"You're a student?"

"We both are. At SCAD."

Which explained the blue streaks in his long hair,
Nate decided.

"And you'd come down this road to give your girlfriend privacy to go to the bathroom." He repeated what
she'd managed to get out.

"Uh, yeah." He shot a look toward the car, as if wondering how much she'd told Nate.

"Look." Nate rocked back on the heels of his eelskin
Tony Lamas. "You're both over eighteen. What you do
on your own time is your business, and I don't care what
you were up to, so long as you weren't breaking the law
in my jurisdiction."

"No, sir!" The kid's Adam's apple bobbed furiously.
He lowered his voice to a just-between-us-guys volume.
"We'd been fooling around for a while."

"And how long would you estimate that *while* was?"

"I don't know." Another shaky swipe of his hand. "I
guess half an hour. Maybe forty-five minutes."

"And you didn't see anyone else on the road?"

"No, sir."

"And you didn't touch the body?"

"No, sir!" He shot an involuntary look back at the
marsh, then looked like he was about to hurl again.

"Look at me," Nate said quietly. Firmly.

The dead woman's long black hair had been caught
up in the roots of a swamp tupelo. Her mouth was open,
as if death had caught her in midscream.

One eye was staring sightlessly upward. The other was
gone, eaten away, Nate figured from the raggedy skin
around it, by crabs or fish.

Her throat appeared to be slit from ear to ear.

It was the second death on the island in the past two

weeks. Last week they'd found an unidentified male floating in the water. His throat, too, had been cut.

They wouldn't know for sure until they got her onto an autopsy table, but what were the chances of the same type of fatal injuries being inflicted by two separate murderers?

Although he wasn't a coroner, Nate knew that the strong ammonia odor rising from the body suggested saponification had already begun. Which meant she'd been in the marsh long enough for bacteria to invade her body.

It also gave Nate the uneasy feeling that he knew exactly who this victim was. Hallie Conroy's husband had reported her missing four weeks ago. Reports from neighbors about frequent loud fights and the fact that Jake Conroy had been rolling around in the sheets at some motel in Somersett when his wife had supposedly gone missing had landed the husband at the top of Nate's suspect list.

Not that he hadn't continued to work the case. The last anyone had seen of the unfortunate Mrs. Conroy was when she'd thrown that tantrum—and a lamp—at the motel before storming off.

They'd found her car, abandoned with two flat tires, not far from the ferry landing the next morning.

The problem was, although Nate didn't have a shred of proof, his spidey sense was telling him that he was meant to find both bodies.

Otherwise, how much trouble would it have been to weigh them down? Or bury them somewhere on the island?

The question was whether the killer was challenging the police, maybe even asking for help—one of those "Here I am, catch me before I kill again" pleas. Or maybe he arrogantly thought he was too smart to be caught by some hick black cop.

Hell, perhaps there wasn't any message involved at all. Maybe the guy just thought so little of his victims he had no problem with tossing them away like used condoms.

A pair of headlights were cutting through the fog, coming this way. Nate guessed it was the medical examiner. Dr. Harlan Honeycutt III, the general practitioner who had delivered most of the citizens of Swann Island for the past forty years, Nate included, hadn't been happy at being dragged out of bed in the middle of the night.

Well, didn't that make two of them?

As it was, Nate was definitely going to have to be on the doorstep when Floral Fantasies opened in a few hours, so he could spring for a big-ass bouquet of pricey red roses, then try to crawl his way back into the good graces of the sexually unsatisfied female he'd left behind in those cooling sheets.

Damn. Another fucking murder. And wasn't that what he needed?

"Okay." Nate pressed his fingers against the bridge of his nose, then directed his attention back to the kid. "Let's start again at the beginning."

12

Word spread like wildfire. As it always did. Although it was the middle of the night, when everyone should've been home in bed, and the body had been found out in the middle of nofuckingwhere, a crowd had begun to gather.

And wasn't he discovering that was part of the fun?

For too many years he'd kept his secret close. Which in its way had been a thrill. But recently he'd begun to consider the unpleasant thought that he really wasn't getting the star attention he deserved.

David Berkowitz had been a pudgy nobody until he became the Son of Sam and kept New York City under siege for thirteen months. And before his execution, pretty boy Ted Bundy had not only become a media darling but had gained even more fame when he consulted with authorities on the Green River Killer case.

Dennis Rader, aka the BTK Strangler, had ended up the most famous (or infamous, depending on your point of view) Cub Scout leader in Boy Scouts of America history. The Zodiac Killer had made international headlines, and people were still writing books and making movies about Saucy Jack the Ripper.

But none of those serial killers had ever—in their darkest, sickest fantasies—come close to his body count.

Which was one of the reasons he'd decided to up the ante.

Show off his work a bit.

Let the local yokels discover that there was—boo!—a spooky monster in their midst.

Let them sweat.

Let them wonder which of them would be next.

After all, he thought, rubbing his hands together, killing was his business.

And business was good.

Although she'd been exhausted when she fell into bed, Sabrina slept only in snatches. And whenever she did manage to drift off, her dreams were filled with dizzying, tilting images of blinding flashes, shattered statues, bloodied bodies, and rain falling on gardens of stone cemeteries.

The scenes shifted, constantly changing, like the facets of a too-dark kaleidoscope, all punctuated by the ear-splitting screech of stone on stone.

Clawing her way out of a nightmare where rescuers drilling away at the fallen stones failed to reach her in time, where her spirit was floating above her broken and lifeless body, she jerked bolt upright in bed and pressed her hand against her heart, which was pounding at least twice as fast as the hammering she could still, strangely, hear.

"It was just a dream." Drenched in sweat, she'd kicked off the damp sheet; her nightshirt was tangled high around her thighs and clung wetly to her body. "You're okay." Her lungs burned as she drew in a deep, ragged breath. "You are *not* dead."

The sun was laying down buttery yellow bars across the bed and floor, reminding her that she'd opened both the shutters and the curtains last night.

Not that there was anyone around for miles, but still . . .

She glanced across the room toward the window.

And screamed when she saw the stranger looking in at her.

13

Christ! Smooth move, Tremayne. Zach cursed himself. Scaring a woman who'd recently had a hotel blown up from under her.

But from what Linc had told him last week, Sabrina Swann wasn't due to arrive on the island for another seven days. So how the hell could he have been expected to know she'd shown up a week early?

Or had she?

Maybe he'd had another blackout.

But one that lasted an entire week?

He might not be all that sure about the timeline, but the one thing he did know was that he wasn't helping the situation by staring into her bedroom window like some Peeping Tom pervert.

He slid the hammer into the loop on his tool belt, went back down the ladder, and tried not to notice that his hands were shaking like a damn leaf.

He blew a long breath through his teeth. Tried to figure out his next move. Tried not to remember when his—and his team's—lives had depended on his ability to make split-second decisions in chaotic conditions.

O-kay. The good thing was that she'd been wearing an oversized soccer shirt. So they wouldn't have to deal with her being embarrassed about him seeing her naked.

The bad thing was that the purple shirt had clung to her body like a second skin, leaving very little to the imagination. Not that he minded, since the body in question, while thinner than it needed to be, still looked pretty damn fine.

Even so, Zach suspected she might not be too pleased to have some guy on a ladder checking her out.

Not that he had been. Not really. Sure, in that frozen moment of surprise, he'd looked. But it had been knee-jerk, instinctive response. The kind any guy might have when presented with a woman sitting in the middle of tangled sheets.

Still . . .

He dragged his hands down his face. Wondered if he should drift away and deal with this tomorrow.

Or next week.

Or hey, how about next year, by which time she'd be gone and the entire stupid incident would be forgotten?

Reminding himself that he'd never been one to run from a situation, Zach held his ground.

And waited.

He did not have to wait long. The huge front door, which everyone on the island knew had come from some crumbling old castle in County Clare, flew open.

She'd thrown on a pair of low-slung jeans that swam on her and a T-shirt the color of ripe raspberries that stopped two inches above the waist of the jeans and revealed a faint line of ribs. Her narrow feet were bare, her toenails unpainted.

She might have just gotten out of bed, but her eyes were wide open. And dark with fear. Which would be understandable even if she hadn't been a recent victim of a terrorist attack.

From the way her fingers were curled around the handle of that big iron skillet, Zach had the impression that she wasn't planning to invite him in for hotcakes.

"Who are you?" Her knuckles whitened. "And what the hell are you doing here?"

She shifted, blocking the door.

Yeah, like a five-foot-four woman who looked as if

the faintest gust of wind would blow her out to sea could stop him from getting into the house if that was what he wanted.

Deep purple smudges, like bruises, shadowed the skin beneath her eyes. Except for the stripes of hectic color along her cheekbones, her too thin face was as pale as snow.

"And why were you looking in my bedroom window?"

"I'm Zach Tremayne."

Guilt turned in his gut for having frightened someone who looked as if she'd already been through too much. Actually, up close, she looked as if she'd been to hell and back, which, if what people were saying about what had happened to her in Italy was even halfway accurate, she pretty much had.

He could certainly fucking identify with that.

"And I'm fixing your roof. We had a frogstrangler of a thunderstorm last week that brought along a lot of hail damage."

He didn't see any reason to mention that the booming thunder, too reminiscent of enemy mortars, had kept him awake and on edge all night.

She glanced up at the roof in question. "The shingles are slate."

"Slate that's over a hundred and fifty years old." He was both surprised and unwillingly intrigued that she was turning out to be tougher than she looked. "The stuff lasts a long time, but it's well past needing to be replaced. As for looking in your window, that was an accident. From what I heard, you weren't expected for another week."

"My plans changed."

She was still jittery. But the knuckles on the hand gripping the skillet were no longer white.

"Zachariah Tremayne," she murmured, more, he thought, to herself than to him. Eyes the color of new spring leaves frosted as the name sank in. "I thought I heard you'd gone off to California and become a Navy SEAL."

"You heard right."

After his father had broken his back falling from a roof, Zach had dropped out of the Admiral Somersett Military Academy and come home to run Tremayne Construction. Once John Tremayne was back on his feet, Zach had taken off for San Diego rather than returning to school.

"So how long were you in the service?"

"One day too long."

Because it was far from his favorite subject, and more because it had been a very long time since he'd experienced this quick, instinctive tug of a man for a woman, Zach indulged himself with a slow, once-over glance.

"You've grown up, New York."

The glasses that had once nearly covered up her small thin face were gone. Her hair had darkened from flyaway corn silk to a rich, warm honey, and her mouth, which had always seemed too large, now seemed just right. In fact, if it hadn't been pulled into such a tight line, it would probably have been a hell of a lot better than just right.

"That would be inevitable, given that it's been sixteen years since we've seen each other." She folded her arms. "So, what's a big bad SEAL doing repairing roofs?"

Hadn't his father been asking the same damn question for the past six months?

"Someone needed to do it before it starts raining inside, which probably wouldn't be all that good for Miss Lucie's antiques."

Christ, he got tired of explaining himself to everyone on the damn island. Which made him wonder if he'd made a mistake coming home. But it wasn't like he'd had a helluva lot of choices.

The pitiful fact was, after that debacle in Afghanistan, the former hotshot Navy SEAL who'd received a Silver

Star for "extraordinary heroism while engaged in action against an enemy of the United States" had nowhere else to go.

"Now that I'm back to being a civilian, working with my hands gives me something to do while I'm weighing my options."

He wondered if that answer sounded as lame to her as it did to him.

From the way she narrowed her eyes and swept a look over him, he suspected it did.

Her gaze drifted to the white pickup parked on the circular brick drive. TREMAYNE GENERAL CONTRACTING SINCE 1917 had been painted on the side of the door in stark, no-nonsense black letters.

"You're working for your father?" She didn't bother to hide her incredulity at that idea.

"Yeah. For the time being, anyway. Though I'm not sure I'll ever live up to his standards."

Her eyes warmed a bit at that, and he thought he saw a hint of a smile touch her lips.

She'd always had a soft spot for his dad.

Zach remembered her first summer on the island, when she'd been all long, skinny legs, pigtails, and Coke-bottle glasses, trailing after John Tremayne, who'd been upgrading the bathrooms and shoring up tilting chimneys.

Normally, for a twelve-year-old boy, an eight-year-old kid—especially one of the female persuasion—wouldn't have garnered a second look, but that hadn't stopped Zach from recognizing a little girl desperate for a father figure.

"I remember when he replaced the banister." Although he knew she'd grown up in boarding schools in New York, Maine, and Switzerland, Zach could hear the faintest trace of Lowcountry South in her soft tone. "His work was fantastic. Even better than the original."

"He's always said sawdust runs in his veins."

Although construction work was something to keep

his mind occupied, Zach didn't enjoy it enough to think it also ran in his, as it had in his father's, grandfather's, and great-grandfather's before him.

"He also liked working at Swannsea because whenever there was a choice, Miss Lucie went with restoration as often as she could, rather than renovating or just gutting things."

"How is he?"

"Same as ever. I swear, he'll still be up on a ladder swinging a hammer when he's ninety. In fact, ever since he heard you were coming back home, he's been wondering if you're going to continue with the plan to expand the house."

"Expand Swannsea?"

"Miss Lucie never told you she was planning to add a twelve-hundred-square-foot sunroom to the east side?"

"No."

"Well, I guess I'll let Titania fill you in."

"Titania?"

"She and Miss Lucie had been planning some changes." Zach belatedly remembered his manners. "I'm real sorry about your grandmother."

Her eyes shuttered over. She lifted a dismissive shoulder.

"So was I." She took a deep breath and went somewhere deep inside herself. "Well, I'd best leave you to your work."

She didn't slam the door. But she came as close as good manners would allow.

Zach blew out a breath as he heard the lock snick on the other side of the heavy plank door. "Glad that went well."

14

Damn, damn, damn!

Sabrina had expected people to talk. She'd known when she decided to return that unless someone on the island was having a hot, illicit affair or a messy divorce— or even juicer, both an affair and a divorce at the same time—that the story of what had happened to her in Florence would probably rank at the top of the list of popular topics to gossip about.

She'd assured herself that she was prepared for that. Especially since, as Zach had pointed out by calling her by the name of the city her artist father had escaped to at twenty-one, despite the fact that her Swann family roots sank deep into the rich loam of the island, she'd always been a relative outsider.

But, she realized as she sagged back against the old oak door, Zachariah Tremayne had caught her totally off guard. Just as he'd always done.

Bad enough that he could look so impossibly hot in that snug T-shirt and faded jeans worn to white in some distractingly interesting places. Worse yet that she'd discovered that male sweat could, indeed, be an aphrodisiac.

He was, incredibly, even better-looking than he'd been back when he was raising hell all over the island. He wasn't all that tall—she'd guess around six feet—but if he was carrying an ounce of fat on that lean, rangy body, he was certainly hiding it well.

His hair was as dark as midnight over the marsh, luxurious waves in all the right places. The perfect length to avoid being too shaggy. The perfect thickness to grab onto and not let go.

No! Do not go there!

His eyes defied description. They were a compelling, kaleidoscopic combination of slate gray and blue, with a touch of hazel around the rim. She'd always thought the shadow-of-a-beard thing he had going on his manly jaw looked contrived on movie stars, but on him it looked just right.

Better than right.

Put the man on a recruitment poster, and the navy wouldn't have any trouble meeting its quota.

He'd seemed more disciplined than the reckless heartbreaker she recalled. Which was a bit of a surprise—although she knew nothing about SEALs, she would've guessed them to be the cowboys of the Special Forces.

Oddly, he had seemed almost too self-controlled. No longer the bad boy who had so captured her unwilling attention that summer of her sixteenth year, today he'd been unfailingly polite, except for that quick glance when he'd checked her out.

But still, if you looked closely enough—and, dammit, she had—Zach had *warrior* written all over him. From the square jaw you could park a tank on, to the rigidly defined row of muscles beneath that sweat-soaked T-shirt, to the ropey sinews of his dark arms.

So what was he doing working as a handyman?

Perhaps he'd been wounded and had to leave the service. He certainly looked healthy enough, though. She hadn't seen anything that would've made him unfit for service.

Not that she'd been looking.

The hell you weren't.

She blew out a slow breath. Okay, so he was even

sexier than he'd been at nineteen. Which was why, when those smoky gray eyes had skimmed over her, he'd started her tingling in places she'd forgotten *could* tingle.

She wondered if he remembered the way she'd thrown herself at him her last night on the island. Hoped that he'd had so many girls before her and women after that humiliating night that he wouldn't remember that she'd flung herself into his manly arms and kissed him with all the fervor of the crazy-in-love sixteen-year-old she'd been then.

The next morning she'd left the island for her freshman year of college, and he'd probably never given her or her inept seduction attempt a second thought.

Sabrina only wished she could say the same thing for herself.

She slid down the door to the floor, drew her knees up to her chest, and wondered why on earth one woman would have needed any more room.

The house was not only already the largest on the island; it was one of the largest in the state of South Carolina. Granted, there didn't seem to be a single flat surface in Swannsea that wasn't cluttered up with tacky Lowcountry souvenirs, knickknacks, and genuine antique collectibles, but if you cleaned the place out, there'd be more than enough space.

Surely the construction wasn't merely about making space for yet more bric-a-brac. So what was going on? And how could she have become so caught up in her own life that she hadn't even thought to ask about her grandmother's?

You can sit on the floor and hold your own little pity party from now until doomsday, darling, the familiar voice scolded. *But it isn't going to change a blessed thing. So, you might as well get off your butt, drive into town, and carry on with your life.*

"Good advice, Gram."

Breathing out a long sigh, Sabrina stood up.

She would take a shower, get dressed, drive into the village, and get on with her life.

Not that Sabrina had any idea what that life had in store for her. But getting off her butt was at least a start.

15

Across the island from Swannsea, thirty-year-old Cleo Gibson was pulling into the driveway of a little white cottage set on stilts.

Being a highly practical woman—she was, after all, a no-nonsense emergency room RN at Somersett's St. Camillus Hospital—Cleo had never believed in love at first sight.

Until her frustrated real estate agent, after months of house hunting, had, in one last-ditch attempt to find something that would suit her picky client, brought her here.

Mine.

The thought had struck like lightning from a clear blue summer sky. The cottage, located on the edge of the marsh, had been listed by Sumner Realty and Development as a "fixer-upper." That, Cleo had discovered, was Realtor-speak for "falling-down wreck."

But the badly peeling paint, sagging shutters, and rusting old car sitting on blocks in front of the cottage hadn't mattered. Neither had the fact that after inspecting the house, John Tremayne reported it needed a new roof, new wiring, new window glazing, new kitchen—well, just about new everything.

The house had spoken to her, as clearly as the voice of God booming from a burning bush.

But softer. More feminine.

Here you are, it had murmured silkily as she climbed

the rickety steps while the cautious agent stayed safely on the ground. *What took you so long? I've been waiting for you.*

The inside had looked even worse than the outside. But instead of the layers of water-stained, peeling wallpaper, Cleo had seen softly sponged walls of sea-glass green that would set off the white plantation shutters she would install. Ignoring the rat droppings on the scarred and pitted floor, she saw smooth hickory planks gleaming in the morning sun.

The views of the rolling dunes topped with sea oats, the glistening sand, and miles of Atlantic Ocean were well worth the cost and trouble it would take to make the home livable. And fortunately, not only was Cleo a practical woman, she was frugal.

After getting rid of that lazy, no-account husband—who'd blown his rare paycheck and too many of hers on those damn gambling cruise boats that were popping up like crabgrass all along the coast—she'd begun putting away money for her own place back on the island where she'd grown up.

Unfortunately, while Swann Island was still a long way from the rampant commercialization of Hilton Head or Kiawah, developers and tourists had begun to discover its beauty, which in turn had caused home values to escalate, nearly pricing her out of the market.

Until now.

She sat in the car for a moment, hands draped over the steering wheel, drinking in the sight of the pretty gray two-bedroom cottage with its sunshine-yellow shutters. Although she doubted she would ever remarry, she'd bought a wicker love seat for the porch and liked to imagine sitting in it on a summer's evening with a beau, sipping sweet tea and watching the lightning bugs flicker amid the star-shaped leaves of the sweet gum tree.

Mine.

She'd lived in the house during the renovation, which didn't prove as much of a problem as she had feared, given that she'd been pulling a lot of double shifts to pay for turning the poor battered beach shack into her dream house.

And recently, since Zachariah Tremayne had come home from the war, he had taken over a lot of the work from his father. Having that former Navy SEAL around to add to the scenery had certainly proven to be no hardship.

She did a little Carolina shag dance as she carried the bags up from the car. She'd spent her morning off at the Buccaneer Outlet Mall in Somersett, and damned if she hadn't snagged a pirate's booty.

Pretty white dinner plates and some purple towels for her bathroom, which was still lacking the soaking tub she dreamed of, but that would come soon. A little crystal dish to put seashells in, two fragrant sea grass baskets for the kitchen, and a trio of crocheted pillows to go on the white iron bed she'd found at a flea market in Charleston.

There were those at the hospital who thought she'd gone crazy. Not so much because she'd bought a home that needed extensive repair. Unlike some places, where people oohed and aahed over new and shiny, Lowcountry folks tended to appreciate the value of history.

What did worry her friends and colleagues was that she'd chosen to live in such an isolated location.

Which, as she'd explained, was exactly what she wanted. The ER was a beehive of activity. Some days, even if she had been able to steal time to stop and think amid all the hustle and bustle around her, she wouldn't have been able to hear her own thoughts.

But here, it was as if time stood still. The moment she returned home at the end of the day she could literally feel her muscles relaxing, her heart slowing, her racing mind beginning to calm.

She had to put down her packages to unlock the door, which she'd painted the bright blue color that her Gullah granny had always said kept away *haints*.

While Cleo had never considered herself the least bit superstitious, since no one had ever proven what, exactly, happens to spirits after death, covering all possible bases seemed the practical thing to do.

She put the baskets on the quartz countertop of the new kitchen island she'd had built, turned on the CD player, then, as the sound track from *Dreamgirls* began pouring out of the speakers, headed down the hall to put away her other treasures.

The bathroom counter held a trio of white candles and a glass jar of sand from what she liked to think of as *her* beach.

She'd hung the towels and filled the new bowl with the shells she'd collected and washed, when, just as Beyoncé was complaining about not feeling at home in her own home, a state that Cleo could blessedly no longer identify with, she heard something—or someone—behind her.

She turned, her heart instinctively leaping into her throat when she saw the man standing in the doorway of her tidy bathroom.

Then it settled. There wasn't anything to be afraid of. Except . . .

"What are you doing here?"

"I brought you a housewarming gift."

Which was nice.

But . . .

Gooseflesh rose on Cleo's arms. At the back of her neck. Although the temperature outside was in the nineties, with the humidity just as high, her skin turned to ice.

She may have been a no-nonsense, practical woman. But she still had a healthy dose of female intuition, and as Beyoncé hit a high note, internal alarms began screeching.

"Well, isn't that sweet of you?"

Stay calm. Do not panic.

"Why don't we go back out into the living room and you can show me what you brought?"

"I'd rather show you here."

With an odd, detached smile that didn't reach his eyes, he pulled a piece of white cord from the front pocket of his slacks. The cord, she noticed through her shock, had been formed into a noose.

Okay, now it's time to worry.

When he grabbed her, long fingers curving around her throat, intending to loop the cord over her head, Cleo had only a fleeting second to decide whether to fight or to go along with the program and hope he'd come here to rape. Not kill.

It was what her mama had always told her to do. Her granny, on the other hand, who remembered when bad things could happen to people of color in this part of the country, had always counseled her to scream like hell and fight like the devil.

Deciding to go with Granny, Cleo grabbed the jar, threw the sand into his face, elbowed him in the ribs as his hands flew to his eyes, and pushed past him.

He was quick. Too quick.

He caught her in the living room and shoved her against the wall.

"You're a very naughty girl, Cleo," he said in a voice that was spookily calm under the circumstances. His eyes swam with moisture as they tried to wash out the scratchy sand. "I'm going to have to punish you for that misbehavior."

He pulled a knife from the same pocket that had held the cord and pressed it against her breast as he slipped the noose over her head, then tugged, tightening it around her neck.

"Now, we're going to walk back into that pretty green bedroom, and you're going to take off your clothes. Then I'm going to rape you."

Oh, God, she wanted to think that was all he had in mind. But this was no stranger danger attack like her colleagues had warned her about, worried about her living out here all alone.

This was someone she knew.

Someone she trusted.

How could he possibly let her get away to tell what he'd done?

As she made her way, with as much feigned meekness as she could muster, back to the bedroom, she suddenly remembered the newscast she'd heard on the car radio about the woman's body being found in the marsh.

And she knew that if she didn't come up with some plan, she would end up the same way.

"You don't have to rape me," she said in what she hoped was a convincingly smoky voice. "All you have to do is ask."

"But what fun would that be?" he asked reasonably. "Now, let's get those clothes off." His voice, which had been eerily pleasant, suddenly snapped like a whip.

He held the knife blade against her jugular as she unbuttoned her blouse, shrugged out of it, and let it fall to her lovely new floor. It wasn't easy shimmying out of her skirt while her entire body trembled, but she managed.

"Nice." His reptilian gaze crawled over her red panties and bra. Wearing sexy underwear beneath the utilitarian scrubs she was forced to spend her days in made her feel more like a girl.

He sliced the bra away with a single flick of the knife. The panties went next.

"Very nice," he amended. "Now, be a good girl and lie down on the bed."

That weird smile faded and suddenly she found herself looking into the face of a very dangerous, very deadly, stone-cold killer.

Cleo lay on her back as instructed, breathing a bit

easier when he released the noose long enough to start taking off his own clothes.

He'd laid the knife on the bedside table.

She thought about using it. Then thought about all the victims she'd seen over the years, people who'd tried to use a weapon against an attacker only to have it turned back on them. Often with fatal results.

She'd taken kickboxing and was stronger than most women her size, since lifting injured patients all day required some serious muscle, but she was still a foot shorter than he was. And at least fifty pounds lighter.

No. The knife was a bad idea.

Still, she thought, as she watched him roll the condom over his rampant erection, she did have one chance.

She waited as he lowered himself over her. Bit her lip as he surged into her, tearing dry tissue.

She could do this, Cleo assured herself as Beyoncé and Eddie Murphy began stepping to the bad side. She could survive.

He was watching her as he plunged in and out, his cold eyes on hers, looking, she knew, for the fear he wanted to see there.

Wanting—needing—him to feel he was in control of the situation, she allowed the tears to flow.

Which, if the increased thrusts of his hips were any indication, only excited him more.

Salty drops of sweat were falling onto her face. Her breasts.

You will survive.

He came silently, without a word. Then crashed down on top of her, panting heavily, his slack mouth against her throat, momentarily letting down his guard.

Which was when she yanked open the drawer of the nightstand, pulled out a small canister, and even knowing that she would be blinded too, aimed the pepper spray at his face.

He leaped off her with a mighty roar.

"Bitch!" He was rubbing wildly at his red eyes with one hand, while slashing out with the knife he'd snatched up with the other. "Nigger cunt!"

Cleo was off the bed like a shot. Her own burning eyes were as useless as his, but she knew the layout of her house, where every stick of furniture was placed, which, she hoped, would give her an advantage.

She raced down the hall, past the kitchen, through the living room, out the door, onto the porch. Holding onto the railing, she found the stairs.

Unfortunately, the keys to the car were in her bag on the kitchen counter, but blinded as she was, she probably would've driven into the marsh anyway. Trying not to listen to the sound of footfalls clattering down the stairs behind her, she took off running toward the road, screeching at the top of her lungs.

She'd almost made it when he caught up enough to lunge for her flowing hair.

Cleo was pulled off her feet. She landed on her back on the sharp shell driveway.

He smelled of sex and sweat and fury as he hovered over her, his face dark with rage.

The knife blade flashed in the bright white light of the noonday sun.

Cleo felt the sharp burn as he buried the steel blade deep in her chest. Heard the sucking sound as he pulled it out.

Then, venting his fury, he stabbed her again.

And again.

And again.

16

One of the absolutes Sabrina had been able to count on while growing up was that whenever she returned to Swann Island, she would find it exactly the same as she'd left it. Which had been reassuring to the child she'd once been.

People talked slower here, so slow there were times it was almost impossible to understand them. They walked slower, too, pacing their entire life to an internal rhythm that only they seemed able to hear.

One thing visitors always commented on when first arriving on the island was the seeming scarcity of buildings. While the town wasn't nearly as large as the city of Somersett across the water, it did possess its share of homes, businesses, and, increasingly, resorts, vacation homes, and even a coastal golf course, where natural dunes gave an entirely new meaning to the notion of a sand trap.

But thanks to a cleverly orchestrated save-the-trees campaign spearheaded by Sabrina's grandmother back in the fifties, the lush green canopy that not only looked fabulous on postcards but also contributed to the survival of birds and other wildlife hadn't been allowed to be bulldozed and replaced with scrawny, look-alike nursery trees, as had been done on so many of the other neighboring barrier islands.

With local zoning laws prohibiting any building higher than the trees, homes and businesses were cleverly hidden behind thick green screens of oak, palmetto, laurel, hickory, red maple, and sweet gum.

Unfortunately, the acres of cotton, rice, and soybeans she'd once driven through to get to the village were being turned over to condo developments, and rows of what appeared to be vacation homes, all painted in pastels, perched on stilts overlooking the sea.

Even the former plantation belonging to her grandmother's cousin was being edged out by a gated golf course community named Plantation Shores, currently under construction. As much as Harlan Honeycutt loved the game, Sabrina doubted he was all that thrilled about that heavy machinery plowing up the field on the other side of their shared property line.

Although time might move slower on the island than on the mainland, the village, which consisted of four narrow, tree-shaded streets arranged around a snowy-white wedding cake of a Victorian bandstand, had undergone some changes.

The Pop Shop, where she and Titania used to flirt with boys over Dr Pepper ice cream floats, was now a microbrewery, and Beatrice's Hair Zone—where Lucie had her regular Saturday-afternoon appointment, come rain or come shine, for forty years—had evolved into the Shores Spa, offering, the gilt calligraphed sign on the window promised, A STRESS-FREE SANCTUARY FROM DAILY LIFE.

"Stress?"

On Swann Island? Isn't that an oxymoron?

Still, there was comforting familiarity in the red-and-white-peppermint-stick barbershop sign rotating outside Leon's Clip Joint; the Lowcountry Market still offered fresh local seafood and picnic baskets to go; and a quartet of old men in bib overalls sat hunkered over checkerboards in the park surrounding the bandstand, as Sabrina suspected elderly men had been doing since before what was known in these parts as the War of Northern Aggression.

And, in the distance, where the street dead-ended at the sea, men and boys dangled lines over the railing of the old wooden pier as fishermen had been doing for more than a century.

She pulled into the angled parking space in front of what had once been the Crab Shack and was now the Wisteria Tea Room and Bakery. A porch, on which leafy green ferns hung, had been added to the side of the building since she'd last been on the island, and every white wicker table was occupied.

Inside, the mouthwatering aromas of fresh-brewed coffee, tasso sizzling in a pan, cinnamon muffins, and myriad other baked goods were swirled around by the ceiling fans that spun lazily from the high white bead-board ceiling.

"Well, someone run out and kill the fatted calf," a wonderfully familiar voice called through the open window between the dining room and kitchen. "The prodigal daughter has finally seen fit to return!"

A tall, willowy African American woman flew out of the swinging doors, a white chef's apron covering a short, tight dress the color of a Carolina sunset that showed off her mile-long legs.

Sabrina laughed as she hugged her childhood friend, breathing in the smells of vanilla, cinnamon, and a sexy, inimitable scent created for Titania Davis by an old Gullah woman who lived out in the marsh.

" 'Bout time you came home." Titania held on to Sabrina's shoulders as she leaned back and swept her dark eyes over her. "Glory, girlfriend, you look like something a cat wouldn't bother to drag in."

"Thanks."

"If you can't count on your best friend to tell you the truth, who can you count on? When was the last time you had something decent to eat?"

"Need I remind you that I've spent the last five years in Tuscany? Which happens to have a reputation for spectacular cuisine?"

"Hah! Anyone can boil up a pot of spaghetti." Titania dismissed the idea with a flick of a delicate wrist. Before Sabrina could open her mouth to say that she wasn't all that hungry, her friend was dragging her through those swinging doors back to the kitchen.

"Sit that skinny ass down over there." Titania waved toward a tall wooden counter covered in waxed white butcher paper. "And prepare to be dazzled."

"I already am." Sabrina perched on a stool painted in the same bright colors as Titania's dress. "You've done wonders with this place."

"Well, it isn't the Wingate Palace, that's for sure." She poured a glass of orange juice from a pitcher, then took a bottle of champagne from the stainless-steel refrigerator. "But it's all mine."

"Just juice is fine," Sabrina said.

"Don't be foolish. We're having mimosas to celebrate, and I won't hear another word."

Although the orange juice was freshly squeezed and the champagne added sparkle, just the sight of those effervescent bubbles gave Sabrina the chills.

She'd been sipping champagne when a religious fanatic driving a bomb disguised as a fish delivery truck had literally turned her life upside down. Ever since, Sabrina had been struggling to find some sense of normalcy. Which was what this trip had been all about.

But if she could be spooked by something as simple and harmless as a mimosa, apparently she still had a ways to go.

She touched the glass to her lips, to be polite. Then, because she didn't want to hurt Titania's feelings, she screwed up her courage and tossed it back, swallowing it down like bad-tasting medicine.

"So," she said after she'd managed to polish it off without shuddering, "why don't you fill me in on what's happening around here? Zachariah Tremayne mentioned something about you having something to do with the addition Lucie had planned to build onto Swannsea?"

"You've seen Zach already?"

"He was fixing the roof when I left."

"Lucky girl. That man was sexy as homemade sin back in high school, but damned if he hasn't grown up to be one seriously scrumptious piece of eye candy."

"I suppose he's good-looking enough. If you like his type."

"Let's see." Titania tapped a fingernail against her lips as she considered that idea. "Tough. Macho. Ripped, rock-hard body to die for, with those world-weary, wounded-soul eyes that make a woman want to kiss the hottie everywhere it hurts and make it feel better."

She pulled a pan of sticky buns out of the commercial oven that had replaced the greasy old grill Sabrina remembered.

"Which, venturing a guess, would mean about ninety-nine-point-nine percent of the women on this planet. Including all the females on this island who've discovered an urgent need for some serious home repair . . . but not you," she said, not bothering to keep the blatant disbelief from her tone.

Sabrina didn't want to talk about the former SEAL. Especially with the only other person besides the man in question who knew her long-ago secret.

"Getting back to the addition at Swannsea—"

Titania shrugged. "It's not that big a deal."

The cinnamon aroma had Sabrina salivating. "Adding twelve hundred square feet to a one-hundred-and-fifty-year-old house isn't exactly a *small* deal."

"You're right. Your grandmother and I had ourselves a business deal going. Which is obviously off the table now."

"What kind of business?"

"She wanted to start running tours at the farm. The way a lot of wineries do? With tastings?" Titania cut one of the oversized buns and placed it on a white plate. "I'd worked out some recipes to serve in a tearoom."

"That's not such a bad idea. It appears, from all the

B and B's and condos I saw on the drive in from Swannsea, that you're getting quite a bit of tourism."

"More than a lot of folks would like. Especially since
Brad Sumner seems determined to pave over the entire island."

"The same Brad Sumner who was working in the Buchanans' fields that last summer I was here?"

"Oh, that boy was plowing something, all right. But it
sure as hell wasn't the Buchanans' cotton. More like
Mrs. Buchanan . . .

"Tea? Or coffee?"

"Although Lucie'd probably consider it heresy, I'll
take coffee." Still jet-lagged, Sabrina needed the
caffeine.

"Coffee it is." Titania poured the dark brew into a
tall white mug that matched the plate.

"Do you really think they were sleeping together?"
Sabrina asked as she sweetened the coffee with brown
sugar crystals from a white bowl that Titania put in front
of her.

"Oh, absolutely. Though I doubt there was much
sleeping goin' on. If you remember, he only worked out
in the fields a couple days before he was promoted to
being their yard boy. I swear, though the house might
not be on Wisteria Lane, it was obvious to everyone in
town that Patsy Buchanan was one desperate housewife."

"I don't remember anything about that." The coffee
was dark and hot and delicious.

"That's not so surprising, given you had your mind all
wrapped around giving away your virginity to a certain
bad boy that summer. Anyway, after you went off to
school, things really heated up. Enough that some people were even suggesting that the two of them had more
than a little to do with Mr. Buchanan's untimely demise
when his John Deere tractor crushed him while he was
changing a tire."

"You're making that up."

"Well, in the interest of full disclosure, Brad was in Somersett when the so-called 'accident' happened. But that didn't stop the talk. Especially after he up and married the merry widow the day after he graduated high school. And a mere six months after Frank Buchanan's funeral."

"Lucie wrote me every week and never said a thing."

"You know she didn't believe in telling tales out of school. Besides, the marriage only lasted a little under three years. Word was that Brad got caught screwing around out on Marsh Road with Mary Sue Easton while his wife was on an overnight shopping trip to Atlanta.

"Well, that caused another scandal, so they went off to Savannah, where Mary Sue has an uncle in the real estate business. Brad got a job working at their agency, and to hear him tell it, he became king of the flip.

"He must have made some money, because they came back home last year and he opened up his own agency. He wasn't back in town a week when he started buying up every piece of property he could get his hands on. And turning a damn good profit, which hasn't earned him all that many friends, since a lot of the land belonged to planters who weren't able to hold on to their farms when property values skyrocketed."

"That's an old story."

Sabrina had even seen it happen in Tuscany as more and more Americans, Brits, and Australians discovered the beauty of the northern Italian countryside.

"Sad, but true. And there are, admittedly, more than a few people who'd just as soon return to antebellum days. But, like Lucie always said, you can't stop progress, which is why she came up with the idea for the tearoom.

"Then, since she was never one to settle for a small idea when a more elaborate one would be better, she decided to make the island, and, of course, Swannsea, a destination wedding location."

"That's not a bad idea at all."

"Agreed. Which was when she decided to build the

addition larger than originally planned. Oh, she was full of fancy plans, including perhaps using some of those extra bedrooms by turning it into a bed-and-breakfast and having house tours hosted by pretty girls in *Gone with the Wind* hoopskirts."

"Well, that's not exactly original. But it's certainly proven popular in other places."

"That's what Lucie figured. She also did an informal poll. As society editor of the *Swannsea Trumpet*, she knew every debutante in the Carolinas and Georgia, and, believe it or not, there appears to be no shortage of women who'll jump at the opportunity to dress up like Scarlett O'Hara."

Sabrina wasn't surprised. It had been one of the things she'd once secretly thought would be fun. Of course, she'd been twelve at the time.

She pulled the sticky bun apart, popped a piece in her mouth, and nearly wept. "Oh. My. God. This is downright sinful."

"It is good, isn't it?" Titania's teeth flashed like pearls in her mocha complexion. "The trick is brushing some of Swann's cinnamon spice tea onto the dough after it rises and then using some more of it in the frosting."

Sabrina took another bite, which was, incredibly, even more delicious than the first. "You could sell these on the Internet and make a fortune."

"Lucie thought the same thing. Though shipping would be a problem, since they really need to be fresh from the oven, which would mean figuring out a way to ship frozen dough. But that would've involved starting up a retail business, which didn't interest either one of us."

She glanced out the opening toward the dining room and the patio beyond. "I can't deny that money is nice to have, but the real fun is watching people enjoy my food."

"I can't imagine anyone not."

The frosting was to die for. Sabrina could feel the bun attaching itself to her hips.

"Lucie's other idea—and it was a good one, I think—was for me to come up with recipes incorporating Swannsea Tea. At first we began with the typical type of lady sandwiches and desserts you'd find in a tearoom, but once she decided to add the weddings, I started working on menus for full meals."

"*All* with tea as an ingredient?"

"That was the plan. And what, we decided, would make Swannsea Tearoom unique."

"Well, it certainly would that." Despite her exhaustion, Sabrina's mind began to spin with possibilities. "Do you do all the testing yourself?"

"Absolutely."

"Then why don't you look like the Goodyear blimp?"

Titania's laugh sounded like silvery bells. "I've been getting regular exercise." Dark eyes danced with laughter that suggested she wasn't talking about Pilates or yoga.

"Who is he?" Amazed to have eaten the entire pecan-glazed bun, Sabrina gave in to temptation and licked her fingers.

"Ah, and don't you know me well?" Another chime of bells. "Nate Spencer."

"Nate? The sheriff's son? I thought he was off fighting terrorism."

"His daddy wanted to retire. He'd bought one of those big ol' motor homes and planned to take off to explore the country with Mrs. Spencer. But you know what a sense of responsibility Nate Senior has. There was no way he was going to turn his badge over to just anyone. So, after Nate's second tour in Iraq, instead of re-upping, he came home and took over his daddy's job."

"And you're pleased about that."

Titania flashed a grin. "As punch."

"He'd be a good sheriff," Sabrina commented.

Unlike his best friend, Zach, Nate had always been a straight-arrow kid. Of course, his father had been incredibly strict, running their home almost like a boot camp. Sabrina remembered telling her grandmother that Nate Senior made his son pass bed inspection every morning. If a quarter didn't bounce on the mattress, the bed had to be ripped apart and remade.

At the time, Lucie had explained that such discipline probably stemmed from the days when a boy of color could get himself in serious trouble for even the slightest slip in control. Although there'd never been a recorded lynching on the island, everyone knew stories about those bad old days.

Titania sobered for a moment, giving Sabrina the impression that their thoughts were running along the same track.

"He's a great sheriff," she said. "Like his daddy, he's tough, and sometimes a little bit more black and white about regulations than some of the good old boys around here would like him to be. But there's not a soul on the island who could deny that he's fair.

"Plus, there's something so damn sexy about a man in uniform." She winked sassily. "Though he's even sexier out of it."

"Please." Sabrina took another sip of the coffee, which was every bit as delicious as the bun. "As much as I like you both, I don't want the mental image of you and the naked sheriff doing the mattress shag imprinted on my mind."

Especially since, for some strange reason, it had her thinking of Zach. SEALs were in the navy. Did that mean they wore those sexy dress white uniforms? And if so, wouldn't Zachariah Tremayne look good enough to eat with a spoon?

Not that she was hungry.

At least not for a man.

Especially not *that* man.

Oh, God, it had been eleven years ago. Please let him not remember the night of her greatest humiliation!

"So, is it serious?"

"Everything's serious to Nate."

"But not to you?"

"I don't know." A shadow moved across Titania's face, coming and going so quickly that if Sabrina hadn't been paying close attention, she might have missed it. "It probably could be. Right now, we're playing it casual."

She began rolling out dough on the wooden counter. "I've had too much on my plate, between this place and Lucie's plan for Swannsea, and trying to get to the nursing home every day to visit Daddy, to even give any thought to long-term planning for my personal life."

Sabrina could certainly identify with that. "I'm so sorry about your father."

Joshua Davis had, like Lucie, always seemed an intricate part of the farm. It was difficult to imagine Swannsea without either one of them.

"Well, that makes two of us." Titania began rolling faster. Harder.

"How's he doing?"

"He has his good days. And his bad. More of the latter, lately. The past couple months he's begun confusing me with my mother." She shook her head. Sighed heavily. "They're not kidding when they call Alzheimer's 'the long good-bye.' "

As hard as it had been to lose Lucie without warning, Sabrina decided that having her grandmother's death drag out over months, and even years, would have been much, much worse.

"From the records Harlan sent me, your brother seems to have taken over his job at the farm without a hitch."

Lucie had named her cousin, Harlan Honeycutt, executor of her estate, and as such he had taken over the financial aspects of running the farm, which Sabrina had inherited. Fortunately, between Harlan and Linc, Swannsea Tea appeared to be in good hands. In fact, she'd been surprised at how much the land and the family business were worth. She certainly would never hit the *Forbes* list of billionaires, but if she did decide not to return to Wingate Hotels, she would have enough to tide her over while she figured out what to do next.

"Well, to be perfectly honest, I think Linc got a lot of experience running the farm while covering up for Dad the past few years," Titania admitted. "Looking back on it, the symptoms were all there, but none of us, not even Lucie, wanted to admit to seeing them.

"Lord, this is a damn depressing conversation." She brushed her hands together. "Let's move on to something else."

"Okay." Since she'd come here to cheer up, Sabrina was as eager to switch topics. "So, dish. Any other juicy scandals going on I should know about?"

"Well, let's see, it's not as if we're the jet-set capital of the South. Or Peyton Place, more's the pity. . . . Oh, remember LeeAnne Cosby?"

"Bleached blonde? Bonded teeth? Miss Buccaneer Days? Pushy, social-climbing mother?"

"That's her. Well, damned if she didn't conveniently get herself pregnant by some New York City hedge fund manager's son whose trust fund alone makes him richer than Croesus even if he never works a day in his life. Which it doesn't appear that he intends to."

"That should've made LeeAnne's mother happy."

"You'd think so, wouldn't you? Well, things were going well enough; LeeAnne's mama had booked the ballroom of the Somersett Wingate Palace Hotel for the reception and practically bought out the entire state of Hawaii having orchids flown over for a tropical-theme wedding.

"Then the groom's mother went and caused herself one helluva stir among the old guard when she showed up at the cathedral for the wedding."

"Was she drunk?"

"Darlin', you know that wouldn't even cause a ripple down here. No, this was something major that had all the blue-haired ladies in an absolute tizzy. I swear, it was the tsunami of social gaffes."

"She got caught in the cathedral cloakroom having sex with the bride's father?"

"Worse." Titania flashed a wicked grin. "Guess what she wore to the wedding?"

Sabrina tried to imagine what could cause the Swann Island matrons to get in a tizzy. "A pantsuit?"

"Well, no. Thankfully, since half the guests probably would've keeled over from heart failure right on the spot. She didn't go that far." She laid the dough out over a pie pan and began covering it with slices of ripe peaches. "She had the unmitigated gall to wear black."

As did most of Italy. "That's not uncommon. These days." Even in America, Sabrina suspected.

"Maybe not in New York City," Titania allowed. "But not only did it give people the idea that she wasn't happy about the nuptials, everyone knows this is jewel-tone country."

The laughter began deep in her belly and rose, rich and warm. As she threw her head back and let it out, Sabrina felt a huge weight begin to lift, ever so slightly, from her shoulders.

"God," she said, dabbing her damp eyes with the corner of the damask napkin Titania had placed on the counter, "it's good to be home."

Her best friend's eyes were equally moist. "Not as good as it is to have you home, girlfriend."

17

It wasn't quite as bad as Sabrina had feared. Oh, there were the inevitable questions at the market. And at Oscar's Gas and Go, where Oscar himself had insisted on filling the tank of her rental car. And, of course, at the Swann Island Bank and Trust, where she'd opened a personal checking account.

Thankfully, although she could hear the murmured rumors following in her wake, Southern manners kept people from being too rudely inquisitive.

Sabrina also knew that as soon as she left each of those establishments, tongues began wagging and phone calls began flying all over town. Because while politeness may have been instilled into Swann Island infants while they were in the cradle, gossip was bred into Southern bones. It was the currency on which small towns operated. And she was the topic of the month.

Zach was on the roof when she arrived back at Swannsea. He was wearing a baseball cap turned around backward and, in deference to the heat, had stripped off the white T-shirt, revealing a mahogany back gleaming with sweat. A back pocket of the jeans was torn, revealing what appeared to be navy blue knit boxer briefs.

Muscles rippled beneath tight dark skin, and biceps bulged as he lifted the heavy hammer, then, with one solid swing, drove a nail into the heavy slate tile. And repeated the procedure.

Since the always lovely island scenery had turned

downright spectacular, Sabrina allowed herself to sit there for a moment and enjoy the view.

He straightened when he heard the car door close. When he turned, she found herself staring at a prime example of raw male power.

A dusting of dark hair arrowed over a rock-hard chest and ripped, corrugated abs, disappearing beneath the waist of those raggedy jeans.

Adding to the drool factor was the tool belt riding gunslinger low on his hips.

When he pulled the cap off and finger-combed those damp, dark waves, Sabrina felt a little flutter in her stomach.

"That didn't take long." His voice was deeper than it had been that summer. Slower. Damn it all to hell, even sexier.

"I've always been a fast shopper," she said mildly, reminding herself as he climbed down the ladder that she was no longer the sixteen-year-old who'd once secretly scribbled "Mrs. Zachariah Tremayne" on the hidden inside of her English literature folder.

She was twenty-seven years old. An adult woman. And adult women did not get all weak in the knees over a sexy-as-hell construction worker, even if he did have a great—make that world-class—butt.

"Now there's an appealing attribute Lucie never mentioned."

Assuring herself that she was not beating a hasty retreat, that she was only hurrying because she didn't want the ice cream she'd bought at the market to melt, she turned to retrieve the box of groceries from the backseat.

"Let me get that for you." Apparently having no concept of personal space, he invaded hers as he reached around her and took hold of the brown cardboard box.

"Thanks, but I can get it myself."

"Of course you can."

He had her effectively caged in. He was also radiating

enough heat to melt not only her pint of Ben and Jerry's Chunky Monkey but the frozen dinner she'd bought to nuke tonight as well.

Deciding that making an issue of it would only reveal how uncomfortable he was making her, thus revealing a vulnerability that she hated feeling, let alone allowing anyone to see, she let go of the sides of the box and ducked beneath his arm.

Damn. He was still close enough that she could see the moisture glistening like diamonds in those dark curls bisecting his chest.

"In case you've forgotten how things work down here, sugar, no Southern gentleman worth his salt would stand by and watch a woman lugging around a heavy box when he's there to do it for her."

"Things may move slower on the island than in the rest of the country, but in case you haven't noticed, the calendar has flipped a few pages beyond the eighteen hundreds."

"Seems I heard something about that." In contrast to her mother's clipped Upper East Side society accent, which she'd pulled out from somewhere deep inside her, his drawl was praline-rich. The tips of his work boots were nearly touching toes bared by her sandals. "But like you said, things move a lot slower down here."

"Interesting that you've been away, what, a dozen years? Yet I'm supposed to believe you fell back into local habits so easily?"

"I was gone eleven years. Give or take a few months. But Swann Island's in the blood. Like this heat." He shifted the box, resting it on a cocked hip. "And the way Southern males, wherever we may end up, maintain a certain fondness for smooth whiskey, fast cars, and hot women."

Now *here* was the wicked bad boy she remembered. The one she'd secretly watched all that long, hot summer. He was radiating the lazy sexuality that back then Sabrina had found both compelling and a little frightening. The weird thing was, she felt pretty much the same way now.

"If we stand out here talking all day, my ice cream's going to melt."

"Wouldn't want that," he said agreeably. His eyes sparkled with what appeared to be amusement. As if he knew what she'd been thinking.

Not that he'd need any superhero mental telepathy skills to read her mind. Sabrina suspected he was accustomed to women looking at him as if he were an all-you-can-eat chocolate buffet.

He backed up and gestured for her to go ahead of him. "Especially since you could use a little more meat on those bones."

She shot him a look over her shoulder and caught him looking at her butt. Which, though she'd jump off the Admiral Somersett Bridge before admitting it, was even skinnier than it had been before the bombing.

"My bones are none of your business."

"I liked your grandmother."

"I doubt you could find anyone on the island who didn't."

She tried to make sense of the non sequitur but couldn't. And, dammit, as he followed her into the kitchen, it appeared he wasn't going to help her out.

"So what does you liking Lucie have to do with my bones?"

He put the box onto the butcher-block counter. "Since she's no longer here to share some home truths, I have the feeling she'd want someone to be honest enough to tell you that you look like hell."

"Well, thank you." She snatched a carton of orange juice from the box, flung open the refrigerator door with more force than necessary, and slammed it down onto a glass shelf. "But for your information, I've already heard that today."

"From Titania."

"And Sissy at the market." She began putting the eggs

into the compartment in the door. "And Oscar at the filling station. And Doro Hemphill at the bank. And let's not forget Betty Lovejoy at the pharmacy," she said between clenched teeth.

Though, granted, only Titania had been as blunt as Zach.

"Damn." She glared down at the bright yellow yolk and gooey egg white streaming over her hand.

"No wonder it broke, the way you were slamming those poor eggs down like you've got a personal grudge against the chicken who laid them."

He pulled a roll of paper towels from the box, tore off a handful, stuck them beneath the faucet, and took hold of her hand.

She snatched it back. "I can do that."

"Fine." He held up both *his* hands and backed off. "And at the risk of getting my head bit off here, may I suggest that maybe it might be a good idea if you sat down and let me finish putting the rest of this stuff away?"

"I don't need your help. Believe it or not, there are people—important people all over the world—who consider me more than a little competent."

"From what Lucie told me about your comet ride through the Wingate Hotel chain, I've not a single doubt of that. But in case you haven't noticed, sweetheart, you seem to have misplaced your magic bracelets."

She was too thin and too pale, and way too on edge. But obviously struggling her damnedest for control, a feeling Zach knew all too well.

Emotions he couldn't quite pin down stirred. Deeper than lust, and, he feared, more dangerous than desire, they were something he'd have to think about later.

"Look." He took hold of her shoulders and used his superior strength to walk her over to one of the kitchen chairs. "Believe it or not, I know what you're feeling."

She tossed up her chin. "You do not."

Interesting. Pink flags were suddenly flying in her

cheeks, suggesting that they might not be talking about the same thing. He wondered if she was remembering back to another time when he'd taken hold of her shoulders. To gently push her away.

"Actually, I do."

After practically shoving her down onto the woven cane seat, he picked up the cardboard carton from the counter where she'd put it while scrubbing the egg gunk off her hands. Her raggedy nails didn't fit with her slender but competent-looking hands. He wondered if they'd been broken off in the bombing.

Or if she'd bitten them that way afterward.

"I've been in that place where you are now," he said mildly. "After your world suddenly falls out from under you, and up becomes down, down up, and you're not sure if your life's ever going to be normal again." He finished putting the rest of the unbroken eggs away. "Whether *you're* ever going to be normal again."

He could tell she was surprised by that announcement. Even more surprised that he'd shared it with her.

And hell, didn't that make two of them?

"I don't want to talk about it."

"Fine. Not that keeping it bottled up seems to be working real well for you."

"It's hard."

"Sure it is. But there's a saying drilled into us SEALs during BUD/S training. 'The only easy day was yesterday.' "

Her eyes had that wounded look again as they reluctantly lifted to his in a way designed to make any guy with blood still stirring in his veins want to leap tall buildings for her. The irony was, there'd been a time when he would have tried to do exactly that without a second thought.

But that was in another life.

"So, if you know how it feels, how did you get past it?"

"Beats me."

Okay, this was now getting *way* too personal for comfort.

He turned away and shoved a box of Rice Krispies onto a pantry shelf. "I'll let you know if and when I do."

He could sense her trying to decide whether or not she wanted to continue this conversation, which, he suspected, might be as difficult for her as it was for him.

The thing to do, he decided, was to shut up, get the rest of her damn groceries put away, then get the hell out of here before he ended up spilling his guts.

Which he hadn't done to anyone.

Not his shrink, not his dad, not even Quinn or Shane, whose lives had also been inexorably changed by that debacle on the mountaintop.

He picked up the trio of little plastic boxes. "What are these for?"

"I heard mice in the attic last night."

"Not so unusual, given that you're right on the swamp. So, I guess you've decided to make pets out of them? Maybe put them in a little cage with a wheel to run on?"

"No." She folded her arms, looking less fragile than she had a moment ago. "I intend to capture them with that peanut butter I bought, then move them to the marsh."

"After which they'll probably beat you back to the house."

"That's my problem. I don't want to kill them if I don't have to."

"Then maybe you ought to think about getting yourself a cat. Let him do the job."

She shuddered at that idea. "I don't want to kill them," she repeated.

Which, Zach figured, made sense. She'd undoubtedly had more experience with death than most civilians.

"Your choice."

"Exactly," she agreed. "May I ask a question?"

Fucking terrific. Wouldn't you know she wasn't going to let the damn subject drop?

Zach's mind was scrambling to come up with an escape route when the front doorbell chimed.

Saved by the bell, he thought as a cooling wave of relief swept over him.

18

Although the original house had blown away in a hurricane and a second had been burned by Union troops during the war, the land on which Whispering Pines stood had been in the Honeycutt family since the seventeen hundreds. There'd been a time when the Honeycutts had owned Nate's ancestors.

Once freed, most of his people had stayed on to work the fields, as they had since being dragged to this country in chains.

They'd had a hardscrabble life, but Nate Senior had risen above his humble roots to become the first Spencer to graduate from high school, the first to go to college, and one of the first black men anywhere in the South to become the law that so many Southern people of color had once feared. Often with good reason.

Even after desegregation, a lot of black people continued to resent the way things had been during the years when cotton was king. And later, during those deadly Jim Crow years. According to some of the old tales Nate had overheard during family reunions, the Spencer family had definitely harbored its share of bitterness.

Then Nate Senior had got himself drafted, landed in a rice paddy on the other side of the world, and by his third tour in 'Nam had figured out that life tended to be a lot easier and you stayed a lot saner if you dealt with the present and looked toward the future, rather than dwelling on a past you couldn't do anything about.

Something Nate had figured out for himself during a deadly posting in Somalia during his Marine days.

Whispering Pines may have been built in the late eighteen hundreds, but it definitely maintained the look of more-prosperous, and indolent (at least indolent for the white folks), antebellum times. In fact, there were those who insisted on calling it Little Swannsea, because it resembled the home of the Swanns, who were cousins to the Honeycutts.

But where Swannsea boasted twenty-seven two-story Doric columns on three sides of the gleaming white house, Whispering Pines had settled for eight one-story pillars in the front. Swannsea had two sets of front steps; Whispering Pines, one. Swannsea, eight chimneys, Whispering Pines, three.

And then, of course, there was the damn golf course development Brad Sumner was building right against the Honeycutt property line.

But even the smaller of the two homes was a palace compared to the tar paper sharecropper's shack without plumbing that Nate Senior had grown up in.

After Reconstruction, when the market for Southern crops plummeted, the Honeycutt men had turned to medicine. For over a hundred years they'd treated patients in a clinic set up in their home, and Nate knew the two doors on the side of the house were for those not-so-long-ago days when "coloreds" and "whites" had bided their time before appointments in separate, and definitely not all that equal, waiting rooms.

Still, he thought, as he climbed the steps to the front door, he supposed the Honeycutt physicians got points for treating their black neighbors, which sure as hell hadn't always been the case over on the mainland.

The doorbell played the opening bars of "Dixie"; a moment later, an elderly housekeeper wearing a black dress with white cuffs and collar and a blindingly bright scarlet, purple, and turquoise turban answered the door.

"Mr. Nate." The Geechee womn greeted him with a

huge smile. She'd been brought to Whispering Pines as a teenager, to care for the doctor from the day he'd been brought home from the hospital as an infant. "How lovely to see you again."

Eugenia Pickney might have been born into a Gullah home, but her diction was pure Lowcountry society white.

"It's good to see you, too, Miss Eugenia." Nate wished he was there under any other circumstances— not that he'd ever been invited to Whispering Pines for any social occasion.

"The doctor's waiting in his operating room."

A euphemism, they both knew, for his autopsy suite, since any actual surgery required by live patients was done off island at Somersett's St. Camillus Hospital.

As he passed the formal parlor on the way to the back of the house, a voice called out to him through an open pocket door.

"Nate Davis. How lovely to see you again." The mistress of the house unwittingly echoed her servant.

Nate stuck his head into the room. The doctor's wife was sitting on a brocade sofa, a needlepoint frame in her lap, a spiffy electric wheelchair by her side. Proving that even the rich didn't get a free pass through life, she'd survived polio as a girl only to have it reappear with a vengeance in her later years.

"Good to see you, too, Miss Lillian."

"If only it weren't for such a somber reason. I swear, I don't know what the world is coming to." She clucked her tongue. "Who'd have ever thought we'd have two murders on Swann Island? Let alone two in such a short period of time."

"It is unfortunate," Nate said, proving himself the master of understatement.

It was a lot more than unfortunate. He knew he was under a microscope, not only because of his color but because he was Big Nate Spencer's son. If he didn't close these cases, and fast, the good citizens of Swann Island would start looking around for another candidate for his badge.

The fact that he didn't want to give it up surprised Nate nearly as much as the fact that he'd agreed to take it in the first place.

"Would you stay for dinner? Eugenia picked up some fresh scallops at the market and has planned a special dessert."

"Thank you, Miss Lillian. I certainly appreciate the invitation, but I'm afraid I have a prior engagement."

It was weird how whenever he got into a conversation with Lillian Honeycutt he started talking like Ashley Wilkes.

Pale blue eyes lit up with feminine interest. "A date?"

"Yes, ma'am."

"With Titania?"

"Yes, ma'am."

"Oh, she's such a lovely girl. And so talented!" She clapped her hands together with pure feminine glee. "I bought some of her ladyfingers for my book club last week and all the ladies raved on and on about them. I swear they were all pea green with envy."

Her hand trembled as she pulled the needle threaded with yarn through the canvas. The picture emerging appeared to be of Whispering Pines in spring, with white dogwoods blooming and red azaleas flaming.

"So, when are you going to make an honest woman of her?"

"Ma'am?"

"When are you going to marry the girl?"

Nate was grateful that his ebony complexion hid the blush he felt burning in his cheeks, and he realized that he'd begun rubbing his shoe on the Oriental carpet. Like a six-year-old called to the principal's office, he was struggling to come up with a response when he was saved by a big, booming voice.

"There you are!" Dr. Harlan Honeycutt, clad in blue scrubs, came down the hall with long, purposeful strides.

He wasn't a tall man, but with his full head of thick white hair, piercing blue eyes, and year-round tan from a penchant for golf, tennis, and sailing, he had a rugged, healthy appearance that Nate figured inspired confidence in his patients. "I was about to start without you."

"It was my fault, Harlan." Lillian broke in before Nate could respond. "I was asking him about his intentions regarding Titania."

"Women." Honeycutt exchanged a what-can-you-do-with-them look with Nate. "If y'all had your way, every male on the planet would be married."

"And wouldn't, just perhaps, the planet be a more civilized place if that were the case?" she countered pertly. She smiled up at her husband. "Marriage hasn't seemed to harm you."

"Now I'm not going to argue with you there, my love."

Putting aside his bluster, he bent down, picked up her hand, and brushed his lips across her knuckles. "However, before you back our good sheriff into an even more uncomfortable corner, he and I have work to do."

"I know." She sighed and her eyes misted up. "It's so tragic." She looked up at Nate. "You will catch this monster, won't you, Nathaniel? So we can stop living in fear?"

Nate jutted out his jaw, unaware that in that moment he was a dead ringer for his father. "I have every intention of having the perpetrator behind bars very soon, ma'am."

He hoped.

"Sorry about my wife putting you on the spot like that," Harlan said as they walked down the hallway. "We've always been fond of Titania. And, of course, her brother." He shook his leonine head. "Hell of a shame about her daddy."

"Yes, it is." Nate also found it a shame that the woman he loved to distraction was using her father's medical condition as an excuse not to discuss their future.

"I've been meaning to get out to visit him, but between you, me, and the fence posts, I keep letting things get in the way because I can't stand the idea of seeing Joshua so diminished."

"I know the feeling." Nate hated everything about the nursing home Titania and Linc had finally been forced to put their father in. But love meant sharing the bad as well as the good. "If it's any consolation, most days he wouldn't recognize you, anyway."

"Still, it'd be the right thing to do."

Since he couldn't disagree with that, Nate said nothing.

The autopsy room was brightly lit and as cold as a meat locker. A white body bag lay on a metal table that, although he didn't know all that much about the field of medical forensics, Nate took to be top of the line.

Which made sense. While not nearly as wealthy as their Swann cousins, the Honeycutts had never done anything in half measures.

"I think I'll go out there this Sunday after church," Harlan said. "Take along some of Eugenia's fried chicken and potato salad. Whenever Lucie'd have barbecues at Swannsea, Joshua couldn't get enough of that chicken."

"Isn't any better," Nate agreed, feeling a little disloyal since, if truth be told, he thought Titania's was more flavorful.

"Did you know," Harlan asked as he handed Nate a bottle of wintergreen oil, "that the first recorded autopsy was of Julius Caesar?"

"No. I'd never heard that."

Although he was all too familiar with the smell of death, and even occasionally relived the battle immortalized in the book and movie *Black Hawk Down* in his sleep, Nate rubbed a bit of the oil beneath his nostrils.

He was going to have to run home, shower, and change clothes before going over to Titania's. Bad enough he'd left her hanging last night. Showing up with the stench of a murder victim on him would probably be the final straw.

"It's true. It was found in the account of Caesar's death written by Gaius Suetonius Tranquillus, aka Suetonius the Gossip."

Harlan tied a heavy rubberized apron over his blue scrubs. "According to Suetonius, the body was examined by a physician named Antistius, who then went to the Forum to inform the senators that Caesar had suffered twenty-three stab wounds, one of which proved fatal."

He took a pair of latex gloves from a box and snapped them on. "While I admittedly never imagined during my gross anatomy class in medical school that part of my career would involve dissecting bodies for scientific purposes, I have to admit that I rather enjoy the link to the past."

"Well, you're living in the right place, then."

"The only place I'd ever want to live." He lowered the zipper on the thick white bag. "As Eudora Welty once said, 'A known past and a sense of place open the doors of the mind.' And Swann Island surely has a plethora of both."

Nate couldn't disagree.

History—the good, the bad, and the ugly—was woven with the present throughout the South, but no more so than here on the island, where first indigo, then rice, then finally sea island cotton had made white planters wealthy beyond their wildest dreams.

By the mid–eighteen hundreds, at the height of the plantation era, most of the island's land and riches had been divided among three families: the Swanns, the Honeycutts, and the Somersetts.

Who, despite reverses after the Civil War brought

down the cotton dynasties, still possessed most of the power and wealth.

The autopsy didn't reveal anything Nate hadn't already suspected. Dental records confirmed that his Jane Doe was indeed Hallie Conroy. Her throat had been cut with the same instrument as the earlier male victim, and she'd been dead when she was thrown into the marsh.

Although her body had begun to putrefy in the warm water, and her café au lait skin made it more difficult to date the bruises by color changes, Harlan suspected some had occurred postmortem.

"Suggesting she was killed elsewhere, then transported to the marsh," Nate murmured, trying to see it, to think it through, as his dad would've done.

"That's how I see it," the doctor concurred.

Where she'd been dumped like yesterday's garbage.

The flesh at her wrists and ankles had been rubbed nearly to the bone in places, suggesting she'd been chained for some time. Which was bad enough. But it was about to get worse.

"See these?" Harlan pointed toward a series of double parallel linear bruises from her shoulders to her ankles, front and back. They were separated by paler, undamaged sections of skin. "These are tramline contusions, caused by impact from a rod-shaped object."

"She was beaten."

"Severely. Over an extended period of time."

"Christ."

Nate took in the dark stripes. The broken fingers. The round scars that looked like burns from a cigarette and a raised letter *S* that had been branded into her left ass cheek. *Slave?*

The she-crab soup he'd eaten for lunch rose into his throat. He forced it back down again.

"She didn't go easy."

"No." Harlan's eyes revealed the same sick horror Nate suspected was reflected in his own. "Unlike our male John Doe, whose death was quick and relatively painless, this young woman suffered a horrific end after what appears to have been an incredibly painful imprisonment."

"Christ," Nate repeated. He skimmed his hand over the hair he kept cropped in its Marine cut.

His phone, which he'd set to mute mode, vibrated against his hip. He'd instructed Dottie, the dispatcher he'd inherited from his father and who often thought she knew more about the sheriffing business than he did, to interrupt only for an emergency.

"I know you said not to disturb you, *Sheriff*." Nate had tried to convince himself that her tone didn't always take on a slightly disapproving note whenever she used his title. As if anyone could possibly attempt to replace Nate Senior. "But a homicide's been called in."

"A homicide?" Nate exchanged a look with Honeycutt, who'd pulled out a crowbar to crack the victim's skull.

"It's Cleo Gibson. She was found murdered outside her house. And, Sheriff"—Dottie's voice dropped to a stage whisper—"according to Deputy Stuart, her head's been near cut off."

The hair on the back of Nate's neck rose in response to that hissed report.

"Tell Stuart to rope off the scene. I'll be right there." He snapped the phone shut. "We've got another one. Cleo Gibson."

Harlan Honeycutt went ghost white beneath his ruddy golfer's tan. "That can't be. I was talking with her yesterday at the hospital. She was giddy as a schoolgirl on laughing gas, telling everyone that now that she had finally had her dream house all fixed up, we were all to be invited to her party.

"In fact, Lillian ordered her a silver serving tray from Treasures, over in Somersett, as a housewarming gift. She and Eugenia were planning to take it over there when they went calling tomorrow."

He shook his head. "There must be a mistake."

"That's always possible. But she and Jeb Stuart dated a few years back. He'd be able to identify her. Especially since she was found outside her house."

"Good God," Harlan breathed.

Good God indeed, Nate thought as he left the artificially chilled room. They'd agreed that Harlan would finish Hallie Conroy's autopsy, then meet him at the scene.

What kind of monster did they have in their midst? Nate wondered as he tore out of the driveway, scattering oyster shells beneath the cruiser's tires.

And how the hell was he going to apprehend him before he killed again?

19

Brad Sumner had definitely changed since that long ago summer he'd supposedly been deadheading the Buchanans' tea roses. Although Titania was right about Sabrina's having had her head clouded with thoughts of Zach, the boy voted the most likely to con you out of your lunch money had been good-looking in a slick, smarmy sort of way that had garnered his share of female attraction.

This man had developed a paunch. His sandy hair was thinning a bit at the temples, and although he was not yet thirty, Sabrina could see the beginning of jowls. The red flush in his cheeks suggested an overindulgence in alcohol rather than too much sun.

"Hello, pretty lady." He flashed her a smile that, if she'd had any lunch money to lose, would have had her holding on to it more tightly. "Long time no see."

"Hello, Brad. This is a surprise."

"I saw you at the bank," he said, "but you left before I got a chance to welcome an old friend home."

"Well, isn't that hospitable of you?"

Sabrina decided not to point out that she doubted he'd ever said a dozen words to her in all the years she'd been coming to the island. Which didn't exactly make them bosom buddies.

Mr. Tall, Dark, and Too Sexy for His Tool Belt chose that moment to come strolling up behind her, chewing on one of the cookies Titania had sent home, looking for all the world as if he belonged here.

"Sumner." Zach nodded.

"Tremayne." The developer's lips narrowed to a thin, disapproving line. "This is a surprise." And not, Sabrina sensed, a pleasant one. "I thought that was your *father's* truck in the driveway."

"It belongs to Tremayne Construction. I work for Tremayne Construction. Ergo, I drive the truck."

"And you're doing work here at Swannsea?"

"Seem to be."

"What kind of work?"

Zach shrugged. Took another bite of the cookie as if he didn't give a rat's ass about this conversation. "This and that."

The tension swirling between them was thick and a little uncomfortable, like the hot and humid air before a summer thunderstorm. Air that was sparked with testosterone.

Zach shot Sabrina a grin. It was wickedly male and, she sensed, intended as much to annoy Brad Sumner as to charm her.

"I'll be back first thing in the morning to see to the flashing, sugar. Then we can discuss Miss Lucie's plans for the new addition."

With that promise hanging in the air, he strolled across the veranda, down the steps, and toward the pickup.

"You're going through with the construction?" Brad asked, clearly surprised.

"I haven't decided yet."

Even as she directed her words to Brad, she couldn't take her eyes off Zach's bare, sweat-slick back and the sexy, drool-inducing way his narrow hips moved in those raggedy jeans.

It wasn't just that the man was ripped; after years working out in hotel gyms, she'd seen more than her

share of buffed-up males. It was, she thought, the knowl-
edge that he'd built his muscles the old-fashioned way—
by hard work and whatever physical training SEALs did
when they weren't killing terrorists—that made his body
downright lust-inspiring.

Damned if Titania hadn't nailed it. Zachariah Tremayne was a tough, macho, serious piece of SEAL eye
candy.

He was also a distraction she couldn't afford.

"I haven't really had time to digest the idea," she said,
dragging her rebellious mind back to the conversation
at hand.

She had no doubt that Lucie could've pulled off such
an ambitious enterprise. But Titania, for all her talent
in the kitchen and enough business skills to keep the
Wisteria Tea Room running, might not be up to the
grand-scale destination wedding/B&B/tearoom/tours idea
her grandmother had come up with.

Since Brad was looking past her into the house, as if
expecting to be invited in, Sabrina bit back a sigh, re-
claimed her own Southern hospitality, and stepped aside.

"Would you like to come in?"

He glanced down at a diamond-studded gold Rolex
that might have fit in if he were, say, a New York City
hip-hop mogul but was definitely overkill for sleepy
Swann Island.

"That'd be great. Thanks. I still have a few minutes
before I have to leave for an appointment with my financial backers in Somersett. I'd like to talk with you
about your plans for Swannsea."

She led him into the formal parlor and was relieved
when he turned down her offer of tea and cookies.

"A great deal depends on Linc," she said, thinking
out loud as she absently straightened a stack of *Southern
Living* magazines that looked about to topple off a mahogany table. She sat down on the Queen Anne chair
covered in purple velvet.

If Lincoln Davis found tours of the plantation and

factory disruptive to the operation of the farm, the entire idea wasn't worth considering. Because even opening the house to overnight guests and the added twist of Titania's using tea in the recipes wouldn't be enough of a draw to make Swannsea all that different from all the other lace-curtained tearooms scattered all over the South.

If she did take on the project, she was definitely going to have to clean out Lucie's stuff. The cardboard box beside the table, filled with bubble-wrapped pieces of shamrock-sprigged Belleek china decorative pieces, suggested that the same thought had occurred to her grandmother.

"I would imagine that it would be difficult, if not impossible, for Lincoln to operate the tours and oversee the actual plantation," Brad said, unwittingly echoing her own thoughts. He paused for a meaningful beat. "Have you even spoken with him about this so-called plan of Miss Lucie's?"

"Not in detail."

Sensing that he had an ulterior motive in asking, and not liking the veiled sarcasm in his use of the term "so-called," Sabrina wasn't about to admit that she'd learned about the idea only a few hours earlier.

"Of course we've talked on the phone," she added. "But with me having been in Florence and him first in South America and now Atlanta, it's been difficult to get together."

"I'm surprised he didn't see fit to be here when his boss arrived home."

"I arrived earlier than expected. Plus, the international conference in Atlanta has been planned for months; it's important to Swann Tea, so I wouldn't want to pull him away. Besides, I'm not exactly his boss."

"You own Swannsea."

"Well, yes. I guess I do." Something she still wasn't used to.

"Which means you also own the tea company. Which, in turn, makes you Davis's boss."

When he put it that way, she couldn't debate it. "Perhaps on an organizational pyramid," she allowed. "But other than liking to drink tea, I really don't know anything about the business."

Which was why, up until now, having been too focused on her own possible promotion, she'd left the details of the farm to Linc and Harlan.

Still, she'd known that eventually she would have to get up to speed so she could understand all those reports the two men kept sending her. Also, while she might not know all that much about the family business, she believed that Linc's latest idea—blending pure cocoa he'd made a deal to buy while down in South America with cinnamon in an herbal tea infusion—could prove hugely popular.

"You could always sell."

"Sell what?"

"The business."

"To whom?"

He shrugged. "To me."

"You?"

Surprise made her tone sharper than she'd intended.

Although there wasn't any solid proof, many historians considered Swann Tea to be America's first tea plantation, established back in the eighteen hundreds when the French explorer and botanist André Michaux had imported the tea plants, along with stunningly beautiful varieties of camellias, gardenias, and azaleas to enhance the formal gardens of wealthy Southern planters.

Margaret Swann, a famous Southern beauty known for her charm, had been a guest at a dinner party in Charleston where Michaux was showing off his garden plan. Before the botanist knew what had hit him, he'd not only agreed to create showplace formal gardens on Swann Island but also surrendered precious tea plants that had been destined for a rival farm on Pawley's Island.

The plantation thrived, and despite all the stories chil-

dren were taught in elementary schools about the colo-
nies' switching to coffee after those patriots up in Boston
held their little tea party, Sabrina's family had supplied
tea to the Continental army during the American
Revolution.

In fact, George Washington had reportedly told Mat-
thew Swann that while he was willing to make many
sacrifices for this fledgling democracy, giving up Swann
Darjeeling was not one of them.

Although the gardens had been burned by Federal
troops during the War Between the States, Annabelle
Swann—another beauty whose husband had died during
brutal hand-to-hand combat in the battle for Fort
Wagner on Morris Island—charmed the officer in command of the mission by roasting Swannsea's last remaining chicken and serving it to him along with two
bottles of port she'd buried in the kitchen garden.

While rumors continued to this day as to exactly how
far Annabelle had been willing to go to save her family
home from the Yankees, the fact was that Swannsea was
one of the few antebellum homes outside of Savannah
to survive the war.

The family's most prized memento of those early years
was a cartoon published in the *Boston Gazette*. A takeoff
on Napoleon's quote about an army marching on its
stomach, it showed the Revolutionary army marching
while drinking Swann Tea. It would be a wonderful item
to frame for the new tearoom, Sabrina thought.

Going one step further, what if they were to build an
attached gift shop and sell replicas? The image could
even appear on postcards sold with boxes of tea and
copies of other Swannsea memorabilia, much of which
was historically valuable enough to draw media attention
if it were all gathered into a collection. Perhaps in a
small museum on the premises?

Which could draw in both professional and amateur
historians and add even more credibility to the idea of
Swannsea as a destination location.

"Sabrina?"

"I'm sorry."

Belatedly realizing he'd been talking to her, Sabrina shook her head to rid it of a mental image of the John Singer Sargent portrait of her great-grandmother that hung at the top of the stairs in the main foyer.

Wouldn't that make a fabulous focal point for the restaurant?

"What did you say?"

"We were discussing you selling Swannsea to me. Well, technically, to my real estate company. We've had great success with Plantation Shores. The entire development sold out before we'd even broken ground."

"Even if I wanted to sell something that has been in my family for over two hundred years, do you have any experience with growing tea?"

"No more than you," he said pointedly. An edge of annoyance revealed a crack in his smoothly polished exterior. "But I wasn't thinking of growing tea."

He looked out the window, toward the fields of tea plants. "As I was explaining to Miss Lucie before her untimely passing, tea's always been a risky proposition down here, what with the possibility of hurricanes. I've never understood why she kept the business running after her husband left."

"Perhaps because not only has the business been successful for two centuries, the Swann name has always been synonymous with the best tea in the world," Sabrina said loyally. "I couldn't imagine Swann Plantation without it."

Granted, according to those spreadsheets Harlan had sent her, sales had dipped in the years after Starbucks got seemingly the entire country hooked on coffee, but tea had been making a strong comeback for the past three quarters.

"Times change," he pointed out—something she knew herself. "Even down here in the South." Another pause. "This is some of the most prime real estate on the eastern seaboard. It would be an ideal location for a golf course."

Surely he wasn't serious? "There are already two courses on the island."

"With more and more tourism, we can always use another. Swannsea would definitely be the jewel in my crown."

His crown? Sabrina nearly had to bite her tongue to keep from pointing out that no one had notified her that Brad had been declared king of Swann Island.

"Some of the most famous course designers in the world are salivating to develop this location, which offers the best of the best," he said, pressing his point. "You've got the beach on one side, then the marsh, then, of course, all the trees, which would make Swannsea one of the more challenging courses in the South. The greens would be where the fields currently are, of course."

He was looking out over the fields in question, hands on his hips, for all the world like a king or emperor surveying his domain.

The only problem was it happened to be *her* domain.

"The fields look pretty green to me right now." They were also lovely, and they stirred an unexpected emotion of belonging deep inside her.

Unlike competing countries, where workers were paid next to nothing to harvest tea by hand, at Swannsea Tea a commercial machine chugged up and down the rows, cutting the top leaves from the shoulder-high bushes.

"Granted, but there's nothing prettier than rolling bent-grass greens." Her dry tone had obviously flown right over his head. "The factory would have to go, of course. But the actual house would stay."

"Well, that's encouraging," she said. "Given that it's a historical home predating the war."

"True. But your grandmother never had it listed on the historical register," he countered, surprising Sabrina by revealing that he had investigated Swannsea's status.

"Lucie was an independent thinker. She always

wanted to maintain the house's historical integrity."
Hence her long-term working relationship with Zach's
father. "But she balked at the idea of being forced to
apply to some historical committee every time she
wanted to make a change to her own home."

Which also explained, Sabrina decided, how she'd
been planning to expand the house without jumping
through historical or zoning hoops.

"Her independent streak turned out to be a bonus,"
Brad agreed. "Since the house is not on the register, its
owner—"

"Who would be me—"

"Who would be you." His smile was meant to charm,
but it reminded Sabrina more of a used-car salesman
trying to convince you to buy the old beater that had
been sitting on his lot for six months. "May I make
a suggestion?"

"What?"

"Come to dinner with me. There's this great new
place in Somersett, on the waterfront—"

"Aren't you married?"

"I am. To a lovely woman I adore to pieces, who, as
it happens, has our first bun in the oven."

"Congratulations," Sabrina said, amazed that anyone
under the age of seventy still used that phrase for pregnancy. Even here in the land of polite sexual euphemisms.

"Mary Sue and I are real excited about the baby," he
said. "But you needn't worry, Sabrina. I'm not inviting
you out on a date. All I'm asking for is an opportunity
to explain my plans. Which I think you'll find attractive."

"I really don't think that's necessary," she said. "Because I've no intention of selling Swannsea."

She didn't need to sit through a meal with Brad Sumner to be told what he was planning to do with Lucie's
home. With her family's home.

She'd bet he was planning to use it as a clubhouse.
The idea of golfers destroying the home's hand-pegged
hickory floors with their cleated shoes was unthinkable.

"At least let me introduce you to my backers." He continued to press his case. "I'm not sure you realize how much money could be involved."

"It's not about the money."

"No offense intended, Sabrina, but that sounds a bit naive for someone who's spent so many years climbing the corporate ladder of an international hotel chain." His tone took on an edge. "It's *always* about the money."

"Not to me." Or to her grandmother.

Although she'd never thought she had a single thing in common with Scarlett O'Hara, whom so many considered the quintessential Southern belle, Sabrina suddenly understood why Margaret Mitchell's headstrong heroine had been willing to do anything it took, even putting on curtains to visit Rhett Butler in jail, to save her beloved Tara.

A thought belatedly occurred to her. "Did you discuss this with Lucie?"

She saw the hesitation flash in his eyes as he tried to decide how much to reveal. Given how small a place Swann Island was, they both knew he wouldn't be able to get away with an out-and-out lie.

"Of course we discussed it."

"And?"

"And, unfortunately, while she professed interest, she died before she had a chance to meet with my partners."

Liar.

Sabrina might have been away from the island for too long. She might, as much as she hated to admit it, even be accused of having neglected her grandmother.

And, granted, things had changed a great deal since the last time she'd been back. But she had not a single doubt that there was no way Lucie would've been willing to turn land that had been in her family for more than two centuries over to this man.

"Times have been tough," he said, as if sensing her arguments. "Profits were down—"

"The company may have experienced a few challenging years. Partly due to skyrocketing real estate taxes."

Harlan had explained that all the new real estate development—such as Plantation Shores—had caused property values to spike, driving many smaller planters out of business.

"But there *were* profits."

She might not have read every clause and subsection of those papers, but she had understood the bottom line. Which had definitely shown what seemed to be a significant profit.

And, thinking about it, hadn't Linc said they'd just ended their best sales quarter in a decade? Thanks to all the media reports about green tea being beneficial to health?

"I'll tell you what," he said. "Why don't I give you some time to think about my offer?" He tossed out an amount in the high seven figures. "Talk with Harlan. And Linc, of course, and I'll get back to you in a couple days."

He'd definitely missed his calling. If not used cars, he could've been the emperor of vinyl siding.

"That's an attractive offer." She suspected a lot of people would jump at it. "But my answer will still be *no*."

Annoyance flashed in his eyes, but a benign, blatantly false smile stayed pasted on his face. Which, she noted, had a weak chin. Especially when compared to Zach's.

He took a thick manila envelope out of his alligator briefcase and laid it on the marble-topped table between them. "It won't hurt to at least look at the preliminary plans." He laid a glossy black business card with raised silver letters on top of the envelope. "Feel free to call me with any questions.

"I don't want to put pressure on you," he said as she walked him out to the veranda, "but my backers aren't patient people. And they're currently looking at other locations."

"On Swann Island?"

"They're partial to Swann, since the land is still less expensive, relatively speaking, but they're also interested in the Isle of Palms, Seabrook Island, and Edisto Island."

All of which, as far as Sabrina was concerned, were welcome to them.

"I'll look at the plans," she said, just wanting to get rid of the man, "but I can't imagine that my answer will change."

She could tell he wasn't happy as he marched back to his snazzy little BMW sports coupe.

Tough.

She thought she'd gotten rid of him, but after he started the engine, he rolled down the driver's-side window.

"There's one other thing you might want to keep in mind," he said.

"What's that?" She braced herself for yet another sales pitch.

"I realize you had feelings for Tremayne back in high school, but as wild as he was then, he's gotten a lot worse. In fact, if even half the stories about what he's done in the so-called line of duty are true, he's downright dangerous."

Sabrina folded her arms. "I wouldn't exactly call fighting terrorism *so-called* line of duty." Having been a victim of a terrorism attack, she was grateful that men like Zach existed.

"Point taken. But fighting the bad guys probably wasn't what got him court-martialed."

Court-martialed? Titania hadn't mentioned that little detail while singing Zach's praises.

"I'm certainly no expert on the military, but I thought special operations were pretty much secret."

"They are. Which is, unfortunately, why no one's exactly sure what happened over there to get him kicked out of the SEALs. Though I have heard rumors of him beating an officer to death with his bare hands."

"I don't believe that."

Zach may have been wild, but there was no way she would believe that the boy who'd been surprisingly tender when turning down her advances could have done such a thing.

"Like I said, they're only rumors." He shrugged. "But the fact remains that he's no longer in the service, and it's no rumor that he was drunk most of the time when he first came back to the island. So, whatever happened, I'm sure your grandmother, if she were still alive, would warn you to stay clear of the guy. Because there's a good chance he's dangerously unstable."

"I'm perfectly capable of taking care of myself. But thank you for your concern."

Which, Sabrina suspected, as she watched him drive back down the oak-lined drive, had a lot more to do with Brad not wanting her to go through with the construction plans than actually caring about her welfare.

20

After the BMW had disappeared from view, Sabrina went back into the house, and although she'd never been one to act on impulse, skimmed through the phone book and had just picked up the receiver to call Zach when the phone rang.

"Darling, I heard you'd come home early. Why on earth didn't you call and let us know you were coming?"

"It was a spur-of-the moment decision." And one she was already getting tired of explaining. "And I only got in last night, Aunt Lillian."

Although Lillian Honeycutt was technically the wife of Lucie's cousin, which, in the complex and interrelated ways of the South, made her, Sabrina thought—though wasn't quite sure—a second cousin twice removed by marriage, for some reason she'd grown up referring to Harlan and Lillian as aunt and uncle.

"But still, if I'd only known, Eugenia and I could have made the house ready for you. Put in some groceries."

"I didn't mind shopping."

"But, after all you've been through, you shouldn't have to. You should be resting."

"I'm not an invalid, Aunt Lillian. I'm fine. Really."

"Darling, you had a building blown up from underneath you."

"Well, there was that."

Sabrina's tone was a great deal drier than the air. She lifted her hair to allow the artificially chilled breeze flowing through the AC vents to cool the back of her neck.

"Honestly, darling, now you remind me of your father. He may have had a clever talent, but he never took anything seriously either."

"I take what happened very seriously. I just don't want to let a single act of terrorism define me."

"Well, I suppose I can understand that," Lillian Honeycutt allowed. "And isn't it exactly how Lucie would behave? Others might have first seen her brass. But I always admired her steel."

"Me, too."

"Your grandmother is sorely missed." Lillian's magnolia voice thickened with loss, and hearing a sniffle on the other end of the line, Sabrina pictured her dabbing her eyes with one of those lace-trimmed handkerchiefs she was never without. "Well, now that you're home, you must come to dinner."

"I'd like that."

It was mostly the truth. She did want to see her aunt and uncle again but had been happily planning to nuke a frozen sesame chicken dinner and then go to bed early with the paperback thriller she'd picked up at the market.

"Fine. I'll send Eugenia's husband, George, to pick you up at seven."

Realizing that her hopes for a quiet evening had been dashed, Sabrina tried one last negotiation ploy. "I'm perfectly capable of driving."

"After what happened to that poor girl, there's no way I'm allowing you out on the road alone after dark."

"What poor girl? And what happened?"

"You haven't heard?"

"No." If she had, she wouldn't have asked.

"Well"—Lillian lowered her voice, as if afraid someone might overhear her— "she was murdered in cold blood. Then her body was thrown into the marsh. As if she were nothing more than a piece of used tissue."

"Oh, my God. That's terrible." Sabrina couldn't recall ever hearing about a murder on Swann Island.

"It's worse. Although Harlan wouldn't share the details—professional ethics and all that, never mind that we've been married forty-three years—Eugenia happened to overhear him talking with Nate Spencer . . . he's the sheriff now. Nate, not Harlan."

"So Titania told me."

"They're such a lovely couple. Why, I was telling Nate just today, when he was here for the autopsy, that it's high time he started thinking seriously of marriage."

"That's one of those things people have to do in their own time."

"True. But I was seventeen when I married my Harlan, and look how well that turned out."

Sabrina couldn't argue that point. Forty-three years was definitely an achievement.

"Well, anyway, the poor dead girl appears to have been tortured."

Sabrina's breath caught. She opened her mouth to accuse her aunt of joking, but slammed it shut before the words slipped out. Murder was definitely nothing that anyone, let alone Lillian Honeycutt, would joke about.

"While chained."

Goose bumps prickled their way up Sabrina's arms. Ice hit her veins, freezing away the feeling of being in a sauna.

Okay. That was downright creepy for anywhere. Let alone the island.

"I'd fret myself to distraction worrying about you," Lillian said.

"We wouldn't want that."

When Lucie had first called with the news that Lillian was suffering from post-polio syndrome, Sabrina had researched the illness online and learned that depression and anxiety were not only common in PS sufferers but could also exacerbate other physical problems. Not a good thing, considering that Lillian was, according to Lucie, also showing signs of Parkinson's disease.

"The car will be there at seven o'clock." Lillian's pleased tone suggested she hadn't expected any other outcome. "Don't worry about dressing up, darling. Although I'd love to throw you a big welcome-home party, this is going to be a casual evening at home with family. I'm so looking forward to seeing you again, Sabrina. It's been far too long."

Sabrina couldn't argue with that.

It was only one evening. At least Lillian didn't run her house on European time—Sabrina figured that if she had to wait until nine o'clock to eat, she'd end up falling asleep before the Honeycutts' longtime housekeeper served the first course.

Fighting off jet lag, she dialed the number she'd initially intended to call.

"Well, that didn't take long." The deep, all-too-familiar male drawl came over the wires and slipped beneath her skin.

"What didn't take long?"

"For Sumner to wear out his welcome."

Did Zach Tremayne have to sound so damn smug? "What makes you think I'm not calling to tell you not to bother to come back tomorrow because I've decided to sell Swannsea to Brad's development company?"

"Never happen."

"Why not?" Even worse than his smugness was the thought that she might be so predictable.

"Because you're obviously an intelligent woman, New York. Plus, you're Lucie's granddaughter. No way are you going to hand over the ancestral home to a pirate like Sumner."

"In case it's slipped your mind, Lucie came from pirate roots."

"And was damn proud of them," he agreed without missing a beat. "In fact, she would've been one helluva privateer herself, back in the day. But guys like Sumner and his cohorts give pirates a bad name.

"Besides, the island already has two golf courses. What the hell does it need with a third?"

Which was exactly what she'd wondered. She'd also never understood the appeal of chasing a little white ball around all day.

"I suspect maybe golfers feel differently. So, you don't play?"

"Nah. I tried it once back in San Diego when I was dating an admiral's daughter. Took me two holes to realize I sucked at the game."

"Really?"

That surprised her. From the way he'd been swinging that hammer, and given that SEALs had to stay active, she'd have guessed that he would be good at all things physical.

Including . . .

Do not think about that! she warned herself when the idea of getting physical with Zachariah Tremayne flashed through her mind.

"Really. I never could figure out whether to hit the ball when the dragon's mouth was open or closed."

Oh, damn. He'd made a joke. A lame one, granted. But heaven help her, it had her wondering if he might be the kind of man who could laugh in bed.

And definitely don't think about him in bed!

"May I ask you a question?"

"Sure. And the answer is yes."

"You don't even know what it is." She wondered what he'd say if she asked about his alleged court-martial.

"Doesn't matter. I can't imagine any man saying no to you, cupcake."

But he once had. She wondered if—hoped—his statement meant he'd forgotten the episode. After all, she suspected he'd had hordes of women all over the world throwing themselves at his feet. And other, more vital parts of his anatomy. Why should he remember her rash behavior?

"Did Lucie work with your father on plans for the addition?"

"As it happens, I have a set of working blueprints in the truck. I can bring them by this evening. Maybe pick up some softshell crabs to eat while we discuss them."

Smooth. Despite her determination to avoid temptation, she felt her lips quirking. "I'm having dinner with Harlan and Lillian tonight. Tomorrow will be soon enough."

"Works for me."

She wasn't interested, Sabrina assured herself later as she turned on the shower. Had no intention of becoming interested. So, why was she irked by the fact that he hadn't pressed her to go out to dinner with him?

It was just as well. She had, after all, come back to the island for some much-needed rest and relaxation. And, unfortunately, although she hated to admit it, there was nothing relaxing about the way Zach Tremayne made her feel.

Swann Island wasn't precisely the same as when she'd last visited. But some things, it appeared, never changed.

"So." She stripped off her clothes and stood beneath the cool water. "Get over it."

Something, she feared, as she smoothed the liquid soap over her body, imagining Zach's hands following that same path, might well be easier said than done.

21

Damned if he wasn't thinking about her. Just as, though he knew she was fighting against admitting it, she was thinking about him. The difference was that while he would bet his left nut that she'd rather have his father be the one to show up in the morning with the blueprints for the Swannsea addition, Zach welcomed the diversion.

Sabrina Swann might have gone up in the world since that summer Lucie had thrown her a sweet sixteen birthday party—from what her grandmother had told him, she was a real hotshot in the international hotel world—but she was still a woman. A woman who'd once kissed him with all the pent-up fervor of a teenager in love.

Okay. Not love.

At sixteen she hadn't even known the meaning of the word. No, what she'd felt for him was good old elemental lust. The same lust that, God help him, had caused his dick to leap to attention when she'd wrapped that lissome young body, barely clad in a teeny-weeny pink bikini, around him and made it all too clear that she was his. If he wanted her.

Which, hell, yes, he had.

But while he might have been reckless and rebellious, he hadn't been suicidal.

Sabrina Swann had been jailbait, pure and simple. And while certainly he'd enjoyed his share of women since losing his virginity to Patsy Buchanan his fifteenth summer, he'd never had sex worth going to jail for.

And even if Nate's dad hadn't thrown him in the pokey, Lucie probably would've gotten that old shotgun out of the gun case in her former husband's den and filled him full of buckshot.

Doing the math, he realized she was now twenty-seven, past the age of consent, and damned if she hadn't been looking at him the same way she had all that long, hot summer. The difference was, back then she hadn't the faintest idea what she was offering.

Since he doubted that she'd hung on to the virginity she'd been so eager to shed, she had to know exactly how a guy felt when a woman looked at him like she was fantasizing jumping his bones.

Just the mental image of her riding him, her slender body glistening with sweat, her long hair tumbling nearly to her bare ass as she arched her back, her tits jutting out, begging for him to take them in his mouth, kicked his libido, which he'd begun to fear had died in those faraway mountains, into high gear.

Before the helo crash that had taken the lives of too many good men and changed his life forever, Zach's mind had mostly focused on two things: his team and sex.

Afterward, while his former team was never far from his mind—particularly since Quinn had also landed here in South Carolina—sex had disappeared below the radar.

Until he'd looked in the window and—sweet Jesus save him—seen Sabrina Swann, nearly naked, with that shirt twisted up to her thighs.

And although he'd done his damnedest to forget how hot she'd looked by sweating buckets and pounding those big fat nails into her slate roof, he was rapidly coming to the conclusion that the image had been indelibly imprinted on his sex-starved brain.

Which meant, unless he wanted to go through life in a horny haze, he was going to have to do something about her.

He'd never been one for entanglements. Though he knew SEALs who'd gotten married, he'd never thought the nature of his work would make him a very good husband.

The business of a warrior was to fight. Period. And when he did fight, he fought to win, because anything less would not only put his team and his mission at risk but could well cost him his life.

From the moment he'd shown up at BUD/S, Zach had trained for that single instant when he would kill or be killed.

At least the Marines and Special Forces went in all cannons blasting, which had never been the SEAL way. SEALs were all about covert operations; if anyone knew you'd been there, you'd fucked up.

And even if the bad guys were terrorist scum who deserved to die, there was no getting around the fact that setting up an ambush was, pure and simple, premeditated murder.

He could envision it now, his wife at some froufrou ladies' tea at the Hotel del Coronado being asked what, exactly, her husband did for a living, and saying, "Oh, my Zach? Why, he's an assassin."

Talk about your conversation killers.

Also, from what he'd observed, the learning curve for a SEAL wife was every bit as steep as for a guy entering the teams. At least the guys were trained for the role; women had to pretty much figure it out for themselves.

He'd watched more than one marriage between two good people disintegrate because the woman hadn't planned on having to put up with the pack behavior of a band of SEAL warriors even when they were off duty.

Women, at least the ones he'd met over the years, liked dating SEALs. Liked it a lot, and being male, and human, he'd taken his share of groupies home from country clubs and dives around the world.

Dating a guy who was always taking off on mysterious missions was probably kind of a rush. But being married to a husband who spent months overseas, was away much of the time training for his next deployment when he was stateside, and didn't come home at six p.m. like other neighborhood husbands did had to be the pits.

You'd think a wife's having a career of her own would ease the problems. But from what he'd seen, from the outside looking in, it could make things even worse. Because when her SEAL did get home from deployment and wanted to spend all his leave time with her, well, likely as not she wasn't going to be able to drop everything and fuck like a sex-crazed bunny twenty-four hours a day.

"Even if you were still in the team, you're not talking about marrying the woman," he reminded himself. "Just getting her naked."

And keeping her that way.

All night long.

Another thing he'd learned in the SEALs was that a failure to plan was a plan for failure.

Flipping open his cell phone, Zach set his plan in motion.

22

Using the accepted definition that a serial killer is someone who commits three or more murders with an emotional cooling-off period between the homicides, Nate had to suspect that was what he was dealing with.

While Cleo Gibson, Hallie Conroy, and the still unidentified John Doe weren't identical killings, there was enough similarity, particularly in the slashed throats—which Harlan believed had all been done with the same type of blade—that Nate tamped down his pride and made a call to the Somersett regional FBI office.

After all, as a former Marine, he was accustomed to working with others, right?

Still, having to call in the feds grated. He was, after all, one of the few. The proud. But he was also pragmatic. If he waited until he had a clearer picture of the situation or, even worse, held back because of his pride, the murderer could claim another victim. Which was not an option.

Apparently it was a slow day, because the pair arrived within the hour: a redhead with mile-long legs who was wearing a charcoal gray suit, and a guy in a black suit and shades who looked as if he'd come from a casting call for *MIB III* or *The Matrix*. His New Jersey accent, straight out of *The Sopranos*, was Nate's first clue that he wasn't a local.

Although MIB, aka Special Agent Frank Angetti, barely skimmed the autopsy reports and Nate's field notes, the redhead, Caitlin Cavanaugh, went through them line by line, stopping every so often to question Nate on some detail. Not that he was much help.

Hell, if he'd had a handle on the case, he wouldn't have called them in the first place.

"Okay." She leaned back in the chair and, lifting her arm at an angle that had her breasts moving in an interesting way beneath her white silk blouse, rubbed the back of her neck. "So victims number one and two were murdered and moved."

"So the medical examiner said," Nate replied.

"But number three's body was found at the murder scene."

Nate nodded. "After an obvious struggle and an attempt to escape."

The canister of pepper spray had told its own tragic story. As had the semen left behind. Nate had sent that pretty white bedspread to the state DNA lab in Columbia, but given the backlog, he figured he might, if he was lucky, get a response back before his retirement party.

He hoped that bringing the feds in would speed things up.

"Pretty risky, attacking a woman in the middle of the day."

"Shows a disorganized UNSUB," MIB declared.

"Or someone who knew the victim," Nate said.

"And the territory," Special Agent Cavanaugh mused, revealing that she wasn't discounting his idea. "She was comfortable enough to let him in—"

"Doesn't mean he knew her," MIB argued. "That serial killer down in Baton Rouge gained access to some of his victims' houses by asking to use the phone."

"Hallie Conroy wasn't killed at home." Nate pointed out what the guy would've known if he'd read the notes. "Her car was found broken down on the side of the road. It's my guess that she was picked up while walking home."

"A crime of opportunity is another sign of a disorganized killer." MIB pressed his point.

"Always a possibility," Caitlin Cavanaugh allowed. "Though he could have been hunting. At night," she stressed. "Which again points to the victim knowing her killer, since I doubt all that many women would get into a car late at night with a total stranger."

"Hookers do it all the time," her partner argued.

"Hallie Conroy was no hooker," Nate said between clenched teeth. "But, according to witnesses at the motel, she was majorly pissed off at finding her husband in bed with another woman. That could be reason enough for a woman not to be thinking clearly."

"Maybe she got into the killer's car looking for a little revenge sex," Special Agent Cavanaugh suggested.

As she crossed her legs, Nate enjoyed a quick flash of camellia-pale thigh.

"Again suggesting that they might have known each other," he said. "Especially given that the population of the island is a little under fifteen hundred people. Not counting the tourists."

"The time period between the killings tends to narrow the possibility of it being a tourist," she said thoughtfully. "At least a short-timer. It should be easy enough to find who's rented a vacation home or condo for a full month."

"I've already got a man working on that." Nate had assigned one of his three deputies to the task of calling every place on the island. So far nothing had panned out. But that didn't mean it wouldn't.

"It's a single white male," MIB declared.

"And you know this how?"

"Whether she needed a ride, or was looking to get fucked, victim two felt safe enough to get into a car with him, on a deserted road, late at night. Plus, most serial killers are single white males."

"But not all." It took an effort to keep his tone even

after having to listen to the implication that a black man driving a car would automatically have been perceived as a threat. "If you want to play the race card, I probably should point out that a black woman might be less likely to get into a car with a white man.

"As for serial killers being mostly single white males, you brought up Derrick Todd Lee, from Baton Rouge. And don't forget Wayne Williams."

Who'd gone undetected for too long because the victims were black children, whom many white law enforcement officers had written off as runaways, accidents, or drug deals gone wrong. Even after a pattern had begun to develop, many people were focused on rumors of a KKK conspiracy. Some, Nate remembered his father saying, had even blamed witches.

"Well, there are always exceptions," MIB allowed testily.

Obviously the fed wasn't used to having his authority questioned. Tough.

"What you're undoubtedly looking for, Sheriff," MIB continued, "is a single white male, with an above-average IQ, who did poorly in school, has a spotty employment record, and works in a job that doesn't require many skills.

"He could come from a deeply troubled family, might have been abandoned at an early age by his father, and grew up with a domineering mother figure, since the rapes point toward a hostility toward women.

"You can expect psychiatric problems, including criminal behavior. As a child your UNSUB probably suffered significant abuse. Physical and most likely sexual, which has instilled in him profound feelings of humiliation and helplessness. Which he makes up for by humiliating others. Thus the branding of your young female victim.

"He'll have also manifested brutality toward animals in his youth in which he rehearsed his later murders, and a precocious interest in deviant sexuality."

"Well, hell, that should make it a snap to locate him,"

Nate drawled, understanding why his father had defined "FBI" as "full of bullshit ideas." "Except for the little fact that besides a stint in the Marines, I've lived here all my life and can't think of a single citizen of Swann Island who fits that very narrow description."

"Those are general characteristics," the redhead—who'd rolled her eyes during her partner's recitation, which made Nate decide that not all feds were dipshits—said. "And while they can be helpful, they can also admittedly divert attention from the actual killer, who, when caught, often appears to be the guy next door."

Which was exactly what Nate was concerned about. According to witnesses, Hallie Conroy had been a loose cannon ever since she'd met the bad boy she'd pissed off her military father by running away with. Even her grieving parents and closest friends had described her as impulsive. And unpredictable.

But Cleo was another case entirely. As an ER worker, she was not only required to keep her head in the midst of chaos, she had to have developed a pretty strong bullshit detector. The fact that someone had managed to get past her defenses indicated that her killer was not only someone she knew but someone she trusted.

"I wish we could do more to help you out, Sheriff," Cavanaugh said. "But you've probably heard of a little problem called terrorism—right now most of our resources are being focused on that.

"Together, Somersett and Charleston harbors receive millions of containers, most of them from foreign countries, coming into port every year. Add to that the Naval Weapons Station with the capacity to handle sixty-two million pounds of explosives, and the two Air Force Air Wing Commands flying several flights a day, and you've got yourself an attractive target. Especially given that bin Laden has purchased several ships specifically for terrorist purposes.

"We were on our way to a Project Seahawk exercise in Charleston when we received your call. As things

stand right now, I'm afraid we're not going to be able
to devote many resources to your possible serial killer."

Having served two tours in Iraq, and another in Afghanistan, Nate knew firsthand about resources being
overextended. He understood that three murders would
seem like small potatoes if a crazed terrorist cell decided
to blow up one of the nation's busiest container ports.

But that didn't mean he had to like it.

He also wondered how many more people would have
to die before the FBI considered their deaths worth
bothering with.

"I understand the need to prioritize. But our state labs
have a long backlog on DNA analysis. A sample from
the third victim's been sent to CODIS. Anything you
could do to move your agency along would be much
appreciated."

MIB opened his mouth, and from his aggressive expression, Nate figured he was about to explain to the
rube cop how the system worked, but the redhead lifted
her hand, cutting off whatever her partner had intended
to say.

"I can't guarantee any results, but I will call the office
in Columbia and see what I can do."

"That's all I can ask."

Actually, he'd like a helluva lot more cooperation, but
remembering what Nate Senior had always said about
beggars not being able to be choosers, he decided to
settle for what he could get.

There was also the fact that, worst-case scenario, he
might need to call Special Agent Caitlin Cavanaugh and
her asshole partner in again. No point in burning
bridges.

"Well, then, I guess that about covers it." She stood
up, smoothed the front of her pin-striped skirt, and held
out her hand. "It's always a privilege to meet an honest-
to-God hero. I wish it could've been under more pleasant conditions."

"I'm no hero." Her nails were buffed to a glossy sheen, her palms smooth.

"Tell that to the people who awarded you a Silver Star for valor."

"I was just another Marine trying to do my job on the battlefield." What it had been was a really ugly ambush in Fallujah. "And I'd give it up in a heartbeat if it could bring back the lives of all the men who died that day." He'd never spoken truer words.

Her smile lit up her eyes. "And that, Sheriff Spencer, is exactly why you're a hero."

Nate walked her out, ignoring the asshole, who was making a point of ignoring him in return. Just your federal taxes at work, he thought as he watched them move toward the black SUV with dual whip antennas that screamed government agent car.

She was about to climb into the driver's seat when she took out a card embossed with the FBI shield from a black leather folder and wrote an additional number on it. "If anything new comes up, give me a call on my cell. That'll be quicker than going through official channels, which could get your murders assigned to someone different. Someone not familiar with the case."

"Thanks." Nate pocketed the card. "I appreciate any help you can provide."

"I've lived here in the Lowcountry since high school. The idea of some cretin killing people in my homeplace pisses me off. Besides"—her eyes smiled again in a way that, if he wasn't already head over heart in love with another woman, would've had Nate calling Special Agent Cait Cavanaugh for reasons that had nothing to do with a suspected serial killer—"we good guys have to stick together."

Since he was in love, not dead, Nate took a fleeting bit of pleasure in watching her climb into the SUV.

After she'd driven away, he checked his watch. Titania would be taking dinner to her father, which gave him another hour before she would show up at his house, looking to work off the stress and unhappiness of the nursing home visit with a round or two of hot, raunchy sex.

She would insist, if pressed, that she was merely scratching an itch. An itch they'd both been working on since those high school days they'd spent rolling around in the bed of his old Dodge pickup parked out in the marsh.

But it had always been more than that for him. And although she continued to refuse to admit it, for reasons he suspected had something to do with her mother having died giving birth to her, Nate knew it meant more to her, too.

So, since his hunger for her was as strong—stronger—than it had been back when he was a hormone-driven teenager and since he was confident that he would eventually convince her to see the light, Nate was willing to take pleasure in what she was offering.

For now.

Meanwhile, he thought with a long, slow sigh, he had three murder victims who needed someone to stand for them.

Which, since his retired, RVing father was currently off in some place called Tucumcari, New Mexico, left him.

Telling himself that it still beat being in the middle of a firefight in the streets of Ramadi, Nate decided to drive out to Cleo's house again. Just to get a feel for the scene and to see if there might be something he'd missed the first time.

23

Because what the Honeycutts might consider casual had always been more formal than the definition used by most of the population, especially here on the island, Sabrina chose a simple sleeveless peach silk shift that belted low on the hip and, as an outward show of exuberance that she was a long way from feeling, put on a dangly pair of earrings.

She frowned as she studied her reflection in the dressing table mirror.

"Too sharp."

The French braid that had appeared both tidy and sophisticated in Florence only served to accentuate the prominent angles in her face, drawing attention to her recent weight loss. She brushed her hair loose, allowing it to fall over her shoulders, softening her features.

Still with time to spare, she walked from room to room, weaving around tables cluttered with Lucie's collectibles and yet more open cardboard boxes, experiencing a flood of memories.

The library was crowded floor to ceiling with books. And not just for show, either. Sabrina knew for a fact that Lucie had read every book in this room. At least once.

She'd always had an open mind, been an eclectic reader. Best-selling thrillers shared space with leatherbound first editions and stacks of well-read paperback romance novels that had given Sabrina her first insight into how love might be between a man and a woman.

Her parents' marriage had certainly been filled with explosive passion, but from what she'd seen, it leaned more toward shouting and door slamming than the long, lingering kisses described in the paperbacks. Just reading about them could curl a teenage girl's toes.

And obviously her grandfather hadn't felt any of that grand, forever-after devotion shared by the couples between those glossy covers, or he wouldn't have deserted his wife.

Not wanting to dwell on negative thoughts, she moved through the double pocket doors at the far end of the library and into the music room.

The gleaming Steinway grand was, as it had been for as long as Sabrina could remember, topped with silver-framed family photos. It was also too, too silent.

How many hours had she spent practicing her scales and finger exercises while Lucie had sat by the Palladian window in a flowered wing chair, offering enthusiastic encouragement although it was obvious to both pianist and listener that Sabrina's talent for music was several levels sub par.

Looking back on it now, she realized that in her continued efforts to discover an artistic talent, she'd been attempting to find some way to connect with her mother and father. To earn their attention. And, more importantly, their approval.

Unfortunately, while she'd been able to play some simple tunes, her left and right hands had refused to cooperate, which always had her bass notes running a quarter beat behind her treble ones.

Totally tone-deaf, she sang off-key, and while she'd grown up to be able to dash off an articulate e-mail or memo, she obviously hadn't inherited the writing talent that had garnered Lucie a successful career not only as a journalist but as the author of half a dozen nonfiction books about Lowcountry life.

She'd taken drama class in the eighth grade with high hopes, and had even won a speaking role in Thornton Wilder's *Our Town*, but on opening night she got stage fright and forgot her lines. Both of them. Which resulted in her getting replaced by her understudy, an orthodontist's daughter from Greenwich, Connecticut.

As for art, well, a chimpanzee with a fistful of crayons could probably do a better landscape.

At fifteen, she'd been in despair of ever finding a talent when Lucie had pointed out that she simply wasn't opening her eyes.

She was organized to a fault. Dependable. Intelligent, with an almost eidetic memory and an affinity for detail. She easily adapted to new situations and was able to get along with all sorts of disparate personalities, talents that had served her well as she'd moved from school to school, skipping both the second and fourth grades.

Later, as she studied both business and hospitality, Sabrina discovered she was also pretty damn good at getting others to follow her lead. Which was how she'd ended up as the general manager of Paradiso Angeli.

For all of an hour before the bombing.

Shaking off the dark memories that had haunted her sleep last night, she went outside to sit on the veranda swing and wait for the driver Lillian was sending for her.

Her first thought, as the car approached, was he was going awfully fast for a limo driver, leaving a rooster tail of dust behind him.

Her second thought was how many red limos had she seen?

No. Not a limo. A convertible. A very red, very mean-looking convertible.

Driven by—and here was no surprise—Swann Island's very own Navy SEAL.

His hair was windblown, and his arms in the short-sleeved polo shirt he was wearing looked about as massive as the limbs of the ancient oak trees lining the driveway. His eyes were shielded by lenses the color of black ice.

As he pulled to an amazingly fast stop, considering the fact that he appeared to be driving just short of the speed of sound, her hormones hiked.

"Hey, New York." His smile was slow, easy, meant to charm females from eight to eighty. "Don't you look as cool as an ice cream parfait."

The fire-engine-red driver's door opened. Long legs wearing creased jeans swiveled out. "And just as tasty."

The rich baritone flowing over her like honey was even more seductive than the smile, making Sabrina realize that if she did decide to pursue Lucie's plan, she was either going to have to insist on Zach's father acting as contractor—which, of course, would only reveal how strongly Zach affected her—or bring her rebellious hormones under control.

"I thought we'd agreed you'd bring the plans over in the morning."

"I intend to." He was walking toward her in a loose-hipped predatory stride that reminded her of a wolf.

No. Not a wolf. A panther.

For God's sake, get a grip on yourself. He's a man. No different from any other.

And if you believe that, next thing you know, you'll be buying that steel suspension bridge soaring over the Somersett River.

"Then what are you doing here?"

"Didn't Miss Lillian tell you she'd be sending a driver?"

"Yes, but—" Comprehension came like a lightning bolt from a clear blue sky. "You're working for her, too?"

"I've done some handyman work. Planed a door for her last week that swelled up in all this humidity. But as it happens, she invited me to dinner tonight, too. So, since poor old George's lumbago kicked in again, I volunteered to play chauffeur."

"What a coincidence," she said dryly.

"A lucky one," he agreed, his grin deepening the cleft in his firm, hero's chin.

Although it was ridiculous, Sabrina didn't want to be alone in a car with him. Even more unsettling was the fact that she couldn't decide which of them she didn't quite trust. Zach? Or herself?

"I assured Aunt Lillian that I'm perfectly capable of driving myself to dinner."

"Of course you are," he agreed easily. "But after what happened to you in Italy, it'd only make sense that she'd worry about you."

"I suppose so." She glanced past him at that outrageous car. "What happened to the truck?"

"I save that for work. This is for fun."

"I'd think that the color red would get you more speeding tickets."

"Probably would, in some places. But down in San Diego, cops pretty much gave me a pass. Especially those who were former military. Besides, most guys secretly lust after a Viper, so I think it's a kick for them to get an up-close-and-personal view of one. As for Nate, well, he's got bigger fish to fry right now."

"So Aunt Lillian told me." She picked up her bag from the wicker table beside the swing, along with the bouquet of Stargazer lilies she'd gathered for Lillian from the garden. "It's hard to think of a murder happening here on the island."

He put a hand on the small of her back as they walked toward the car. Since the touch seemed more casual than seductive, she didn't want to draw attention to another hormonal jolt by moving away.

"Harder still to think of three."

That stopped her. She turned and looked up at him, damning the dark glasses that kept her from seeing his eyes. "Are you serious?"

"Murder's nothing to joke about."

"No." Wasn't that what she'd said to herself when Lillian had told her about that poor young woman?

Three murders? How was that possible?

"Are they all women?"

"Two women, if today's news is accurate. And one man."

"Are they connected?"

"I haven't spoken with Nate since the third body was found. But it sounds as if they might be."

"That's so impossible to believe." She shuddered as gooseflesh rose on her arms. Began walking again. "Poor Nate. When this gets out, the press from the mainland is going to be all over this place."

"Like white on rice." He opened the passenger door.

Her espadrille wedges made it even more difficult to slide into the low-slung seat without flashing him.

"You know what I said this morning about your bones being too thin?" he asked after he'd come around the front of the vented hood and climbed into the car's cockpit.

"I seem to recall something about that." And it still irked.

"I was wrong. You've got some pair of pins on you, New York."

Unlike the throaty purr of the European sports cars she was used to hearing, this one had the deep, low dangerous growl of a hungry lion.

"Thank you." She hoped her coolly polite tone belied the renewed tangle of nerves.

"And the way they go all the way up to your neck." He punched the gas. "Gives a guy ideas."

As she wondered exactly how much of her lace panties he'd seen, a mighty surge of acceleration pushed her back against the seat. "A Southern gentleman wouldn't bring that up."

"That may be." He turned his head and skimmed a provocative look over her. "But he'd sure as hell be thinking it. And in the interest of fair warning, I'm no Southern gentleman."

"Gracious." It felt as if they were approaching the

speed of sound; wind whipped at her hair. "I never would have noticed that little fact if you hadn't pointed it out to me."

"The lady has an edge after all." A chuckle rumbled from deep in his broad chest. "This could be an interesting summer. You and me working together."

"That hasn't been decided yet."

"Well, I guess I'm going to have to convince you."

"The key word is *working*," she pointed out. "So you may as well quit hitting on me."

"I'm not hitting on you."

"Then what do you call it?" And why, if she didn't want him to, was she disappointed that she might have misread his signals?

His lips quirked as he shot her another quick look.

"Like I said, I'm *thinking* about hitting on you."

"Then I might as well warn you right out, I've never been interested in mindless sex."

Damn. Had that prim, stick-up-her-ass tone come out of her mouth?

"Neither have I."

She snorted at that outrageous claim. He'd been a Navy SEAL, for Pete's sake.

"Believe me, New York, if we do end up in bed, I'm going to want your mind fully engaged." He caught her left hand, laced their fingers together, and squeezed lightly. "At least in the beginning."

Deciding that to pull her hand away would make her seem even more uptight, Sabrina left it where it was. But as they raced through the alley of Spanish moss–draped oaks, turning them into a green blur, she reminded herself, yet again, that she was no longer the naive teenage girl she once had been.

She'd traveled the world. Had sex with lots of men. Well, okay, maybe she could count her lovers on one hand, but still, dealing with all those hot-blooded Italians in Florence had given her a great deal of experience in fending off amorous males.

This former bad boy turned SEAL turned construction worker shouldn't make her stomach flutter and her pulse skip.

He shouldn't.

But, dammit, he did.

Which was one more thing she was going to have to think about.

24

While Swannsea reflected the eclectic and eccentric tastes of its former owner, Whispering Pines possessed all the ambience of a baronial manor.

Gilt-framed paintings of what Zach supposed were ancestors hung on silk-draped walls. Ornate satin-upholstered furniture rested on a carpet that looked a lot like those Zach had seen in one of Saddam Hussein's many palaces. Except the carpet in the Honeycutt library was twice as large.

"Darling! It's so lovely to finally have you back home again where you belong!" Lillian Honeycutt beamed her pleasure from her wheelchair as an elderly African American man clad in a white dinner jacket led Zach and Sabrina into a room paneled in glossy bird's-eye maple.

"It's good to be home," Sabrina said as she bent down and kissed her aunt's cheek. Zach suspected that their hostess's long double string of pearls had cost more than his first car.

"And I'm so glad you could join us as well, Zachariah."

"It was a pleasure to be invited, Miss Lillian," he responded, taking the woman's extended hand and lifting it to his lips in his best Southern gentlemanly manner.

Which caused Sabrina to roll her eyes.

"Well, I, for one, certainly feel better knowing that our Sabrina is in good hands." The older woman turned her smile from Zach to her husband, who was standing next to a wet bar across the room. "Don't you, Harlan?"

"Absolutely," the doctor said. "Any would-be killer foolish enough to tangle with a U.S. Navy SEAL would find himself in serious trouble."

"Former SEAL," Zach felt obliged to point out.

"Doesn't matter. Having served myself, I can say there's no such thing as a former Marine. Which, I suspect, is the same way SEALs view themselves."

"That's pretty much the case," Zach agreed.

"I thought so. What can I get you two to drink?"

"White wine would be fine for me," Sabrina said.

"We've a lovely Sauvignon Blanc that Eugenia and I discovered while shopping along Somersett Harbor the other day," Lillian said.

Sabrina nodded. "That'd be great."

"And for you, Tremayne?"

"Bourbon, if you have it." He hadn't had hard liquor since returning home, but doubting the doctor would have an O'Doul's on tap, Zach decided one glass wouldn't hurt.

"Of course we do." Of course. It was, after all, the South. "Got a fine sipping Jim Beam's Choice, if that's all right?"

"Absolutely, sir."

The Cadillac of bourbons. Zach had paid forty-nine thousand afghanis on the black market for a bottle once the surviving members of the team had made it back to Kabul. Which, at the time, he'd figured was still a bargain for a whiskey that retailed for three hundred bucks back in the States.

After handing Sabrina and his wife their wine, the doctor used a set of sterling silver tongs to take some ice from a silver bucket, put the cubes in a heavy glass, added bitters, and poured the whiskey from a decanter whose cut-crystal pattern matched the old-fashioned glass.

"To having our dear Sabrina back home again," Lillian said, raising her glass in a toast.

"I'll drink to that," Zach said.

The twenty-year-old whiskey was rich and smooth from the wine casks it had been finished in. Unfortunately, the first sip sent an avalanche of memories crashing down on him.

Plan A—which had been to land safely, climb the mountain, and call in the bombers to blow up the tango stronghold—was shot. Plan B would have been to stay inside, using the helo as shelter, but that wasn't an option, given the flames, because the fuel tank could end up blowing them all sky-high. There were now so many holes in the metal side, Zach figured the helo looked like a giant camouflage-painted colander.

Which left them with Plan C.

Evacuate the bird before she blew.

The bitch was, things weren't all that much better outside. There were Rangers and Marines scattered about on the ground. Through his goggles, their blood, spattered across the snow, took on an eerie green fluorescent tint.

Too many were not moving. A Marine was sprawled with his boots still on the ramp, his torso in the snow, blood pooling beneath his helmet.

A pair of Rangers huddled beneath the ramp, which made more sense than the strategy of their teammates who were getting picked off like flies as they ran—make that waded—through the snow. With all the fire, there was no time to dig foxholes.

If the enemy is in range, so are you.

There is no second place in a gunfight. Winners kill, losers get killed.

With those maxims from SEAL training ringing in his head, Zach stepped over the fallen Marine, then leaped off the ramp.

And—damn—landed in a drift up to his crotch.

One of their problems was that Shane had, by necessity, crash-landed the Chinook in a clearing. The good news was that the enemy seemed to be shooting not from a nearby grove of trees but from a hidden bunker dug into the mountain.

Hell, the day his team couldn't take out one enemy bunker was the day Zach would trade his kick-ass cammies for a school crossing guard's uniform back home on Swann Island.

The air was filled with the fruity aroma of cordite and the overwhelming scent of pine oil from the bullet-shredded trees as he charged through the snow, unloading the magazine of his M4 in a continuous burst . . .

"Are you all right?" murmured a voice that managed to make itself heard through the gunfire and screams of the wounded.

Dragging himself out of the all-too-vivid memory, Zach found himself looking down into a pair of concerned green eyes looking back up at him from beneath furrowed brows.

"Sure. Why?"

"Because you seemed to sort of space out."

He rotated his shoulders, which felt as hard as boulders. Shit. He was royally screwed. Not knowing exactly what had happened, he figured there was no point in lying.

He rubbed the heel of his hand against his chaotic heart. "For how long?"

"Don't worry." Her voice was gentle. Her hand was on his bare arm, her light touch soothing. "It was only a second. And since Uncle Harlan received a phone call at the same time, no one noticed."

Across the room the doctor was talking on a cell phone while his wife looked on, her expression resigned.

"You noticed."

He might be in the library of a Southern mansion, but his blood was still as cold as if he were back in the

Afghan mountains. Where, as he continued to hear gunfire, Zach realized a part of him still was.

You. Will. Not. Disintegrate.

"True," she admitted.

He looked for fear in her soulful gaze. Or worse yet, pity. What he thought he saw was, amazingly, understanding.

"But I'm not telling."

Zach considered tossing back the rest of the whiskey he never should have tasted in the first place. Instead, he put the glass down on the inlaid wood table beside the sofa.

"Thanks."

"Don't mention it."

Wouldn't it be cool if it were that easy?

If the entire incident could be dropped.

Gone.

Forgotten.

But Zach knew the chances of that happening were about, oh, a gazillion to one. Because, first of all, Sabrina Swann was a woman, and he'd never met one of her kind yet who didn't want to talk a subject to death.

And second, if he was going to end up working on Swannsea, she had the right to know that sure, he had some problems. But he was getting help for them. And she didn't have to worry about him going postal and shooting everyone on the island.

"Do you have to leave?" Lillian Honeycutt was asking her husband. Her plaintive tone drew Zach's attention back to his host and hostess.

"We've some time," Harlan said soothingly. "This is Becky Wainright's first child, so she and her husband are a little unnerved by the prospect of her giving birth. Her contractions are, so far, very weak and irregular, so I suspect they're merely Braxton Hicks."

"I imagine it's difficult for an inexperienced mother to be able to tell the difference between false labor and the real thing," Lillian said sympathetically.

"Absolutely." Harlan nodded. "I suggested she put something in her stomach—tea and toast—and take a walk. Moving around will often stop the contractions.

"Meanwhile, in the event they are the real deal, or if, as so often happens, the parents panic and go to the hospital, I'll call St. Camillus and let them know they may have a patient showing up tonight."

He turned toward Zach. "If you wouldn't mind escorting my wife into the dining room, I'll join you as soon as I take care of this."

"It would be my pleasure, sir," Zach said.

Catching Sabrina's knowing look, he had the feeling she knew he'd rather take on an entire terrorist cell than have to sit through an evening of politely inane dinner conversation after that flashback.

"Don't worry," she murmured as he pushed the wheelchair into the dining room. "It'll be over before you know it."

"Yeah," Zach muttered back. "I hear that's what they say about firing squads."

25

The sun had set over Somersett Harbor, casting Whispering Pines into shadows. But the night scope on the long-range rifle, along with the chandelier that turned the dining room nearly as bright as midday, allowed the man to observe the scene undetected.

Even if Tremayne and the Swann girl hadn't been seated next to each other, it would have been impossible to miss the connection between them. The brush of her hand against his arm, his light caress of her thigh beneath the tablecloth, the way they'd look at each other when they thought no one was noticing.

Interesting.

He'd been watching the former SEAL for weeks, planning his mission with the attention the Joint Chiefs ought to use when preparing to invade a foreign country.

Which admittedly would have been easier back when the guy was drinking himself into oblivion.

The problem with that was he hadn't wanted Tremayne dead drunk. He wanted the bastard dead.

But he also wanted him sober enough to be fully aware of what was happening to him.

And why.

Then, proving that timing was fucking everything, damned if the guy hadn't sobered up just when he'd been about to make his move. Which had thrown a monkey wrench into his plans.

Fortunately, all those months in a rat-infested prison cell had taught the man a lot about patience.

So he waited.

And watched.

And proving that it was true about a window opening when a door slammed shut, it appeared the big tough SEAL might have a new weakness.

One more easily exploited than the booze.

What would happen, the man wondered, if he allowed things to play out a little longer? What if Tremayne started to care for the woman who'd so obviously caught his attention?

What if—while it was admittedly a stretch, it *could* happen—he fell in love?

Only to have her taken away from him?

It was, the man thought as he watched his enemy skim a finger down the back of Sabrina Swann's slender hand, an intriguing possibility.

26

Although Lillian had described the evening as a casual family supper at home, to Zach's mind there was nothing casual about a dining table large enough to seat twelve covered with a snowy white cloth and gleaming with an impressive array of gold-edged china, heavy sterling silver, and crystal.

The she-crab soup, spinach salad, and sautéed local sea scallops over creamy white grits served with a lobster butter sauce were the best meal he'd ever tasted.

But it was difficult to keep his mind on the food and conversation while memories of that damn flashback lingered in his mind. Even more difficult was concentrating when the woman sitting next to him smelled like heaven and kept casually touching him. Not to flirt, but to reassure.

Which he would've found humiliating if he hadn't enjoyed it so much.

"So, Sabrina," Harlan said, "what's this I hear about you taking on Lucie's cockamamie plan to expand Swannsea?"

"I'm merely considering it, Uncle Harlan." If she was at all offended by his less than flattering question, her calm tone didn't reveal it.

"Does that mean you're planning to stay here on the island?"

"Well, not permanently, but—"

"Then how could you possibly expect to run a hands-on enterprise like that?"

"Harlan," Lillian murmured warningly.

"Well, *someone* has to say something," he blustered. "Granted, my cousin was a force on the island, and while she had many clever ideas, in my opinion this wasn't one of them."

"Lincoln and Titania both seemed to approve," Lillian said.

"Linc did?" Sabrina asked.

"Well, we didn't get into details, but when Eugenia and I stopped by one afternoon last month to pick up some of that lovely herbal infusion tea he's been making, I mentioned it to him and he seemed to think it was worth considering."

"He was undoubtedly merely being polite," Harlan said. "And it's not the least bit surprising that both Lincoln and Titania would be boosters. They would, after all, both benefit from the additional revenue it'd bring in."

"I seriously doubt that's Titania's motivation," Sabrina said mildly. "She seems quite happy, and satisfied running the Wisteria Tea Room and Bakery."

"Oh, that's such a lovely restaurant!" Lillian said. "I'll admit I never cared to go there when it was the Crab Shack, but Eugenia and I do so enjoy stopping by to indulge in Titania's desserts. In fact, we're having her delicious Lady Baltimore cake tonight."

She leaned forward a bit across the table, toward Zach. "Which, of course, isn't from Baltimore at all, as some Yankees like to claim, but originated right here in South Carolina, at a tea shop in Charleston."

"Is that so?" Zach asked politely.

"Oh, yes. According to the story, the cake was first baked by Alicia Rhett Mayberry, for a novelist who was so enraptured with its taste that he titled his next book *Lady Baltimore*."

"The point I was attempting to make, my dear"—

Harlan reentered the sidetracked conversation, saving
Zach from having to respond to the cake story—"is that
very few people could say no to my cousin once she set
her mind to something."

"I haven't spoken with Linc yet," Sabrina said, "but
I've been friends with Titania for nearly twenty years
and have never known her to let anyone steamroller her.
And I have to second what Aunt Lillian said about her
seeming enthusiastic about the idea of incorporating
Swann Tea into her recipes."

"That's all well and good." Zach could tell that Harlan, who was of a generation of physicians treated like
gods by their patients, wasn't accustomed to being argued with. "But that doesn't mean she has the ability to
run a business as complex as Swann Tea."

"But that's what her brother is doing." Lillian apparently hadn't received the never-question-the-doctor
memo.

"And very well, too," Harlan allowed. A bit reluctantly, Zach thought. "His idea to add herbal infusions
is paying off nicely. But that doesn't mean he's going to
be amenable to having hoards of tourists tramping all
through the tea fields."

"I strongly doubt that's what Lucie had in mind," Sabrina, who also appeared to have missed the memo, said.

"She told me she was thinking of buses for the tourists," Lillian volunteered. "To keep them from wander-
ing all over the fields. Or perhaps, in the beginning,
something like those cute little fringe-topped Jeeps. You
know, Harlan, like the one we rode in during our trip
to Hawaii that winter."

"It would still be disruptive." He harrumphed. "And
costly." He speared Zach with a look. "I saw a bill from
Tremayne Construction for blueprints."

"I believe my father and Miss Lucie worked with a
Somersett architect on those," Zach said.

"And the plans call for an additional thousand
square feet?"

"Twelve hundred, sir."

"Which would be built where?"

"Off the solarium."

"There's a garden there."

"Yes, sir."

"Are you aware of the fact that a great many of those plants come from stock that predates the Revolution?"

"Yes, sir," Zach repeated, even as the doctor's tone grated. All the years in the military had taught him to temper his response to those who outranked him. Except for that one time . . .

"But Lucie found a landscape architect at USC who believes he can transplant them without much loss. The greenhouse out back next to what used to be the summer kitchen is already being used for regermination."

The older man shook his head. His white brows beetled. "I understand that you're at loose ends right now, Sabrina, dear. And that being the case, throwing yourself into a project like this might seem like the thing to do to take your mind off your problems. However, as executor of your grandmother's estate—"

"Speaking of Lucie's estate, darling"—Lillian broke in again—"has Earl Gardner gotten hold of you?"

He felt Sabrina stiffen at the name of the island's mayor. "I've heard from him. He sent his condolences."

"Did he happen to mention a memorial service?"

"I believe it might have come up."

"I know Lucie's feelings about a funeral," Lillian said, blithely forging on. "I can't fully appreciate or approve of them, but Harlan and I felt obligated to follow the instructions in the will she'd left with her lawyer."

"I'm sure she would've appreciated that."

"I hope she does."

No one in the room could have missed Lillian's use of the present tense. Obviously she felt her husband's cousin's spirit lived on. Perhaps in some bright and shining place with winged choruses of angels playing harps.

Zach found himself wishing that he had even an iota

of the older woman's faith. But he'd witnessed a lot of death and not once had he seen anything resembling all those stories he'd heard of a soul rising up from the now useless body.

"But," Lillian continued, "a memorial service is *not* the same thing as a funeral. There are no depressing dirges or lowering of caskets into the ground, or tossing of dirt. It's not just Earl Gardner who's pressing for some sort of service, Sabrina. Nearly everyone on the island wants to do something to commemorate a remarkable woman's remarkable life."

Sabrina lifted her fingers to her temple. "I understand, but—"

"The service is going to happen with or without your consent, Sabrina," Harlan declared. "Wouldn't it be better for us to at least try to make it a party Lucie would enjoy?"

"I don't know." She was obviously conflicted.

The ring of Harlan's cell phone cut off any further discussion. For now.

"It's my service again." He took in the caller ID screen. "I'll need to take this call."

"I have to admit, dear," Lillian said to Sabrina as Harlan strode from the room, "that as much as I can understand my husband's reservations about the tea tours, and even shared some of my concerns with Lucie when she first began planning the enterprise, I'm fully in favor of anything that will keep you here, even if only for a short time."

She turned toward Zach. "Don't you agree, Zachariah?"

Knowing a lot about land mines, Zach could recognize a conversational minefield when he stumbled into one.

"I'm sure Sabrina would do a bang-up job of any project she took on," he said diplomatically.

"Well, of course she would," Lillian said. "In that respect, she definitely takes after her grandmother. As I keep trying to tell Harlan, but—"

"I'm sorry, dear." The man in question was back, seeming less irritated than when the call came in. "But duty calls. It seems Becky's going to be a mother by morning after all."

"It's her first," Lillian reminded him unnecessarily. "You should at least have time for dessert."

"Her water broke," he said simply.

"I should have married George Martindale," Lillian huffed prettily. "I doubt a dermatologist ever has to make house calls."

"Ah, but if you'd married my medical school rival, my love"—he skimmed a long-fingered hand down her hair—"you'd be living in Boise."

She lifted her still-firm chin. "I recall Idaho being lovely that time we were skiing in Sun Valley."

"Spectacular scenery, with great powder," Harlan allowed. "But it's not Swann Island."

"True enough." She sighed. Tilted her head so he could kiss her cheek. "I won't wait up."

"I'm sorry," he repeated. "And I promise to give some more thought to what we've been discussing."

"I've been wanting Harlan to retire," Lillian revealed. "But he doesn't know what he'd do with himself now that he's sworn off golf."

"You have?" Sabrina sounded surprised at that revelation.

"Ever since that jackass Sumner started building his damn course right up against my property line." A dark cloud moved over the handsome face. "That's when I realized that I'd been responsible for other people having their privacy ruined just so I could hit a little white ball around on the grass. But that boy's going to find out he's tangled with the wrong person. Because first thing tomorrow, Judge Karr is going to issue an injunction stopping construction."

"On what grounds?" Sabrina asked.

"On the grounds that he didn't properly survey the property."

"He's building on Whispering Pines property?"

"Probably not," Harlan allowed reluctantly. "It's merely a legal maneuver my attorney came up with to slow things down."

"But as soon as he gets a proper survey, won't he go back to work?"

"Not if we pull another tactic out of the hat. My plan is to stall long enough to drive the bastard into bankruptcy." His face had gone as red as a sunset over the marsh, and a vein pulsed at his temple.

"Now, dear," Lillian said soothingly, "remember your blood pressure. I've been trying to get him to take up boating," she divulged. "Margaret Palmer and her husband recently took a trip down the Intracoastal Waterway to Miami. This summer they're planning to take the route north to Norfolk."

She sighed again, reminding Zach of a little girl with her nose pressed up against a Macy's Christmas window.

Her husband's expression softened, making Zach wonder what it must be like to stay with one woman for over forty years. Although he'd never been one for long-term commitments, oddly, at this moment he found himself almost envying the doctor.

Not for the wealth and respect his profession had brought him but for the love Zach saw shining in his wife's eyes as she gazed up at him.

"I told you I'd think about it." He skimmed a hand over her shoulder. "Now I really need to get to the hospital."

He said his good-byes and was off.

"I do adore my husband," Lillian said. "But if you'll take a word of advice from an old married woman, darling," she said to Sabrina, "unless you enjoy spending a great deal of time alone, never wed a doctor." She smiled up at Zach. "Contractors don't work at night, do they?"

He would have had to be deaf to miss the meaning of that question. "My father spent a lot of evenings going over blueprints and plans. But, no, I don't recall him ever going out to a job site after dark.''

"Well.'' Her mood, which had deflated a bit with that phone call, definitely perked up. "Isn't that nice to know.'' She beamed her satisfaction.

Feeling a noose tightening around his neck, Zach felt like jumping up and kissing Eugenia when the housekeeper chose that moment to arrive with the frothy white three-layer Lady Baltimore cake.

27

"I owe you one," Zach said as they drove back to Swannsea.

"Actually I think we're even. Thanks for standing up for my abilities to Harlan."

He shrugged. "It was the truth. If you decide to tackle Lucie's tasting tour and tea shop, I'm sure you'll make a go of it." He glanced over at her. "So, you haven't made a decision yet?"

"I still need to talk with Linc. But I really want to make sure that we have someone for the job of coordinating the tours, because there's no way I'd take him away from the actual running of the farm."

"Makes sense to me. As for Harlan, I suspect he's accustomed to having his opinions always being taken as gospel."

"That's pretty much been the case, I suppose. When I was a little girl, I thought he must be what God sounded like."

"The doctor definitely has a presence, all right."

"Then there's also the fact that he's always hated change. Sometimes I suspect he was born in the wrong century, that he would've been happier living in antebellum times."

"No stretch at all to picture him being lord of the manor, sitting on the veranda, sippin' mint juleps, surveying his domain," Zach agreed.

"Which, as much as he hates it, probably gives him

something in common with Brad," Sabrina said, remembering the gleam in the developer's eye as he'd looked over Swannsea's tea plants.

"Should be interesting, watching him take on Sumner's land grab. My money's on Harlan. That's a bitch about Miss Lillian being in that wheelchair."

"Isn't it sad? She first had polio as a child, but recovered, grew up and married Harlan while he was still in medical school, and except for the fact that she was never able to have children—though no one knew if that was some sort of aftereffect from the polio or merely a coincidence—she seems happy."

"That's too bad about the kids. But it looks as if they've had a good marriage."

"Doesn't it? And, of course, even with this new onset of Parkinson's, she's always kept busy with her various charities."

"I know." He glanced up as headlights flashed in his rearview mirror. Sabrina saw his fingers tighten on the steering wheel. "Tremayne Construction agreed to work on a house for the local Habitat for Humanity program that she heads up."

"That's nice." And something she could easily imagine his father doing.

John Tremayne was a nice man. Strong enough to be gentle. She remembered the butterscotch candy pieces he'd always carried in his shirt pocket. And how he always smelled of Old Spice, and the coffee he drank by the gallon, even in the sweltering heat of a Swann Island summer.

"Apparently Dad's been doing a Habitat house every year for the past decade," Zach said as he turned down the lane toward Swannsea. When the car behind them continued on, he visibly relaxed. "He says Lucie talked him into it."

"Like Harlan said, not many people could say no to my grandmother."

"Not Pop, that's for sure."

"They were close."

Sabrina remembered overhearing speculation when she was in her teens about exactly how close Lucie Swann might have been with the man who always seemed to be fixing something around Swannsea.

"Odd as it seems," he confirmed, "considering the differences in their social status, they were best friends."

"I suppose that makes sense, since they probably had more in common than people might have thought at first glance. After all, they both ended up alone about the same time."

It had been the summer she'd turned twelve. Sabrina remembered well because it had happened during a time when she and Titania had been practiced their kissing techniques. In Sabrina's imagination, the back of her hand had always been Zachariah Tremayne's mouth.

At the time she hadn't understood the scandal that had caused her grandfather to desert her grandmother. Coincidentally, that same week, Zach's mother had run off, leaving only a brief typewritten note behind.

She also remembered rumors about Robert Swann and Laura Tremayne having run off together. Rumors that were proven false after Zach's mother sent him a postcard from California, where apparently she'd gotten a job as a cocktail waitress in a bowling alley not far from Disneyland.

"Pop has never been one to share his feelings, but I think he misses Lucie." Zach pulled into the circular drive in front of the steps leading up to the pillared veranda and cut the engine. "A lot."

"He's not alone there."

Sabrina looked up at the house, which, tonight, because she'd forgotten to leave any lights on, looked lonely. As if mourning its mistress.

"Well, thank you." She reached for the passenger door handle. "Although I really could have driven myself, I enjoyed the evening."

Wasn't that a surprise?

"That makes two of us." He sounded every bit as surprised as she was. "But, in case you've forgotten how things work down here, New York, a Southern gentleman always walks a lady to the door."

"I seem to recall you saying something about not being a gentleman."

"Maybe it's situational."

The waxing moon, a little fuller tonight, cast a silvery glow over the landscape. A soft breeze wafted in from the sea, blending a tang of salt with the sweet fragrance of Confederate jasmine. There was an intimacy to the dark, and the night, and the company, that had her feeling freer to share her thoughts than she might have been in the bright light of day.

"I sort of know how it is," she murmured as they climbed the steps.

"How what is?"

They both knew what she was talking about.

"PTSD."

He didn't immediately respond. She hadn't really expected him to, but decided this was one of those in for a penny, in for a pound situations.

She sat down in the swing. "The flashbacks."

Again, nothing. But he did sit down beside her.

"I don't remember the actual bombing," she said. "Just what I was doing right before."

"Which was?" He put an arm around her shoulder and started the swing swaying a bit.

"I was drinking champagne, celebrating getting promoted to manager, which had been my goal since I'd graduated college, feeling a little guilty about not having gotten back to see Lucie before she died, and—"

She slammed her mouth shut.

Too late.

"And?" His fingers idly played with the ends of her hair.

Sabrina shrugged. "And thinking that perhaps I'd

been concentrating on my work too much for too long. That perhaps my life could be fuller." No way was she going to admit she'd decided to take a lover.

"I suspect most everyone feels that way from time to time."

"I suppose so."

Which was partly what this little trip home was about. Although Lucie had ensured that Sabrina never would have to work again, no way could she imagine herself living a life without some purpose. After all, her grandmother had worked until the day she died.

In fact, according to Harlan, who'd called Sabrina with the news, she'd been found collapsed over her computer keyboard, working on a column about the Buccaneer Days ball.

But running a hotel took a great deal of patience, concentration, and the ability to take multitasking to a new and higher level. It also often required 24/7 attention.

And as much as Sabrina hated to admit it, even to herself—*especially* to herself—the bombing had left her feeling unnaturally fragile, and returning at less than full strength wouldn't be fair to Eve Bouvier, who had been so good to her, or to the guests at whatever hotel she would be transferred to.

"I guess, in your old job as a SEAL, if you didn't fully concentrate on your work, you could end up dead."

"Sometimes people ended up dead even if you *did* give it your all."

There was a new, sharp edge to his voice. She glanced up at him and watched as his eyes flashed, hot and dark. And, she thought with a slight involuntary shiver, deadly.

"Are you cold?" He stopped the swing's back-and-forth movement. "Do you want to go in?"

Those warrior eyes didn't miss a thing. "No."

She shook her head. Relaxed, knowing, that despite

what Brad had said about Zach's temper, she wasn't in any danger from this man who was concerned about her comfort.

"I guess a ghost walked over my grave." She began swinging again. "I'd forgotten how quiet nights are here."

"Not exactly the big city," he agreed. "So what happened?"

"It's not that big a deal." She looked out over the marsh.

"Sabrina." He tipped a finger beneath her chin and turned her gaze back to his. "I'd say getting blown up is a very big deal. But if you don't want to talk about it—"

"It's okay."

She didn't really want to even think about it, but she was dying to ask him what, exactly, had brought him back to the island, and she figured that to do that she owed him quid pro quo.

"As I said, I don't recall the particulars before the bombing. I remember tossing and turning the night before, because my end-of-probation meeting was the next day. I spent more time than usual dressing for the meeting.

"I remember drinking countless cups of coffee. The staff wishing me good luck all day, my secretary's page that the review committee was ready for me. Oddly, I can't recall being told I'd gotten the job, but the champagne is clear in my mind.

"Everything between drinking it and when I woke up in the dark, buried beneath tons of stone, is lost. The doctor said I might get it back." She shrugged. "Or not."

"Christ."

His arm was still around her shoulder. He drew her closer and, heaven help her, it felt right. Not sexy, just right. Not exactly comforting right. Just, well, *right*. As if she belonged in his arms here on Swannsea's veranda. Almost if they belonged here together.

"There was a woman buried somewhere on the other side of the stones. She was panicky because she didn't know where her children were."

It had helped, somewhat, for a time, establishing a connection with another human being in the dark.

"Their names were Brandon and Jess. The daughter, Jess, was named after their father. He'd taken them out for gelato, to give his wife a bit of peace and quiet."

Even now Sabrina could hear the frantic wail of sirens, taste the smoke acrid with chemicals and melting plastic.

"As it turned out, her husband and children were fine. Or as fine as they could be, after losing their wife and mother."

When the woman had stopped sobbing a few minutes into their conversation, Sabrina had feared the worst. Which, she'd later learned, was the case.

"It's a miracle you weren't killed."

"Funny you should put it that way, since it turned out that the reason I didn't die was that this huge marble copy of the *Pietà* in the lobby landed in a way that protected me from falling rubble. A lot of people believed that being saved by a statue of the Virgin Mary holding her crucified son was proof of a miracle."

"Which undoubtedly got you a lot of attention, especially in such a Catholic country. Attention you probably didn't need right then."

"Tell me about it."

She supposed she shouldn't be surprised that he so understood her situation—after all, she'd claimed to understand his. But Sabrina couldn't have foreseen that he immediately grasped what had become even more unsettling than the bombing itself.

"Eve Whitfield Bouvier—she's the owner of the Wingate Palace chain—and her husband came to Florence and stayed while we attended all the funerals."

Zach swore softly. "You didn't have to do that. After what you'd been through."

"That's the same thing Eve and Gabriel told me. But

I was alive, while so many others weren't. And since I'd been promoted to manager of the hotel when that bomber struck, it was my responsibility."

"No one would have blamed you for not going to them all," he said between his teeth. "Christ, I can't imagine how tough that would've been on you."

"It wasn't easy."

Talk about your understatement.

She'd collected thirty-eight funeral cards.

The sound-alike eulogies, the melancholy hymns, the aromas of burning candle wax, frankincense, and incense had all blurred together, with their solemn borders, black tassels, and pictures of sad-eyed saints.

"After the first few days I went numb. Which left me feeling even guiltier."

Yet inside that cottonlike cocoon of numbness, her tangled nerves had felt tight and hot beneath her skin, ready to pop and fray. Sometimes, like that moment last night, when she'd thought she heard someone moving around in the attic, they still did.

"Survivor guilt's a bitch."

He said it in a way that had her suspecting he knew all about it firsthand, surprising her yet again at the once impossible idea of the two of them having much in common.

"So I was told by all the grief counselors who flew in from around the globe."

They'd assured her that her reaction to the bombing was perfectly normal. That it would take time, and therapy, but eventually she'd get back to normal.

Totally drained—physically, mentally, and emotionally— Sabrina hadn't argued. But deep down inside, she secretly wondered if she would ever feel normal again.

"As the so-called miracle of the Paradiso Angeli, I suddenly had this huge spotlight on me. I couldn't so much as walk to the *mercato* without people staring at me. Whispering about me."

Or wanting to touch her, as if to transfer a bit of her miracle power to themselves.

"One morning, just as we'd gotten out of the car that Eve's husband, Gabriel, had rented, a woman held up her baby for me to bless."

The infant had been wearing a long white lace dress and a frilly bonnet, like a baptismal gown.

"That was when I decided to come home."

"Good call."

"So." Sabrina exhaled a long breath and realized she felt a bit better for having shared the story. Not good. But better.

Enough so to garner the courage to ask him the question she'd been wondering about all evening.

"Having shared my darkest experience, I have to ask—is it true what Brad's telling people? That you were court-martialed?"

"Now, why am I not surprised he was in such a hurry to tell you about that?" he said dryly. "The subject of a court-martial *was* mentioned. But the whole thing ended up being dropped when I agreed to leave the team."

Which couldn't have been easy. "Why was there a *thing* at all?"

"Maybe because the military brass gets a little annoyed when a noncom threatens a superior officer." As he took his arm from around her shoulder, his hand unconsciously folded into a fist. "In my case, the officer in question was a general."

"You said 'threatened.' Does that mean you didn't try to kill him?"

"I didn't lay a finger on him."

"I didn't think so." The teenager he'd once been had possessed a temper. From what she'd seen of the man, Zach had acquired a great deal of self-control during the intervening years.

"But only because I knew that if I allowed myself to

punch him in his supercilious face just once, I wouldn't have stopped until I'd killed the son of a bitch."

"I don't believe that." She hadn't bought the idea when Brad had thrown it at her, and she didn't buy it now.

"That's where you're wrong, New York."

The man who had quietly stroked her hair, her shoulder, and nuzzled the top of her head with his chin while she'd shared her story was gone. Replaced by the hardened SEAL she was beginning to recognize.

"The only reason I didn't send the bastard to hell, where he belonged and will hopefully someday end up, was that I didn't want Dad to have to spend the rest of his days visiting his son on Fort Leavenworth's death row."

Sabrina didn't believe Zach capable of such an act, but she decided against arguing.

"What happened?" she asked instead. "To make you want to kill him in the first place?"

His exhaled breath was longer, deeper, than hers had been. He also had gone inside himself. Sabrina could see NO TRESPASSING signs posted all around him.

"It's a long story. And it's late."

"I told you mine."

A ghost of a smile appeared at the corner of his lips. "If you want to play that game, I can think of a lot more fun ways to show and tell."

"Good try. But I'm serious."

"Yeah. I could tell that." He rolled his broad shoulders. "But, like I said, it's a long story. For another time."

Seeming uncomfortable with the direction the conversation had taken, Zach stood up and held out his hand. "Where's your key?"

"This is Swann Island," she said. "No one locks doors here."

"I'll bet the house was locked when you first arrived."

"Well, yes, but I assumed that was because it'd been sitting empty."

"More likely because things have changed around here. When you were at Titania's, how many people did you recognize in the restaurant?"

She paused a moment to consider that. "None."

"I rest my case. It's not just locals anymore. I'll bet you never left your doors or windows unlocked in Florence."

"Well, of course not. It's a big city."

"Like I said, with all the strangers, there's no point in taking stupid chances."

"Are you calling me stupid?"

"Sorry." The mood had definitely changed. "Bad choice of words." He opened the heavy door. "But you of all people should know that the world isn't always safe."

"True." She lifted her chin. "But I'm also not going to run around like Chicken Little waiting for the sky to fall in on me."

"Maybe you could shoot for a middle ground," he suggested. "I'll see you in the morning. Meanwhile, lock this door behind me."

"Yessir." She shot him a quick salute, closed the door in his face, and twisted the lock.

"And don't forget to latch the chain," he called out.

Cursing beneath her breath, she slid the chain into the slot, kicked off her heels, and headed upstairs to bed.

28

Where the hell had she hidden it?

The problem was, the task was like looking for the proverbial needle in a haystack. It had been bad enough before the granddaughter suddenly showed up on the island before he'd had time to find the envelope, which could be hidden anywhere in this obscenely massive house.

Now he was forced to spend his nights creeping around in the dark like some second-story man from a bad jewel-theft movie.

But what he was seeking was far more valuable than diamonds or emeralds. Because if Sabrina Swann found the damning evidence before he did, he would end up strapped to a gurney in the Broad River Correctional Facility's death chamber with needles in his veins.

He had to find it.

Or, he thought as he moved the flashlight over the library walls, trying to figure out which, if any, of the hundreds of books Lucie Somersett Swann had hidden the envelope in, perhaps there was an easier way out of this problem.

He could kill the granddaughter.

Like he'd done with the old bitch, who'd had the bad luck to die before he could learn where she'd hidden the damn photos. Proving that it was true what they said about best-laid plans . . .

He'd always known the photographs and tapes were

a risk. But, dammit, wasn't that half the fun? Being able to look back and remember the good times?

Books and movies about serial murders were all the time alleging that serial killers were insane because they kept trophies, or souvenirs, of their crimes.

But the profilers, who thought themselves so damn smart, had it wrong. It wasn't crazy to want to document good times. Why else did people take videos of themselves having sex, or bore everyone at work with their snapshots of Disney World vacations?

Everyone needed a hobby. Some people played golf, others went fishing, some liked to needlepoint, and others got off on traveling.

He liked having himself a hot little sex slave. He liked bending her to his will. Liked making her do things she'd never, ever, imagined doing in her darkest dreams.

He especially liked punishing her, not because she'd disobeyed him but because that was the way she learned that he was the Master. And as such, he could treat his slave any damn way he wanted.

Even forcing her to have sex with other men. And afterward, making her watch him kill those men in front of her.

Hell, he didn't need photographs. Not when just the memory of watching the blood gush from that homeless loser's jugular all over her chained, naked body, then feeling the hot, slick, wet slide of it against his own flesh as he'd taken her hard and fast, was enough to make him hard even now.

Too horny to wait until he got home, assured from the stillness in the house that the granddaughter had gone to sleep, he sprawled in one of the bark brown leather chairs and unzipped his pants, releasing his throbbing dick. He wrapped his fingers around it, felt it jump beneath his touch like a downed electrical wire in a thunderstorm.

With the sound of Hallie Conroy's terrified screams reverberating in his mind and urging him on, he leaned his head against the chair and arched his back. It only took him three quick strokes to come.

His body stiffened, then jerked as the orgasm, nearly as powerful as that first time, exploded. With erotically violent visions flashing in his mind like strobe lights, he allowed his mind and his body to empty.

The crash was deafening, yanking him back to reality.

Shit. His foot had kicked the base of a floor lamp, knocking it over, breaking the stained-glass shade.

And damn it all to hell, if that wasn't bad enough, from upstairs, in her bedroom overhead, he heard Sabrina Swann's feet hit the floor.

29

Zach had always been able to sleep anywhere. Anytime. He'd learned during his first week of SEALs BUD/S training to take a "combat nap" standing up. Even that helo going down hadn't changed things. Oh, his sleep might be tortured with memories of the aftermath of the crash in nightmares, but he still possessed the ability to fall like a rock into sleep the minute he hit the rack.

Until tonight.

Because, dammit, he kept imagining Sabrina in that pink fairy-tale-princess canopied bed. But, unlike when he'd inadvertently seen her, she wasn't alone. In his *Penthouse Forum* fantasies, he was with her.

Her long blond hair flowed over her bare shoulders, reaching nearly to pert breasts that, unlike so many pumped-up silicone ones that were a dime a dozen these days, fit perfectly in his hands. Her rosy nipples pebbled like berries beneath the erotic onslaught of his lips. His tongue. His teeth.

In his fantasy, her lean body was warm and welcoming; her arms and legs wrapped around his hips as she urged him, "Please, Zach, take me now."

He could picture her as clearly as if he were lying with her now. Her flesh would be silvered by the moonlight streaming in through the open window; her soft lips, swollen and dark from shared kisses, would be parted as she murmured his name over and over; and her remarkable green eyes would widen as he surged into her, claiming her. Totally.

"Shit." He glared down at the erection that, if he didn't manage to get his mind on something—or someone—else, was going to cause him to spend the rest of the night in a cold shower.

She's just a woman. He repeated the words that were quickly becoming his own personal mantra over and over again in his sex-hungry mind. *Just like any other.*

Yeah. Sure.

He could try to convince himself of that from now until doomsday, but it didn't stop the erotic images of Sabrina Swann, hot and naked and *his*, from burning in his mind and his loins.

He splayed his right hand across his chest and felt the increased beat of his heart beneath his fingertips as he imagined her straddling him, her lush pink lips trailing hot, wet kisses down his body. Zach was about to cave in to the woman hunger ripping away at him and take care of things himself when the sudden shrill demand of the cell phone on the bedside table shattered the sexual fantasy.

The caller ID said "Lucie Swann." Which was, of course, impossible. Which would only mean one person.

He snatched it up. "You're supposed to be sleeping." His voice was rough with need. "Though if you're calling for phone sex, I'm certainly up for that."

Literally.

There was a long pause on the other end of the line. A special kind of quiet that had the hairs at the back of his neck standing on end.

"Sabrina?"

"I'm sorry." She sounded very far away. "This was a mistake."

"What?"

"Calling you. For some reason, maybe because of our conversation earlier, you were the first person who

popped into my mind. Which I know is going to sound
foolish, but I was scared, and—"

His erection instantly deflated. He sat bolt upright.
"What happened?"

"It's not important." Her shaky tone said otherwise.

"Are you in any immediate danger?"

Out of bed in a nanosecond, he scooped up the jeans
he'd dropped earlier and yanked them up his legs.

"Of course not, but—"

"Where are you?"

"In the house. In my bedroom. Which was another
stupid thing. If someone *was* in the house, going upstairs
was not the brightest idea I've ever had."

Someone in the house? "Lock the bedroom door.
Then call 911."

"I'm sure it's nothing. I was just edgy after our talking
about the bombing, and I overreacted when that crash
downstairs woke me up."

"Call 911," he repeated, pulling out his do-not-fuck-
with-me SEAL tone. "And lock the door. It'll take me
ten, fifteen minutes to get there."

"Really, Zach—"

"Ten minutes," he repeated. Then hung up before she
wasted more time by arguing.

He made it in eight. By the time the red Viper came
tearing up in front of the house, Sabrina was already
regretting having called him. What was it about the man
that had her behaving so impulsively?

She left the bedroom, went downstairs and out onto
the veranda. "I'm sorry. I never should have bothered
you."

"Of course you should have." His long legs ate up the
driveway. "What happened?"

Could she feel any more foolish? "A lamp broke. And
there are some books scattered around on the desk and
some tables that I could've sworn weren't there earlier."

"In the library?" If he was surprised to have gotten an emergency SOS over a broken lamp and some clutter, he didn't reveal it.

"Yes. As I said, I was asleep, and I heard this loud crash, and when I came downstairs a floor lamp was on its side. The glass had shattered."

"That explains the blood on your feet."

Blood? Sabrina looked down and saw the crimson smears. "I must've stepped on a piece of glass."

"That'd be my guess." He scooped her up.

"I'm perfectly capable of standing on my own two feet," she insisted.

"Wouldn't want you to push it in deeper," he said reasonably as he carried her back into the house. "You could slice a tendon."

He plunked her down onto a wooden chair. "Sit. And don't move from this spot while I search the place."

"Do you have a dog?"

"No." He seemed surprised by the question. "Why?"

She gave him a sweet, false smile. "Because you certainly seem to have the vocabulary down. *Sit. Stay.* If we do end up sleeping together, I hope you won't expect me to fetch your paper in the morning, because I'm afraid you're going to be very disappointed."

His grin was a quick slash of white that made her think of the pirates that used to sail the waters around Swann Island.

"Believe me, New York, *when* I wake up with you wrapped around me, reading the news is going to be the furthest thing from my mind. Meanwhile, wait here for Nate while I start searching the house."

"Don't you think this is overkill? I obviously overreacted."

"That could well be what Hallie Conroy thought. Or Cleo Gibson."

Sabrina's blood suddenly turned as cold as it had when she'd first heard that crash downstairs. "You don't think their killer was in my house?"

"I've no idea. It's unlikely." He pulled an ugly gun from the back of his jeans. "But how likely is it that a serial killer would show up on the island in the first place?"

Having no idea what to say to that, Sabrina decided against arguing.

"Be careful," she said instead.

"Don't worry." He winked, although his expression remained sober. "I'm a professional, remember?"

30

Swannsea was not a small house. By the time Zach and Nate, who showed up less than five minutes after Zach, finished searching every room, Sabrina had cleaned the blood off her foot, put some antiseptic on it, and covered the cut with a Band-Aid she'd found in a first-aid kit beneath the sink.

"I thought I told you to stay put," Zach said between his teeth.

"I thought I told you I'm not very good at taking orders." Not nearly as good as he seemed to be about issuing them. "Besides, the cut wasn't any big deal. It was only a sliver of glass and easily taken care of. Since I didn't hear gunfire, can I assume neither of you found a maniac killer hiding in a closet?"

"No," Nate said. "Whoever he was, he's long gone. The logical explanation is that it was someone looking to make a quick buck selling some of your grandmother's stuff. But what bothers me is that he didn't take some of the more expensive, easy-to-fence items. Like the laptop, or the camera that was in one of the desk drawers."

Nate skimmed his hand over his short hair. "Do you know of anyone who'd have a grudge against you?"

"I can't imagine who. I've only been home a little over a day," she said.

"There's Sumner," Zach said.

"What about him?"

Nate changed in front of Sabrina's eyes from the reassuring man who'd shown up at the house to a no-nonsense, take-charge sheriff. Observing those sharp, hard, dark eyes, she could easily imagine him as a Marine.

"It's nothing. Not really," she insisted, as Zach looked ready to argue. "He dropped by wanting to talk with me about buying Swannsea farm. I told him it wasn't for sale. End of story."

"That you know of," Zach pointed out. "The guy's always been a weasel. It'd be just like him to try to scare you out."

"That's ridiculous," Sabrina scoffed. Then she noticed that Nate didn't exactly jump in to back her up. "Isn't it?" she asked the sheriff.

"Probably," he said. But she could tell he was considering the idea. "I'm still going to want to come back and dust for prints tomorrow."

Sabrina wondered if he was planning to compare them with any prints he might have found in that murdered woman's house. Wasn't that a comforting thought?

"I'm starting to feel as if I fell down the rabbit hole when that bomb went off," she admitted.

"Give it time." Zach glanced out over the moon-silvered landscape, as if still watching for bad guys. "And you don't need to worry about being alone tonight. Because you won't be."

"You're staying?"

He exchanged a look with Nate. "A horde of vandals couldn't drag me away."

"You've made your point. I'll definitely lock all the doors from now on."

"Locks are only a first deterrent," Zach said. "There's not one made that a determined thief can't get past. The locks on this place would be a breeze. I could probably bust them in under two seconds."

"I'm not sure I should've heard that," Nate said mildly. He turned to Sabrina. "He has a point. You can replace them in the morning. Meanwhile, it's better to be safe than sorry."

Sabrina watched Zach walk the sheriff out to his SUV. Even as they talked, they both scanned the property, every muscle in their bodies seeming on red alert. They might have left the service, but it was obvious that both were warriors still.

Understanding for the first time why her grandmother had always believed there was nothing a stout cup of tea couldn't fix, Sabrina put on a kettle.

"I'm making tea," she said when Zach returned to the kitchen. "Would you like some?"

"Sure."

She took two Earl Grey tea bags from a wooden box on the counter and placed them in a pair of cups she took from a glass-fronted cabinet. "And while we're waiting for the water to boil, you can tell me what happened in Afghanistan."

"Like I said. It's late." Seeming uncomfortable, he took the kettle, which had begun to whistle, from the range and poured the boiling water over the bags. "And it's not exactly a bedtime story.

"But I *can* tell you that I thought about you." He held one of the cups toward her. It looked very small in his large dark hand. "A lot, actually."

"Right." She perched on one of the stools at the island counter. "Like I'd made such an impression on you during all those summers I spent on the island."

"Maybe not all those years," he allowed. "But you definitely got my attention that last night. When you came to my apartment over Gus's gas station and offered yourself to me—"

"Oh, God." She felt the blush rise in her·cheeks. "I was hoping you'd slept with so many women over the years, you would've forgotten that."

"Yeah, you'd think that, wouldn't you?"

He sounded a bit surprised himself, though Sabrina

couldn't help noticing that he didn't contradict her about all those women he'd gone to bed with.

"I even wondered about that a few times. Usually when the team would find ourselves in a shit sandwich." He grimaced. "Sorry, that's sort of a military term—"

"I get the gist. And I've heard a lot more, most recently from a hot-tempered sous-chef I had to fire, who could curse in four languages, so it'd take a lot more than that to offend me."

"Okay. Anyway, although I'm sorry as hell to have brought it up, for some reason I'd think back on you, so neat and clean and tidy." Which was definitely not the memory she'd intended to leave him with.

He leaned back against the opposite counter, facing her as he crossed his long legs at the ankles. "Did I ever tell you how, every time I saw you, I wanted to mess you up?"

"No. But that's a bit of a revelation, since at the time I hadn't realized you'd seen me at all. Except to be really, really annoyed that time your dad took me fishing with the two of you."

"Yeah. I was majorly pissed." His lips quirked as he remembered. "Especially when you whimpered like a girl when you had to touch that night crawler."

"I *was* a girl." She'd been eight. "And it was slimy."

"If you didn't want to bait a hook, you shouldn't have whined to come along."

"I didn't whine. Well, maybe a little," she amended at his sideways look. "But how was I supposed to know catching fish involved worms?"

His father had baited the hook for her, Sabrina recalled. Then helped her pull in the six-inch shark that had gotten itself hooked.

She also remembered her relief when John Tremayne put it back into the water.

"Point taken. I guess, when you put it that way, you were pretty much a fish out of water, so to speak."

"Anyone ever tell you that your jokes are, well, a little lame?"

"Not and lived to tell about it."

Despite what Brad had said about Zach being dangerous, she didn't believe that.

"Getting back to my point, there'd be times, when we'd be out on some mission and for some reason I'd think about you looking all clean and white, and well, I guess 'pure' would be the best word, and I'd remember what I was fighting for."

How on earth did a woman respond to such a statement? "That's very flattering."

He shrugged. "It's the truth. In some weird way I never bothered to think about it all that much, because I was afraid if I overanalyzed it, you'd vanish, like a hot dream you lose when you wake up. And I wouldn't be able to get you back."

Sabrina wondered if, just possibly, *this* could be a dream.

Stalling, she took another sip of the light golden tea, savoring the bright taste. Unlike many competitors, who used the bergamot orange oil to mask the lack of flavor from inferior, less-expensive black tea in their Earl Grey blends, Swann Tea had always used only the most select leaves from bushes grown here on the farm.

A farm she vowed Brad Sumner would never get his hands on.

"I thought soldiers fought for the guys in the foxhole on either side of them."

"That's when the bullets are flying. When you're hauling your ass up some godforsaken mountain in some shithole of a place in the middle of winter, when you can't tell the good guys from the bad guys, and most of both of those groups think *you're* the bad guy, which puts a big target on your back, it helps to have something larger to focus on.

"Guys with families have it harder in one way, because they have more to worry about back home while they're away. But they also have it easier in another way, because they're not just fighting for the flag and apple pie, but for their wives and kids.

"I had you in your spotless white dresses and long blond Alice in Wonderland hair. I know it sounds like I was smoking some really crazy shit, but you came to symbolize innocence. What the world could be if people in charge didn't keep fucking it up with their power trips."

"Since you're the one who brought it up," she murmured, "I think this is where I point out that if you hadn't turned me down, I wouldn't have been all that innocent."

"You were jailbait."

"Is that the only reason you sent me packing?" She'd often wondered.

"Partly. It wasn't that I wasn't tempted. Hell, what guy wouldn't have been to have a luscious blonde wearing nothing but a come-hither smile and an itsy-bitsy pink bikini throwing herself at him? But the thing is, New York, you represented a complication I couldn't handle at twenty."

"What about now? Is that still how you see me?"

"Are you looking to be flattered? Or do you want the truth?"

"I want you to be honest." *Better to know than to wonder.*

"Then I'd have to say I still view you as a helluva complication. But"—he held up a hand when she opened her mouth to respond—"I also see you as the sexy woman I want to fuck blind."

Oh, God. That was exactly what she wanted, too.

"Well, that's certainly romantic."

"If you wanted poetry, you should've asked for it. Not that you would've gotten any, since my repertoire, with the exception of Robert Service's *The Cremation of Sam McGee*, which I had to memorize in the seventh grade, is pretty much limited to dirty limericks and marching cadences. But you said you wanted the truth," he reminded her.

Sabrina had never been an impulsive woman. She'd always been a planner. A list maker, weighing the pros and cons of every move.

Twice in her life she'd made a spur-of-the-moment decision. The first was when she'd practically begged this man to take her virginity. Which she'd ultimately ended up giving away two years later on the narrow bed of her dorm room to an unimaginative TA in her statistics class.

The second time had been when she'd called the airline and booked a ticket home to Swann Island.

Which had brought her full circle, right back to the man who'd triggered rash decision number one.

"Well." Deciding she'd wondered long enough, and throwing caution to the winds, she looked him straight in the eye. "I'm legal now."

31

Good point, Zach thought as he took in the anticipation written over her face in bold, unmistakable strokes.

In that forthright way he remembered so well, she was letting him know flat out that he could have her. Which was exactly what he'd been thinking since he'd first accidentally looked in her bedroom window.

But then what?

Even as he told himself he was playing with fire, Zach allowed his gaze to drift from her eyes to brush over her mouth, lingering on her lips, which parted on a soft, inviting sigh.

He had only to move. A slight shifting of his head and their mouths would meet.

He paused, a desperate man caught on the edge of a jagged, treacherous cliff. One more step and they'd both go tumbling off.

Right into a pit of quicksand.

But perhaps, he mused, tracing the shape of her slightly parted lips with the roughened pad of his thumb, it might be worth it.

He tossed back the cooling tea, put the cup on the counter, and lowered his mouth to hers.

Her lips were warm and sweet and avid, as she immediately began kissing him back with such fervor that their teeth clinked.

His thumb tugged downward on her chin, allowing his tongue access to her lips. She twined her arms around his neck as he deepened the kiss, degree by simmering degree. Her tongue mated with his; her straining breasts pressed against his chest,

Heat smoldered at the base of his spine, creating a low, deep pull in his groin. The more he drank, the more he wanted. Lord help him, he couldn't get enough of her.

But still he refused to rush, taking his time, drinking from her lips with a slow, lingering pleasure that made it seem as if time had stopped just for him.

For them.

Zach was used to having his body burn in response to a willing woman. He was accustomed to a woman's touch making his blood hot, and he knew the ability of a woman's clever mouth to fog his mind.

But this was different.

Kissing Sabrina touched him in some elemental way, a way he'd never been touched before.

He'd always prided himself on his ability to shut off his emotions when there was a job to be done. He'd even managed to stop himself from killing that son of a bitch three-star when the team had finally gotten off that godforsaken mountain thirty-six hours after the copter crash.

But nothing could have prepared him for the tenderness flooding through him as he pulled her off the stool and drew her closer, sinking deeper and deeper into the prolonged kiss.

As she arched against him, needing, demanding more, Zach knew that another moment of this and he'd be lost.

Greed. Hunger. Need. They rose like ancient demons, battering at him, and as his aroused body screamed for relief, Zach contemplated going for it.

Common sense, along with a strong survival instinct that had kept him alive against all odds during his SEAL team days, told him that despite her bold words, unless she'd done a one-eighty turnaround in the past eleven years, Sabrina wasn't a woman to rush into sex without weighing the consequences.

Which meant, since she didn't seem to be considering them now, she would have to deal with them later.

Which meant *he* would, as well.

Zach was no stranger to danger, to risk. He'd lived with it, and most of the time had even enjoyed it. But this woman and the feelings she stirred in him represented more risk than he'd ever known. He'd always recognized his own strengths, his own weaknesses.

And right now, even as he ached for her, even as he fought to remember that part of the reason he'd left the navy and returned home to Swann Island was that he didn't want anyone in his life, Zach was forced to admit that Sabrina Swann represented a major weakness. One he couldn't afford. Not while his own life was in such flux.

Which was why he drew back, denying the clamorous demands of his mutinous body.

"We'd better get you to bed." He paused a beat, giving himself time to change his mind. "Alone."

"Why?" She stared at him, breathless, confusion and lingering passion swirling in her eyes.

She was also visibly exhausted. Her complexion, which had always been fair, even during those summers spent beneath the hot Southern sun, gave her the look of fragile bone china.

"Because you look dead on your feet, and when I take you to bed, New York, I fully intend for it to last all night. And since I'm an equal-opportunity lover, I'm going to want you to be fully engaged. Which means you'll need to be well rested."

He took both her hands in his and stood up. "Which is why, as attractive as the offer is, sugar, I'm going to have to take a rain check."

"Houston, the ego has landed." Given that she'd had only a single glass of wine tonight, Zach knew it was fatigue, not alcohol, slurring her words. "I don't recall offering you any rain check."

"I'll take my chances." Linking their fingers together,

he led her out of the kitchen. "Need some help getting upstairs?"

"I can make it." Those luscious lips he could still taste turned down in a frown. "I never would have expected this from you, Zachariah Tremayne," she said on a huff of feminine pique.

Zach laughed.

At her. At himself.

At this ridiculous situation.

"Damned if that doesn't make two of us."

The lady was not only gorgeous—she was smart as a whip and gutsy as hell. Which made her, in Zach's view, damn near perfect.

Which meant that if he didn't find a flaw pretty soon, he was sunk.

32

Wondering how such a chaste kiss could leave her so needy, Sabrina dragged herself up the stairs, brushed her teeth, and fell into bed.

Even as she reminded herself that before the bombing she'd been a strong, independent woman, that she didn't need a bodyguard, she couldn't deny that it was comforting knowing Zach was downstairs.

Was he thinking about her? Wishing he was here in her bed, ravishing her blind instead of sitting alone in the dark?

And speaking of the dark, surprisingly, she didn't feel afraid.

Which, being a logical, levelheaded woman, she realized was precisely because there was an armed SEAL in the house.

Not just any SEAL.

Zach. And his strong, solid presence allowed her to truly relax for the first time in weeks.

Closing her eyes, breathing out a long, slow sigh, Sabrina tuned out.

Frustrated by a lack of sleep, which for once had nothing to do with war flashbacks, Zach had almost convinced himself that his uncharacteristic emotional connection to Lucie's delectable granddaughter was nothing more than a hormonal response to a sexually appealing woman.

Especially given how long it had been since he'd slept with any woman.

Take one attractive, sweet-smelling blonde and a hormone-driven male, stir in a bit of danger, shake well, and it was only natural you'd come up with a sex connection.

That, at least, is what Zach had kept telling himself all night.

What he'd almost managed to believe.

Until the woman who'd caused him so much emotional and sexual turmoil entered the kitchen looking like a summer garden in a brightly flowered halter top and crisp white slacks.

She also looked as if she'd gotten some sleep. Which made one of them.

"Good morning." Her smile, while only a bit tentative, brightened her moss green eyes.

" 'Morning." He poured some orange juice from the carton he'd watched her put away yesterday. Had that been only twenty-four hours ago? It seemed like a week. Month. Year. "Sleep well?"

"Very well, thank you." She took the glass he handed her and sipped. "How about you?"

"Like a rock," he lied.

"I owe you an apology." She perched on a barstool and crossed those legs that appeared to go all the way up to her ears. "For keeping you up just because I got skitterish about things going bump in the night."

"I got used to going without sleep in the SEALs. Besides, there was no point taking chances. Especially since you never know who Lucie might've given keys to over the years. I had one. So did Dad. And Linc. The former housekeeper. And the service Harlan hired to come in once a week, and—"

"I get your point. Knowing Lucie, there could be keys all over the island."

"Which is why we're going to change the locks."

"You won't find me arguing about that." She slid off

the stool and poured herself a cup of coffee he'd made from the carafe, then stirred in some milk and not one, not two, but three spoonfuls of sugar.

"I'm amazed you have any teeth left."

She flashed those gleaming whites at him. "I have tough teeth. And the rest of me is definitely tougher than I look."

"Yeah, I kind of figured that out for myself, seeing as how you had a seven-story building fall down on you and lived to tell about it."

"Only you."

He arched a brow, inviting elaboration.

"Except for the grief shrink in Florence, who wouldn't sign me out of the hospital until I agreed to a session, and some various international security types from the CIA and Interpol, I've talked with only you about the bombing."

She walked over to the window and looked out over the fields of tea plants. "I'm still not sure why."

"Maybe because I'm a good listener."

She glanced back over her shoulder. "Maybe. But more likely because you, of all people, can understand."

"That too."

"But here's the thing." Her teeth were worrying her bottom lip. He confused her, Zach realized. Which was only fair, since she was confusing the hell out of him. "I've never dwelled in the past. Or even the present. I prefer to look ahead."

"Lucie always said you weren't one to stop and smell the roses."

She frowned. "You make being goal-oriented sound like a fault."

Feeling a near-obsessive urge to rub those lines between her brows with his thumb, Zach slipped his hands into the pockets of his jeans to keep them out of trouble.

"It wasn't a judgment call, New York. Just a statement."

Hadn't he been the same way? Until these past few months when he'd been uncharacteristically drifting.

"Well, as I was saying, I don't believe in looking back."

"Hard to get anywhere when you're looking at life in a rearview mirror."

"Exactly."

Relief flooded into those remarkable eyes, making him wonder if she'd always been so open with her emotions. He decided this, too, was a lingering effect from the bombing. If she'd always had every thought written across her face in bold script she couldn't have risen as high and fast as she had at Wingate hotels.

"So, while I won't deny that it felt good to get that night off my chest, I also don't want to dwell on it."

"Put it away in a lockbox."

"Exactly," she repeated with a firm nod, openly satisfied by her mistaken belief that they were on the same page.

Which was where she'd gone wrong. He could tell her, from personal experience, that compartmentalizing, which had always worked dandy for him in the past, had its limits.

But since he doubted she would believe him—he certainly wouldn't have bought the idea himself a year ago—he decided she would have to find that out for herself.

"And now that it's officially behind me, I'm going to move on with my life."

"You're going back to work?"

"In a way." She polished off the coffee and put the cup in the dishwasher. "I don't suppose you brought the blueprints with you last night?"

"I had other things on my mind."

"That's okay. I need to go into town, find out from Harlan how to draw money from the Swann Tea account. What was the figure Lucie and your father agreed on?"

Although she hadn't been engaged in any construction in the States since her stint in new hotel development six years ago, the amount he named certainly sounded fair and reasonable.

"Okay. I'll also run by the bank and arrange for bridge financing to cover your draws, if Linc doesn't have any strong objection to the plan. And, of course, I'll need to let Titania know she's going to be working her tail off for the next few months.

"Why don't I meet you back here around"—she glanced at her watch—"two."

"I'm not wild about the idea of you running all over the island by yourself."

"Oh, for heaven's sake." Her frustrated breath ruffled her bangs. "It's daylight. What could happen?"

"Try asking Cleo that," he suggested mildly. "Oh, wait." He put up a hand as if the thought had just occurred to him. "You can't ask her, can you? Because some maniac serial killer rapist stabbed her to death."

"There's no need to be sarcastic."

"No." He pressed his fingers against the bridge of his nose and tried to keep his mind from conjuring up the image of the nurse's body that Nate had described. "You're absolutely right. My tone disrespected a good woman, and I didn't mean to do that.

"However"—he pressed on when she opened her mouth to interrupt—"that doesn't make my point any less valid. Cleo was killed in the middle of the day. Seemingly by someone she knew."

"How do you know that?"

"Nate told me last night. Signs point to her having let her killer into her house."

The cute little house he'd helped her bring back from near-dead, the same one for which only last week he'd planed her bedroom door, which, like the ones at Whispering Pines, had begun sticking due to a spike in humidity.

"Well." She blew out another breath that trembled slightly. "That *is* unsettling. But so long as I don't let anyone in my car while I'm out, I can't see I'm in any danger. And here's the thing." She cocked her head, lifted her chin in that way he was beginning to recognize. "I'm hiring a contractor, Zach. Not a bodyguard."

"Maybe you should."

"And wouldn't that get everyone talking?"

"Gossip is a lot less painful than murder."

"Wow." She folded her arms. "If you'll wait a minute, I'll dig up a pen and write that down."

He liked the little spark of temper that flashed in her eyes and brightened her cheeks. The bombing may have gotten her down for a time, but no way could anyone count this lady out.

He dug into his pocket and pulled out a mechanical pencil. "Be my guest."

"Cute." Her lips twitched. Just a little. "It's a SEAL thing, isn't it?"

"What?"

"You probably get off on being the big macho superhero who rushes in to rescue the damsel in distress."

"You couldn't be more off base."

"Really?" She arched a challenging brow.

"Really. I came back to the island because I was through with saving the world. And everyone in it."

"Oh." Her eyes swept over his face as she took that in. "Well." She snatched her bag from the counter by the kitchen door. "You know, if I promise to take reasonable care, and you, in turn, promise to lighten up and not hover over me, we might possibly get through this construction job without driving each other crazy."

Driving her crazy, Zach thought, as he stood at the window and watched her drive away, was exactly what he intended to do.

But not right away. He'd spent a lot of time—okay, too much time—thinking about her last night and had come to the conclusion that despite the obvious chemistry between them, the timing sucked.

She still had issues.

He still had issues.

If he was looking for a blow-your-mind release, he'd go for it.

But as the tall case clock in Swannsea's foyer had noisily ticked away the minutes and hours last night, he'd decided to deliberately slow things down.

See what developed.

After all, he wasn't going anywhere.

And neither, it appeared, was she.

33

Having struck out at finding anyone on the island who'd seen Cleo the day she was murdered, Nate decided that after dusting Swannsea for prints, he would drive over to Somersett in hopes of finding the clerk who had waited on her. As he was preparing to head out, his dispatcher appeared in his office doorway.

"There's someone to see you, Sheriff," she announced, her mouth pulled into a line as tight as her salt-and-pepper perm. "A woman." Her eyes narrowed behind the bifocals. "That redhead who claims to be an FBI agent."

Nate reminded himself that patience was reputed to be a virtue.

"Perhaps that's because she *is* a special agent," he suggested.

"Well, she's no Efrem Zimbalist, Junior, that's for sure," Dottie Taylor sniffed.

"Why don't you send her in, please, Mrs. Taylor."

Deciding there was nothing to be gained by pointing out that Efrem Zimbalist had only played an FBI agent on TV, Nate stood up behind the battered desk, which, along with his disapproving dispatcher and a paroled-murderer janitor, was a legacy from his father.

"Good morning, Sheriff." She breezed into the room on a long-legged stride, bringing with her the fresh, clean scent of soap.

"Special Agent."

"Oh, please." After a brief handshake, she sat down and crossed her legs with an impatient swish. "Let's make it simple. I'm Cait. And you're Nate. And, wow, how about that, we rhyme."

"Seem to." Taking his own seat behind the desk, he glanced past her toward the door. "Where's your partner?"

"With any luck he's gone back to the mother ship. And for the record, it's nuns who always travel in pairs. Not FBI agents."

"I'll keep that in mind."

Despite today's gray and white suit, she was about as far from a nun as a woman could get. Once again it crossed his mind that if he weren't already involved with the woman of his dreams, he definitely wouldn't mind spending a lot of time consulting with Special Agent Cait Cavanaugh.

"What can I do for you?"

"It's more what I can do for you." She reached into her black leather bag and pulled out a thumb drive. "I've been thinking about your case."

"While protecting the ports from terrorism?"

"No, while forced to spend the day at the port with the most boring and sexist man on this planet. Anyway, I had my office run a check for all women between the ages of eighteen and forty reported missing in the Low-country over the last decade. Also all unclaimed female bodies."

"And?"

"And, unsurprisingly, there were quite a few. In the hundreds, actually."

"That's unsurprising?" Nate hadn't thought he was easily shocked.

"Unfortunately. Males are more frequently killed in acts of violence. Street fights, drug deals, two guys get into a drunken argument, that sort of thing. Which, even if there aren't any witnesses, the bodies are generally fresh and more easily identifiable.

"Whereas murdered females are more likely to be victims of abduction. Their bodies are often hidden, or left to the elements."

"Like in a marsh."

"Exactly. They decompose, which makes them more difficult to identify. The news, however, was better for the missing females. Most of them showed up within a few days or weeks."

"You say 'most.' "

"There are still some unclosed cases. Some which point toward a significant-other homicide, but those aren't always easy to prove. But here's the thing. One of the women reported missing in Somersett was a prostitute."

"That doesn't seem unusual, given her occupation."

Nate watched movies. Read thrillers. Prostitutes often seemed to be victims of serial killers, given that they not only indulged in risky behavior but lived below the radar, in a world where people wouldn't necessarily go searching for them if they didn't show up for work one day.

"True. What's unusual is this woman had a friend who reported her missing. A friend who claimed to have escaped a guy who'd taken her home, supposedly for an all-nighter, and put her in a cage."

"That is interesting."

"Isn't it? And if that doesn't get your cop spidey sense tingling, try this: The woman had an *S* burned into her left butt cheek."

Every atom in Nate's body went on alert. "And this was when?"

"Three years ago."

"And no one thought this was worth investigating?"

"Unfortunately, no. Because the woman in question was already covered in ink, which, to the officer who took the complaint, indicated that she might be into weird body enhancements."

"Some people consider a tattoo an enhancement." Nate decided not to mention the eagle globe and anchor he'd had inked over his heart while on his first liberty in Singapore. "But a brand would seem to be pushing the envelope."

"For most people. But apparently this woman, and her missing friend, were the go-to gals if you were looking to purchase a little S&M entertainment."

She rubbed the back of her neck, appearing uneasy with this conversation. "Look, I agree—the complaint shouldn't have been dropped. But you have to understand, at the time the department was dealing with a serial arsonist and innocent people were dying. The missing woman fell through the cracks." She shook her head. "She shouldn't have. But she did."

"And her body never showed up?"

"Not that anyone knows of."

"Which doesn't exactly fit this case." Nate wondered how unusual a brand was in the S&M community and guessed it wasn't impossibly uncommon.

"No. But it's close enough you might want to go through the files I downloaded and see how many more you can find that fit the profile. I would've, but—"

"You have ports to protect."

"Yeah. Which is hugely important, although I have to admit that after all the years as a cop, I miss working more-active cases. But that's neither here nor there.

"I took time to call a friend who works in the bureau's Behavioral Science Unit. I minored in psychology, so I was jazzed when the Somersett, Georgetown, and Charleston PDs got together and had him come teach a weeklong class back when I was on the force.

"Although he wanted me to stress that profiling is an art, not really a science, from what I told him about what I knew of your case, he thinks it's very possible that your UNSUB's been at this a while."

"A while." And hadn't been caught. Wasn't that encouraging?

"It's just his gut. But he did give me some suggestions to pass on to you. Some things to look for."

"I'm grateful for any help I can get."

She tilted her head. "That's unusual. Most local cops get, shall we say, a bit *territorial* when the feds show up."

"I spent fifteen years in the Marine Corps. We worked in teams. Seems this is pretty much the same thing. But the good news is that no one's shooting at me." So far.

"Like I said, it's unusual." She paused a beat. Glanced down at her leather-banded watch. Then looked at him with frank feminine interest. "I've got a meeting with some politician types in Columbia, but I should be back by six. What would you think about continuing this discussion over dinner?"

Timing, Nate thought with a wry inward smile, was, indeed, everything. There was a time he would've jumped at the invitation, which, unless every instinct he possessed had gone on the blink, was as much personal as it was professional.

"Sorry, but I have plans."

She tilted her head. Studied him some more. "Serious plans?"

"Let's say I remain hopeful."

"It figures." She flashed a dazzling smile. Then, as if turning off a switch, moved the conversation back onto its professional track.

"A lot of serial killers have been found to have antisocial personality disorder."

"Killing strangers isn't the most social activity," he agreed.

"True. And the fact that at least one of your victims apparently knew her assailant points to some of the traits—manipulativeness and even glibness—that allowed him to get close."

"Ted Bundy was reported to be charming."

"Exactly." She nodded. "But if this has been going on a while, there are other traits my friend suggested might have surfaced. A persistent violation of social norms, breaking laws, low frustration tolerance, aggression, drug abuse."

"Things that would tend to garner attention from authorities."

"Exactly. Which is why it's possible—and remember, this is merely a hypothesis—that you're dealing with someone with a narcissistic personality disorder. Which means you might want to be looking for a guy who has a greatly exaggerated sense of being special, who limits his personal and professional associations only to those he deems worthy."

"Except when he decides to kill," Nate said.

"Good point," she allowed. "But that's part of the deal." She leaned forward to stress her next statement. "The narcissist is so caught up in his own self-importance, he doesn't develop empathy, which makes him more able to cause suffering to those he doesn't view as his equals.

"He could exhibit a sense of entitlement. And engage in arrogant behavior, but at the same time, my friend said, since narcissism is the beating heart of pyschopathy, the narcissist resembles the antisocial guy in that he can also be glib and manipulative. Which is not only how he attracts his victims but how he avoids getting caught. Sometimes for decades."

"Well." Nate blew out a long breath. Rubbed the back of his neck. No way was his killer going to get away for that long. "Sounds like all I have to do is go over to the Palmetto Golf and Tennis Club and round up all the men on the course."

"Swann Island, for all its outward calm, is populated with more than its share of overachievers," she agreed. "Which makes sense, given how expensive oceanfront property's gotten. Though, of course, someone from the mainland could've decided to start using your little island paradise as a dumping ground.

"But even if I hadn't taken that class and called my friend, back in my cop days, if I thought this UNSUB had been around a while, I probably wouldn't be looking for some homeless psychopath who's acting on impulse."

"It's hard to keep a woman in a cage when you're living under a bridge," Nate murmured, as much to himself as to her.

"There is that." She stood up. "Well, that's all I've got."

Nate stood up as well, came around his desk. "It's a huge help. I appreciate it."

"No problem. Like I said, I minored in psychology, so this case intrigues me. I hope you'll keep me updated."

"Absolutely," he said as he walked her out of his office and past the narrowed, watchful eyes of his dispatcher.

She was about to leave, then turned in the doorway leading to the street. "Tell her she's a lucky woman."

He didn't have to ask who she was talking about. "I've been trying to do exactly that."

"Well." She gave him another one of those quick once-over looks, from the top of his head down to his boots, then back up again, her gaze meeting his with the frankness that he suspected had served her well as a cop but might cause problems in the more structured environs of the FBI. "If she isn't easily convinced, you've got my number."

He indulged in watching her walk out to the black SUV. The lady definitely had a nice ass. And from the lack of a ring on her left hand and the dinner invitation, it seemed she was unattached.

Wondering what was wrong with the men over in Somersett to let Caitlin Cavanaugh get away, and drawn by the siren call of those files the sexy special agent had brought him, Nate glanced up at the round white wall clock and decided he had time to take a cursory look.

Thirty minutes later, his blood was running cold as he realized that his murders were just the tip of a very deadly iceberg.

34

"Shut up!" Titania's fork paused on the way to her mouth. "You and Zachariah Tremayne spent the night together?"

"Why don't you let me call the *Trumpet*?" Sabrina said dryly. "Then you can issue a press release. Save everyone in this restaurant from having to spread the word one person at a time."

Declaring that eating at Wisteria was too much like work, Titania had insisted they go to the Palmetto Golf and Tennis Club to celebrate their collaboration. The moment the Keira Knightley–look-alike hostess led them to the umbrella-topped table, Sabrina realized exactly how long it had been since she'd had a girl lunch.

And how badly she needed one. Even though the first part of the conversation dwelt on last night's possible break-in, which wasn't exactly a fun topic.

"Besides, we didn't exactly spend the night together." She began searching through her seafood salad for elusive lobster. "I was in my bedroom. And he stayed downstairs."

"Now there's a waste." Titania flashed a flirtatious smile toward the quartet of men at a nearby table who'd been trying to catch her eye since they'd come off the emerald green golf course. Sabrina knew she didn't mean anything by it; her friend had, by her own account, been a flirt in the cradle. "Are you telling me you weren't even the slightest bit tempted to do a little tepee creeping?"

"More than a little."

Sabrina took a sip of the crisp, straw-colored house wine and made a mental note to ask the waiter the label. It would be nice to stock for those who wanted something a little stronger than tea with their finger sandwiches and petits fours.

"Especially after that kiss."

They could also add it to the wine list available for those wedding receptions Lucie had planned.

"Kiss?" The golfers were immediately forgotten. Titania leaned across the table. "What kiss?" she hissed, remembering Sabrina's warning to keep the private conversation exactly that. *Private.*

She grinned. Yes, this lunch had been a perfect idea. She only wished she'd been the one to think of it. "The make-your-knees-weak-and-your-head-spin kiss we shared after he drove me home from dinner at Harlan and Lillian's."

Titania leaned back in the white wicker chair, twirled her own glass of Sauvignon Blanc, and gave Sabrina a long, deep look. "As soon as Nate told me about what happened last night, which is, by the way, really creepy, I wanted to call you but he said to wait until he knew something.

"Then, when he got back to the house, he assured me you were okay and going back to bed. So I decided, since we were having lunch, it could wait. But he didn't mention a single word about Zach staying at the house. Or that you were in danger."

"I honestly don't think I was." Sabrina stabbed a bay shrimp and tried not to think about what Nate had said about the laptop and camera not having been stolen.

"So, I guess finding that your house had been broken into was what derailed the love train?"

"No." Sabrina shifted her gaze to the court, where a hunky tennis pro was hitting balls to an overweight fiftysomething guy who looked on the verge of keeling over as he huffed and puffed after them. "That happened before we went into the house. I was more than willing, but Zach turned me down."

"No way." Titania's doe brown eyes widened.

"Way." Sabrina sighed. "It was probably just as well, since it would just be one more complication I don't want to deal with."

"Like you and the hottie SEAL working together with all that unsatiated lust zapping around the two of you isn't going to be a complication?"

"Good point." And one she'd been thinking about all morning.

"Well, then, there's obviously only one thing to do."

"What's that?"

Titania crossed her long, dark legs, causing one of the men—blindingly decked out in green knickers covered with pink flamingos and a fuchsia surfboard aloha shirt—to choke on his beer.

"You'll have to seduce him."

Before Sabrina could respond to that suggestion, Titania said, "Oh, shit. Don't turn around."

"All right." Feigning casualness, Sabrina plucked a roll from the basket between them. "Who is it?"

"Remember Misty Mannington?"

"Oh, please, not Misty the Man-eater." Sabrina needed an encounter with her childhood nemesis like she needed a yeast infection.

"In the flesh." Titania's carmine-tinted lips widened in a bright, patently false smile. "And so much of it is showing."

"Well, if it isn't Lucie's jet-setting New York granddaughter." The exaggerated Southern drawl ripped at Sabrina's last nerve like razor wire. "Home from the Continent."

Sabrina exchanged a look with Titania. Did anyone call Europe the Continent anymore?

She looked up at the woman wearing a white halter

top that barely contained size double-D breasts that had
definitely been plumped up from the Cs she'd flashed at
all the boys back in high school, a flirty white skirt that
strained across her hips, and snowy tennis shoes with
those little half socks that have balls on the back.

Revealing that Misty knew how to accessorize with
the best of them, the fuzzy little balls were exactly the
same bubblegum pink color as the gloss she'd smeared
over her collagen-enhanced, bee-stung lips.

"Hello, Misty. How are you?" Sabrina inquired
neutrally.

"Oh, as fine as fine can be."

A diamond the size of Alaska glittered like a glacier
on her right hand as she pushed her rhinestone-studded
Chanel sunglasses onto the top of her artfully tousled
and rigidly sprayed blond hair. More diamonds, set off
by pink tourmalines, sparkled in a trio of tennis
bracelets.

"But the important question, Sabrina, dear, is how
are *you*?"

Placing a hand tipped in acrylic nails that echoed her
lip gloss on Sabrina's shoulder, she leaned down to air-
kiss cheeks, nearly smothering Sabrina in a musky cloud
of Obsession.

"I was so shocked to hear about that terrible thing
that happened to you. We were all so relieved that you
survived, bless your heart."

Sabrina may not have been born and bred in the
bosom of the Confederacy, but she *had* spent all those
summers on Swann Island, which was more than enough
time to understand the underlying meaning of that all-
encompassing phrase.

Truth be told, a well-bred Southern belle could say
any ugly thing at all, such as "Why, that Sally Mae would
spread her legs for the entire front line of the USC
Gamecock football team, but given that her family's always been poor white trash, she can't help being a slut,"

so long as she made sure to tack on "bless her heart."
Or, equally as effective, "poor thing."

"Your concern is so sweet, Misty," Titania replied.

"And much appreciated," Sabrina said.

"Well, it's a relief you survived. I swear, if I'd been
blown up, then buried alive, I'd still be eating Valium
like M&M's. After all you've been through, aren't you
nervous about staying out there at that big old empty
house by yourself?"

"Not at all." No way was Sabrina going to reveal she
hadn't been alone.

"Aren't you the bravest thing? Why, I'd be as nervous
as a cat on a hot tin roof. I suppose you'll be going back
to work soon?" Her voice went up a bit on the end of
the statement, turning it into a question.

"Actually, I'm considering staying on the island."

"Really?" An arch blond brow lifted. Lips pursed.
"Well, aren't you just full of surprises?"

Misty stepped back and looked Sabrina over with the
sharp, appraising gaze of a female checking out any possible competition.

"You're certainly not looking any the worse for
wear," she announced. "Considering. And gracious, it
must be lovely to be skinny enough to wear white
pants."

She ran her hands over lush hips that used to have
boys walking into walls when she'd sashay by in her
perky little cheerleader skirt. "Why, with all the weight
I put on after having my darling twin baby girls, if I so
much as tried to squeeze into an outfit like that, my
behind would look like two cats in a gunnysack fighting
to get out."

Her blue eyes glinted like steel sabers in the bright
noon sun as they took another swift scan. "While you,
on the other hand, I swear, are every bit as skinny as
you were back in middle school." Her magnolia tone
was laced with delicious female malice. "How ever did

you manage such a feat, living over there in the land of perpetual pasta?"

"I guess I got lucky and inherited Lucie's metabolism."

"And didn't Lucie Somersett always have energy? I swear, she was always racing here and there, never stopping to take so much as a breath. Which is, I suppose, how she got so overextended."

"I hadn't realized she had," Sabrina said evenly.

"Well, now, I wouldn't want to talk ill of the dead," Misty began in a conspiratorial tone as she sat down at the table without waiting for an invitation that neither Sabrina nor Titania would have ever in this lifetime extended.

"Then don't," Titania suggested.

"Well, I wasn't going to be ugly." Pink Angelina Jolie lips pouted. "It's just that I was surprised when she failed to write up my wedding in her column in the *Trumpet*."

"Perhaps she thought she'd given you enough ink with the first two weddings," Titania suggested sweetly. "And given that number three didn't make it to the first anniversary, I'd say she saved you some embarrassment."

"You needn't be snide, Titania Davis." Misty paused for a lethal moment. "Just because Nate Spencer hasn't seen fit to make an honest woman of you is no reason for you to be jealous of those of us who prefer a more traditional, committed relationship."

She looked up, scanned the terrace. "Oh, there's my party." She waggled bubblegum fingertips at Brad Sumner, who was seated at a table across the terrace. "Well, it was lovely seeing you again, Sabrina, dear."

Her smile was as false as her breasts. "You know, I belong to a book club that meets once a month. We'd absolutely be tickled to have you join us. If you do decide to stay on the island for a while."

"Thanks for the invitation. I'll give it some thought," Sabrina lied. She'd rather go skinny-dipping with sharks than spend an evening with Misty the Man-eater Mannington. "What are you reading?"

"Reading?" Her expression turned as vacuous as Sabrina remembered her mind to be.

"Your book club."

"Oh." She smiled. "That." She tilted her head as if considering the matter. "I'm not sure. Oprah hasn't announced the title yet."

This time she directed her finger waggling to Sabrina, openly ignoring Titania. "Well, toodle-oo. I'm in the phone book; give me a jingle and we'll set something up."

"Will do," Sabrina said. As soon as the devil strapped on a pair of figure skates and began doing triple axels in hell.

Misty had begun weaving her way through the crush of tables, when Titania called out to her, causing her to turn back.

"What?" she asked on an edge of impatience.

"I meant to tell you, I really like what you've done with your hair."

"Really?" She lifted a hand toward the mass of lacquered blond waves.

"Absolutely." Titania's grin could have lit up Swann Island for a month of Sundays. "If I were you, I wouldn't pay any attention to all those mean-spirited gossips who say it makes you look as if you belong leaning against a lamppost and propositioning sailors on the Somersett waterfront."

Color even brighter than her nails flooded into Misty's cheeks. Her mouth moved, but nothing came out.

"If she dies of apoplexy right here on the spot, I sure as hell hope the fact that you're sleeping with the sheriff will keep you out of the slammer," Sabrina murmured.

"It'd be worth going to jail for," Titania returned as Misty spun back around, taking out a tray of mojitos a T-shirted hunk of a waiter was carrying from the bar.

Radiating satisfaction as the horrified young man

began madly dabbing at Misty's Playmate breasts with a handful of cocktail napkins, Titania took nearly as big a bite out of her sandwich as she'd taken from Misty's hide.

"Make an honest woman of me, my ass," she muttered around a mouth of crab cake. "As for a committed relationship, any man insane enough to get anywhere near that bitch barracuda belongs in a rubber room at Somersett Sanitarium. And did you see that tan? It's gotta be a spray job."

"If it isn't, she's going to look like a raisin by the time she's forty. But I'm more interested in what she's doing with Brad Sumner."

"I'd say that's more than a little obvious," Titania said. "Given her history of collecting alimony the way my eight-year-old goddaughter collects American Girl dolls, and from that bait of an outfit she's poured herself into, I'd guess she's casting around for husband number four."

"But Brad's married."

"That's never seemed to stop him from playing around. Don't forget, he was screwing wife number two while married to the first one. And, as a matter of fact, Cleo told me he hit on her when she went to his office to sign the papers to buy her house. And again last month, when he brought his wife into the ER after she'd eaten some bad shellfish. Can you believe a man coming on to another woman while his wife is puking her guts out?"

"That is low." Sabrina thought back to the vibes she'd gotten from him. "But I guess I'm not surprised, in his case." Something occurred to her. "I wonder if Nate knows?"

"I told him. Not because I think Sumner is the one who killed Cleo—I mean, let's face it, taking a life has got to require some kind of nerve, which Brad boy doesn't have—but it seemed like evidence. Not that it'd hold up in a court of law, since I believe it'd be hearsay, but still . . ."

"Does Nate consider him a suspect?"

What if it had been Brad in the house last night? What if he'd come in planning to kill her so he could somehow get his greedy, grasping, developer hands on Swannsea?

If she died, her grandmother's estate would go to Harlan. Who, if last night's conversation was any indication, might not be all that enthusiastic about keeping the tea company going.

Though, given how angry he was about Plantation Shores being built right next to Whispering Pines, she couldn't see him ever selling to Brad's company.

Maybe Zach was right. Maybe Brad *was* trying to scare her away, hoping that if he unsettled her enough, she'd want to dump the house, and the business, and leave.

"I've no idea what Nate's thinking." Titania shrugged her bare shoulders. "The man's frustratingly close-mouthed when it comes to his work. But I'd be shocked if the Swann Island Slasher turns out to be Brad."

"The Swann Island Slasher?"

"You didn't read this morning's *Trumpet*?"

"I've been a little distracted. Besides, checking out whose cousin is visiting from Raleigh and reviews of the Junior League cookbook wasn't exactly at the top of my priority list."

"Oh, the paper's changed a lot since you were last here. It covers real news now. At least local news, like elections and police logs and school board meetings, that sort of thing. There's this new editor, David Henley, who keeps saying he's determined to drag us into the twenti-eth century."

"Uh, I don't want to be picky, but this is the twenty-first."

"Of course it is. But, you know, you have to take

change one step at a time down here. Anyway, he's a
Yankee from D.C. who—"

"Unless the country had a massive land shift after I
moved to Italy, Washington's still south of the Mason-
Dixon Line."

"Well, geographically maybe. But, honey, it was, after
all, the home of the Union army." She bit into a sweet
potato French fry. "So, you want to tell me how that
counts as Southern?"

Sabrina had often thought that one of the reasons
she'd slid so easily into Florentine life was that she'd
spent so much time in a place that continued to keep
one foot firmly rooted in the past. In that respect, Italy
hadn't been all that different from the American South.

"A Union army that set your people free," she
pointed out.

"Well, there is that. Anyway, the *Trumpet*'s new editor, who is, by the way, a bit of a hottie, despite his
deplorable yuppie taste in clothes, apparently decided
our local killer needed a catchy nickname. Personally, I
find it rather unoriginal for a so-called wordsmith to
come up with, but it's already been picked up by the AP
and is starting to pop up on blogs all over the Internet."

"Oh, my God. Nate must be furious."

"Well, I'm not one to share domestic details. But he
did promise to fix that fist-sized hole in my kitchen
wall."

Sabrina glanced around the patio at the well-dressed
people enjoying the sunny summer day. And, now that
the fuss over the spilled mojitos had settled down, each
other's company.

A lazy black and yellow bumblebee buzzed over the
snowy white blossoms of the butterfly bush hedge; carefree children on vacation called out "Marco Polo" from
the turquoise waters of the pool; golfers strolled across
acres of emerald green lawn, while only a few feet away,
a dragonfly hovered over the terra-cotta swan fountain,
drinking from the tumbling clear water.

The idyllic scene could have washed off the canvas of *Sunday Afternoon on the Island of La Grande Jatte*, had Georges Seurat been painting here rather than on that island in the Seine.

"It's going to turn the island into a media circus."

"That's precisely what Nate fears. Which could make it more difficult to catch the killer. Nate's afraid he'll go underground for a while until the heat's off. Or even move on."

"And start killing somewhere else."

Sabrina shook her head. Even as she felt sympathy for Nate, she couldn't overlook the irony that she'd come back to the island seeking peace and quiet after nearly being killed, only to find that danger had followed her home.

35

Silver Shores Manor was a state-of-the-art facility designed by an award-winning team of architects, interior designers, and health-care professionals who were, if the manor's glossy brochure was to be believed, award-winning experts in the care of Alzheimer's patients.

Although it cost an arm and a leg, at least it tried to be more than a warehouse for those patients waiting to die, unlike all the others Titania had looked at during her six-month search for a safe and nurturing environment for her father.

Not that he would know anything about his surroundings.

But she would. As would Linc, who admittedly was footing more of the cost than she was. Then again, his salary at Swann Tea was triple what she cleared from the Wisteria Tea Room and Bakery, and besides, wasn't she the one who visited every single damn evening?

Not that Joshua Davis would even notice if she failed to show up.

But for all the sassy image she put forth to the world, Titania was, down deep, old-fashioned enough to know she'd never forgive herself if, when the blessed day came on which her father finally found peace, she couldn't look back and say honestly, if only to herself, that she'd done the best she could.

The walls were painted in bright primary colors, the

better, the administrator who'd taken her on her initial tour had explained, to stimulate residents' minds. At Silver Shores, Titania learned, the patients were never called "patients"—they were "residents." As if, she'd thought at the time, the manor was merely some high-priced retirement condo development.

Paintings of scenes from the World War II era during which most of the residents had grown up were displayed on the walls of six hallways that radiated outward like the rays of the sun around the central nursing center located at the core of the building.

Family members were encouraged to bring in photos documenting the residents' lives, the idea being that seeing familiar images would stimulate memories. Or perhaps encourage conversations that might lead to recapturing memories lost in the mists of damaged minds.

Duke Ellington was taking the A train as Titania entered the building. Music—Glenn Miller, Les Brown, Tommy Dorsey, and all the other greats of the Big Band Era—continually drifted from speakers hidden in those bright red, yellow, and blue walls. She'd been fascinated at one event when elderly residents who hadn't spoken for months were not only able to remember the words to "Sentimental Journey" and "Boogie Woogie Bugle Boy," but sang along.

Unfortunately, once the player piano was turned off, the singing stopped. Like water turned off at a tap.

Wondering if, when her generation started arriving at Silver Shores, the speakers would be belting out Metallica, Barenaked Ladies, and Jon Bon Jovi, Titania waved a hello to the guard seated in his booth next to the locked door. The bank of TV screens in front of him allowed visual access to every room on all the hallways, which on one level she found an awful invasion of privacy. But, she'd realized as she signed the papers committing her father to the facility, a necessary one.

Despite all the optimistic and well-meaning efforts to

make Silver Shores cheery and homey, it was still, to those forced to accompany loved ones on this long, fatal journey, as cheerful as, well . . . an Alzheimer's home.

No amount of bright paint or pretty pictures could hide the scents of disinfectant, despair, and impending death. No music could hide the cries of once vital members of the greatest generation whose minds were tragically trapped in nightmares they no longer had the words to describe.

She found her father in the lounge, sitting in his wheelchair in front of the large-screen plasma TV that someone had tuned to a cable news station. Terrific, she thought as she watched some apartment building burning somewhere. Wasn't that just what these people needed to see? Weren't their own lives tragic enough?

After clicking through the channels until she found perky Rachael Ray demonstrating how to prepare an entire meal in thirty minutes, she went over, bent down, and gave him a big hug.

" 'Bout time you got here, girl," he said. "What took you so long? I've been waiting all day for you."

"You have?"

She sat down on the ottoman next to the chair. Her father had good days and bad. Lately more of the bad, sliding downhill into horrid. Hope that this was one of the rare good ones fluttered like hummingbird wings in Titania's heart.

"Sure as heck have. What happened? Miz Swann keep you working late at Swannsea again?"

Her heart plummeted. "No."

"She's been making you work too many hours." His worried eyes swept over her face. No, not *her* face. Her mother's face. "Maybe I ought to say something to her about it. Tell her that you're expecting."

He nodded with more decisiveness than she'd witnessed in months. Which would have been encouraging, were he not back in 1981.

"Daddy—"

"Now, I know you don't want to tell her about the baby just yet," he said, overriding her planned words, "but Miz Lucie's a good woman, Mel. She'd never fire you for starting a family. Didn't she loan us that down payment on this house when we got married last year, so we'd have room for a nursery?"

He took her cold hand in both of his, lifting it to his lips. "You'll see. It'll be all right. Why, I bet she's gonna be near as happy about our baby as we are."

"I'm sure she will."

She gave up, knowing that arguing would do no good and deciding that believing he was having this moment with the mother she'd never known might bring some joy into his dismal life. She gave him a watery smile.

"You'll see," he said. His face, so much darker than hers, offered reassurance. And unqualified love. He reached out and brushed at the tears streaming down her face with a tender fingertip. "What you crying 'bout, baby doll?"

She drew in a ragged breath, swiped at her wet cheeks with her hands. "Nothing, Joshua," she said past the painful lump in her throat. "I guess it's just baby hormones."

And a broken heart.

36

"I'm fine," Sabrina insisted yet again.

Only to humor Lillian, she'd dropped by Whispering Pines after lunch for a checkup.

Harlan patted her knee, as if she were eight years old again and had fallen off her bike.

"Of course you're right as rain." He put the black cuff back in its drawer. "Though you could afford to lose a few blood pressure points."

"It's not that high. And it's only stress."

"My point exactly. I'm prescribing morning walks and afternoon naps."

The walks she could do. Even enjoy. But naps?

"I haven't taken a nap since I was eighteen months old."

Of course, she couldn't remember being that young, but she could recall her mother mentioning that the nanny complained about that fact.

"Well, it should be a nice change of pace," he said mildly. "How are you sleeping?"

"Like a baby."

It wasn't really a lie. She knew from having friends who'd become new mothers that lots of babies didn't sleep all night.

His harrumph as he picked up her chart suggested he didn't believe her. He skimmed the notes that Ida Thornbill, who'd been his office nurse since before Sabrina had been born, had written down.

"You could put on a few pounds."

"You know what they say about a woman never being too rich or too thin," she quipped, not wanting to admit that the number on the scale had surprised her.

And not in a good way.

He slid his wire-framed reading glasses down his nose and gave her a long, studied look. "You're already rich enough. But there's naturally slender and there's anorexic. You were always the first. But you're on a slippery slope, young lady." He waggled a finger at her. "If you're not careful, you could slide into the second category."

He made a notation on the chart. "While you're out on that daily walk, stop by Wisteria and have Titania feed you."

"I'm perfectly capable of feeding myself."

"You mean nuking diet frozen dinners."

"Sissy's obviously a snitch." She'd known the clerk at the market was gossipy, but this was stepping over the line.

"True. But a well-meaning one."

"Did she tell you I also bought ice cream?"

"Chunky Monkey," he said approvingly. "Which is a start."

"Aren't you supposed to be recommending fresh fruits and vegetables?"

"There are bananas in your ice cream. That's one serving of fruit."

"Hahaha."

"I'm not joking."

He wasn't? Of course, she thought, she was in the South, where people had never met a veggie they didn't think was better deep-fried.

"What kind of doctor are you?"

"A good one." He picked up a prescription pad and scribbled a few lines. "Who cares about my patients, especially when they're family." He put the pen back in the pocket of the lab coat and tore off a script. "Here you go. I believe they'll have everything you need at the market."

She snatched the piece of paper from his outstretched hand. "A liquid food supplement?" Oh, yuck.

"Being underweight also indicates you're undernourished. That and a bottle of multipurpose vitamins should get you back up to fighting weight."

"And if I don't want to fight?"

"You're going to be working with Zach Tremayne, aren't you?"

She slid off the examining table, tucked the script into her bag, and snapped it shut. "I haven't decided yet."

"Well, you know how I feel about it. I still think you'd be taking on too much."

"Did you know Brad Sumner wants to buy Swannsea?"

"So Lucie told me. The bastard even had the nerve to make me an offer the day after she died. But I told him I'd rather burn the fields than let him get his hands on them."

"I feel the same way."

"However, Sumner's not the only option. As it happens, we've had offers from two major tea companies, both interested in acquiring the business."

"And, of course, you told them no."

He didn't immediately answer.

"Uncle Harlan?"

He blew out a breath. "I was waiting until you got home to discuss the situation with you."

"There's nothing to discuss. Whatever I decide to do about Lucie's teahouse idea, neither Swann Tea nor Swannsea is for sale."

"You're like your grandmother, always operating in damn-the-torpedoes-full-steam-ahead mode. You'd probably end up with migraines and an ulcer if you didn't have some project to tackle."

"I don't see you retiring," she said pointedly.

"Touché." Chuckling, he draped an arm around her

shoulders and led her to the door. "Ever hear of a guy named Aristotle?"

"Of course."

"Well, he recommended moderation in all things. That's not such bad advice."

She couldn't help smiling at that. "I'll keep it in mind."

"You do that." He winked. "Your Aunt Lillian worries."

"Well," Sabrina asked that evening, "what do you think?"

Lincoln Davis, Titania's brother, leaned back and took a long pull on the bottle of AmberBock beer Sabrina had greeted him with.

After he'd updated her on the details of the Atlanta conference—from which he'd returned with a dozen new major corporate clients—they'd turned to the blueprints John Tremayne had drawn up. The ones Zach had brought by that afternoon.

The minute she'd seen the computerized three-dimensional drawings, she'd fallen in love with the plan, and although she'd been ambivalent in the beginning, she now found herself desperately hoping Linc would share her enthusiasm.

"Same thing I thought when your grandmother showed them to me. It's a damn good job of adding on while keeping the house's historical integrity."

"I know that," Sabrina said, trying to stifle her impatience. "Do you believe the entire concept is doable? From a business standpoint?"

"Sure. So long as you hire a really good manager."

"Actually, I'm thinking of taking over that job myself."

He spared her a look. "It's going to take some time to get off the ground."

"I'm aware of that."

"And while Swannsea is something to be damn proud

of, it's not exactly in the class of the international Wingate Palace hotel chain. 'Where—"

" 'Deluxe will no longer do.' " She finished the famous slogan. "I'm disappointed in you, Linc."

"Me?" He set the beer aside. "Why?"

"Because it seems as if I've known you forever, and I never would have taken you for a snob."

"Me?" he said again, flinging a dark hand against his chest. "Where did that come from?"

"Well, the fact that you felt the need to point out that Swannsea isn't the Wingate chain suggests that some people might consider it inferior. I certainly don't."

"Hell, Sabrina." He brushed his hand over his closely cropped black hair. "You know I didn't mean that. I merely figured that after all these years of jet-setting around the world and hobnobbing with kings and sheikhs and such, you might find the island, and Swannsea, well, a little tame."

She laughed when an image of Zach popped into her mind. " 'Tame' isn't the word I'd use. 'Peaceful' comes closer." At least if you discounted serial killers and the thief who broke into her house last night. "But it's apples and oranges, Linc. Wingate hotels are the best in the world at what they do. Swann Tea may not be the biggest tea company in the world, but we make the best tea."

She tapped the eraser end of her pencil on the blueprints, loving the way the architect had made the windows able to be quickly changed out to screens for nice days.

"I loved my work at Wingate, but from the day I arrived, I jumped on a one-way track and kept moving forward without giving thought to anything beyond making the next goal and reaching the next level.

"This unplanned break has allowed me to realize that by the time I was appointed manager, I only ever actually interacted with guests when I was called upon to solve a problem. Which, while I don't like to boast, I'd gotten very good at, if I do say so myself—"

"It's not braggin' if it's true," he said easily. "And Lucie definitely was all the time telling us how good you were at your job."

"My grandmother was prejudiced. But the thing is, I got into the hotel business because I enjoyed creating an enjoyable, comfortable environment for people. I like the idea of putting 'hospitable' back into the hospitality business.

"So, let's you, Titania, and I make Swannsea the best destination location in the Lowcountry."

Amazingly, an idea she never would have considered two months ago, one she'd only found rather intriguing three days ago, now seemed like something she'd been waiting to do all her life.

"Sounds like a plan. And one that'd make your grand-mamma real happy." He lifted the bottle. "To Lucie Swann."

She, in turn, lifted her gilt-rimmed teacup and clicked it against the bottle's neck. "To Lucie."

"You gonna call Zach?"

"I guess I should. So he can start getting a crew together."

Sabrina rolled up the plans, put the rubber band around them, and stuck them back in the cardboard tube.

"I do have some questions about a few details," she said. "Such as the crown molding in the tearoom. And the floors in the tearoom and museum. Also, Titania told me she'd like to add an island topped with a marble slab for rolling out pastry dough in the kitchen."

He nodded. "Good to get those little details straightened out right away, before construction starts."

She thought she heard laughter in his tone. Knew she saw it in his bright eyes.

"I'm not fooling you for a minute, am I?"

"Nope," he admitted. "But then again, my sister called to fill me in while I was down in Atlanta, so I had sort of a head start, so to speak."

"Any feelings I might possibly have for Zach are not why I've decided to follow up on Lucie's dream."

He immediately sobered. "I'd never think that of you, Sabrina. Or of Zach."

"Okay." She blew out a breath. "Well. It looks as if we're in business."

She watched him walk out to the SUV parked in the circular crushed-shell drive, then picked up the phone to call Zach but decided no, that pretending to call about floors, or molding, or countertops, or any of the million other things that would be bound to dominate their conversation for the next several months was the coward's way out.

"He thinks of you as a planner," she reminded herself. "A plotter. Who makes lists and checks things off one by one. A boring, unimaginative drone who's never done an impulsive thing in your life. Well, at least not since you were sixteen."

The disgusting thing was, that was mostly true. She'd chosen her path early in life and never wavered, never looked off to the side to see if there might be something more exciting. More pleasurable.

Unlike those people who found the unfamiliarity of hotels unsettling, to Sabrina a hotel had always been the closest thing, other than Swannsea, to home. It was where she'd caught up with her parents during those brief school breaks when they would send her plane tickets and deign to spend a few days with their only daughter.

Most of her time had been spent with the hotel staff, since her mother was a firm believer in using social occasions for networking and her father was always up for a party. Probably because with his larger-than-life personality, he'd always held center stage.

But being ignored hadn't bothered her all that much,

because when they weren't out, they were always sleeping until noon, and fighting hangovers and each other the rest of the time.

Meanwhile, she was treated to behind-the-scenes hotel life, which she found both fascinating and reassuring because, she discovered, a well-run hotel—and her parents frequented only the best—made everything seem effortless, with every contingency planned for.

By the time she was ten years old, she'd decided that if such a precise system worked for running a hotel, why couldn't it work for her life?

For the most part it had. What she hadn't planned for was losing both her parents and her grandmother unexpectedly, having a suicide bomber decide to make his radical statement at her hotel, and ending up back here on the island at the same time as Zach Tremayne.

Zach, who undoubtedly considered her one of the most boring, rigid women he'd ever met in his life.

"There's nothing wrong with being organized," she assured herself. "I'll bet SEALs never go off on a mission without a detailed battle plan."

Still, how long had it been since she'd done something not only impulsive but reckless?

How about eleven years?

Well, maybe it was time.

37

She wasn't going to try to seduce him, as Titania had suggested. She'd already gone that route and failed in the attempt. Not just once, but twice.

"But there's no point in not letting the man see what he turned down," she decided as she went upstairs to the bathroom, started the water running in the tub, then threw in a handful of a light floral springtime scent that had a tang of lemon to spice it up.

Which was precisely what she intended to do with her life.

Although she'd shaved her legs that morning, she did so again, thinking that if she was going to stay here on Swann Island, she should probably pay a visit to the Shores Spa and allow some sadist to attack her with hot wax.

And wow, wasn't that something to look forward to?

She smoothed lotion all over her body, then, although she usually dashed through her makeup, took the time to line both her eyes and her lips.

If she were to be honest, she would have to admit that all the people who'd been telling her she was too pale were right.

But that wasn't a problem tonight.

A flush left from the warm bath, highlighted by sexual expectation, had added a soft rose hue to her cheeks.

She thought about curling her hair, then remembered

she didn't own any hot rollers. Which was just as well, because she feared if she tried, she could end up with big hair like Misty.

Which is definitely not *the look you're going for.*

Unfortunately, the scant wardrobe she'd brought home from Italy didn't offer many choices. The black suit would be perfect if she were on her way to either a board meeting or yet another funeral.

Jeans were too casual. Besides, the ones she'd bought after the bombing had skinny legs, which meant they could be a bitch to get out of without her looking like a not-so-graceful snake shedding its skin.

A friend—the concierge of the Paradiso Angeli, who'd shared an apartment across town with one of the desk clerks—had dug into her own closet and donated a long, flowing dress in deep shades of burgundy and red, with an off-the-shoulder top that brought to mind gypsies dancing around campfires.

The look worked perfectly on the dark-eyed, ebony-haired Italian woman, but Sabrina feared she would never be able to pull it off without feeling as if she were on her way to a costume party.

And then she saw it. A slip of a dress that Eve Bouvier had talked her into trying on in a small designer boutique on the Via Vigna Nuova. The short baby-doll dress had spaghetti straps that bared her shoulders, and the kaleidoscope of bright Pucci print colors somehow managed to make her look—and, more importantly, feel—sexy and carefree. Almost frivolous.

Exactly like the type of woman who would impulsively seduce a man.

Because the dress called for them, she slipped on a pair of skyscraper-high sling-back turquoise sandals that the clerk—who turned out to be from across the Alps in Grenoble and was dripping with French sangfroid—had insisted she must buy to go with the dress.

Sabrina took a quick spin in front of the mirror.

Licked her lips, which she'd tinted a pink shade lighter
than Misty's bubblegum, and skimmed a palm over her
hips.

"Zach Tremayne, eat your heart out."

Satisfied with her transformation, Sabrina ran down
the stairs and out of Swannsea before she could change
her mind.

The man watched her race out of the house, down the
steps, and across the drive. Her skimpy dress and fuck-
me shoes—how did women manage to walk in those
damn things, let alone run?—announced her intentions
as clearly as if she had a flashing neon sign over her
head.

He watched the car back out of the carriage house,
then tear down the drive through the arched canopy of
oaks.

He'd pulled his black gimme cap low over his face to
shield it from reflecting moonlight; he would have preferred face camouflage, but that would have been hard
to explain if someone saw him driving through town or,
worse yet, if he got stopped by a cop for some reason.
Especially with everyone so jumpy, looking out for a
serial killer.

As he made his way to the car he'd backed into a
stand of tupelos alongside the highway, he was willing
to bet the farm that she was on her way to Tremayne's.
Which, being even more isolated than this place, could
provide a perfect opportunity to get them alone
together.

The idea of making the former SEAL watch his lover
die a slow, painful death was appealing. It also would
be, the man decided, his grim smile flashing momentarily, the perfect last vision for Zach Tremayne to take
with him to hell.

38

Sabrina stopped at the market and picked up a bottle of champagne, deftly dodging Sissy's attempts to learn what, exactly, she might be celebrating. No way was she going to allow the woman who considered herself Swann Island's very own Paul Revere to spread the word that Miss Lucie's granddaughter was off to Zach's house. At night. With alcohol.

Headlights shone in her rearview mirror as she headed toward the beach, momentarily blinding her. She reached up and tilted it slightly to cut the glare.

Thanks to the wonders of modern technology, tracking Zach down proved a breeze.

She'd taken out her BlackBerry while driving to the village, and, since he'd gotten a South Carolina driver's license when he moved back to the island, Google had kicked up the address of his house in five-point-three seconds.

With that information in hand, the GPS in her rental car obligingly provided not only a map but voice directions as well.

The house, set on one of the few isolated stretches of beach left on the island, was an old planter's style, made of cypress planks and set on piers to allow for the ebb and flow of the water beneath it.

She could hear the radio through the open windows—Toby Keith was claiming that while he might not be

as good as he once was, he was as good *once* as he
ever was.

Champagne in hand, Sabrina climbed the steps and,
since there didn't seem to be a doorbell, knocked on the
door, trying to look more casual than she felt, in case
he checked her out through the peephole.

Inside the house, the radio went silent.

A moment later, she could hear the three heavy locks
being unfastened.

Then the door opened and there he was, backlit by
the living-room light, looking beyond scrumptious in a
snug gray T-shirt and another pair of jeans as raggedy
as the ones he'd worn while fixing Swannsea's roof.

His feet were bare. And, heaven help her, as sexy as
the rest of him.

If he was at all surprised to see her standing on his
porch, he didn't show it. Merely glanced at the heavy
green bottle in her hand and asked, "Are we celebrating something?"

"I hope so." Her breathless voice was as unfamiliar
as the wild and reckless feelings hammering away at her.

They stood that way, Zach looking down at her, Sabrina looking up at him, for what seemed forever.

Finally, he moved aside. "Why don't you come on
in, then?"

"Okay."

Wasn't that brilliantly sexy repartee?

The front room turned out to be a living room/kitchen
combination. The only furniture was an oversized guy
couch, a TV, and a table that looked as if it had been
rescued from a Salvation Army Dumpster.

"Nice place," she lied. In truth, it was depressing.

"It belongs to my dad. He bought the property and
house as a rental retirement investment a long time ago
before prices skyrocketed."

"Well, that was certainly thinking ahead."

So, where's the bedroom?

No! That was way too Misty Man-eater.

Besides, Sabrina reminded herself, she hadn't come here to have sex with Zach. While she honestly wanted to celebrate her life-altering decision, she also intended to make him regret not having followed up on that hot kiss this morning.

So what she needed was a clever, sexy line that would have him thinking of her not as some perfect paragon of purity, or a too-easily-spooked terrorist victim, but a hot chick who could rock his big bad SEAL world.

"Linc's back," she said. That was *so* not it.

"That's good." His eyes were dark and focused on hers in a way that suggested he wasn't any more interested in this conversation than she was.

"He voted thumbs-up."

"More good news. So, the reason you've come bearing French bubbly is to launch the new project?"

"It seemed like a good idea."

"It's a great idea." He took the bottle from her hand, went around the counter, and with his eyes still on hers, tore off the foil covering the cork. "Construction projects are always a challenge."

"I realize that."

"I figured you would. Given what Lucie said about all the work you were overseeing at that hotel in Florence." He took two water glasses down from the open shelf. "Sorry. I don't have any flutes."

"Those are fine." Sabrina chastised herself for not having thought of that. Of course, as it was turning out, she hadn't really thought through this make-the-man-grovel plan, either.

See what happens when you don't plan ahead?

"There's also the fact that this project comes with an additional built-in challenge."

Holding the bottle in one hand, he began slowly turning the cork with the other. Watching him, imagining those dark hands creating havoc on every inch of her naked body, was enough to make the muscles in Sabrina's belly quiver.

"Oh?"

"I've never had any problem separating lust from work before," he said conversationally. The cork eased out with a tiny whispered hiss and a trail of white vapor. "Of course, in the interest of full disclosure, lust was never an issue working with a SEAL team. And there aren't that many women working construction, even these days. At least none whose bones I've wanted to jump."

"You had your chance," she reminded him. Great. Now she sounded petulant.

"You know what they say about timing." Golden bubbles rose as he poured the champagne into the glasses. "It wasn't right this morning."

"And it is now?"

"Probably not. But I spent the day thinking."

"About me?" Could this get any worse? Now she sounded like a needy high school freshman hoping the quarterback would ask her to the prom.

"About you. And me. And us together."

"And?"

"And I decided that although you and I've got a history between us, we don't really know one another."

Sabrina jerked a bare shoulder. "And I'm supposed to believe you've never slept with a woman you didn't know?"

"No. I've been known to tumble into some strange beds on occasion. But again, we're back to that situation of having to work together."

"So." Tamping down her pique, asking herself why she'd bothered wasting her time coming here tonight, she snatched up one of the glasses of champagne and took a long sip, narrowing her eyes as she met his gaze over the heavy glass rim. "What you're saying is you want me. But you're going to regretfully resist temptation."

"No." The dark heat in his eyes gilded with a glint of laughter as he took the glass from her hand and deliberately replaced it on the counter. "What I'm saying is that the solution, as I see it, is to get to know one another really, really quickly."

He closed the small gap between them. Skimmed a finger over her shoulder, leaving a trail of heat. "Beginning now."

His light caress moved down her arm until he'd linked their hands together and brought them to his lips. "So, New York, if you're still in the mood for seduction—and given the way you're dressed, I have to sorta suspect you are—I sure as hell won't stop you."

"I wanted to make you crawl." She trembled—both her voice and her body—as he brushed his firmly cut mouth across her knuckles.

"I can do that."

She laughed a little at his easy, obliging tone. Then went up on her toes, brushed a light kiss against his lips and was rewarded when he slanted his head and deepened it, not enough to wrest away control but to let her know he was fully engaged with the program.

Encouraged, she slipped her fingers beneath his T-shirt and ran her hands around to his back, pressing into his flesh, delighting in the steely strength of muscle.

"I love your body." She trailed her hands down his sides, around to his chest.

"It's all yours." The male need in his ragged tone was echoed in the galloping beat of his heart beneath her fingertips.

She'd had only a sip of champagne, but she was already intoxicated with the exquisite power she found herself able to wield over this man she suspected was not accustomed to surrendering control.

"But you're wearing too many clothes." She caught hold of the bottom of the T-shirt and pulled it up over his chest.

He helped her pull the shirt over his head, but when he reached out to skim a finger along the top edge of her dress, she stepped away.

"Not yet."

She could tell it wasn't his first choice, but he nevertheless dropped his hands to his sides.

She splayed her hands over his bared chest. When she pressed an openmouthed kiss against that dark flesh, he sucked in a sharp breath.

Even as she was aching for him to take her, here and now, Sabrina forced herself to keep the pace slow.

She skimmed her lips up his chest, over his broad shoulders, then lingered at his throat, where she imagined she could taste the heat of his pulse, before moving up to his mouth again. Her tongue tangled with his, playing a little game of thrust and parry.

"Sabrina." He moaned her name, part oath, part prayer. "For God's sake, let's at least move this to the bedroom, so I don't end up taking you on the table."

She laughed at that idea, which didn't sound so bad. "In case you've forgotten, *I'm* the one taking *you*."

She touched a fingertip to her tongue and trailed it down his burning-hot chest, amazed it didn't sizzle. "But I'm willing to change venues. For now, anyway."

She linked her fingers with his. "So lead the way."

39

The bedroom, like what little of the house she'd seen, revealed nothing of the man who lived here. The walls, painted in a standard rental house beige-white, showed rectangles where paintings had once hung. The carpet, an industrial-grade beige Berber, had undoubtedly been chosen more for utilitarian purposes than looks, and when he flicked the wall switch, the ceiling light was bright enough to make her blink.

"I don't suppose you have any candles?" she asked, her confidence flagging a bit.

The scene shimmering in her mind, when she'd imagined making love with this man, had been misty-edged, lit by the flattering soft glow of candles, everything occurring in exquisite slow motion. There'd be music playing. Something bluesy, but underscored with a sexy percussive beat.

She had to laugh at herself, just a little, as she realized her fantasy had, in fact, been a soft porn video.

But still . . .

"There are some in the mudroom, for power failures," he said. "But please tell me you're not going to make me go look for them now."

"No." She could do this, Sabrina assured herself, even as she fought to keep the mood from slipping away.

"How about a compromise?"

He went over to the window and pulled up the shade, allowing the moonlight to stream in.

Then, thank you, God, he turned off the damn light.
"Better?"

"Much. Thanks." She managed a faint smile. "You
probably think I'm foolish, worrying about such a silly
thing, but I've never done this before—"

"Never had sex?"

"Never seduced anyone."

"Well, so far, for a novice you're showing incredible
instincts." He ducked his head and brushed his lips
against hers. "Must be you're a natural."

"Maybe I am."

It wasn't her, Sabrina knew, as much as him. Because
she'd certainly never been inclined to seduce anyone
else.

"As for thinking you're foolish—" He skimmed the
back of his hand down her face. Kissed her again, a
nibbling little peck that made her want more. Much,
much more. "As it happens, I think you're perfect."

The way he was looking at her had her believing him.

"As it happens," she echoed him on a deep, throaty
laugh, recklessly taking hold of the waistband of his
jeans and tugging him closer, "I think the same thing
about you."

She rubbed her silk-covered breasts against his bare
chest.

"I've been dreaming of this," she admitted.

"Well, that makes two of us."

"So you say now." With a daring that would shock
her later when she looked back on it, she moved her
hand around to his butt and squeezed. "I seem to recall
you mentioning something last night about me repre-
senting virgin innocence."

"You did." When he took her lips with his again, Sabrina sighed and felt herself yielding to him. "That was
before I came home and discovered how well you'd
grown up."

He fisted a hand in her hair and tugged her head back

enough to look down at her. "I know you're the one
running the show here, but am I allowed to say that
that's a great dress?"

"I'm glad you like it."

"I love it. It's probably the most fantastic dress I've
ever seen."

He skimmed a roughened fingertip along the crest of
her breasts, then, with a casual flick of the wrist, sent
first one thin strap and then the other sliding off her
bare shoulders. "But the thing is, darlin', right now I'd
like it even better if you'd take it off."

His eyes were dark and hungry. Looking at him looking at her, for the first time in her life, Sabrina knew
what it meant to crave.

"Since you asked so nicely."

She reached around her back and lowered the zipper
with one hand, holding the dress against her chest with
the other.

Then let it drop to the pine plank floor.

Zach blew out a long, slow breath as he took in the
sight of her, clad in a strapless bit of white satin and
lace she'd bought at the same shop where Eve and the
saleswoman had pressured her into the dress and shoes.

He lifted his eyes to the ceiling. "Thank you, God."

She laughed, feeling her anxiety dissolve. If she'd
thought about it beforehand, she would have imagined
she'd feel incredibly nervous standing in front of him in
a skimpy bit of lingerie and high heels. But instead, she
felt amazingly, uncharacteristically sexy.

A little like those sirens that ancient sailors used to
insist dwelt on the coral reefs off the coast.

Or like Eve, tempting Adam with that shiny red apple.

"It'd probably be more appropriate to thank all the
poor nuns who undoubtedly went blind making the
lace," she said.

His grin was quick, but his eyes hot. "Ah, but don't
forget who they work for."

Before she could discern his intention, he pulled her down onto the king-sized bed. Which moved like breakers beneath them.

"A water bed?" Sabrina was so surprised she forgot to complain about him seizing control.

"I know. It's ridiculously seventies." He rolled over on top of her. "I can't even claim it's retro, because it came with the place."

His lips glided over her flesh. "I hope you're not prone to seasickness."

"Not that I know of," she managed as he tugged the strapless lace down. "But in case you've forgotten, I'm supposed to be seducing you."

"Congratulations." His tongue dampened first one breast, then the other. "You've succeeded. I've been totally seduced since I first saw you sitting in the middle of that fairy-tale bed, looking like a sexy princess waiting for Prince Charming to show up.

"Not that anyone would ever describe me as Prince Charming." Her back arched as his mouth closed around a nipple and tugged. "But you get my drift."

As if he weren't already creating havoc in both her mind and her body, his calloused hand, feeling like the finest-grade sandpaper, stroked the back of her knee. "Christ, your skin is soft," he murmured as his mouth went to work on the other nipple.

His caressing touch moved higher. Up the back of her leg. "Like gardenia petals warmed in the sun."

He was saying something else, but as that wickedly clever hand slipped around her leg and began moving up the ultrasensitive skin of her inner thigh, there was such a roaring in Sabrina's head—like the sea during a violent storm—that she couldn't hear it.

Which was why, when Zach suddenly climbed off the bed, creating more sloshing of waves, Sabrina's first thought was that as impossible as it seemed, he was going to stop.

But then she realized he wanted to take off his jeans,

and, as delicious as that rough denim felt rubbing up against her body, she wanted them gone, too.

He pulled the jeans and knit boxer briefs down together, kicked them aside, and reached into the drawer of the bedside table to grab a handful of condoms, which he scattered across the scarred tabletop.

"You were expecting this," she said.

"I was hopeful." The glint in his eyes spoke volumes.

"Also optimistic," she murmured.

"It's a long night." If he was at all uncomfortable, standing there fully aroused, he showed no sign of it. But why should he be? Sabrina asked herself as he casually ripped open one of the red foil packets.

Zachariah Tremayne was a superb example of a perfect male form. In fact, if he'd been around in Renaissance days, all the tourists who flocked to Florence to gape at Michelangelo's famous *David* sculpture, would have been looking at Zachariah Tremayne instead of some anonymous model.

"Wait." Okay, so it was more croak than sexy Southern drawl. But the hand she held out toward him was remarkably steady, considering that rockets were going off inside her. "Let me."

He might have been more experienced than she. He might have known more positions, been more comfortable with his body. But there was no way he could hide his body's response to her soft request.

"There's not a man on God's green earth who would turn that offer down." The humor faded from his eyes, replaced by what appeared to be pure, unadulterated lust.

When she took his rampant sex in her hands and slipped her mouth over him, the dark shadows of dread that had been hovering over her in the weeks since the bombing disintegrated.

There was only now.

Only Zach.

"I know you're supposed to be calling the shots here,

sugar," he said, tangling his hands in her hair to pull her away, even as his hips thrust forward. "But if you keep that up, we're going to have an early blastoff."

"We wouldn't want that." Though the idea of making him lose control was certainly a heady one.

He broke the erotic contact and collapsed on the bed beside her, his mouth claiming hers with a jolting shock of possessiveness that she felt in every atom of her body.

He stripped away the pretty white lace and satin. The pace quickened. Hands that had been content to loiter now moved more urgently. Tender kisses grew eager. Hungry.

As nervous as her mind had been, Sabrina's body had been ready for this since she'd first pulled his shirt off.

No. Before that. Since she'd thrown open that heavy front door at Swannsea and seen him standing there in the bright morning glare of summer sun looking like some gilded god.

Which was why, the instant he cupped her, hard, she shattered, pouring into his hand.

"More," he demanded, plunging his fingers deep inside her.

How had it happened? How had she totally lost control of this situation?

And why should she care? When the assault on her senses was so wild and deliciously decadent?

She pistoned her hips, urging him on, shuddering, sobbing, as he brought her to another, higher, harsher peak.

"More," he said again.

"I can't."

"You can." He slid down her body and clamped his mouth between her legs.

As he took her, with teeth and tongue and lips, Sabrina's body, which she would have sworn he'd exhausted, leaped back to life.

She writhed.

Strained.

Dragged her hands through those silky dark waves,

splaying her fingers against the back of his head as she arched against his mouth.

This sharp, hard climax sent shock waves outward from that hot, slick core.

But he wasn't finished yet.

Bracing over her, muscles quivering, Zach desperately struggled to hold on to what scant control he had left.

She was so strong, so unrelentingly goal-oriented, it was easy to overlook how delicate she was. How soft. How sweet.

Her long lashes rested on cheeks stained with heat. Her lips were parted, the faint breath escaping them as shallow as his own.

"Sabrina." She stirred when he touched his lips to hers. "Look at me."

Her eyes, when she opened them, were soft and dazed. "I'm sorry. You haven't . . . I wasn't sleeping, really, I was just . . ." Her lips curved in a dreamy, satiated smile. "Sort of floating." She lifted her lips to his. "Back to earth . . . But as fabulous as that rocket-ship ride was, I want you, Zachariah Tremayne."

She wrapped one long, smooth leg around his hip. "All of you."

Her warm and inviting smile sent emotions rushing into Zach's throat. And his heart. Myriad, indefinable emotions that expanded to fill all those dark and empty places inside him.

Filling him as no other woman ever had.

As no other woman ever could.

The thought staggered him.

"I want you, too." He kissed her again. And for the first time since he'd landed back on American soil, Zach felt as if he'd come home.

Which was why he said the words he'd never said to any woman in his life.

"And I need you."

Her mossy green eyes darkened to emerald and shone with what, goddammit, he feared were tears.

*Smooth move, Tremayne. Why make a woman scream
with passion when you can make her cry?*

Her hands, which had been twisting the sheets by her
side into hot tangled knots, rose to link around his neck.

Smiling through what were, indeed, tears, she said,
"Then take me."

Zach needed no second invitation.

Beyond words, rather than plunge as his body had
been shouting at him to do, he slipped into her, filling
her, even as he filled himself.

Completing them both.

When he began to move, she matched his long,
smooth strokes perfectly, deeper, and faster, arms, legs,
and hearts entwined as she flew with him into the mists.

And this time, when she returned to earth, Zach was
with her.

40

Titania was going to flat-out kill him. But not immediately, Nate decided. No, being of the female persuasion, and having come from a long line of Geechee stock, she'd probably be into the vengeance thing.

Maybe she'd have one of those old aunties of hers who lived out in the marsh put a spell on him. One that would, as she'd once threatened during a particularly expressive tantrum, cause his dick to turn dry as dust and blow away out across the Atlantic, where minuscule particles would fall into the ocean and be gobbled up by fish.

Or—another suggestion at the time—she would have her kitchen helper, Njanu, whose name was supposedly Kenyan for "bull" (which fit, since he was about six-foot-eight and had to weigh over three hundred pounds, all of it muscle) cut off that very same dick with a rusty carving knife and feed it to the gators out in the swamp.

The only reason Nate had taken that idea seriously was that anyone with eyes in his head could tell that Njanu had a major crush on his employer and would probably have not a single qualm about getting rid of any guy who made her unhappy. Especially one that he undoubtedly considered competition.

Even knowing it had only been Titania's temper talking, that she would never follow through on the threats, both prospects nevertheless had sent Nate's gonads up to his tonsils.

Hopefully, she'd do what she always did when he was called out at night. Punish him with the silent treatment for a day or two. Before she let him take her in a wild, no-holds-barred round of makeup sex.

Even so, he knew he was pushing his luck, leaving her in bed three nights in a row.

"Great way to convince her to marry you," he ground out as he drove through the rain that had blown in from the sea.

And hell, this wasn't even for a murder, like the call the other night. Or a break-in, like at Swannsea. It was for a damn domestic dispute, which was, hands down, his least favorite part of the job.

Ida Mae and Angus Thornton had been married for sixty-odd years, "odd" being the definitive word. And every few months during each of those years, according to the mountain of manila folders filled with complaints, one or both of them would get tanked and start destroying stuff.

This time Ida Mae, who was loudly accusing Angus of making eyes at that chippie pharmacist who'd rung up his Viagra at the Palmetto Pharmacy, had doused the model pirate ships her husband had made over the past two decades with kerosene and started a bonfire in the front yard.

A neighbor, concerned when the flames looked as if they might spread to his roof, had called in the disturbance.

Unfortunately, of Nate's three deputies, one was in bed with chicken pox contracted from his six-year-old daughter, another was in Spartanburg attending a family reunion, and the third was handling a drunk-and-disorderly down at The Stewed Clam.

Which, Nate had tried to explain to a very pissed-off Titania, left him to play Dr. Phil.

He was on his way home with a Hershey bar he'd picked up at Oscar's Gas and Go, hoping the chocolate might help ease his way back into both his woman's good graces and her bed, when he passed a car parked on the side of the road near the turnoff to Zach Tremayne's rental house.

At first he figured it'd been abandoned.

"Most likely broke down." The driver had probably decided to walk home and call for a tow in the morning.

Then, remembering those two SCAD students who'd stumbled across Hallie Conroy's body, Nate decided he'd better stop and check to make sure there was nothing going on in the backseat.

Not that he was the sex police—far from it, being able to remember his own hormone-driven days—but kids making out in the middle of nowhere while a crazed serial killer was on the loose were a horror flick waiting to happen.

He made a U-turn. Pulled up behind the car and turned on his flashers.

As he walked toward the driver's door, Nate unsnapped his holster flap.

Because you just never knew.

Sabrina had realized, as she drove to Zach's house, that her behavior was reckless. That it would change things. But she'd managed to convince herself that getting the sexual tension out of the way would make it easier for them to work together.

After all, they were both adults, both unattached without any committed relationships hovering on the horizon. It was, after all, the logical thing to do.

She'd spent a lot of time wondering what it would be like to make love with Zachariah Tremayne.

Well, after more than a decade, she'd found out.

It had been even hotter and more thrilling than she'd imagined.

It had left her feeling a little bruised. A little battered.

And absolutely blissful.

Which was the part that terrified her.

Because, for that suspended moment after Zach had

told her he needed her, Sabrina had felt cherished. Like one of those pieces of Swarovski crystal her mother had collected. And, unfortunately, about as fragile.

She hadn't wanted him to care about her. She'd only wanted him to, as he'd so less than eloquently put it, fuck her blind.

She'd come here seeking sex. Not a relationship. And definitely not love.

Love?

Who was talking about love?

So, he'd used that really scary *n* word. But "need" encompassed a vast range of things. People needed air to breathe, food to eat, and yes, at that moment they'd both needed an intimate physical connection with another human being.

That's all it was.

All Sabrina would allow it to be.

Besides, sex for sex's sake wasn't all that bad. In fact, with the right man, at the right time, it could be fabulous.

She laughed at that idea.

"Something funny?" He rolled over, pulling her with him so she was sprawled across his chest.

"I was thinking how good I feel," she hedged, feeling a little foolish for not having realized she'd laughed out loud, but she felt she covered well.

"Again, you're not going to get any argument from me." He ran one of those rough broad hands that had created such havoc over every inch of her body down her back, from her shoulders to her butt. "But 'good' is a vast understatement. I'd say you feel abso-fucking-lutely terrific."

She laughed again, feeling wonderfully, foolishly like the schoolgirl she'd once been.

"I should go."

"Well, now, sugar, you're going to have to rethink that decision." He cupped her breast, his thumb rubbing against her nipple, his mouth nuzzling her neck. "Because we're just getting started."

"We can't." She came close to purring as his mouth roamed down her throat. "I can't . . . Oh, God."

That wonderful wicked mouth began creating a trail of sparks, over her breasts, down her torso, her stomach, continuing south.

Outside, a light rain was tapping on the green tin roof. Inside, things were beginning to heat up again.

"Surely you can't . . . I mean, this soon . . ."

"Wanna bet?"

He shifted positions again, overpowering her, trapping her body beneath his.

"You're the one who started this, New York. So you're going to have to stick around until I'm finished with you."

When his hand pressed against her, a sexual charge, just this side of pain, shot through her body like a lightning bolt.

"And when do you think that might be?"

Her skin, which had cooled in the misty afterglow of lovemaking, was hot again, the blood running beneath it feeling as if it had begun to boil.

"I've no idea." As wet as she was hot, she flowed over his hand. "But I do know I'm nowhere near done yet."

"Good," she gasped as his fingers dove into the heat of her.

It was all either of them said for a very long time.

41

Damn! Just what he needed, fucking Barney Fife showing up just as he'd been about to make his move.

The man tossed the Beretta 9 mm into a pile of dead leaves and, forcing down his frustration, strolled casually back toward the car. Leaving it parked on the side of the road had been careless, but he'd been afraid if he drove it into the bushes, he would end up sinking into this godforsaken, mosquito-infested swamp.

"Good evening, Officer," he said with what he thought was a believable blend of innocence and confusion. "Is there a problem?"

"That's what I was about to ask you." The Maglite focused on his face. "I noticed your car and thought you might need a tow."

"No." A cooling wave of relief washed over him. "Although it's embarrassing as hell, and I probably broke some island decency law, I just stopped to take a piss." He smiled, one guy to another. "I never should've had that second beer down at The Stewed Clam."

The damn sheriff did not return his smile but merely said, "May I see your driver's license and registration, please?"

"Sure." He started to reach into his back pocket, then paused. "I'm taking my wallet out."

"Fine. Just do it nice and slow, okay?"

"Absolutely." He pulled out the nylon billfold, flipped it open to the window ID, and held it up.

The flashlight shifted. Dark eyes studied the photo, then looked back up at his face.

"And your registration?"

"That's in the car."

As he moved to open the driver's door, he calculated the chances of grabbing that Glock the cop was wearing on his belt and ending this right now.

Problem was, it was so goddamn quiet they'd probably be able to hear the shot all the way to town.

Which would blow any element of surprise.

But if he did let this hick sheriff live, tonight's plan for Tremayne was down the crapper.

The bottom line, he decided, was that he hadn't come all this way to turn into a cop killer. He'd come to seek vengeance.

Which he still had every intention of doing.

But, it appeared, not tonight.

Do you feel lucky, Sheriff? he thought on a riff of the old Dirty Harry line.

He took the registration out of the glove compartment and handed it over.

The sheriff took another long look.

"You're a long way from California."

"Got a divorce." That much was the truth. His entire life had pretty much gone to shit after Mission Enduring Goatfuck in Afghanistan. "Decided it was time for a change of venue." Another true statement. Oo-rah, he was on a role.

The dark head nodded, taking that in as the sheriff's gaze skimmed over him, pausing for a heartbeat on the full-color Marine Corps seal tattooed on his forearm.

Sweat began to pool beneath his arms. His crotch. The palms of his hands and the back of his neck. And not just because the air was thick enough to fucking drink.

Just when he was thinking he might have to neutralize the guy after all, the sheriff returned the piece of paper.

"Be careful driving home," he advised. "There aren't a lot of streetlights on the island, because we're pretty

big on sea turtle protection around here, so it's real easy
to run off these rural roads. Especially if you've been
drinking."

"Two beers," Sergeant Richard Cunningham, USMC,
swore, holding up two fingers in confirmation. "Over a
two-hour period while I watched the Braves game on TV."

"Well, like I said, drive safe. And Semper Fi."

The sheriff gave a little two-fingered salute, then
turned and walked back to the patrol car.

Releasing a long, relieved breath, Gunney unzipped
his pants and sent a long stream of urine he'd nearly
pissed in his pants against the tire.

Then, cursing his bad timing, he reluctantly followed
the sheriff back into town.

"I have to go," Sabrina murmured.

"Hmmph."

Zach had dozed off and was indulging in the hottest
imaginable dream, involving the woman currently cud-
dled next to him, a tropical lagoon, some ripe passion
fruit, and a grass hula skirt.

He drew her closer, spooning, his erection pressed
against the cleft of that sweet butt.

"Zach." She wiggled a bit, which only proved more
of a turn-on. "I have to go."

"Okay." He rolled over onto his back, releasing her.
"I'll keep the bed warm."

"No." She pulled the sheet off him. "I meant leave."

"Leave?" He reluctantly hitched himself up in bed
and shot a glance at the window. "It's the middle of
the night."

"It's almost morning."

"Almost." He ran a hand over her shoulder, cupped
her pert breast, which was a perfect fit for his palm.
"The sun won't be up for another two hours." He
looked past her to the clock radio on the bedside table.
"At least."

"That's my point." She slapped his hand away. "You

know how everyone on the island talks. No way am I going to let them see me driving back to Swannsea in broad daylight after spending the night at your house."

"Who's going to know where you're going or coming from?" Undeterred, he trailed a finger up her leg. "Maybe you went out for coffee." Through the soft curls between her thighs, which proved her a true blonde. "A bagel."

"In that dress?" She waved a hand toward the bit of bright silk that still lay where she'd dropped it on the floor hours earlier.

"Could be worse. I could've given in to the temptation to rip it off and you'd have to drive home naked." He leaned forward and took a little nip of her shoulder. "Stay fifteen more minutes."

"Zach . . ."

"Ten."

"Dammit," she complained. But he could hear the rising desire in her soft voice, felt it in the way her body had begun to move beneath his stroking touch.

"Okay, make it eight."

Considering he still had a hard-on from that sex dream, Zach figured he could go from zero to sixty in about thirty seconds, but as far as he knew he'd never left a woman unsatisfied and he wasn't about to begin with this one.

"You're incorrigible." Even as her lush lips said no, her hips were lifting toward his touch.

"I know," he soothed.

As he took her mouth in a long, deep kiss, he reached for another condom, a little surprised at how many they'd gone through. If they could only bottle what Sabrina Swann had done to his libido, they'd both be gazillionaires several times over.

She sighed, broke off the kiss, and took the packet from his hand.

"Lucky for you that I've always had a thing for bad boys."

Her touch, as she smoothed the rubber over him, nearly had him exploding. Make that two seconds.

He pulled her on top of him, filling her as her body clutched at him.

"Lucky for both of us," he managed as she began to ride him, the same glorious way she had in that dream the other night.

Zach had no idea where this unexpected thing between them would lead. But the one thing he did know was that for now, as he looked up at her silvered in the moonlight, straddling him, back arched, eyes closed, hair streaming down her back like a shimmering pale waterfall, he was, hands down, the luckiest man on the planet.

42

"Well." Sabrina stretched like a sleek Siamese who'd just finished lapping up a particularly sweet bowlful of cream. "As much as I'd love to never move again, I really do need to leave."

Keeping her in his bed forever didn't seem like such a bad idea. But even as Zach reluctantly decided that tying her to the bed might be overkill and wouldn't exactly inspire trust, he also understood that despite having traveled and worked all over the world, Sabrina remembered how small towns worked. And was, surprisingly, turning out to be enough of a small-town Southern girl not to want to give people any more to talk about.

"I'll follow you home."

"You needn't do that."

He slipped his hand beneath her hair, cupped her neck, and brushed his lips against hers. "Even if there wasn't some crazy guy out there, like I told you, my Southern gentleman act is situational. And seeing a lady home after she's spent most of the night heating up my sheets is definitely one of those situations."

"Got a lot of ladies dropping by to heat up your sheets, do you?" she murmured as her lips clung.

Before he could answer, she jerked away. "I'm sorry." She held up a hand as color waved in her cheeks and across her breasts. "Forget I asked that. It slipped out." Her smile was weak and embarrassed. "It's your fault for clouding my mind so I can't think straight."

"Stay a little longer and we'll see if we can cloud it some more," he suggested as he nuzzled that sweet curve of her neck where it met her shoulder.

A delighted laugh burst out of her. "You've no idea how tempted I am to do exactly that," she said as she left the tangled sheets. "But I really have a lot to do today."

"Such as?"

He crossed his arms behind his head, enjoying the sight of her gathering up her scattered clothes.

"I need to arrange for some construction financing at the bank. Then, since I'm going to be staying, I'll have to pick up more groceries. And take the ferry over to Somersett to buy some clothes."

He sighed with a bit of regret as she pulled that pretty white lacy thing back up her legs and tucked her breasts away. "That dress you wore last night was real fine. And that flowery halter thing you were wearing earlier?"

He shook his hand and waggled his brows. "Hot."

Speaking of hot, he was surprised they hadn't started the water to boiling in the bed.

"I'm so pleased you approve."

Sweet Jesus. He swallowed back a groan when she bent over to retrieve the dress, giving him a dandy view of her fine ass.

Granted, she could still use a bit more meat on her bones. But what she had was definitely prime.

"Neither is exactly business attire, though." She pulled the brightly colored silk over her head, arranged the skinny little straps, then glanced over at him. "You're still in bed."

"Damn, Gus Melton's right. You are one smart cookie, New York." He grinned. "I'm planning to get up as soon as you're ready. Meanwhile, I was just taking some time to enjoy the view. And thinking how much fun it's going to be next time I take your clothes off you again."

She snorted at that. Then tossed her head in a way

that had him remembering how that silky blond hair had felt draped over his thighs as she'd taken him deep into her sweet, succulent mouth.

"If you're going to insist on following me, let's go." She bent down and pulled the sheet off him, revealing the hard-on that was sticking up like a tent pole.

"That's amazing."

"Well, now, thank you kindly for the compliment."

"I wasn't talking about your, uh, *penis*." And wasn't she as cute as a speckled pup when she blushed at saying the *p* word out loud? "After all, if you've seen one, you've pretty much seen them all."

She shrugged with a casualness he didn't buy for a minute. "What I was referring to," she said in a cool tone that she might use to chastise a hotel desk clerk for poor service, "was how you could have any stamina left."

"The day I don't respond to a sexy, naked woman is the day I climb to the top of the Admiral Somersett Bridge and throw myself into the river."

He flashed his best bad-boy grin. The one that had always worked wonders in bars from San Diego to Singapore and too many ports in between to count.

"I don't suppose you'd like to come back to bed and help me out." He patted the mattress. "Seeing as how you're responsible for my little problem in the first place."

"Why don't you simply try a little mind over matter?"

Zach couldn't remember the last time he'd enjoyed himself as much as he had the last eight hours. "Well, now, see, here's the thing, sugar."

He'd never thought of himself as a stereotypical good old Southern boy, but he wasn't beyond playing that card in the right circumstances.

"It's my *mind* that's the matter. Because it keeps painting these hot pictures of you. Like when you dropped that dress and were standing there in nothing but those high-heeled shoes and that skimpy bit of lacy underwear. Or when you climbed on top and were riding me—"

"I get the point." She cut him off with a quick slice of that silky smooth hand that had certainly not been the least bit shy as it managed to find all his hot spots. Some even he hadn't known he had.

She bent again, picked up his jeans, and tossed them at him. "If you want to come, get dressed."

He snatched them out the air.

Gone was the sexy siren who'd nearly set his water bed on fire. In her place was the high-powered executive who'd shot like a comet through the management ranks of one of the most famous hotel chains in the world.

He sighed mightily as he yanked the jeans on, thinking of grabbing a quick nap when he got home again from Swannsea.

Unless, of course, she invited him to stay. In which case, sleep was overrated.

43

Sabrina wasn't really afraid. After all, what were the chances of some crazed killer choosing her for his next target? Even if he was still on the island, which was unlikely. You'd think that, having called attention to himself, he'd want to move on to a larger city, where he wouldn't stand out.

Somewhere like Somersett. Charleston. Or even Savannah. Once the media latched on to the Swann Island Slasher story, everyone would be watching every move every stranger made.

Still, she couldn't deny that there was something comforting about having Zach follow her back to Swannsea.

The sun was hovering below the eastern horizon when they got to the house, casting a soft lavender pink glow over the still-dark sky. A few valiant stars winked overhead, but the sound of birdsong from the marsh announced the approaching dawn.

She pulled up in front of the carriage house, but before she could get out of the car, Zach was already lifting the heavy wooden door.

She knew better than to object when he insisted on walking her to the front door. Which she was glad she'd remembered to lock, because she was in too mellow a mood for another safety lecture.

"I had a lovely time," she was appalled to hear herself saying, as if she'd spent the hours attending a ladies' tea. "Thank you."

Could it get any worse?

His lips quirked. "I think I'm supposed to be thanking you. Since you managed to cover just about every item on my top ten things I want to do with Sabrina Swann list."

"You have a list?"

"In here." He tapped his temple.

"You said 'just about.' "

"Well, there are a couple more items I'm hoping we can discuss down the road," he said, answering her unspoken question.

"Such as?"

"I don't imagine you could pick up one of those French maid outfits while you're shopping over in Somersett?"

"I'm disappointed," she said, even as her blood spiked at the idea. "I would've thought a man of your vast experience had moved beyond such an ordinarily prurient fantasy."

"What can I say?" He pulled her into his arms and touched his smiling lips to hers, which curved in response. "Men are slugs."

"True." She lifted a hand, played with the dark waves she could still feel skimming over her breasts. "But I suppose you do have your uses."

"Feel free to use me anytime your little ol' heart desires."

She could feel herself melting, like a beeswax candle left too long in the hot Carolina sun. "How would you like to come to dinner?"

"Dinner?" He pulled his head back. "Like real food that doesn't come in a box or a take-out bag?"

"That's pretty much what I had in mind. I'm not exactly Julia Child, and I can't touch Titania's talent, but I've spent enough time in hotel kitchens to know how to grill a steak and bake a potato."

"Be still, my heart." He tapped his fingers against his

chest. "Man food." He kissed her again. "Roger that. I think I love you, New York."

Even as the robust kiss caused the blood to drain from her head, Sabrina assured herself that he didn't really mean it. The same way his earlier "need" could have so many different interpretations, "love" also meant so many things.

You could love fettuccine Alfredo. Love an icy glass of fresh-squeezed lemonade on a hot summer day. She herself loved fluffy kittens, the Three Tenors, and Italian shoes.

Zach hadn't meant anything personal. Or romantic. Obviously he, like most men, loved steak and potatoes.

Which was why, although she seldom ate red meat, she'd proposed it in the first place.

"I take it 'roger that' is SEAL talk for 'yes'?"

"Usually. This time it means, 'You're a goddess and I count myself the luckiest male in the universe to be permitted to worship at your feet.'"

"Well." She laughed when he dropped down on one knee and kissed the top of her foot. "That's quite flattering. But a simple yes would have been sufficient."

"But not as heartfelt." He stood up and looked inclined to kiss her again when he suddenly slapped a palm against his forehead. "Damn."

"What?"

"I forgot. I've got a thing tonight."

A thing. Like a date. Of course he did. Just because they'd spent the last few hours fucking each other blind didn't give either one of them proprietary rights over the other.

"Don't worry about it." She forced a smile that she feared looked as fake as it felt. "I haven't even bought the steak, and it's not that I was asking you over for, like, a date or anything. I thought we could talk about the plans for Swannsea, and—"

Oh, God. She was babbling. She *never* babbled. Not

ever! Not even after being pulled out from under her hotel.

"Sabrina." He touched a finger to her lips. "I can't think of anything I'd rather do than spend time with you. But I've got this semimonthly poker game, and—"

A poker game? He was turning down red meat and hot sex for a damn poker game?

"Of course." Her already fake smile turned cool. "I can understand why you wouldn't want to miss that."

"Dammit." He plowed a frustrated hand through his hair. "Would you let me explain?"

Wishing she'd gone inside the house when they'd first arrived, she gave him a go ahead gesture.

"That's very good." He nodded. "That duchess-to-peon wave thing you've got going there," he explained when she arched a brow, inviting elaboration. "Makes a man want to grovel, even when he hasn't done anything wrong. But here's the thing," he said quickly, cutting off any response. "It's with my dad."

"Oh." That was, she considered, somewhat different than drinking beer, eating unhealthy snack foods, and belching with a bunch of guy pals.

"He's the one who started them after I got back, because he figured I needed something to get me out of the house. And out of the bottle."

"Oh." All right, that was a *great* deal different.

"And, in case you're wondering, it wasn't drinking I was having a problem with. But living. Now that I'm sort of remembering how to do that, an occasional beer hasn't proven a problem. Though," he said consideringly, "after that flashback at Harlan and Lillian's, I guess I'll stay clear of bourbon.

"So, although I'm doing okay these days, and a lot better the last couple days"—he tugged playfully on the ends of her hair—"I think he still feels the need to keep tabs on me. Plus, though he'd probably never admit it, I suspect he enjoys getting together with the guys. Especially since he's seemed at loose ends since Lucie passed."

"Oh, damn." She felt her eyes filling. "You had to do it, didn't you?"

"Do what?" The sun rising out of the Atlantic had gilded everything in a brilliant pink and gold glow that allowed her to see what appeared to be panic in his eyes.

"Are you crying about Lucie, because, damn, Sabrina, I didn't realize bringing her up . . . shit." This time he plowed both hands through his hair. "I mean, we've talked about her a couple times since you got back, and you've seemed okay with it, but—"

"I'm not crying because of my grandmother, idiot."

Although she'd never hit anyone in her entire life, Sabrina smacked a fist against his shoulder and felt the shock, like hitting a concrete wall, reverberate up her arm.

"If I *was* crying, which I damn well am not, because I never, ever cry, it's because you're being so fucking nice!"

She also never said the *f* word.

What *was* this man doing to her mind?

"Being nice is a bad thing?" No longer panicky, he now looked confused.

"It is when I want to think of you as some oversexed bad-boy SEAL who I'm going to sleep with from time to time while you build an addition on my grandmother's house. Of course you need to play cards with your father. We can have the steak some other night."

"If you're sure."

"Positive." Lifting a hand to his shoulder, she went up on her toes, and this time it was she who kissed him.

Deepening the kiss, he planted his palms against her butt and drew her closer against him. "What time do you go to bed?"

"My schedule's been screwed up since I got back, but usually somewhere between eleven and midnight."

He began planting light little kisses from one side of her mouth to the other. "What would you say if I came by about ten thirty? With dessert?"

She refused to play coy. "I'd say yes."

"Terrific." He captured her mouth one last time, a quick, hard kiss that left her head spinning.

She watched him take the steps two at a time. He was, she noticed with a smile, whistling.

"Oh, one more thing," he said before he climbed into that ridiculous red muscle car. "For the record, I sure don't have any problem with you thinking of me as some oversexed bad-boy SEAL you're going to be sleeping with while I'm building an addition onto your grandmother's house."

44

"Are you certain you want to do this?"

Jeremy Macon frowned at Sabrina across the wide expanse of mahogany desk, which had been polished to a mirror sheen. The banker, whose cotton ball white hair, mustache, and goatee made him look as if he were channeling Colonel Sanders, was known as a man who appreciated life, and it showed in the belly straining against the front of the blue shirt he was wearing with his white summer seersucker suit that he donned every year from Memorial Day to Labor Day.

"Are you suggesting you don't think it's a good investment?"

Although she'd grown accustomed to dealing with millions of dollars during her years with the Wingate chain, Sabrina was surprised to be so nervous. It was different when you were talking about your own money.

"Oh, I didn't say that." He waved her concerns away with a pudgy hand that looked as if it had never done anything more physical than swing a golf club.

He cleared his throat. Folded his hands over the expanse of his stomach. "As I told your grandmother when she first came to me with the idea, it could be very successful.

"However," he tacked on with a frown, "it would also require a great deal of hands-on involvement."

"I understand that. I'm prepared to give it my best shot." Sabrina rubbed an uncharacteristically damp hand on the skirt of her suit. "After all, I do know a bit about the hospitality industry." Her smile was meant to reassure.

"Well, of course you do." He plucked a pencil from the round walnut holder on the corner of his desk and began passing it from hand to hand. "And to hear Lucie tell it, you've been doing a bang-up job for Wingate. But surely you're not thinking of giving it all up to run a little tea shop here on Swann Island?"

"It wouldn't be just a tea shop." She leaned forward and tapped a fingernail on the manila folder he'd yet to open. "If you'll notice, along with the proposed budget that Tremayne Construction has given me, there's also a projected P&L for not just the tea shop but also the gift shop and tours."

"But you're not planning to charge for the tours?"

"No. They're merely a draw to get people to the farm so they can spend their money. And hopefully become loyal Swann Tea customers."

He finally opened the folder and skimmed the pages. "It appears you've put an impressive amount of work into this."

"Lucie and Titania created the concept," Sabrina said. "I merely tweaked it a bit. Such as adding the museum and the carriage rides."

"Both nice touches," he allowed. "But they'd make for even more work."

"I've never been afraid of work."

"Of course not. Still, Swannsea isn't exactly the fast lane." He closed the folder again and clasped his pudgy hands on top of it. "May I ask if you've thought about selling?"

Bingo. Sabrina was tempted to glance up over her head to check out the lightbulb that had flashed on. "To Brad Sumner's development company, perhaps?"

"Brad's been doing a great deal of work on the island," the banker said. "And so far he appears to have the Midas touch."

"How lovely for Brad." Sabrina leaned back in the

chair on the visitor's side of the desk, crossed her legs with a swish, and folded her arms across her silk blouse.

"However, I've no intention of selling the farm. If you have problems with my request for construction financing, although I'd prefer to do business with a local bank—"

"Oh, no," he said swiftly. "My family and your family have been doing business together since before the war." Meaning, Sabrina knew, not the current war, but the Civil War. "It was merely a suggestion."

The smile beneath that white mustache was a bit smarmy for her taste, but Sabrina had learned very early on that it wasn't absolutely necessary to like someone to do business with him.

"Even if I wanted to sell Swannsea, I wouldn't dare," she said mildly. "Because Lucie would come back and haunt me."

His belly shook as he chuckled at that. "I hear you." His expression sobered as he began playing with the pencil again.

"Lucie's death was not only a loss for the entire island, but for me personally," he confided.

"It seems everyone felt close to her." She hadn't been able to go anywhere in town without someone wanting to share an anecdote about her grandmother.

"Some more than others." A spark of what appeared to be anger flashed in his pale blue eyes. Then was just as quickly contained. "I asked her out a few times, after your grandfather took off. But she always turned me down."

"I'm sorry."

"So was I. I always thought she married beneath her when she chose Robert Swann."

"There was a problem between you and my grandfather." Sabrina remembered it now.

"More than a problem. He took advantage of our friendship to bilk the bank out of nearly a million dollars in a check-kiting scheme."

There was an audible snap. Both their eyes went to the broken yellow pencil.

He put the two pieces down and shook his head,

"The man definitely didn't deserve Lucie. Which is what I told her at the time."

"I didn't know." Pressing a finger to her temple, where a headache had begun to threaten, Sabrina wondered how they'd gotten on this topic.

"I know Lucie always considered you a dear friend." She had no idea if that was true, but figured it wouldn't hurt to say. It wasn't as if her grandmother was around to correct her.

"I would have been more than a friend if she'd let me. Did she ever tell you I'd proposed?"

"Marriage?" Okay, now they were getting into some really strange territory.

"Exactly. Not long after Robert took off. And several other times over the years. But she would never go through with the legal work that would have made her a free woman."

"I'd no idea." That was definitely true. "I suppose she decided marriage wasn't for her." It was definitely time to get this conversation back on track. "So—we have a deal?"

"Absolutely." He, too, seemed relieved to ditch the unpleasant stroll down memory lane. "I'll have my girl get the papers drawn up. They should be ready by Monday afternoon."

"Thank you." Cringing inwardly at his chauvinism, Sabrina stood up and held out her hand.

Well. This made it official.

As she left the bank, which, like so many others in the South, was yet another Tara replica, she felt a giddy little thrill at the thought that she was now running her very own business.

She would make a success of it. Despite Brad hovering like a vulture, despite Jeremy Macon's less than enthusiastic response to the plan, despite Harlan's outright objections, she would make this work. Make Swannsea the most desired destination spot on the island.

Not just the island.

How about the entire Lowcountry?

Maybe this was just the beginning.

Her mind raced as she imagined Swannsea resorts scattered around the country. Why think small? How about the *world*?

She could establish a brand, build on it—but no franchises. No, that's how you start losing control, and once that happens, quality can slide downhill fast.

One of the reasons Wingate was even stronger now than it had been when Eve Bouvier's father had established his first hotel in New Orleans was that Eve kept her finger on the pulse of every aspect of the family business.

Which was what Sabrina intended to do with Swannsea.

She laughed as she realized that, once again, she was racing ahead of herself.

Part of her reason for having decided to stay on Swann Island was to slow down. To learn to balance work and play.

And speaking of play . . .

Taking out her BlackBerry, she made a notation on her memo pad to stop by the Somersett Victoria's Secret.

The memory of how Zach had looked at her last night as she stood in front of him in that white teddy and high heels created a definite zing.

Looking forward to surprising him tonight with some new bit of sexy lingerie, Sabrina didn't notice the car parked two slots down from hers.

Or the man watching her intently from beneath the bill of a black USMC cap.

45

If there was one thing being in the SEALs had taught Zach, it was how to bluff. More than once, when he'd gone undercover in what the government euphemistically called "trouble spots" all over the world, his life had depended on it.

Trouble was, except for Nate Spencer, the other guys sitting at John Tremayne's kitchen table had been SEALs too.

Normally he could watch for tells. Those little signs that gave away what hands his opponents drew. But in this crowd, except for the former Marine occasionally scratching his right thumbnail when he drew a good card, there were no damn tells to read.

"So," he asked as he shuffled the cards, "how's the investigation going?"

"Nowhere." Nate frowned. And not, Zach figured, because of the cards he'd picked up. "I called in the FBI, but they're all tied up with terrorism shit, so a guy slashing throats apparently didn't come real high up on their official hit parade."

He tossed a chip into the center of the table. "One of them was an asshole. The other, Special Agent Cavanaugh, did at least make some calls for me. And seems to care about the case."

"Cavanaugh?" Quinn, who'd come over from Somersett for the game, glanced up from his cards. "Caitlin Cavanaugh?"

"Yeah," Nate said. "You know her?"

"Irish milkmaid skin, eyes as blue as a County Kerry lake, legs that go all the way up to her ears, red hair, and a temper to match?"

"I don't know about the temper. But you called the rest right."

"Wow. Cait Cavanaugh a fed." Quinn rubbed his unshaven jaw. "Who'd have thunk it?"

"You know her?" Nate asked again.

"I went out with her roommate a few times when I came here on leave over the holidays a few years ago." He glanced over at Zach. "I recall setting you up on a blind date with her for New Year's Eve."

"Yeah, I remember." Zach grinned. "I also remember that while she and I got along fine, she hated your guts."

"Yeah." He shrugged. "Some women have no taste."

"Are we playing cards, ladies? Or talking about women who got away?" John Tremayne complained.

"I'll call." Quinn tossed a chip into the pot, then added two more. "And raise. And for the record, Cait didn't get away."

"Because you never had her in the first place." Zach drew a card. Three kings and two sixes.

"What makes you think I wanted her?"

Liking his full house, Zach raised the ante two chips more. "Wasn't a guy who met Cait Cavanaugh who didn't wonder if she'd be as much of a firecracker in bed as she was out of it."

"Sounds like a man who found out," Nate said.

"I've never been one to kiss and tell." Zach flashed a grin.

"Jesus." John lit up a cigar and puffed out his frustration in clouds of acrid smoke that Zach figured would really go over well when he showed up at Sabrina's later tonight. "I don't know what the hell's wrong with your generation. Whatever happened to guys talking about guns, sharing war stories, and telling lies about the size of fish?"

"Because the war stories are too fresh, guns have pretty much lost their appeal once you've had some turned on you, and women smell a whole lot better than fish?" Quinn suggested.

"Along with the fact that women are a lot more of a challenge." Zach looked across the table at his father and tried to read the bluff.

"That's for fucking sure," Nate grumbled as the pile of chips in the center of the table grew.

"What's the matter?" Zach asked. "Titania got you reading bride magazines and pushing you toward the altar?"

"For your information, frog boy, I've never read a bride magazine yet and hope to hell I can die saying that," Nate shot back. "But as it happens, *I'm* the one pushing *her*."

"You *want* to get married?" Quinn looked poleaxed by that idea.

"Yeah. I do. But she's dragging her feet."

"Women." Zach shook his head. "Just when you think you've got them figured out, they turn around and act like guys."

"I'm out." Quinn threw down his cards, got up from the table, took another beer from the refrigerator, and unscrewed the cap. "Speaking of acting like guys," he said to Zach, "have you given any more thought to my proposition?"

"No."

"What proposition?" John asked.

"I offered him a job," Quinn said.

"I've got a job," Zach said, his jaw tight.

"Working as a carpenter?" Quinn countered with obvious disbelief.

"Something wrong with construction?" John challenged.

"Hell, no. It's just a little—" Quinn paused, as if seeking the right word. "Staid," he decided.

"I like staid," Zach said mildly. He gave his father another hard stare. As good as he was at the bluff, his

pop had always been better. "It suits me." *What the hell.*
He tossed another pile of chips into the center of the
table. "I'll raise."

"This has gotten too high for my blood." Nate laid
down his cards.

"What job?" John pressed for an answer.

"It's for this international security firm you've probably never heard of—the Phoenix Team."

"Sure, I've heard of them." John pursed his lips as he
studied his cards, puffed a bit more. "Done some work
for them from time to time, too."

"Fuck that." Zach blinked, his mind momentarily
yanked off the game. "Where? When?"

"Here and there. Off and on."

"Your dad happens to be one of Phoenix Team's favorite operatives," Quinn offered around a piece of pepperoni pizza.

Cards momentarily forgotten, Zach narrowed his eyes.
"You never said a goddamn thing."

"Maybe that's why they call them *clandestine* operations," John said dryly. "And it's not like I'm running
around some jungle with an automatic weapon. I mostly
work in logistics."

"Logistics." And here he'd been working like hell to
follow in his father's outwardly settled-down footsteps.
"Christ. I can't believe I didn't know about this."

"You weren't around when I signed on with them."

"I've been back home six effin' months."

"Well, yeah. But you had, as they say these days, *issues* to deal with, so I decided the time wasn't right to
bring it up. You gonna play? Or fold?"

"You're bluffing," Zach determined. Apparently
about a lot more than cards. "The thing is, whether
you've got enough guts to act on your convictions."

"I always do."

John Tremayne's eyes were as flinty as blue steel.
Looking at them, Zach realized that despite the lines
fanning out from them and the gray scattered at his tem-

ples that hadn't been there last time he'd been home, his old man was, deep down inside, that same hardened Navy SEAL who'd done three tours in 'Nam and had, if the rumors he'd heard while at BUD/S training were even halfway true, gained a reputation for leading night raids into Cambodia.

"Hell." Zach folded.

"Good move." John put the cigar down on a saucer he'd been using as an ashtray and began scooping up the pile of chips. "If you'd have kept it up, you would've lost your shirt and I'd have probably ended up having to give you an advance on your salary."

"I've got money," Zach grumbled.

"Yeah." His father's smile flashed beneath his gray mustache. "But the night's still young, buddy boy."

46

Misty Mannington checked her makeup one last time in the rearview mirror. Fluffed her hair, frowning as she remembered what Titania Davis had said about her.

"Like that bitch would know anything about getting a man."

After all, Titania was all of what, twenty-seven, twenty-eight years old and still hadn't caught herself a husband. Oh, everyone back at Swann Island High School had known Nate Spencer would crawl naked on his hands and knees over broken glass from one end of the island to the other for the girl.

But had she given him so much as a tumble?

Hell, no. Full of big ideas, after sending him off to the Marines without so much as accepting an engagement ring, she'd gone off and gotten herself some sort of fancy culinary degree from the Art Institute of Charleston.

But apparently even that wasn't enough, because after six months making pastry at the Somersett Wingate Palace hotel, she'd gone to Paris, France, of all places, where she'd attended the Ritz Escoffier Culinary School, which to Misty sounded like a froufrou name for one of those technical schools, like the ones that were always advertising on daytime TV about how to become a dog groomer or air-conditioner repairman, but everyone sure seemed to act all impressed by that degree she hung on the wall of her tacky little restaurant.

And so what if she'd come back home speaking, ladi-dah, French? Why, Misty didn't know a single solitary soul on the island she could talk it with.

All that time Titania hadn't seemed to give any men a tumble, which had more than a few people, including Sissy down at the market—who usually could be counted on to know just about everything about everyone— wondering if she might be one of those lesbians.

Like Ellen DeGeneres. Or Rosie O'Donnell.

Gus Melton, who'd run the Gas and Go since before Misty was born, thought that would be a purely pitiful loss.

Which was when Sissy had passed on what she'd heard about one argument that had supposedly taken place at The Stewed Clam. Leon Foster, who cut hair down at Leon's Clip Joint, offered the opinion that he wasn't sure black girls could even *be* lesbians, a suspicion that Pete Sullivan, who'd been given a job by Nate Spencer's daddy after getting out of prison, had declared flat-out crazy, claiming that being black or white didn't have a dad-blamed thing to do with which way a person swung.

To which Leon countered that he guessed Pete probably knew a lot about the subject, being as how he'd spent all those years taking prison showers.

Well, hadn't that caused a ruckus? Which had ended up with both Pete and Leon spending a night at the same jail Pete spent his days sweeping up.

Shortly after that, Nate Senior had retired and Nate had come home from the Marines to take over being sheriff, and damned if he hadn't grown up to be one fine hunk of a male specimen.

And, it appeared, still crazy as a damn loon about Titania, who, it turned out, apparently wasn't a lesbian after all, but heaven knows what filthy habits she'd picked up from all those foreigners.

Fortunately, Nate had the good taste to understand that there's the kind of women you just have sex with.

And the other kind you marry.

Thank the good Lord Misty's mother had brought her up to be the second kind.

The problem was, even with the best plastic surgeon in Charleston on her speed dial, Misty knew that the little preventative nips and tucks she considered along the same lines as having a pedicure or her roots done at the salon weren't going to be enough to hold back the clock forever.

She was, after all, coming up on thirty, and while the alimony from her second, and third, husbands kept her in the style to which she'd become accustomed (unfortunately, husband number one had been a love match and poor as dirt, and hadn't she learned that lesson the hard way?), she didn't have any money put away for her old age.

Like thirty-five.

Or, and oh, God, she didn't even want to contemplate it, *forty.*

Which was what tonight was all about.

She'd been stringing husband candidate number four along now for the past two months. Teasing him enough to keep him interested, but not going all the way because she knew she wasn't the only woman he kept on the side, and the one thing she didn't want to do was to give him the impression that she was like all the others—the kind of girl he could fuck, then feel free to walk away from.

After all, as her mama had drilled into her, why would a man buy a cow if he could get the cream for free?

Some women might consider the fact that he was married a bit of a roadblock to an engagement, but having maneuvered her way around that very same roadblock on two previous occasions, Misty didn't view it as any more of a bother than those asphalt bumps the island council had stuck down on Oceanside Avenue last year to keep drunk spring breakers from speeding and crushing those darling baby turtles as they went crawling out to sea.

Misty didn't believe the man she was meeting tonight

truly loved his wife. Oh, she'd been through enough breakups and signed enough pre-nups to understand it was hard on him to make the choice, given how tangled their finances were and such.

And, of course, there was the inevitable scandal.

But these days scandals were a dime a dozen. Why, how many wives and mistresses had Donald Trump gone through? And the networks even gave him his very own TV show.

Money was the perfume that made the stink of scandal go away.

And Lord knows, the man she was going to be spending the next few days in bed with had bushels of it.

And, soon, so would she.

Fortunately, her girls were visiting their father—and his new wife, aka the tacky bimbo slut secretary—in London, which meant Misty didn't have to deal with tedious explanations to the nanny about where she was going or how to reach her in case of an emergency.

She pulled her sporty Mercedes convertible into the designated meeting spot.

His car was already there, which she took as an indication that he'd been waiting for her.

Which showed he was anxious. And wasn't that just the way she wanted him?

Which was also why she'd shown up ten minutes late.

The driver's door opened as she parked next to him.

She opened her own door and swiveled her legs out in a way designed to capture his attention. Although there weren't any streetlights, enough moonlight was filtering through the clouds to cast a silvery sheen on long legs shown to their best advantage in a pair of stiletto hooker heels, and a strapless, skintight black dress that stopped bare inches below her crotch.

He let out a long, low whistle.

"Did you put on that dress you're barely wearing for me?"

She glanced around as she took his hand and let him help her out of the low-slung car.

"Do you see anyone else around here, sugar?" she asked, on the same mint julep drawl that had captured the fancy of husband number three. Of course, he'd been an oilman from Denver, where a Southern accent was more of a sexy novelty.

"Just you, darlin'." He pulled her close, letting her feel how effective the dress was proving to be.

Misty went up on her toes and gave him a kiss brimming with promises of things to come. Then dangled the keys in front of him. "My suitcase is in the trunk."

He clicked the remote and lifted out of the trunk the pretty blue and chocolate polka-dot Hartmann bag she'd bought in Charleston for this occasion. "No one could ever accuse you of packing light," he said with an indulgent smile.

"Well, since you wouldn't tell me where we're going, I wanted to prepare for any contingency," she purred as he transferred the bag to his own trunk.

"Ah, but I seem to recall telling you that you wouldn't be needing any clothes."

He squeezed her breast roughly. Hard enough to make her flinch.

Well. Wasn't this a surprise?

Apparently she'd miscalculated. Just a bit. He'd always been such a smooth, gentlemanly type. Far more Ashley Wilkes than Rhett Butler.

Still, Misty could handle this. After all, her second husband had been into Atlanta's underground S&M scene. Which had paid off quite handsomely, since the cardiologist to the city's rich and influential wouldn't have wanted his Buckhead neighbors to know that he got off having his trophy wife dress up in black leather and thigh-high boots and whip him with a cat-o'-nine-tails in front of all those other perverts during parties in the home's soundproofed basement dungeon.

"Oh, dear," she said, on a sexy, tremulous whimper she figured he wanted to hear. "How ever did you know?"

"Know what?"

"That I've been a naughty girl." She was trapped between the car door and his increasingly aroused body.

"Have you now?" His free hand delved beneath her skirt, cupping her already moist panties. "What would you suggest I do about that?"

"I don't know."

This time her whimper was for real as he pinched her nipple, the pressure painful enough to bring tears to her eyes.

So there'd been a change in plans. Obviously she was going to have to work for her reward.

Still, she reminded herself what her physical trainer was always telling her: *No pain, no gain.*

Her teeth, which had cost her a fortune in caps, worried a bottom lip still stinging a bit from yesterday's collagen injection.

"Perhaps punish me?"

He smiled. A slow, feral flash of white that did not meet his eyes.

"That can be arranged."

Her tremor, as he reached past her and opened the passenger door, was only partly feigned.

Misty was so busy giving herself a little pep talk, assuring herself that she could handle this unexpected situation, and him, the same way she'd handled all the other men in her life, that as she slid into the bucket seat with another seductive flash of thigh, she failed to notice that the overhead dome light had not come on.

47

"Well?" Quinn asked later that evening.

"Deep subject," Zach replied.

Inside the house where he'd grown up, the game was still going on. His dad had been pretty much mopping up the floor with all of them, and Zach, wanting a break from the cheap stink sticks John Tremayne had always insisted on buying, even when he could afford better, had gone out onto the deck that looked over the marsh.

"Sorry about springing your dad's involvement on you like that. But John wanted to keep his work with Phoenix Team quiet."

Zach jerked a shoulder. "Yeah, why tell his own son? When he can play war games with you?"

Quinn rocked back on his heels and slipped his hands into his front pockets. "It was his call. I think he wanted to give you a chance to get back on your feet without feeling any pressure from him."

"I put my damn guns away."

"Good for you."

"And this doesn't change anything. I'm not interested in playing bodyguard for some CEO who makes more than the gross national product of most countries."

"Phoenix Team's about a lot more than doing bodyguard work, but since you don't want to talk about it, there's no point in going into detail about the logistics."

"I don't get it." Zach turned toward his longtime best

friend. "You sold your book. You can't need the money."

Quinn laughed at that. "Stories of my wealth are highly exaggerated. Hell, if you factor in benefits, I was making more in the military."

"But you still left."

"Well, yeah. After Afghanistan playing soldier lost its appeal." He shrugged again. "But writing in notebooks during breaks from missions and training was one thing. Sitting in front of a computer all day long is beyond tedious. So, keeping my hand in by taking on a freelance job from time to time allows me to keep my skills up.

"Besides"—his grin flashed in the dark—"if I'm late getting a manuscript in, I can always use the excuse I was off on a top-secret mission to save the world."

"Good luck with that."

Zach had nearly come to the conclusion that the world, or at least a large part of it, might not deserve saving.

Quinn tilted his head back, jangled the change in his pocket, and contemplated the night sky. "Amazing, isn't it?"

"What?"

"Those stars are the same ones shining over the Kush. But the two places are as different as night and day."

"You ever think about that?" Zach asked. He'd never brought it up before, because the truth was he hadn't been ready to talk about it.

"Just every day. Since it's what my second book's about."

"You're shitting me."

"Nope."

"Jesus." As an egret, startled by the sharp tone, suddenly shot up from the water and soared over the marsh, Zach blew out a breath and wondered how many other things people had been keeping from him. "Is this one going to be nonfiction?"

"Fiction. Sometimes you can put even more truth in a story that way."

"Jesus," Zach repeated, wondering how the hell Quinn could relive that mission day after day.

Quinn rubbed the back of his neck. "I was in Washington last week," he said with studied casualness. "Stopped by Walter Reed."

Zach's gut clenched. "How's he doing?"

He did not have to say the name. They both knew exactly who Quinn was talking about.

"Damn well, all things considered. He's been doing a lot of PT and should get his permanent prosthesis any day. You should see what they're doing now. It's amazing. He's gonna be pretty much the Bionic Man, though he says he's already looking forward to going to Halloween parties as a pirate this year."

Zach had to laugh at that. "Typical joker cowboy."

"Yeah. It was good to see. He's considering going back into JAG."

"The way he's always arguing, he'd make a good lawyer."

Shane Garrett had argued against that last flight, but, once overruled by the brass, he'd done his job as well as he'd been able to under the circumstances. Zach figured if anyone else had been flying that Chinook, none of them would have made it out of those mountains alive.

"He also has an offer to teach military law at the academy over in Somersett if he decides to opt out. Which he doesn't need to, because the army doesn't rotate guys out the way they used to. Hell, from what he told me, there are four-star amputees in war zones these days."

"Good for them."

Zach couldn't figure out why anyone lucky enough to be handed a get-out-of-war card would want to go back. But then again, there were a lot of things that didn't make sense to him these days.

"He was offered his old gig back flying birds, but he's afraid that if he ever crashed again he could put guys at risk trying to evacuate him."

He paused.

Zach braced himself for what was coming next.

"He asked about you."

Great. Lay on the guilt, why don't you?

"He's worried about you," Quinn said when Zach didn't immediately respond. "I told him you're on the road back."

"Thanks."

"He's also worried that you're blaming yourself."

"It was my job to carry out the fucking mission," Zach said through clenched teeth.

"Which you did. Better than anyone else could have done. It wasn't your fault the operation was a clusterfuck from the get-go."

"Look, I'm glad he's okay, I feel like the asshole shit of all time for not visiting as often as I should, but what's done is done, and if you don't mind, I'd just as soon not talk about it, okay?"

"Sure," Quinn said mildly. Like a lot of big guys Zach had met over the years, Quinn was pretty mellow; it took a lot to rile the former SEAL sniper turned military novelist. "You know, you wouldn't have to go out on a mission in the field. Phoenix Team has a lot of need for consultants. Remember Nick Broussard?"

"Sure. He was in our BUD/S class."

"Well, he left the navy to take care of some personal stuff when his dad died in New Orleans, and then went off sailing around the Pacific for a time. But he discovered retirement can get boring real fast, so he recently signed on as an operative. And his wife's working as a consultant."

"Broussard got married?" Zach had never met anyone less likely to tie the knot.

"Yeah. To a former homicide cop. She's a dynamo at logistics."

"Good for the both of them. I hope you'll all be very happy together. But the answer is still no."

"Your call. But if you ever change your mind, you know where to find me."

"Don't hold your breath."

48

"I don't understand," Misty sobbed. "Why are you doing this to me?"

"Because I can," the man she'd pinned all her hopes and renewed dreams on said calmly.

She wasn't some wide-eyed innocent. She'd willingly given up her virginity to Jimmy Ray Turner for a sterling silver charm bracelet when she was thirteen, and had never looked back. She'd been married several times, and she did, on occasion, even enjoy a bit of rough sex, though the getting-sweaty part was nasty and something she preferred to do without.

Back in her Buckhead days, she'd known that some women seemed to get off on being tied up and even lashed, though she'd been vastly relieved that because of her husband's predilections, she ended up on the delivering end rather than the receiving end of that black leather whip.

But this was different. Although he'd raped her more times than she could count, she sensed that this wasn't really about sex.

It was about power.

Which she could understand, because she'd certainly wielded it herself over enough men in her life.

Oh, God. What if all those people who were all the time going on and on about karma were right?

What if, heaven help her, she was getting the comeuppance that more than one cheated-on wife had threatened her with?

"You're my slave," he said with a calm that Misty found even scarier than all the whips and chains hanging on the wall. "I can do anything I want with you."

He dipped the cloth back into the basin of warm water and continued washing the blood and vomit off the body he'd ravaged.

"You may as well get used to it."

"You're h-h-him, aren't you?"

The question came out on a croak, due to her throat being rough from when he'd nearly choked her to death by squeezing her neck until she'd passed out.

After she'd come to, the stickiness between her legs had been proof that he'd come while she'd been unconscious.

"T-t-the k-k-killer."

"You mean the Swann Island Slasher?" He chuckled. "Clever name, isn't it? I'm quite pleased with it. I also wonder how long it'll be before the national media pick it up and run with it."

He put the cloth back in the basin and began fussing with her matted hair. "You use too damn much gunk on this." He picked up a handful and yanked painfully. "And it's bleached to straw. I don't like my slaves all tarted up."

It was the second time this week someone had criticized her hair. Not wanting to challenge him, Misty didn't respond.

"You need a shower."

"Oh, yes."

Relief surged through her. In order to give her a proper shower, he'd have to let her out of this cage. If she was out of the cage, maybe she could escape.

"I'd do anything for a shower."

She gazed up at him through lowered lashes, the way Vivien Leigh had when playing Scarlett flirting with the Tarleton twins at the barbecue at Twelve Oaks. Misty had begun practicing that expression in the mirror back when she'd been in grammar school and had yet to meet a male it didn't work on.

"Absolutely anything," she cooed.

Smack! He struck her cheek with the back of his hand. Hard enough to snap her head and rattle her teeth. Before she could catch her breath to cry out, he hit the other cheek, whipping her head the other way.

"Obviously you still don't understand the program," he said with exaggerated patience. "You'll do anything, absolutely anything"—his falsetto tone mocked her words—"I tell you to do. *Nothing* is up for negotiation."

She flinched as a fist went sailing by her head and realized he'd purposely missed because right now he wanted to terrify her more than hurt her.

He was succeeding.

"That's what being a slave is all about," he said. "Now hold out your arm."

Even knowing what was coming next, Misty did as instructed. Hesitation, she'd already learned, could prove costly.

Not to mention painful.

He closed the heavy metal shackle around first one wrist and then the other. Then fastened both ends of the chain to the bars.

"My wife is going out this afternoon. It's her book club day. But you already know that, don't you?" he asked with a wicked laugh.

He ran his hand over her freshly cleansed flesh, from her bruised throat, over the raised red welts covering her breasts, down her stomach, which roiled at his touch.

"I wonder if anyone will miss you? Worry about you? Maybe even call the sheriff."

Misty screamed as he harshly shoved his fingers into her torn and burning body. But she knew it wouldn't do any good. He'd already warned her that the windowless room where she was being held captive had been soundproofed.

"It would be nice to think that someone would be coming to help you, wouldn't it?" he asked.

Her teeth were worrying her bottom lip as she looked mutely up at him.

"I asked you a question, slave." He struck her again, this time a fist to her jaw. Misty felt the shock as the molar came out, tasted blood in her mouth.

She nodded.

"Yes, it would be lovely. But unfortunately for you, there's not a woman in this town or, hell, probably the entire Lowcountry who gives a flying fuck what happens to you.

"In fact," he said, "I'll bet there are a lot of them who'd be willing to pay to stand in line to use that whip."

The terrible thing was Misty feared it might be true.

She'd always put her efforts toward seducing men, never befriending women, who'd never been any use to her.

Which meant that no one would notice if she disappeared off the face of the earth. And worse yet, anyone who might happen to notice wouldn't care.

"After she leaves, we'll go to the house."

He folded up the tripod and packed the video camera into the black leather duffel bag he'd brought with him.

"I'll let you take a shower. Then I'll fuck you in that sweet, tight little ass. In the master's bed."

She had to know. "A-a-a-re you going to k-k-kill me?"

He paused as he gathered up the liquid soap and basin. Looked down at her as if seriously considering the matter.

"That all depends on you," he said finally. "If you're a good girl and learn to please me properly, I may decide to keep you."

He gave her another of those chilling smiles that didn't reach his eyes.

Then he left, turning off the overhead light, leaving her all alone again in the tomblike darkness.

49

Sabrina was admittedly surprised at how well she and Zach worked together. Of course, during the day he was the ultimate professional, running his crew with almost military precision. Which wasn't surprising, she supposed. Given his SEAL background.

They also fit well together in so many other ways. And not just in bed. They were comfortable in each other's space, he could make her laugh, and their evening walks on the beach and moonlight swims were becoming her favorite parts of the day.

A week after she'd gone to the bank, she was standing in what had for nearly two hundred years been a garden, getting her picture taken for the *Trumpet* with Zach, John Tremayne, Linc, Titania, and, of course, Jeremy Macon, who was making sure to get a plug in for his bank, which was only fair, since he was providing the financing.

According to Linc's records, Swann Tea had the funds to finance the construction, but as Sabrina had learned, it was always preferable to use someone else's money.

In addition to those involved in the project, Harlan, and Lillian, and even Nate had shown up. As had reporters from Somersett, Beaufort, and other towns scattered throughout the Lowcountry, who, unsurprisingly, were proving far more interested in the Swann Island Slasher than the prospect of yet another Southern tearoom.

There were tourists, perhaps, attracted, by the crowd.

And, for some reason, though about as welcome as ants at a Memorial Day picnic, Brad Sumner was also in attendance.

"Okay, Ms. Swann," David Henley, the *Trumpet*'s new editor and, it appeared, chief photographer, said. "If you could put your foot on the shovel."

He fiddled with the focus some more while the smile grew stiff on Sabrina's face.

"That's perfect. Now, Mr. Tremayne, Zach, if you could scoot in a little closer—"

"No problem," Zach said, putting an arm around Sabrina's waist and leaning in so he could murmur in her ear. "In fact I have plans to get a helluva lot closer this evening."

She laughed, not so much because of what he'd said, but because of how the prospect made her feel.

She was still insisting on at least keeping up appearances, which meant that he hadn't yet spent the entire night, but he might as well have, because he usually left her bed at dawn, then returned to Swannsea at eight with the crew that had begun setting the stakes for the new foundation.

"Perfect," Henley said with satisfaction. The camera clicked.

"May I have a few moments, Ms. Swann?" he asked as he pulled out a long, slender notepad. "I'd like to ask you a few questions for the paper."

She sighed inwardly. In her previous job, she'd always been available to talk with the press. She hadn't necessarily enjoyed the experience, but neither had she disliked it.

Promotion, which was what all interviews really were, after all, had been just one more aspect of the job, and occasionally—such as when that Australian hip-hop group had gotten drunk in the lobby bar and decided to crash a wedding reception at the hotel in Melbourne—it could provide a valuable opportunity to spin a negative story in as positive a light as possible.

"I always enjoy talking about Swann Tea," she said with a smile, as Zach went off to speak to the bulldozer operator, who was waiting to break ground.

"I was hoping we could discuss your experience in Florence."

Wasn't that exactly what she'd feared? Especially from the newspaper editor who she suspected was sensationalizing the murders to earn himself national recognition.

"Really?" She feigned surprise. "But that's such old news."

"I thought we'd cover it as more a personality-profile piece. You know, local girl goes off to seek her fortune, gets attacked by terrorists, and escapes the rat race to return to her hometown."

"Well, I suppose that's the *TV Guide* program description version," she allowed with a smile as fake as her surprise. "But it's a bit more complicated than that."

"Now, see, that's exactly what I want to get into." He pressed on. "The complexities of your decision. I believe the *Trumpet*'s readers would like the paper to peel away the many layers of Sabrina Swann. To get down to the inner woman. The survivor who has overcome so many challenges in her life."

"I don't believe I've faced that many challenges," she said mildly. "Certainly no more than anyone else."

"You lost both your parents, who, from what I've read, weren't exactly the most stable of individuals. You were sent to boarding schools around the world—"

"My parents were artists," she said. "I suspect that made them a bit more emotional than, say, an accountant. Or a hotel manager. Or even," she added with a forced smile, "a newspaper editor. And I was fortunate to receive an excellent education."

Sensing that he was going to turn this into a poor little rich girl story, which hers so wasn't, she glanced desperately over toward Zach, but he was busy talking with his father and the crew, so there wouldn't be any help coming from him.

Nor from Harlan. After giving her a brief wave and a sympathetic lift of his eyebrows, he began pushing Lillian back to their wheelchair-accessible van.

"I was merely in the wrong place at the wrong time. Which doesn't make me much of a story."

"Why don't you let me be the judge of that?" Henley suggested. "I realize there are other members of the press who'd only be wanting some puff PR stuff from you, but I really want to go deeper.

"Is there somewhere we can conduct this interview in private? Perhaps over dinner? My wife doesn't know that many people here yet and she misses entertaining."

"I suspect having a husband show up with an unexpected guest isn't a wife's favorite thing in the world," Sabrina replied, dodging the unexpected dinner invitation. "As for the interview—"

"Oh, isn't this too, too fabulous!" As if conjured up from her wildest wishes, Titania suddenly appeared, gave Sabrina a huge hug, and turned her million-watt smile on the editor.

"This is definitely a red-letter day for Swann Island," she gushed. "I do hope you got lots and lots of photographs for your paper."

"I believe I have enough. I was just discussing with Ms. Swann—"

"Oh, darling, now, you needn't be so formal." She ran a glossy coral fingernail down the front of his rumpled sport coat. "We're very casual here on the island. I'm sure Sabrina wouldn't mind if you called her by her first name. Would you, Sabrina?" she asked.

"Not at all. And as much as I'd love to discuss the exciting new plans for Swannsea, there's really something I need to talk to my contractor about."

"Oh, you go right ahead and take care of business." Titania wagged her hand, then linked arms with Henley. "I'll be pleased as punch to fill David in on all the details. Have you tried the chocolate mint brownies, sugar?

We've got a table set up on the back veranda for friends
and family, and, of course, our favorite members of the
press, to celebrate this auspicious occasion.

"The brownies are one of my personal favorite recipes
that we're going to be featuring at the Swannsea Tearoom. Of course we use our own mint tea in the recipe,
and, I swear, they are to die for . . .

"Where did I hear you're from, darlin'? New York,
or Philadelphia, or some such place?"

"Washington," Sabrina heard Henley say as Titania
dragged him away.

Not that it took much effort. Sabrina had grown up
watching men become pixilated by her stunningly beautiful, animated best friend.

"I knew it was one of those Yankee cities," Titania
said.

"Quite a wingman you've got there," Zach said. He'd
left the crew and met Sabrina as she was coming over
to him.

"I owe her. She rescued me from an interview about
the bombing."

"You'd think that'd be old news."

They both watched as the couple disappeared around
the side of the house.

"That's what I thought, too," Sabrina said. "But he
said he wanted to get to know the real me. Peel away
the layers, so to speak."

"That's my job. Anyone else goes peeling on you, I'll
have to break their hands."

He was standing a respectable distance away, hands
safely in the pocket of work jeans that, while faded, were
not as raggedy as the ones he usually wore, making Sabrina think he'd made the effort for her special day.

He was wearing sunglasses, which kept her from
seeing his eyes, but from the way his baritone voice
roughened, she knew he was thinking back on that dress
she'd bought to wear out to last night's dinner in Somer-

sett. The snug, peach-hued dress that he'd had to literally peel off her body.

Which had been precisely her intention when she'd
bought it.

"You're bad."

"Just the way you like me."

"Absolutely the way I like you."

"You know I didn't mean it, right?"

"Mean what?"

It was happening again. That mind-stealing phero-
mone cloud that always seemed to surround them whenever they were together.

"What I said. About breaking his hands."

"Well, of course I know that." She blew out a breath.

"I wanted to make sure. After what Sumner told
you."

"Oh, forget about him."

She glanced over at where he'd been standing, but
apparently he'd left. "He only said that about you to try
to get me to sell Swannsea."

"Which didn't work, so what the hell was the guy
doing here today?"

"Maybe he was hoping I'd change my mind at the
last minute."

His grunt suggested he wasn't all that willing to take
anything about Brad Sumner at face value.

Supposing that looking for hidden motives was part
and parcel of being a SEAL, she patted his arm.

"I have to go circulate," she said. "How about we stay
in tonight? Fix ourselves a Lowcountry boil, drink some
wine, watch a DVD, make love—"

"Change the order around to making love while supper boils and, hey, what the hell, after the movie, too,
and you've got yourself a date, sugar."

She laughed. "Men are so easy."

"You're damn right I am. Where you're concerned,
anyway." Because they both knew his crew was watch-

ing, he skimmed a finger down the slope of her nose. "See you later."

"Later," she agreed, wondering why such a light, non-sexual caress could have her nearly melting into a hot puddle of need.

She enjoyed watching his tight butt in those faded jeans as he walked back to where they'd already begun digging up Lucie's old garden plot.

Halfway there, he turned. "What DVD did you have in mind?"

"I picked up an oldie but goodie yesterday at the Video Express. What would you say to *Goldfinger*?"

"I'd say it's the best Bond movie ever and the reason Connery owns 007." His grin suggested he'd been expecting a chick-flick romance. "Lowcountry boil and Bond. I don't suppose you'd marry me? Have my children?"

"I'm a little busy today." It was a joke. That's all. So why did that foolish question make her nerves spike? "But I'll take it under advisement."

"I'll have to see what I can do to convince you," he said with a laugh.

See? Sabrina told herself. *It's only a stupid joke.*

The man operating the heavy yellow bulldozer impressed Sabrina with his ability to seemingly turn the machine on a dime. She observed him for a moment, always impressed by anyone who could do any job well.

It was one of the things that had made her a good hotel manager. From the busboys sweeping the crumbs off the tablecloths between courses without unduly disturbing the diners, to the way the valet parking attendants always remembered what guest belonged with which car, to the classical music the housekeeping staff tuned the radio to after cleaning a room, she'd always tried never to miss a detail.

Which was why, when she took in the U.S. Marine Corps cap the bulldozer operator was wearing, she wondered if he had learned to operate construction machinery in the service. She'd never given it all that much thought before the war, but surely someone had to put up all those tents and build all those camps.

As she continued on around to the back veranda, she made a mental note to remember to thank Zach, or his father, for assigning such a professional to her job.

50

It was cold. As cold as Zach, who was currently hunkered down behind a dead donkey that had the misfortune to become a casualty of war, had ever felt it.

Not helping was the wind that was whipping off the mountain, freezing his skin even through the PCU— protective combat uniform—he was wearing.

He was going to call in air support and, although it had gotten light enough to take off his NVGs, he would also try for another helo so they could get the hell off the mountain.

Because obviously this mission was going to have to be scrubbed.

If the terrorist they'd been sent to find didn't know they were on the ground, by the number of signal lights that had begun glowing on the mountain, he damn well would by the time they could reach his bat cave.

The radio, about the size of a cell phone, was delicate at any time, even more so in extreme temperatures. When the batteries got cold, it could either not work or malfunction, something you didn't want when you were calling in jets to start bombing tangos. He pulled out the batteries and stuck them inside the PCU under his armpit to warm them up.

The old military cliché that no battle plan survives first contact with the enemy was definitely proving true in this case.

One problem—okay, they had a lot of problems, but

one of the worst was that Zach didn't need to check his handy-dandy J-Fire reference guide to know that they were too near the enemy for close air support. No way was command going to risk a friendly-fire incident.

Which was a good thing. Unless said tangos happened to be whipping your ass, which, Zach told the men hunkered down with him, meant that you had three choices: (1) die by enemy fire, (2) die by friendly fire, or (3) get rid of the damn enemy fire.

"Looks like door number three," Zach said as the Kalashnikovs' muzzles flashed from the bunker. He put the batteries back in the radio.

"The only choice," Quinn agreed, brushing away enough of the snowdrift with a gloved hand to allow him to kneel on the rocky ground.

Lifted his rifle and shot off two rounds before the rifle jammed.

From the bunker, the enemy began firing more rounds. "Damn!"

As Quinn worked to clear his weapon, Zach, Shane, who'd picked up a rifle from a fallen Ranger, and a Marine sniper who'd joined them behind the donkey, began returning fire.

"Oo-rah!" the Marine shouted as he picked off a tango who'd made the mistake of lifting his head.

One shot. One kill. The kid had learned his lesson well.

"Good shot," Zach said.

"Used to shoot squirrels back home." The Marine's grin lit up his freckled Opie Taylor face. "But this is a lot more fun."

Fun? Christ, Zach thought, had he ever been that young?

He also hoped to hell the kid would still think so once this day was over.

One of the guerrillas popped up like a jack-in-the-box; putting the red laser dot in the center of his chest, Zach squeezed the trigger, sending the fighter tumbling back into the bunker.

Which earned another fusillade of fire that shredded trees and made holes in the snow all around them.

Lucky for us the assholes are all such bad shots.

The thought had no sooner popped into Zach's head than another tango rose and got off a round that flew about a mile over their heads.

"My turn," Shane said. Lying on his stomach, with his bad leg stretched out behind him, he fired.

Two down.

The bunker was turning out to be like a damn clown car. When another terrorist leaped out and started running toward them, Quinn, his gun now unjammed, called dibs.

With a preternatural calm that told Zach he'd gone into his spooky sniper zone, ignoring the RPG that suddenly zoomed over their heads, he picked the runner off with a single shot.

Then, the muzzle of his M4 barking its resistance inches from Zach's head—which would leave him deaf in his right ear for the next three months—he nailed the next two with practiced ease.

"We've got them on the run now!" Opie shouted, enthusiastically firing off another round at the bunker.

Fuck. Quinn and Zach exchanged a look.

Shane cursed.

Now the kid had done it.

Didn't the Marines teach their jarheads about the fate thing?

About the Titanic *moment?*

During his first year in the navy, Zach had been dragged to that flick by a woman whose pants he was intending to get into at the end of the evening.

As soon as the captain had assured a lushly curvaceous Kate Winslet—who in Zach's mind had been the only reason to watch the movie—that the gigantic ship couldn't sink, even if Zach hadn't known the story ahead of time, he would've recognized the exact moment of hubris when all those passengers became, well, sunk.

Do. Not. Fuck. With. Fate.

Sure enough, right on cue, a belt-fed machine gun suddenly appeared from beneath some piled-up branches and dark-colored tarpaulins and began splitting the air with a murderous hail of bullets that took out a clutch of Rangers who'd been hunkered beneath a rock outcropping.

"Hell with this," Zach said. "I'm gonna frag 'em."

As so often happened when adrenaline was surging, time slowed to frame-by-frame moments.

While the Marine and Quinn continued to blast away at the bunker, Zach fired a fragmentation grenade that hit the trap, bounced back into a deep drift of snow, and exploded without doing any damage.

He fired another that flew through the branches of the remaining tree beside the bunker and, again, detonated harmlessly.

Okay. He had three left.

After the third went wide, he loaded a fourth, aimed at the machine gun's muzzle flash, then pulled the trigger.

The grenade hit the snow right below the muzzle. And, dammit all to hell, didn't go off.

"This isn't working," he told Quinn.

"And your first clue was?" Quinn asked as he blasted off another round.

Hot brass from the spent cartridges was flying wildly around in the air. One of them hit Zach in the face and burned his cheek even through the insulated balaclava he was wearing.

Fun?

He didn't think so.

While SEALs might be more loosey-goosey when it came to the chain of command than other units, with the LT dead, Zach was officially in charge of whatever mission he could manage to cobble together here.

As things stood, they were sitting ducks.

The helo hadn't blown yet, but it would, which would probably take out whatever Rangers and Marines hunkered beneath it.

Meanwhile, hands and arms kept reaching up and shooting without aiming, pointing guns and hoping for the best. Depending on how much ammo the enemy in the bunker had—and Zach suspected it was a lot—they could keep shooting all day.

He knew a lot of guys thought of the enemy as nothing but a bunch of insane religious fanatic goatherders, but having aced a training course in the military and geopolitical history of this region, Zach knew better.

These were the same people—well, not the actual individuals but countrymen with the same ambitions—who'd beaten the British army's butts in the eighteen hundreds, fought for and won their independence in the early nineteen hundreds, and after years of brutal warfare, sent the Russians packing in the late part of the last century.

They were tough, ruthless, and driven.

And today they were trying to kill not just him but the members of his team.

Which meant they had to go.

Now.

The only possible answer was an assault on the bunker.

It was risky, but unless they did something soon, no one was going to get off this mountain.

And meanwhile, the snow around Shane's leg was beginning to look like a frozen strawberry margarita.

"Okay, this is what we're going to do," Zach announced. "See that ledge over there?" he asked Quinn, pointing toward an outcropping of rock behind and about five feet above the bunker.

"Yeah."

"We're going to give you cover, while you go around and climb up on it. Then you're going to fire point-blank down on those sons of bitches."

Quinn's teeth flashed a feral smile in the mouth opening of the black balaclava. "Roger that, Chief."

Without hesitation, he began rolling across the snow while Zach, Shane, and Opie opened fire.

As the machine gun kept blasting away, more guys

popped up, playing cat-and-mouse, with those damn AK-47s the Russians had left behind. The red tracers hitting all around the six-foot-five-inch SEAL looked like an outbreak of measles on the white snow.

"Damn," the Marine said admiringly as he risked a glance at Quinn while continuing to blast away. "That is one crazy dude."

"That's a no-shitter."

But weren't they all at least partly nuts? Because when you came right down to it, what sane person would join a circus where you were guaranteed to always be cold, wet, hungry, and exhausted, and where, if you screwed up, you and/or the guys around you could get turned into pink vapor?

And that was on a good day.

The other Marines and Rangers, hunkered together around the downed bird, figured out what was going on and began throwing grenades and firing at the bunker, all the guns sounding like gigantic plastic packing bubbles popping as snow flew and more trees splintered.

Damned if Quinn hadn't made it.

Zach watched as the sniper scaled the rocks, stood up on the ledge like John Fucking Wayne, and began blasting away.

It could have been seconds. Minutes. Hell, hours for all Zach knew, but finally the sniper lifted his weapon and stopped shooting.

Hundreds of spent brass rounds and empty magazines littered the once pristine snow.

And suddenly the mountainside went as blessedly still as a church on Monday morning.

"Shit!" A scream shattered the silence. "I'm hit."

Sabrina was back on the island of Lido—a quaint, seven-mile strip of land separating the Venetian lagoon from the Adriatic Sea. Going European, which was something she'd never before had the nerve to do, she was clad solely in a skimpy thong bikini bottom, soaking up the golden rays of the sun while a movie-star-sexy carpenter rubbed sunblock all over her body.

She sighed as his wickedly clever hands, roughened from swinging a heavy hammer all day, stroked their way across her shoulders, down her back, over her bared bottom, along the inside of her thighs, spreading oil and sensual warmth everywhere he touched.

When he turned her in his arms, a lock of dark hair fell across his mahogany forehead. As Sabrina reached up to brush it away, she drank in the tropical scent of coconuts, heard the ebb and flow of the tide, the soft sigh of the salt-tinged breeze, the sudden shout that jerked her from sleep.

Disoriented and afraid, she leaped out of bed and rushed for the light switch by the bedroom door, her heart hammering so hard and so fast she feared that if the Swann Island Slasher didn't kill her, a heart attack might.

The light from the white cottage-style chandelier overhead revealed Zach, sitting bolt upright in the canopied bed that she hadn't yet gotten around to replacing.

"Zach?" She returned to the bed and touched his shoulder.

He was soaking wet. And shaking. His eyes were wide open, but she knew that he was not seeing the ballet-slipper-pink walls or the teenage memorabilia she'd been too busy to put away.

"It's okay." The mattress sighed as she sat down beside him and put an arm around his stiff body while brushing his damp hair back from his forehead with her free hand. "You're here. With me. On Swann Island."

His skin was so cold. And as rapidly as her own heart was beating, his, which she could feel against her breasts, was pounding at least three times as fast.

"Sabrina?"

His eyes focused slowly. As she stroked his back with a soothing touch, she watched him gradually return from whatever horrific place he'd been. Back to Swannsea.

And her.

"Hell." He dragged an unsteady hand through the hair she'd smoothed. "I'm sorry. I must've scared you to death."

"It was quite a wake-up call," she admitted, skimming a finger over his tight, frowning lips. "For a minute I thought maybe the Slasher—never mind, you don't need to hear about that. I'm more concerned about you."

He jerked a shoulder. "I'm fine."

Her heart wrung with sympathy. Sabrina suspected he was embarrassed. In his manly world of poker, pickups, and guns—big ones that shot nails *and* bullets—the guy was supposed to be the strong one.

He was not supposed to be the one screaming with night terrors.

"No, you're not fine at all."

She wanted to press his head against her breast, to comfort him, to protect him from whatever ghosts still haunted his sleep.

But understanding that that wasn't what he needed, Sabrina forced herself to back away and play the scene cool.

"News flash, Tremayne," she said, leaving the bed again to pull her robe from the closet. "If you think I'm one of those Southern belles given to vapors, who expects a man to leap tall buildings in a single bound for me, you're mistaken."

"Damn," he countered, his voice edged with an encouraging touch of the dry humor she'd come to expect from him. "And here I thought all females were suckers for Superman."

"None of the ones I know. In the first place, the outfit is ridiculous." She slipped into the robe and belted it. "And the romantic concept was clearly created by a man because there's not a woman on the face of the earth who wouldn't immediately figure out that Clark Kent is really the guy with the big red *S* on his chest that she keeps mooning over.

"But the real reason he doesn't do a thing for me—though I have to admit Christopher Reeve made me willing to reconsider my position, at least while I was in the theater—is that I've always preferred Batman."

"A guy living in a cave turns you on?"

"Well, given the choice, I'd prefer to spend my time upstairs in Wayne Mansion. But my point is that beneath that bazillionaire male charm Bruce Wayne shows to the world, Batman's edgier. Darker. But with more vulnerabilities that make him more human. More appealing."

"And that's how you see me?"

"Absolutely." She glanced at the clock on the bedside table. "It's hours before breakfast and I'm hungry. Are you up for some tea and some of those mint brownies Titania left behind?"

"You do realize that SEALs are taught not to fall for the old trick of enemy interrogators using food as a ploy?"

"I'd never heard of that before, but it makes sense. You do realize that I'm not the enemy, don't you?"

"Yeah. That's one thing I'm sure about these days."

She beamed. Inside and out. "Exactly what you're supposed to say." Although it wasn't easy, Sabrina was determined to play this light. Not to protect her own heart, but his. "See, there's that charm I was talking about."

She held out a hand. "Come downstairs with me."

She'd learned from experience that it often helped to leave the nightmares behind in bed. "And if you want to talk about it, fine. If you don't, that's fine, too."

Bending down, she touched her mouth to his and felt him giving in as she nibbled and nipped at his firm lips.

"You realize, of course," he said as he slipped a hand down the front of her robe and cupped a breast, "that we're also trained to resist sexual come-ons from beautifully seductive females."

"And, gracious, you're doing so well with that, too. You must have been valedictorian of your BUD/S class."

She was pleased when he laughed.

"You're good for me," he said.

"Ditto," she said back. It was true. "So let's go have some tea and conversation. And then, sailor," she said, "if you play your cards right, you're going to get very, very lucky."

He removed his hand from the robe.

The laughter faded from his eyes, replaced by a seriousness that despite some already heavy discussions over the seven—make that almost eight—days they'd been together, she'd not yet witnessed from him.

"I already am."

51

He turned down the chamomile that she offered for its soothing properties, claiming he'd rather eat the bark off the tulip tree outside the window. But although Sabrina suspected that he would prefer something stronger, he accepted the more robust Irish breakfast tea.

She'd believed him when he'd told her that he didn't have a problem with alcohol, but nevertheless she admired his self-control in not giving in to the temptation to have a drink because he needed one.

Because he seemed to be feeling closed in, despite the spaciousness of the house, she immediately agreed when he suggested going outside.

Which was how they came to be sitting on the same swing where she'd told him her bombing story only a few nights ago. Strangely, once she'd shared the terror, it had seemed to diminish.

She suspected that the memories of the event, and the effect it had on her, would never entirely go away. But at least she was beginning to move on, and her thoughts—and dreams—were filled more with hope and positive visions than with bad.

He told her about his concerns regarding the logistics of the mission from the beginning. About the crash, which sounded horrific, and all the good and brave men who'd been ambushed, gunned down as they'd run off the helicopter.

He went on to tell her about his close friend, Shane Garrett, who, despite being wounded, had still managed to land the helicopter in a way that gave them at least a chance for survival.

Sabrina suspected that Zach was giving her the abbreviated, highly censored, PG-13 version of the subsequent battle, which was just as well, since although she wanted to be strong for him, she wasn't certain how much detail she could handle.

"There was this Marine," he said. "He was maybe eighteen, nineteen, tops. I thought of him as Opie, because he reminded me of that kid on the *Andy Griffith Show*."

"Ron Howard."

"Yeah. He was short and skinny with a face covered with freckles. He was also one helluva shot."

"You said 'was.' "

"Yeah." He dragged a hand down his face. "It was almost over. We'd taken the tangos out, and I was starting to breathe again when the kid began screaming. He must've stood up to fire sometime during the battle, because he'd gotten hit below his chest plate. In the pelvis.

"Which is one of the worst places you can get shot, because the aorta splits low in the abdomen, forming left and right arteries, which branch into the exterior and deep femoral vessels, which are the primary arteries for blood to the lower half of the body."

"I didn't know that."

He shrugged. "Neither did I. Not the precise medical details, anyway. We all have first-aid training and can field-dress our own wounds if necessary, but I learned a helluva lot more than I wanted to that day.

"Lucas Chaffee, he was our team medic, got some IVs going and was literally squeezing the bag with both hands to push the replacement fluid into him.

"He must've gone through six bags, but the blood kept spurting. By now the kid had figured out he had an arterial bleed, but instead of screaming bloody hell like most guys would be doing, he stayed amazingly calm."

"Maybe he was in shock," she suggested, remembering how, when she'd been pulled from the rubble and had seen all the chaos around her, it had seemed strangely as if she'd been watching a movie. As if none of it was real.

"That's what I thought, too. Meanwhile, Lucas is going nuts, because it's like trying to turn off a fire hose and he knows that the only way he's going to save this kid is to clamp off the artery. Which means going into the wound."

"With his hands?" A chill ran up her spine.

"Yeah. It had to have hurt like hell, because Lucas couldn't give him any morphine, because of the altitude and the fact that he'd lost so much blood his pressure was too low. Morphine could've killed him.

"Anyway, Shane and Quinn and I held the kid down and took turns pressing on his abdomen, to keep pressure over the artery while Lucas started spelunking through all this skin and fat—not that there was much of that, because the kid, along with being skinny, was in great shape—and muscle, but it must've retracted into his abdomen, because he couldn't find it."

"Oh, God."

Sabrina pressed one hand over her mouth, the other against her own stomach, which clenched at the thought of what they were all going through. She'd seen war movies; had even managed to sit through *Saving Private Ryan*, but this was so very different.

"I called in for an evac helo, but command was firm about not flying in the daylight."

"But you said it was barely dawn."

"Yeah. But the military lives by the rules of combat engagement, and on this mission, the rules stated that no planes flew within thirty minutes of sunrise. So, putting another bird down before nightfall was out of the question, because as far as they were concerned, the LZ was still hot, so they couldn't risk having another helicopter shot down."

"That's horrible!"

"That's combat," he said mildly. "And they were probably right, because we were getting some intel from the fixed wings heading back to base from high-altitude bombing runs that they were seeing a lot of guys who didn't look like friendlies headed down the mountain our way.

"The commander did tell me to keep him apprised of the situation, though. And that they'd be there as soon as they could."

Sabrina's curse was rich and ripe and caused Zach's lips to curve up, just a bit, at the corners.

"The only thing left to do was to cut into the abdomen and hunt down the artery and clamp it. But the kid was going into shock and every time Lucas dug around for it, he lost more blood, so there wasn't any way he could survive being opened up without a transfusion."

"On the battlefield? Can that be done?"

"Sure. If you do a direct, person-to-person transfusion. It's risky, because it's only done as a last resort, which means the recipient is already in a world of hurt, but if you've got a match, sometimes you've got to go for it."

"And he found a match?"

"Yeah."

From the way he jerked a shoulder, Sabrina guessed exactly who that match had been. "It was you, wasn't it?"

He shrugged again. "I'm type O. Which makes me a universal donor."

Stunned beyond words, she could only shake her head at the risk Zach had taken.

"He would've done the same thing for me," Zach said, giving her a much clearer idea of that fighting-for-the-men-in-the-foxholes-on-either-side-of-you concept. "Any guy in that bunker would've.

"Lucas decided to risk giving him some of the morphine, and he managed to find the artery and clamp it off. But even with the transfusion, the kid had lost so much blood, his survival chances still didn't look all that hot.

"Quinn went around and took ponchos off some of the troops we'd lost because they didn't need them anymore and this Marine did.

"By then the wind was blowing pretty hard, and since we didn't want to risk taking him back into the helo, we decided to move him into the bunker."

Sabrina was starting to get the picture that *we* meant Zach.

"We took Shane, too, because although he'd fought like hell during the gun battle, he wasn't looking too good, either. Lucas had shoved some Curlex, that's a kind of bandage, into his leg to stop the bleeding, but it was obvious that if we didn't get him on a surgical table pretty soon, he wasn't going to make it out of those mountains alive."

He blew out a harsh breath. Tossed back the now cool tea he hadn't yet touched and put the empty cup down on the table next to the swing.

"There's some wine left from dinner," she said, changing her mind about offering him alcohol. Hell, she could use a drink right about now.

"Maybe later. I'm almost done."

He rubbed the back of his neck.

"So, we got them into the bunker and covered them up with insulation from the helo, and the ponchos, and some pine boughs the surviving Marines gathered from all the trees that had been shot up.

"The kid knew he was going to die. Oh, we told him he'd be okay, but everyone in that damn bunker knew it was a lie, so we all sat there and listened while he told us about his mother, who'd died of ovarian cancer when he was nine, so he'd had to go live with his grandmother in Kentucky, because his daddy was a Marine, and he couldn't very well be on active duty if he had to stay home and be a single father to Opie.

"You could tell he was proud of his dad, who was a gunnery sergeant deployed in Iraq. That's why he became a Marine. To follow in his father's boot steps."

"Something I suspect you could identify with," Sabrina said softly.

"Yeah. Totally . . .

"Anyway, I don't know how long he talked, but he told us all about this girl he had back home in Salt Lick, Kentucky, which is where his family was from and where his granny still lived. She—the girl, not his grandmother—was going to beauty school to be a hairdresser, because she figured she'd be able to get work fixing hair wherever he got posted after they got married.

"They were going to have two kids. And a pair of bluetick hounds, because his granddaddy had raised them, and he figured his boys could go hunting with them, same as he had growing up."

"And if he'd had daughters?"

"Shane asked him about that." He managed another of those faint half smiles at the memory. "He's from out west," he revealed. "Where folks are more likely to speak their mind. At least he sure as hell always has.

"Anyway, the kid seemed surprised by that idea. Then he said that if he had girls, he'd have to lock them in a closet as soon as they went into puberty and keep them away from boys until they were thirty.

"Or maybe, he said, he'd switch over to the Catholics, so he could lock them away in some convent. We all had ourselves a good laugh about that."

He sighed. "It was kind of cool for a few minutes; sort of like sitting around the barracks, or even back in school, shooting the bull. Made the war outside seem like something that was happening to someone else, if that makes any sense."

"I think it was nice you had that time," Sabrina said. "That you gave him that time. Since I'm getting the distinct impression he didn't make it home alive?"

"No. We'd finished laughing about the convent thing, and the idea of a born-again Pentecostal converting to Catholicism, like that was going to happen in this lifetime, just to keep his babies away from horny Marines and SEALs like us, when out of the goddamn blue he asked us to pray with him."

Zach leaned his head against the back of the swing and closed his eyes. "Of course there wasn't a guy in that bunker who was going to refuse what we all knew was a last request.

"So Shane, who was an altar boy when he was a kid and knows that sort of Bible stuff, recited the Twenty-third Psalm, the one about not fearing walking through the shadow of death?"

"I know it." Sabrina's eyes filled.

"Well, he seemed to like that. Then we all said the Lord's Prayer together. And because I guess he could tell a lot of us were about to lose it at that point, he assured us that we didn't have to worry about him, because he'd been brought up to love God.

"Which was when Shane told him that God loved him, too . . .

"And that was that. He sort of smiled, and was gone."

He shook his head and, as if he couldn't hold the stress in anymore, got up, walked over to the end of the veranda and put his hands on the railing and stared out over the swamp.

As she wiped the moisture off her cheeks, Sabrina wondered what he was seeing.

The rain had stopped; a light breeze ruffled the palmetto fronds.

"It was weird. Outside there were Rangers and Marines lying all over the ground. Dead as Marley's damn ghost. You'd think that would've been worse, because of the sheer numbers—"

"But this was personal," she said quietly. "Because you connected emotionally. Which had to be more difficult. More painful."

"Yeah." He plowed his hands through his hair. "There was this show that spun off from *The Andy Griffith Show*, that used to play on Nick at Nite, where Gomer Pyle goes off and becomes a Marine.

"Well, in one episode Opie got mad at Andy after he'd gotten a licking for doing something, I can't remember what, but he ran away to Camp Pendleton to join the Marines, too.

"Of course Andy, who was fit to be tied, came out to California and fetched him back home to Mayberry. I remember thinking that it was too bad this Opie's dad hadn't taken him back to Kentucky when he announced he wanted to run off and become a jarhead."

"He wasn't a child. Well, perhaps he was still a teenager," she allowed at his sharp look. "But he was proud of his father, who was undoubtedly proud of him. And I'll bet he was proud of being a Marine."

"Well, of course he was." Zach glanced back over his shoulder at her, sounding surprised she'd even have to ask.

"Well, then."

"His name turned out to be Richie. Richie Cunningham, which I thought was goddamn ironic, being how that's the name of the kid Howard went on to play on *Happy Days* after all those years being Opie."

She stood up and went over to him. When he turned around, she took his hands in hers, uncurled the tight fists and lifted them to brush soft kisses against his knuckles.

"As tragic as his death is, at least, thanks to you and the others, he didn't die without comfort."

"I hadn't thought of it that way."

"Well, you should. What about the pilot?" she dared ask, dreading the answer. "Shane?"

When a shadow moved across Zach's eyes, she remembered what he'd said about those bomber pilots reporting the enemy moving down the mountain toward them and braced herself for another personalized tale of tragedy.

"He's back in Washington," he answered after a pause. "In D.C., not the state. In fact, Quinn talked to him last week. He's thinking of taking a teaching job at ASMA."

He'd told her, during the early part of the story, about how he'd dropped out of the military academy after his father's accident.

He'd also told her about Quinn McKade's book, which she'd decided she was going to put on tomorrow's shopping list. Military novels weren't her usual choice in reading. In fact, she'd never read one in her life. Had never intended to.

But she wanted to read Quinn's because she hoped it would give her more insight into Zach.

"That would be nice. For the three of you to be living near each other again."

"Yeah. I guess."

There was something else there. Something he wasn't telling her.

Another story, Sabrina thought. For another day.

Hadn't they relived enough sorrow for one evening?

Zach would continue to grieve. As would she.

In their own fashion and individual time. Overcoming a deep personal loss wasn't anything that could be rushed.

Meanwhile, she realized, sometimes a woman had to be the strong one.

Leaning her head against his shoulder, Sabrina breathed in the scent of soap and warm skin and was engulfed with tenderness. Along with the need to soothe the rawness she sensed was still aching so painfully inside him.

She lifted her palms, framing his face. His beautiful, tortured face.

"Come with me," she murmured. "I want to take you somewhere."

He covered her hands with his. "Where?"

She smiled as she kissed him lightly. With sweetness. And promise.

"Somewhere wonderful."

52

Sabrina took him up the *Gone with the Wind* staircase Lucie had always talked about her someday walking down as a bride.

Undressed him with a tenderness born of the love she could no longer deny. At least to herself.

She eased him down on the bed. Then, after lighting a fat beeswax candle, she slipped out of the robe, lay down beside him, and skimmed kisses—soft as feathers, warm as a summer sun—over his face.

His jaw.

His brow.

Down his throat.

Across his broad, knotted shoulders, which had carried more burdens than any man she'd ever known.

His chest.

Her hands followed the gentle trail her lips had blazed, stroking, comforting, soothing his tension away. Banishing the shadows, if only for this shimmering, suspended time.

Yesterday spun away, the future was light-years from now.

There was only the present.

Only Zach.

When he reached for her, she shifted away, not to tease but to give her time, to give them *both* time, to banish whatever ghosts and demons were haunting him.

It had begun to rain. She could hear the patter of it

on the terrace outside the French doors of the bedroom. Fog drifted in from the sea, and rose from the marsh, swathing Swannsea in a gauzy white blanket that clung to the windows and added to the intimacy.

She glided her palms up taut, muscled thighs, drawing a rough sound from deep in his throat. When she skimmed her tongue against a raised white appendectomy scar, he shuddered.

But still, even as he surrendered to her soft seduction, she could feel his steely control beneath the surface. He never entirely let it go, Sabrina realized. It was as much a part of him as that sexy cleft in his broad chin, his remarkable bluish-gray kaleidoscopic eyes, his wavy dark hair that instinctively drew a woman's fingers to it.

"Do you know what you do to me when you touch me like that?" he groaned as she dipped the tip of her tongue into his navel.

"No." Her fingernail stroked the hot flesh right above dark curls and beneath the scar. She may have relaxed him a bit, but that didn't stop him from being fully, magnificently aroused. "Tell me."

Expecting something along the lines of she made him so hot he was going to explode, or he wanted to fuck her brains out, his next words caught Sabrina totally off guard.

"You make me feel as if you've lit a lamp inside me." He brushed her long slide of hair over her shoulder, his hand now steady and sure. "As if, so long as you're by my side, I'll never be in the dark again."

Sabrina's hands paused. Tears sprang to her eyes; her breath hitched. A lump rose in her throat, blocking any words, even if she had known how to respond to such a profound statement. Which she didn't.

"Damn." His eyes, swirling with myriad emotions, met hers. And held. "There I go. Making you cry again."

"It's okay," she said on an unsteady laugh. "They're good tears."

She sniffled, lowered her cheek to his chest, and realized that their hearts, like their minds, were, at this moment, in perfect harmony. "That's the most amazing thing anyone's ever said to me."

"Then I'm glad I said it." He took her in his arms and rolled over onto his side, facing her, settling her so her leg was over his. "Because I've never felt as amazing as I feel with you."

He slid into her, a smooth, silky glide, as if they'd been created solely, perfectly, for one another.

The shared climax rose, slowly, a long, lingering swell.

And as the candle burned down and the soft Southern rain continued to fall, with arms and legs entwined, they rode the wave together.

He was going to have to kill her. He'd known that from the beginning, of course. All of them eventually had to die. Not only because they became more high-maintenance as they weakened but because he possessed a low boredom threshold. Once a slave was broken, her fear, which he'd always found so exciting, was replaced by her weary acceptance of her fate.

And what fun was that?

He'd always preferred to have two, or even three, slaves at a time. Once, he'd been up to half a dozen, which had proven a mistake, as they'd gotten together and attempted a rebellion. Which, of course, he'd immediately quashed, and the mutinous bitches had paid for their behavior.

In the end, each had begged him to put her out of her misery.

He'd killed five of them, one at a time, forcing the others to watch.

But he'd left one alive to warn the new acquisitions.

That experience had taught him not to be greedy. After all, two was a more manageable number. It also ensured that his needs were well satisfied, which kept him from behaving impulsively, the way he had with that damn ER nurse.

Killing Cleo Gibson at her house, in broad daylight, had been a risk. Which, at the time, had admittedly added to the rush. But it was also unreasonably dangerous.

Unfortunately, he'd allowed himself to get sidetracked by other life issues. But the obvious solution was to acquire additional property before he rid himself of the whiny, weepy Mannington bitch.

Better yet, he could force his new slave to kill his current one. Wouldn't that be fun?

As he lay there in the dark and began making plans, erotic images of the two naked female slaves fighting to the death sent blood flooding from his brain to pool hotly in his groin.

53

The day burned bright and sunny and filled with promise. As she sat across the table from Zach in the breakfast nook, Sabrina felt as lighthearted as if she'd swallowed a tankful of helium. In fact, she wouldn't have been at all surprised if she suddenly went floating up into the bright blue sky.

"You realize," he said, as he held out a bright red strawberry, "this is the first time you haven't kicked me out of your bed in the middle of the night."

"Hmm." Her teeth closed around the berry, taking it from his hand. She'd been eating strawberries all her life; she'd even spent many hours of her childhood picking them in Lucie's kitchen garden. But never had she appreciated what an aphrodisiac they could be. "Perhaps that's because I was otherwise occupied."

The hazel ring around his eyes gleamed like the morning sun. "You and me both, sugar."

He glanced out the window at the trucks that were beginning to arrive onsite. "You do realize that people will talk?"

"They're already talking."

She scooped some whipped cream from the bowl in the center of the table, held out her finger and felt the vibrations through her entire body as he sucked it off.

"Might as well give them something to talk about," Sabrina said, uncurling her toes. She sighed. "I suppose we'd better get to work."

"Or, I could declare a holiday, give everyone the day off, and we could go out in my boat."

"You have a boat?"

"A cruiser I brought from San Diego. I usually use it for fishing, but we could go down to Key West, drink some margaritas, make mad passionate love, and see if I can make you scream again."

"I did not scream." She felt the color rise in her cheeks.

"Well, not technically," he said, as he took his mug and bowl and put them in the dishwasher. "It was more of a long, ragged wail. And you called out my name. At least three, maybe four times."

"I seem to recall you shouting *my* name a lot louder."

Heaven help her, she was even feeling sappy putting her cup next to his in the dishwasher rack. It almost made them seem like . . . well, a couple.

"Got me on that one," he said with a quick, easy grin. "So, what do you say?" He looped the dish towel around her neck and pulled her close for a quick kiss. "Run away to Margaritaville? Or be grown-ups and go to work?"

There'd been a time, only a few weeks go, when that would have been a no-brainer. But that was before she'd returned to the island.

Before Zach Tremayne had captured her heart.

"If we don't stay on schedule, we'll end up owing Swann Island Bank and Trust a hefty late penalty. And why do I think Jeremy Macon would love any opportunity to foreclose?"

"And wow, just happen to sell to Sumner?" he asked.

"Great minds." She skimmed a fingernail along his jaw. "I suppose it wouldn't hurt to take a short lunch break later."

"Gotta keep our stamina up," he agreed.

"Absolutely." She laughed, nipping playfully at his lips while the driver whose skills she'd admired backed his bulldozer off the trailer.

Although Zach's invitation to escape to Florida had been so, so tempting, it was time to get back to business.

Richard "Gunney" Cunningham, Sr., watched as they came out of the house together. Although they weren't touching, it was obvious they'd spent the night fucking.

Something Richie was never going to experience again.

Why should Zachariah Tremayne, whose fault it was that clusterfuck on the Kush had gone so fatally wrong, be alive?

While his only son, who, dammit, had been continuing an honorable family tradition, was lying dead in the cold dark ground beneath a white cross in Arlington Cemetery.

From that memorable November day in 1775, when John Jacob Cunningham had gotten together at the Tun Tavern in Philadelphia with a group of other patriots with long rifles and humongous balls to form the Marine Corps, Cunningham males had fought in "every clime and place" from the shores of Tripoli to the halls of Montezuma, to Khe Sanh to Beirut, finally ending up in Baghdad and Afghanistan.

John Jacob had been killed in an assault at Fort George on Penobscot Bay, Maine, in 1779. His son, Samuel, had helped defend Washington in the Battle of Bladensburg in 1814, and *his* twin sons—Jeremiah and Daniel—had fought in the Second Seminole War and waded ashore with the army in Veracruz, Mexico.

He himself had spent six long, unforgettable months in the Saigon Hilton before a deal had been cut with Hanoi to release POWs.

Whenever America needed a U.S. Marine, anywhere in the world, a Cunningham male had always been there to answer the call.

"The Marines have landed and have the situation well in hand" was not a cliché in his family. It was a Cunningham fact of life.

And now, thanks to that fucking SEAL, their long, proud line had come to a screeching halt.

Richie would never get to spend some hot summer night in a pretty girl's arms.

He'd never get married, never have those sons he'd always talked about. Boys who, since they'd never be born, would never get to go squirrel and possum hunting with their dogs, the way Richie had always loved to do.

He'd been Deadeye Dick with a rifle, which was how he got picked, his first day at boot camp, to be the deadliest weapon on earth: a Marine and his rifle.

Those overrated navy frogmen only went back to WW Two. While the Marines were fucking older than the U.S. of A.

"In a face-off, there's no contest," Gunney muttered to himself as he started up the big yellow Cat. Tremayne may be younger, but hell, he was a Marine.

Want to win your war?
Tell it to the Marines!
Oo-rah!

So intent was he on planning what, exactly, he was going to say to Tremayne, *do* to him, before he killed him, that at first he didn't notice the commotion.

It was only when one of the Mexicans, who'd been wheeling away the excess dirt, jumped up onto the bulldozer, grabbed hold of the cage and shouted in Spanish for him to stop, that Gunney finally noticed the skeleton his bulldozer blade had uncovered.

54

Standing outside the yellow crime scene tape that had been used to cordon off the excavation, Sabrina, with Zach's arm around her shoulder, watched in stunned disbelief as a crew that Nate had called in from the state law enforcement division to assist with the investigation combed the site with metal detectors and sifted soil within grid areas created by staking out string in twelve-inch squares.

"Surely it's not part of the recent murders," she said to no one in particular.

"I'm no forensic techie, but the bones look old," Special Agent Caitlin Cavanaugh commented.

Although at this point the FBI didn't have any jurisdiction here, the agent said she'd been intrigued enough to drop by after Nate had also called her.

Or maybe, Sabrina mused, the lanky redhead was more interested in the sheriff than in his crime scene.

Wouldn't Titania love that?

"See how the skull's downhill from the rest of the body?" the agent pointed out, as casually as if she dealt with dead people every day.

Which, Sabrina realized, she might.

"The garden was built on an incline, and since the skull's usually the first part to become separated from the rest of the body, because all the orifices provide such an attractive location for maggot activity—"

A faint, ragged moan flew out of Sabrina's mouth before she could call it back. She pressed an arm against her stomach, which had pitched at the gory images those words had conjured up.

"Perhaps you should go inside and sit down, Sabrina, dear," Harlan, who'd been called to the scene in his capacity as medical examiner, said solicitously. "You're looking a little pale."

She was sick to death of hearing that.

"I'm fine," she snapped, more sharply than she'd intended, knowing from the way his face fell that he'd only been concerned for her. Both as a family member and as her doctor.

She placed a hand on his sleeve. "Really."

"Sorry," Caitlin Cavanaugh said with a grimace. "I get so fascinated by this stuff, I tend to forget I'm talking to civilians."

"No problem," Sabrina said. "Really," she insisted yet again as she felt Zach looking down at her with the same concern Harlan had displayed. She lifted her chin and instructed her mutinous stomach to stay put. "You were saying?"

While decaying bodies might be at the bottom of her list of conversational topics, they were still preferable to discussing the post-bombing state of her health.

The agent gave her a probing look, then shrugged.

"Well, anyway," she continued, "a lot of times something about teeth that come out postmortem will help us learn the identity of the person. Maybe a filling, a crown, that sort of thing.

"When the skull's several feet away, as it happens to be in this case, teeth will usually be found somewhere between the skull and the body."

She glanced over at Sabrina again. "Are you sure you wouldn't like to go inside, Ms. Swann?"

"I'm fine."

Swannsea was her home. Her legacy. Which meant that this situation, as unsavory as it was, was her responsibility.

"Sheriff Spencer said you don't have any idea who it could be?"

"No idea at all." Sabrina shook her head. "There's been a private cemetery on the grounds of Swannsea for more than a century. Since shortly after the Civil War. There'd be no reason for any family member to be buried in my grandmother's garden."

"Maybe it wasn't a family member," the agent suggested. "Maybe it happened during the war. Perhaps some Union soldier came by to do a little looting and plundering, faced a bit of local opposition, and didn't make it back across the Mason-Dixon Line alive."

"That's a bit of a stretch, isn't it, Cait?" Zach suggested mildly. "Maybe you ought to get together with Quinn and collaborate on a thriller."

She snorted. "Wouldn't that be something?" she scoffed. "Then the police would be investigating a new homicide, since there's no way McKade and I could be in the same room for ten minutes without one of us killing the other."

"Not to hear him tell it," Nate murmured as one of the techs put a bit of soil into a screw-top plastic bottle.

"What?" Cait Cavanaugh's head spun toward him.

Sabrina wasn't quite sure how Zach knew the former Somersett homicide detective turned FBI special agent, but when he'd introduced her as an old friend, she'd gotten the impression that there was definitely some personal history there.

When something alien stirred, something she reluctantly recognized as jealousy, Sabrina tamped it back down.

If there'd been anything important between them, he would tell her. And if Caitlin Cavanaugh and Zach *had* had a romantic relationship, it was in the past.

Bygones.

"It wasn't any big deal." Zach jumped in to help Nate, who was looking as if he wished he'd kept his big mouth shut. "We were playing cards the other night and Nate mentioned having talked to you about his serial killer. Which was when Quinn casually said something about having dated your roommate."

"That was a long time ago," Caitlin said briskly, effectively slamming the door on that topic of conversation.

She frowned and folded her arms across the front of her charcoal suit that had to be uncomfortably hot, even though it was summer weight. But Sabrina didn't think heat had anything to do with the color staining those chiseled cheekbones.

"If any teeth would be found between the body and the, uh, skull"—Sabrina had trouble saying the word out loud—"why are they sifting dirt from all over the site?"

"Because you never know what a killer will drop," Nate said, showing he'd done his homework. "A cigarette butt, maybe even a receipt showing a date and time, anything that could prove helpful in apprehending him."

"If the bad guys weren't stupid, we'd never catch them," Caitlin agreed. "We tend to use the same basic principles and procedures that archaeologists do when they come across the ruins of some ancient civilization, or dinosaur bones. But because we don't have the same luxuries of time in law enforcement, we have to work faster. Which means also working smart.

"We studied a crime scene at the academy where the killer had knelt down beside his victim—who happened to be a twelve-year-old girl he'd nabbed on her way home from school—and ended up leaving an impression of his palm in the dirt.

"Well, it was red Georgia clay, which left enough of a readable ridge that we were able to track him down by his fingerprints."

"That's amazing." Harlan, apparently in medical examiner mode, was clearly impressed.

Sabrina, who'd never watched *CSI* or any of those other copycat forensic shows because they grossed her out, silently agreed.

"It is rare," the agent admitted.

She rocked back on her pumps, which, while a staid FBI black, were Bruno Maglis. Having always considered the Italian designer a shoe god, Sabrina decided that this made her and the special agent, at least in one respect, kindred spirits.

"But you never know," Caitlin Cavanaugh continued. "Which is why it's important to process it like any other crime scene. There's also the chance that stuff fell from the victim's pockets, or maybe there's some jewelry, something that will help identify him."

"Or her," Harlan said.

"Or her," the agent concurred.

As if on cue, one of the technicians sifting the soil shouted, "I've got something."

The captain in charge of the crime scene took the evidence in a gloved hand and carried it over to where the others were standing.

"Would you happen to recognize this, Ms. Swann?" he asked on a drawl that spoke of Piedmont roots.

"I'm afraid not."

It was a man's gold ring. Heavy yellow gold, with a framed crest she didn't recognize, three Greek letters engraved on one side of the crest, and a date—1958— on the other. Which, she thought, definitely disproved Caitlin Cavanaugh's imaginative murdered-Yankee-soldier hypothesis.

"I don't recall ever seeing it before."

Sabrina was trying to remember her Greek alphabet when Harlan gasped.

"Oh, my God!" he said. "It's Robert's."

"Robert?" the SLED captain asked.

Zach, whose expression rarely gave away his feelings, appeared as stunned as Sabrina felt. "Robert Swann?"

"My grandfather?"

It was impossible. The man who had deserted Lucie in the middle of the night to escape being prosecuted for a bank fraud might be dead.

He could have died in a car crash on a freeway somewhere in California, or keeled over from a heart attack while making love to some woman half his age in Las Vegas. Or even been eaten by a shark while surfing off the Australian coast.

But to have been murdered in cold blood?

And buried in Lucie's garden all these years?

The very thought was inconceivable.

Wasn't it?

"It's a Sigma Alpha Epsilon fraternity ring," Harlan said.

"Are you sure?" Caitlin asked.

"Of course," he said, regaining a bit of his physician's authoritative tone. "We were fraternity brothers at USC." He held out a visibly shaking hand. "I have the same ring."

It was, to Sabrina's eyes, identical. Same yellow gold, same crest, same initials.

"Okay," she said on a short, exhaled breath as white spots, like snowflakes, began swirling in front of her eyes. "I believe I'd like to sit down now."

55

Titania had been practicing her patience. If she was going to be in a relationship with a law enforcement officer—and it appeared she was—then she was going to have to become accustomed to his being called out at all hours of the day and night.

If she wanted a nine-to-fiver, she may as well sleep with a banker, like Jeremy Macon's son, Dennis, who for the past two years had been hitting on her every afternoon when she deposited the day's receipts.

It wasn't that Dennis was so terrible. Oh, he was a little dumpy, due to all the hours spent behind a desk, but he certainly wasn't obese, like his father. His sandy hair was beginning to thin at the temples, and his attempt to hide it with a comb-over definitely wasn't working.

But all in all, a girl could do worse. If she didn't mind spending the rest of her life bored senseless.

It might be showing her shallow side, but Titania liked the fact that Nate hadn't let himself go since leaving the Marines. That his body was as hard and ripped as it had been when he'd been one of the few. The proud.

And despite being antiwar on principle, she had to admit that that pistol he wore on his hip like some old-time gunslinger was flat-out sexy.

He was also intelligent, which was a plus, because while she was clever enough to know that looks faded, brains didn't (at least most times, anyway), and even if the sex was off the Richter scale—which with Nate it definitely was—if she couldn't talk to a man out of bed, well, she didn't want him *in* her bed in the first place.

She also had to admit that beneath that hottie Marine body and fitted khaki uniform was a genuinely sweet man. Which was why, although she wasn't about to tell him yet, she'd fallen in love with him.

But even loving him didn't mean that she was happy about him having left a message on her voice mail telling her that something had come up and he was probably going to have to cancel their movie date.

Hoping it wasn't yet another murder, she took a deep breath and braced herself as she entered Silver Shores Manor.

The first thing she noticed, other than that smell, which, heaven help her, she was getting used to, was that the TV was tuned to the news again.

Wondering how many times she had to tell the staff that murder and mayhem weren't beneficial to the residents' peace of mind, she was about to change the channel when she saw her hunk sheriff on the screen.

And even more surprising, Nate appeared to be standing in front of Swannsea.

Oh, please, God, she thought as she sank down into an empty vinyl chair beside her father's wheelchair, don't let anything have happened to Sabrina!

Nate was talking about a body being found. Blessedly, not a woman's body. One that appeared to have been buried a very long time ago.

Joshua Davis muttered something under his breath.

"What, Daddy?" she asked absently as Nate was explaining that SLED would be sending the bones to the crime lab and it could take time to get a positive identification.

"I said, it's Robert," he said in a stage whisper. "That bastard Robert Swann."

Her father had always been the sweetest, most gentle man she'd ever known in her life. She adored him to pieces, and he was why, she realized now, as she took his hand in hers and tried to unfold his fingers, which had tightened into a stiff claw, she'd responded to those same traits in Nate Spencer.

"Daddy," she soothed, "you can't possibly know that."

Though, given how Lucie's husband had mysteriously disappeared in the middle of the night, Titania supposed there was an outside possibility he'd guessed right.

Poor Sabrina! She must be beside herself.

"It's him," he said, with more authority in his tone than she'd heard in years. "I figured he'd surface one of these days."

He shook his head with what appeared to be very real regret. Looked out the window for a very long time.

"You have to understand, Mel," he said, once again calling her by her mother's name. "I did it for you."

"Did what, Daddy?"

He stared at her for a long time, making her think that she'd lost him again, even deeper into that labyrinth of what had once been a quick and clever mind. So clever that Lucie Swann, ignoring warnings about the potential perils of giving a black man so much control over her business holdings, had put him in charge of Swann Tea.

"I killed him, Mel." Those clawlike fingers squeezed hers until she feared he'd break them. "I killed that lowlife bastard, Robert Swann."

56

"Are you sure you're all right?" Zach asked.

"I'm fine," Sabrina assured him.

Or at least as fine as she could be, given that she still felt like she was in a state of shock.

She was standing at the bedroom window, looking down on the dug-up garden, trying to make sense of what had happened earlier. Fortunately, a three-alarm warehouse fire in Somersett had sent all the reporters who'd been hovering over Swannsea like vultures rushing back onto the ferry for the mainland.

"All these years," she murmured. "Everyone thought my grandfather had taken off. But he never left at all."

She wondered how long it would take to forget the sight of that headless skeleton of her grandfather. How about never?

"Apparently not." His turn to comfort, he came up behind her and wrapped his arms around her waist.

"Who do you think killed him?"

"I wouldn't venture a guess. But rumors at the time had him not the most faithful of husbands. And jealousy is always a motive."

"I remember talk about him and Patsy Buchanan," she allowed. "I didn't exactly understand it at the time, but later, well . . ."

She took a deep breath. Wished she could cry, but the time for tears was long past. "And she and her husband did get a divorce, and he left town not long after that."

"Six months." Zach knew because that was when he
and Patsy had had their little fling. "But he also pissed
off some investors with that real estate scam he tried to
pull off."

"Especially Jeremy Macon. You know, Macon tried
to talk me out of this project."

"He wasn't alone. Sumner was pressuring you to sell
to him. Harlan was lobbying against the plan at dinner.
Hell, even Linc told me he had reservations."

"Well, Harlan may not be wild about the idea, but he
and my grandfather were close friends. There was no
reason for him to kill him. Brad's my age, so he would've
been too young. And we can certainly take Linc off the
suspect list, since not only could he never kill anyone,
but he wouldn't have been old enough, either."

"He's four years older than I am. Which would've
made him twenty that summer. And anyone can kill.
With the right motive."

She turned in his arms and glanced up at him. "I
couldn't."

"Not even if you were a mother? To save the life of
your child if, say, he or she was kidnapped?"

"Well, of course, but—"

"I'm not saying it wouldn't be understandable." He
stroked her hair. "Or even justifiable. Just that everyone
operates under their own sense of situational morality."

Sabrina closed her eyes as she considered that idea
and decided it would be necessary for a soldier to view
life through such a dark prism. She also hoped she'd
never be put in a situation where she had to discover
her own personal capacity for taking a life.

"Well, it wasn't him."

"Of course it wasn't. I was just playing devil's
advocate."

"I can't see Macon having the nerve," she mused.

"Doesn't take a lot of nerve to hire someone to do
your dirty work for you."

"No." And wasn't that an ugly thought?

"There's another possibility," Zach said. "He could be one of the so-called slasher's victims."

Icy fingers of fear skittered up her spine. "Surely Nate's not seriously considering that?"

"He's not leaping to any conclusions. But he's not ruling it out, either."

"But that would mean that someone—who could live among us—has been killing people for over a decade."

"Apparently, according to some files Cait Cavanaugh dug up for Nate, there's evidence pointing toward that. Which is why he went on TV tonight and offered that twenty-thousand-dollar reward Harlan put up for any information leading to an arrest."

The chill that had skimmed up her spine spread through her veins, causing her to shiver.

"I need a shower." Not just to warm up but to wash the sense of murder away. At least for a little while. She reached for his hand. Held on tight. "Will you come with me?"

"Funny you should mention that, sugar." He lowered his head and claimed her mouth in a long, breath-stealing kiss. "Coming with you was exactly what I had in mind."

57

"He didn't do it."

"How do you know?"

"Because I know your father," Nate said patiently. "And I know what it takes to kill another human being. Joshua doesn't have it in him."

"You only know the frail, dying old man," Titania argued. Seemingly unable to remain still, she'd been pacing the floor for the last twenty minutes.

"I've known him as long as I've known you," he said. "Which, may I point out, is all my life. My mama took care of you while your father was at work at Swannsea. You and I took baths together, for Chrissakes."

"We were babies." Her high heels clattered an impatient staccato on the wood floor. Her skirt swirled around her legs as she made a swift, violent turn. "No more than toddlers."

"And even then I thought you were the most beautiful thing I'd ever seen. Even prettier than the angel on top of the Christmas tree."

"Don't you dare be calm when I'm not, Nate Spencer!" she shouted. "And don't patronize me."

"I wouldn't dare try." What he *would* dare was to step in front of her and put his hands on her shoulders. "My point, and I *do* have one, is that I've been part of your family, and you've been part of mine, all of our lives. I know your father as well as my own.

"Hell, I like him a whole lot better. And I know, with

every fiber of my being, that Joshua did not kill Robert Swann."

"He claimed Robert raped my mother. Back when she was a housemaid at Swannsea and he was outside working in the tea factory."

"For your mother's sake, I hope to hell that wasn't true."

"Do you think Robert Swann was capable of rape?"

"I've no idea. Unlike you, I never spent any time at the farm. I barely knew the guy."

"Whether he did or not, if my father believes it's true, that's a motive for murder."

She pulled away and began pacing again.

"Jesus, Mary, and Joseph!" Nate felt his hard-won patience beginning to unravel. "No one is looking at your father for motives or anything else. He's not even on the cops' radar screen." He caught her again. By her sexy, curvy hips this time. "So how about we keep it that way?"

"You're willing to compromise an investigation?" She arched a perfectly formed black brow. "For your lover?"

"No." He ran a hand down her hair. Cupped her cheek. "I'm willing to put up with wild, unsubstantiated conjecture about a murder case from the woman I love."

To Nate's horror, her dark chocolate eyes began to swim with moisture. "He believes I'm Robert's child. That he and my mother agreed to keep silent about how she got pregnant. That he'd raise me as his own—"

"Which he did," he reminded her.

"Which he did," she allowed. "And I'll always love him for it, and I'll always be grateful, but what if he's telling the truth about having killed Lucie's husband after my mother died giving birth to me? Can you imagine the grief he must have suffered when she died in childbirth? The anger he'd have felt if the child who'd killed her had been born of a rape by their employer?"

Tears were streaming down her face in silver ribbons.

"It would have been horrible." He brushed a tear

away with the pad of his thumb. "But first of all, you didn't kill your mother. Pregnancy's always a risk, and unfortunately, your mother was one of the unlucky ones. But even if any of the story of your paternity's true, Joshua wouldn't have—*couldn't* have—committed murder."

Her makeup, which she always applied with a clever artist's hand, had washed off her face. Her eyeliner and mascara had created raccoon circles around her eyes, and she'd not only chewed off all her lipstick but her teeth were worrying deep impressions into her lower lip.

And her hair, which he remembered his mother combing that foul-smelling straightener through before her first day of school, was a wild ebony corona around her head.

She looked like a madwoman in one of those operas she was always dragging him to in Charleston. At this moment, he would not have been at all surprised if she dropped to her knees on his living-room floor and began belting out an aria.

She was, when it came to business, one of the most practical people, male or female, he'd ever met.

When it came to the rest of her life, Titania had a tendency toward the overdramatic. It was one of the many things he loved about her and just one aspect of her considerable charm.

"Look. Here's the thing," he said, holding her gently and smoothing his hand up and down her back. "Maybe Robert Swann's your biological father. Maybe not. If that's an issue, it's easy enough to find out with a DNA test.

"Maybe your father fantasized about killing him back then. But I'll bet anything that's all it was. A fantasy. Maybe the damn idea got filed away back there in some dark, hidden corner of his brain, and now it's popped out. And he believes it's true the same way he believed, after watching *ET* last month, that aliens from outer space had landed in the Silver Shores parking lot.

"And," he said, pressing a kiss against her brow, "I

intend to prove that there's no way he could've killed Swann." He handed her a tissue from a box on the counter.

"How?" she asked, as she swiped at the tears, smearing the black streaks even more.

Because he could feel the tenseness easing out of her beneath his hands, Nate decided it would be safe to smile.

"Because I'm going to apprehend the real bad guy."

"That would do it." She sniffled. Then managed a small, wobbly, very un-Titanialike smile of her own. "You're so good to me, Nathaniel Spencer."

" 'Bout time you noticed!"

She was clearly shocked when he scooped her into his arms. "What do you think you're doing?" she demanded, in a way that assured him that she was already on her way to getting her Titania mojo back.

"I'm taking you to bed," he said. "Where I'm going to be very, very good to you."

He kicked open the bedroom door with his boot. "And then maybe, once you're all warmed up, you'll find out exactly how bad I can be."

58

"I want you to know—I didn't kill the bastard."

"Hell, Dad, of course you didn't!" Zach stared at his father, shocked that he would even consider that his own son would think such a thing.

They were in the kitchen of the house Zach had grown up in.

Sabrina had assured him that she really would be okay if he left her alone for just a short time, and she'd promised to lock the doors and activate the new security device he'd installed after the break-in, so he had driven over here after receiving his father's call.

"Not that I didn't want to," John said. "Because the guy was pond scum and treated his wife like shit, the way he was always screwing around on her. But she'd already told him that she wanted a divorce when he took off. Or at least when everyone thought he'd taken off."

"*I* know you didn't do it. *You* know you didn't do it—"

"What about Sabrina?"

"Sabrina? Hell, she'd be more likely to believe Santa Claus had entered into a conspiracy with the Tooth Fairy to kill her grandfather than to suspect you. You were the closest thing to a father she ever had. She adored you. Still does, for that matter."

"Even after the night crawler incident?"

Zach laughed and felt the welcome release of tension. "Yeah, even after that."

His father silently traced the initials Zach had cut into the kitchen table with the K-Bar knife he'd bought with money he'd made pulling weeds for Lucie Swann back when he was nine. In that same garden where her husband had been found this morning.

His father hadn't been thrilled by his decorating efforts, and Zach hadn't been able to sit down for two days.

"The thing is," John said, "people are going to talk."

Zach shrugged. "So, let them. Sticks and stones and all that."

"You got any pull with Nate?"

"What kind of pull?"

"I can't be questioned about the murder."

Zach was confused. "Why not? We both know you don't have anything to hide."

"Well, now"—John skimmed a hand over his buzz cut—"that's not exactly the case."

"Christ Jesus," Zach said, his frustration building. "Want to cut to the chase and get to what you called me over here to tell me?"

"If I'm asked where I was that night Robert Swann disappeared, I'm going to have to lie."

"Okay." Could his old man drag this out any more? "Putting aside the problem about the nitpicky little legalities against lying to the police about a capital crime, why?"

"Because I was with Lucie."

"Lucie was in Somersett. Covering some fancy dress ball at the Wingate Palace for the *Trumpet*."

"Lucie *was* in Somersett. She *was* in the Wingate hotel. But she didn't spend the entire night in the ballroom."

Comprehension struck. "Because she was with you?"

"Because she was with me," John confirmed.

It was Zach's turn to plow his hand through his hair. "You're a regular treasure trove of secrets, aren't you, Pop?"

"Wait until you and Sabrina have kids. See if you tell them everything," John suggested. "Then we'll talk about keeping private stuff exactly that. Private."

He had a point. Still, it was a little weird thinking about his father having a sex life. With Sabrina's grandmother, for Christ's sake.

"How long did the affair last?"

"It started before her marriage to the scum. First time we were together was the night before her wedding."

"Jeez, Pop!" Zach exhaled a sharp breath. Then held up a hand. "Sorry. It's not my place to judge."

Especially given his youthful indiscretions with Mrs. Buchanan, Swann Island's very own desperate housewife. Whose husband had, until the Buchanans' divorce, happened to be his high school football coach.

"I was drunk, like I was most of the time in those days, and she had a case of pre-wedding jitters when we met at the bar in Somersett, where her girlfriends were throwing her a bachelorette party. We both figured it was a one-night thing.

"But then, a few years later, she helped me climb out of the pit I fell into after your mother took off. Which, by the way, she had every right to do, because I'd come back from 'Nam a real mess. I drank a lot, smoked a lot of dope. Even screwed around some with Patsy Buchanan."

Oops.

"I never struck your mother. Not like I learned later that bastard Swann did Lucie. But, like I said, I came back pretty fucked up. The last straw was when I started staying up all night patrolling the perimeter of the yard."

"Armed?"

"No point in doing guard duty if you're not carrying a weapon," his father said dryly.

"We probably would've had problems anyway, because we'd drifted apart while I was away in the SEALs, and neither of us was the other's great love. But your mother deserved better, and I'll always be sorry I couldn't be the husband she thought she was getting when she married that kid in the dress white uniform."

"The whites get them every time," Zach agreed. Comprehension dawned. "Lucie was, wasn't she? Your great love?"

"She was the sun around which my entire universe revolved," John confessed. "If we'd met sooner in life, who knows? She married Robert Swann because, like I said, I sure as hell wasn't any prize back then. And because she'd made a promise to marry him.

"The damn ironic thing was that although we'd become best friends, we didn't sleep together again until the night it now turns out someone gave the scum exactly what he deserved."

"You're going to have to tell that story to Nate. If you're called in for questioning."

"I told you. I won't do that."

"Why the hell not?"

"Because I'm not going to sully a good woman's reputation."

Zach couldn't believe it. Well, actually, he could, because as crazy as it sounded, he could see himself doing the same damn thing. Reputation was everything down here in the Lowcountry. And, like he'd said the other night during the poker game, a gentleman didn't kiss and tell.

"It's not going to get to that," Zach said. He wasn't sure what he was going to do, but he damn well wasn't going to allow his father to take the rap for a murder he'd no way committed.

"We'll call Quinn," he decided.

"What the hell for?"

"He said Phoenix Team is a full-service agency. You work for them."

"I only freelance."

"Doesn't matter. Nate's undoubtedly willing to take all the help he can get to close this case fast. SLED has a lot of other cases they're juggling, and even if Cait is interested enough in the mystery to do a little digging on the side, it might not be enough to keep the FBI spotlight from shining on you.

"So, since we know you didn't do it, we'll let Quinn's mighty Phoenix Team prove it."

"That's not such a bad idea," John said.

"That's why I came up with it," Zach replied.

59

One of the few downsides to owning a restaurant that specialized in breakfast was you had to get up before dawn to begin the daily baking. Although Titania assured Nate she was more than capable of driving herself to work, ever since Cleo Gibson's murder he'd insisted on following her to the Wisteria Tea Room.

She'd been at work for an hour when there was a knock at the back door. With her mind still rerunning sexy scenes from Nate's masterful lovemaking and assuming it was the deliveryman from Surfside Dairy, she wiped her hands on her apron.

"Who is it?" she called out.

The familiar voice that answered was surprising, but certainly not threatening. Concerned, she opened the door.

He grabbed her, covered her mouth with a damp cloth. As she struggled against his superior strength, Titania breathed in a sweet scent.

Then everything went dark.

"Imagine that," Lillian Honeycutt murmured, as she sat in the sunroom of Whispering Pines with her husband later that afternoon. "Here everyone thought Robert deserted Lucie, but it turns out that he never left Swannsea at all."

She took a sip of the mint julep Harlan had mixed for

her. "To think of him having been buried in the garden all this time."

She ran her finger around the rim of the glass and shook her head. She'd had her roots touched up today, and since the weather was turning so warm, Mr. Dennis, her stylist, had tucked her still-blond hair into a classic French roll that kept it off her neck.

"I suppose it would be tacky to mention that it may finally explain why Lucie's hydrangeas always had blossoms twice the size that any of the other members of the garden club were ever able to achieve."

"You could never be tacky, dear." He smiled benevolently. "Though the suggestion that Robert Swann has been fertilizing Lucie's bedding plants may be a bit inappropriate under the circumstances."

"I suppose you're right." She took another sip. And sighed. "But you weren't the one losing to her year after year at the annual Flowerfest . . . Though, to be fair, I suppose she wasn't exactly cheating. Given that she had no way of knowing Robert was lying beneath those bushes."

Her brow furrowed as she considered that idea. "You don't think she *did* know, do you?"

"I have no idea." He took a sip of his bourbon and branch water. "I suppose anything's possible."

"There's bound to be gossip about a fatal love triangle," she mused. "Between Lucie, Robert, and John Tremayne."

"Tremayne doesn't appear to be the type to kill another man."

"Harlan, John Tremayne was a Navy SEAL in Vietnam. That's what he did for a living. Kill people."

"Well, it's always a possibility, of course," he allowed.

"He wouldn't be the first man to commit murder out of an act of passion. Nor would he be the first to have a black-widow female talk him into getting rid of a spouse."

Despite the gravity of the subject, Harlan laughed at that description. "Lucie Swann, a black widow?"

"You're the one who pointed out the other night, when Zach and Sabrina came to dinner, that no one was ever able to say no to Lucie."

"I wasn't referring to murder."

"I realize that, dear." She took another, longer drink. "I was merely thinking out loud."

"There was certainly no love lost between Robert and Jeremy Macon," Harlan said, offering another suspect. "Especially after Robert played him for a sucker."

"Yes. I always felt sorry for poor Jeremy. After all, he never was the sharpest piece of cutlery in the drawer. And although he didn't lose the bank, his reputation suffered a great deal. I'm not sure he's ever fully recovered from the scandal."

"A man's name is the most important thing he possesses," Harlan agreed. He smiled at his wife over the rim of his glass. "Except, of course, his charming spouse."

She smiled back. "That's very charming of you, Harlan."

"I meant it. You're very dear to me, Lillian. I couldn't have wished for a better wife."

"I know, dear."

A companionable silence settled over the plant-filled sunroom as they sipped their drinks and contemplated the events of the past few days.

"You killed him, didn't you, Harlan?" Lillian asked with absolute calm.

Her gaze was directed out the window at her formal English garden. At the puffy snowball hydrangeas, which, like everything else about Whispering Pines, had always come in second place to Swannsea.

"Yes."

She nodded. Took another sip. "And Lucie. She didn't die of a natural heart attack, did she?"

"No."

She sighed. "I suspected as much."

Turning back toward him, she took another, longer sip. "And now you're going to kill me as well."

He nodded. "Yes, dear."

He took the empty glass from her hand. Filled it to the brim.

"I'm glad. Because I fear all this ugliness is going to explode into a dreadful scandal and I'm not sure I'd survive it. Or even want to, for that matter. Especially given the fact that I haven't been looking forward to facing end-stage Parkinson's."

"I never meant to hurt you."

"You never have." Her smile was touched with regret. "You could have, of course. If you'd chosen to. I wouldn't have objected. But you never saw me that way. Never wanted me in such a base, sexual fashion."

"You were my wife. You belonged on a pedestal."

"Even if it grew very lonely up there?"

She'd no sooner asked the question than she waved it away with a beringed hand. "Never mind."

She looked out at the garden again, at the butterflies flitting around the bloodred flowers of the passion vine, and then continued to drink the doctored julep.

"My mother warned me, on the night before you and I were married, that men have certain needs. Needs their wives may not always be able to satisfy."

She sighed again.

Lifted a hand to her temple.

And missed her head by several inches.

"It's not going to be painful, is it?"

He appeared affronted by the very suggestion. "Of course not. You're my wife, Lillian. I've always loved you."

"And I you." The empty glass fell from her hand. "Would you do one last thing for me, Harlan?"

"Anything."

A sad, private smile touched her lips. "If only that had been true, we might not be in this situation."

She reached out her hand. "Would you take me to bed?"

For the first time since they'd begun this conversation, he appeared uncomfortable. "Lillian. Dear."

She trilled a laugh. Her breathing was getting slower. It was getting more difficult to focus her thoughts. To form the words.

"I'm not asking you to make love to me, darling. I'm merely asking you to lie with me. And hold me."

"Of course." He picked her up from the wicker sofa into his arms. Carried her down the hall and up the stairs.

By the time he'd reached the bedroom they'd shared for more than forty years, she was gone.

He placed her on the mahogany sleigh bed. Smoothed the hair that had escaped its tidy twist away from her face. Folded her hands.

He bent down and kissed her cooling lips.

Then he left the room, closing the door behind him.

60

Confused and disoriented, Titania felt as if she'd swallowed all the plough mud in the marsh, maniacs were banging away with jackhammers behind her eyes, and her shoulders felt as if they were being pulled out of their sockets.

As her exploring fingers discovered the metal bars, she realized, with a shock, that she was chained.

Inside a cage?

"It's about time you woke up," an all-too-familiar voice complained.

That clinched it. This was only a dream. Make that a nightmare. If she concentrated really, really hard she would wake up beside Nate and they'd make some slow morning love before getting up and going to work.

"Misty?" *Please let this be a nightmare.*

"It's me. And guess what, bitch? You're in the same fucking insane boat I'm in."

She'd never been able to tolerate the woman on a good day. With her head pounding, and metal cutting into her wrists, Titania was in no mood to attempt to be polite. "Would you just shut the hell up? And tell me where we are."

"You don't know?"

"If I knew I wouldn't ask, now, would I?"

"You're in the slave quarters at Whispering Pines."

"I am not."

"Are too," Misty shot back.

They could have been two kindergarteners facing off in a sandbox. Not that Titania could see Misty's face. It was so dark she doubted she could've seen her own hand in front of her own face. If she'd even been able to lift it, which she couldn't because it was chained to the damn bars.

"Nothing personal, Misty, but I'd really like to wake up now, so if you wouldn't mind getting the hell out of my nightmare."

"It's not a friggin' nightmare!" Misty shrieked.

No. If it were, that would've woken her up for sure.

"I can't remember how I got here."

"He probably drugged you. That's what he did to me. Well, some of the time. Most of the time he likes his slaves to be wide-awake. So we know exactly what he's doing to us.

"Believe me, you're going to wish you could develop amnesia pretty soon," she said. "If you live that long. The fact that he brought you here after killing his wife tells me that we're both pretty much toast."

"Harlan killed Lillian?"

"That's what he told me. Why would he lie?"

"You don't sound very upset about the prospect of dying."

Not that Titania was going to be killed. Because she had faith that Nate would find her. And when he did, she was going to quit playing hard to get and drag that man to the nearest altar at the very first opportunity.

"After you've been here a while, you'll realize it's not dying that's scary," Misty warned. "It's living like this that's the real nightmare."

"But why is he doing this? I don't understand."

Harlan Honeycutt wasn't some insane torturer who kidnapped women, locked them in cages, and chained them to the bars. He was a loving husband. A successful doctor. Admired and respected throughout the Lowcountry.

Which was why, against Nate's warning, she'd stupidly opened the kitchen door to him.

"You know those women?" Misty's voice cut through Titania's swirling thoughts. "The ones with the slit throats?"

"Of course." The reason for the question sank in. "You can't be serious. Harlan couldn't possibly be the Swann Island Slasher."

"Wanna bet?" Misty asked as the heavy door swung open with a fingernails-on-the-blackboard screech that was straight out of a horror movie.

A blindingly bright light suddenly came on overhead.

"I'm very disappointed in you, slave." Harlan Honeycutt's familiar voice tsked-tsked. "Telling all our little secrets."

Titania found Misty's transformation in mere days beyond comprehension.

Her hair, no longer its bright, sunny hue, had been dyed a flat black shade that was echoed in the shadows beneath her sunken eyes. She looked gaunt and pale, more like a wraith than the obnoxious sex kitten she'd been only days ago.

Realizing that Misty the Man-eater hadn't been exaggerating about the danger she'd landed herself in, Titania swallowed the metallic taste of terror that rose in her throat.

61

The call came in at six a.m., after Njanu had shown up at the Wisteria Tea Room for work and found the kitchen door unlocked, the dough for the cinnamon rolls risen so long it had collapsed into the deep bowl, a mug of cold coffee on the counter, and Titania nowhere to be found.

Although there were no signs of a struggle or violence of any kind, her purse, which Nate knew she would never have left behind, was in its usual place in the bottom drawer of her office desk. Her locked car was in the parking lot.

Fighting back a panic worse than he'd felt when his platoon was attacked in Fallujah's "ambush alley," Nate forced himself to stay calm as he organized the search, bringing in not only his own deputies but the same SLED officers who'd shown up when Robert Swann's body had been discovered.

Unsurprisingly, Zach was one of the first on the scene, accompanied by his father, Quinn, and other members of Phoenix Team. Rounding out the group were Special Agent Caitlin Cavanaugh, MIB, and two additional agents she'd requested from the Charleston FBI office. Meanwhile, troopers from SCDPS had set up a barricade and checkpoint on the single road leading to the ferry terminal.

Since the ferry crew had reported that no cars had

crossed the harbor that morning, she had to still be on the island.

"We'll find her," Zach assured Nate as they divided all the volunteers who'd shown up into search teams.

"No question," Nate agreed.

And when they did, she'd be alive and well. He refused to allow himself to think otherwise.

Eight hours later, working a grid pattern, they still hadn't found her. Not helping was the tropical depression moving in from the Bahamas, bringing rain that soaked the searchers to the bone.

"Quinn and I'll take the jon boat to this quadrant out in the marsh," Zach said as they met back at the command center set up in the sheriff's office. "Check out some of the fishing camps."

"Good idea," Cait Cavanaugh, who'd come back for yet more coffee, said. "We'll move farther south along the coastal shoreline."

"Tide's coming in," Quinn cautioned.

She gave him a look, replaced the stainless-steel top on the thermos, and walked out the door.

Even as concerned as Nate was about Titania, it had not escaped his notice that while the special agent had, despite the dire circumstances of their meeting, appeared glad to see Zach again, she hadn't said a single word to Quinn.

The former SEAL sniper shook his head. Although he did his best to hide it, his frustration was obvious as he yanked his hat down low on his forehead and went back out into the rain.

Although she'd desperately wanted to join the searchers, Sabrina reluctantly admitted that both Nate and Harlan had a point when they insisted that since she was not yet back at full strength, she had no business traipsing all over the island in the rain. Especially when she could be equally useful working with Njanu to keep the search teams alert and well nourished with gallons of coffee and plenty of sandwiches.

She was on the way back from the market after buying another twenty-five loaves of bread—knowing that Titania would cringe at the idea of store-bought—when her cell phone rang.

Hoping that it was news about Titania, she flipped it open without first checking the caller ID.

"Sabrina, dear," Harlan said, not bothering with any greeting, "I have a problem."

Don't we all.

"It's Lillian. She's very upset by all this, and it's allowed her imagination to run away with her, which can be an unfortunate side effect of all the medication she's on. While I've assured her that you're fine and safe, I'm afraid she won't be convinced that I'm telling her the truth unless she sees for herself that you're all right."

Sabrina glanced down at her watch. As much as she cared for the woman she'd always called Aunt Lillian, she needed to get back to the command center.

"It'll only take a few moments," he assured her, as if reading her mind.

Not wanting to suffer regrets about being too busy for Lillian as she had with Lucie, Sabrina decided a few minutes wouldn't exactly mean the difference between life and death.

"I'll come right over," she said.

"Thank you, darling," he said, his obvious relief telling her she'd done the right thing. "You've no idea how much this means to me."

62

"I don't understand."

Even as she tried to process what had happened to her once she'd arrived at Whispering Pines, Sabrina kept her tone soft, her expression guileless, struggling to keep Harlan from seeing her revulsion.

The last thing she remembered was him leading her into the sunroom. Then, somehow, she'd ended up in a cage in the old slave quarters, where, to her shock, she'd found he was also holding Misty Mannington and Titania prisoner in separate cages.

The good news was they were all still alive. And if Sabrina had anything to do with it, they'd stay that way.

"This has to be a mistake." Her heart was in her throat, making it difficult to get the words out. A blinding headache pulsed lightning bolts behind her eyes.

"My only mistake was not taking your damn grandfather out, tying concrete around his ankles, and dumping him into the sea," he said. "But I didn't have much time before daylight, and the gardener had finished turning over the soil for spring, so it seemed a sensible solution at the time."

Sensible didn't exist in the same universe as this man. How had he managed to live among them every day without anyone knowing how evil he was?

"Why did you kill him?"

"Because he suddenly found his conscience. Oh, it was all right when he was playing plantation master and whipping the girls I'd collect for us. Or raping and branding them."

Branding?

"Of course," Sabrina said weakly as a naked Misty whimpered at his description. Horrified, she realized that explained the oozing scab on the other woman's bottom.

"He also enjoyed when I brought home a Russian container ship pilot I met at a bar on the Somersett waterfront. It was the first time I'd allowed an outsider to join our little game. We made him the overseer.

"Unfortunately, he wasn't quite as rough as he could have been, certainly not as much of a disciplinarian as I am, which was a surprise, given that Russians have a reputation for being fairly brutal—

"But Robert enjoyed himself, just the same. Until he got squeamish at the end."

"The end?"

Sabrina exchanged a look with Titania, who, thankfully, except for a black eye and a nasty bruise along her cheekbone, seemed to be surviving far better than Misty. Of course, unless Sabrina had been unconscious longer than the time it had taken Harlan to move her from the sunroom, her best friend had been a prisoner for only a day.

"Well, now, we couldn't let the man leave, could we?" he asked reasonably. "Because he'd be bound to tell someone. And they'd tell someone, and so on, and so on, and our lovely game would end."

"So you killed him." Just as he'd done with that man who'd recently been found in the marsh.

"Slit his throat with a scalpel. It was quick and smooth and painless. But I could tell the murder disturbed Robert. And then two nights later, I also dispatched the girl, who'd gotten tedious anyway, since she seemed to have lost the ability to speak. All she would do was tremble and make these pitiful whimpering sounds."

A lot, Sabrina realized, like the ones Misty had begun making. Which didn't give Sabrina a great deal of con-

fidence about how much help the other woman would
be in whatever escape plan she and Titania could come
up with.

"Is that what you're going to do to me?" she asked.
"Whip me? Rape me?"

It sounded like the title of a snuff film.

"Of course not!" Appearing shocked, he ran the back
of his hand down her cheek. "You're family."

"So was my grandfather."

"Only by marriage. *Lucie* was my cousin. Which was
why, I have to admit, it was difficult to dispatch her."

The Florence suicide bomber began to seem rational
by comparison. The more Harlan explained and rational-
ized his horrific crimes, the more Sabrina's blood chilled.
But if she could only keep him talking, she might be
able to figure out a way to get out of here. A way to
get them all out of here.

"My grandmother's death wasn't natural." It wasn't a
question, but he answered it anyway.

"No. I had to kill her after she came to me with photographs she'd found while packing things away in the attic
to get ready for the construction. Robert, it appeared,
wasn't very discreet. Unfortunately she died of the so-
dium pentothal I gave her, before she could tell me
where she'd hidden them.

"Her mistake was that she gave me twenty-four hours
to turn myself in before she went to Nate Spencer herself. Naturally, I couldn't let her do that."

"Naturally," Sabrina murmured, even as she was
heartsick at this revelation.

"It's interesting," he observed, in that same spookily
conversational tone, "that you'd ask the very same question about Lucie that Lillian asked me only this
morning."

"And what did you tell her?"

Stall.

"Why, the truth, of course," he said with some surprise. "You don't stay married to a woman for more than forty years by lying to her."

"So Lillian knew? About my grandfather? And the women?"

"Apparently so. Which surprised me. Then again," he said, "they always say that the best marriages are where the partners keep a few secrets from their spouses."

"So I've heard."

Forget about what she'd told Zach about having fallen down the rabbit hole after the bombing. She'd now made it all the way to the lowest circle of hell.

"Does she know that you've taken me hostage?"

"No. I'm afraid she's beyond knowing anything."

"You murdered your own wife?"

"It was a mercy killing," he said, a bit defensively, Sabrina thought. "One she asked for. But 'hostage' is such a harsh word." He rubbed his chin. "I don't suppose you'd accept the idea of being my guest?"

"Gee, Harlan, you know, that sounds real peachy. But, while I admittedly haven't read all of the Miss Manners columns, I sure don't remember one that mentioned caging your guest and putting them in shackles."

"You have a point," he allowed. "But what else would you have me do with you? I couldn't risk you finding those photographs."

"Take me—take *us*," she corrected, "upstairs. If you truly intend to kill us—"

"Oh, I do," he assured her.

"Then let Titania write a note to Nate. And I need to write to Zach. I haven't told him yet that I love him, and I hate the idea of him never knowing how I felt."

"That's remarkably maudlin. But you do bring up an intriguing idea."

"What's that?" So far she hadn't been the least bit wild about any of his ideas.

"Can you type?"

"Of course. Doesn't everyone these days?"

"I don't. I've always had secretaries and nurses to transcribe my medical records. And Lillian always took care of personal correspondence. Not that she believed a typewritten note was appropriate for most personal occasions, but she did learn in school, when women were taught proper secretarial skills.

"So, here's what we'll do. I'll let you come upstairs and write your precious sweetheart note to your lover. And then I'll dictate my story to you. Because, although I have documentation, with photos and videotapes, it will be better for historians if I tell about my work in my own words."

He nodded, obviously pleased with that idea.

"You want to get into the history books."

"Of course. With Bundy, and the Boston Strangler, the Son of Sam, and all those other notorious serial killers—not that they ever reached my impressive body count."

He was, Sabrina could tell by his tone, vastly proud of that.

She also realized she'd gained a bargaining chip.

"I'll do it," she said, "if Titania and Misty can come with me."

"You don't have a choice," he pointed out. "You'll do what I say or die."

She shrugged. "I'm going to die anyway. The location doesn't make that much of a difference."

"What about that note you were so eager to write?"

"If Zach doesn't know how I feel about him, he's probably not the right man for me anyway."

But she knew he was. Had known it at sixteen, and knew it even more surely now.

He laughed at that. "You're a very pragmatic young woman. In that way you remind me a great deal of your grandmother. But Lucie proved more of a fighter at the end."

He shook his head. "She did not go as easily as Lillian into that good night."

With the drugs still in her system, and her head pounding, the idea of her grandmother's last moments on earth nearly had Sabrina passing out.

Or throwing up.

Or both.

"How did you get away with it?" she asked. A split second later, she'd answered her own question. "Because you're the medical examiner. You can put whatever you want on the death certificate."

"I always knew you were a clever girl."

He took a key from the pocket of his slacks and unfastened her shackles, then did the same for Titania, who, unsurprisingly, stubbornly didn't so much as rub her wrists. Unlike Misty, who crumpled to the steel floor of the cage like a rag doll.

"Get her up," Harlan snapped. "And let's get going. We have a manifesto to write."

63

"Is she a genius or what?" Zach asked the four men in the car with him as they raced toward Whispering Pines. He would've preferred the Viper, but they wouldn't all fit in it, and this was a team effort.

"A genius," John agreed. "Which bodes well for the intelligence of my future grandchildren."

"Don't rush the guy," Quinn said. "He hasn't even gotten the lady to say yes, yet."

"Piece of cake," Zach said.

So long as he could keep her alive long enough to propose.

No! He wasn't going to let himself think those old dark negative thoughts.

Thanks to Sabrina's having called him on her Black-Berry and leaving it on after she slipped it into the pocket of that full gypsy skirt she'd been wearing the last time he'd seen her, they'd been able to track her to her location.

It was also how they were able to hear Harlan's description of at least some of his alleged dozens of murders. And how they knew that so far, Sabrina, Titania, and that ditzy Misty Mannington were still alive.

In a bit of good luck, thanks to having planed Lillian Honeycutt's humidity-swollen doors, Zach knew exactly where Harlan's second-floor office was located.

Of course, he could be planning to write his murder book for the masses in the library. But remembering back on their evening there, Zach couldn't recall a computer in the room. Which he hoped meant that Honeycutt would be holding the women in the office.

To avoid any surprises, given that the house had been added on to several times over the years, Zach's father had found the blueprints for Whispering Pines in the island's building-permits files. Not wanting to waste valuable time going down to the office and having Nate flash his badge at some bureaucrat, Zach had simply hacked into the database.

Then he told Quinn that Phoenix Team really ought to solicit the island government account, because the average third grader could hack his way into that site.

"Okay. Let's synchronize our watches."

The line might sound corny to civilians watching it in the movies, but it wasn't at all humorous to the former military men, who knew the importance of split-second timing while carrying out a mission.

Watches were set. Positions assigned.

Nate, John, and Zach would storm the room, Nate and John from the interior hallway and Zach coming down from the roof, then kicking open the French doors that opened out onto a small balcony, which, though not nearly as large as the veranda, would still prevent him from having to crash through the glass of a window.

Although he would've preferred taking Harlan out himself for what he'd done to Sabrina, her grandmother, and Titania, Zach had planned enough missions to know it was best to go with the experts. And when it came to snipers, there were none better than SEAL specialist Quinn McKade.

Today Zach wasn't about to settle for anything less than the best.

Whatever he'd drugged her with was still fogging her mind enough that Sabrina was having difficulty keeping up with Harlan's rambling narrative of murders going back nearly forty years.

Like so many children who'd grown up in the South of the nineteen forties and fifties, he'd been taught that the War Between the States had been a states' rights issue. Very little attention had been given to the actual dirty commerce of slavery.

Which was why it wasn't until Harlan's sophomore year of high school—when a history teacher who'd moved to Swann Island from Vermont to escape the seemingly endless winters had assigned her students a paper on the slave auctions that had taken place in Savannah, Charleston, Richmond, Somersett, and other cities all over the South—that he viewed, for the very first time, a woodcarving of a naked, bound African woman being led by a rope to the auction block.

The fifteen-year-old boy became instantly, painfully, aroused.

In the beginning, he would find the occasional girl who would be willing to get naked, stand on a barrel, and allow him to point out her feminine attributes to imaginary buyers.

But when even the most adventurous balked at rougher play, he had turned to prostitutes, during his college years, which was when Robert Swann had joined the game.

Until the whippings and brandings, rapes, and other degrading acts of humiliation were no longer enough. When the first murder occurred, Robert had dropped out. And had died for his defection.

Unfortunately, though, he hadn't gotten rid of the photographs taken over those years. Photographs that had gotten Lucie killed.

"I don't understand why no one ever knew," Sabrina dared to ask as she sensed he was getting to the end of his rambling tale of madness and murder.

"Because I chose my slaves carefully," he explained. "Usually hookers or women who the authorities wouldn't look for very hard. Women with histories of promiscuity, adultery. Addictions. That sort of thing."

"But from what I've heard, that nurse, Cleo Gibson, didn't fit your profile."

"No. She was an impulsive kill. She'd been so excited the day before at the hospital, talking about her pretty little bedroom in her pretty little house, that I decided to fit in a play date."

Sabrina wondered what kind of monster could smile at the memory of terrorizing a woman, raping her, and finally stabbing her multiple times, then leaving her naked corpse on the road.

"As for dispensing with their bodies, that was simple." He waved a hand toward the window, back toward the old slave quarters, which he'd turned into torture chambers. "I simply buried them with all the other slaves, from when Whispering Pines was a working indigo plantation.

"It was only when Sumner starting building his fucking golf course right next to my fence line that I had to find a new place to dump them."

Which was, according to reports, precisely what he'd done. Dump them, like yesterday's garbage.

"You won't get away with this," she said mildly.

Strangely, a calm had come over her, allowing her to remain outwardly composed, carry on a conversation, and type up the story of this man's insanity, while her brain was scrambling trying to come up with escape routes.

"I don't intend to," he said, his tone as mild as hers. "Just as I had no intention of leaving my dear wife alive to face all the media circus and scandal that would have surely killed her slowly and painfully, given her weakened condition. I have no desire to end up with a needle in my arm in the state execution chamber."

He reached past her into a desk drawer and pulled out a revolver.

"Once I kill you, your friend, and that sniveling slave over there"—he waved the revolver toward Misty—"I'll take my own life.

"It's been a good run. I've had an extraordinary life. One most men could only dream of."

As he looked over her shoulder at the computer monitor, Sabrina caught a glimpse of something out of the corner of her eye.

No. Not *something*. *Someone*.

Even as her heart hitched, she fought to keep her voice calm.

"So, no regrets?"

"Not a one," he replied.

Zach was outside the French doors, hand up, fingers counting down.

A sideways glance toward Titania revealed that she'd seen him, too.

One.

Two.

On the count of three, both doors to the office burst open.

John dove for Misty, covering her trembling body with his, while at the same time Nate and Zach dragged Titania and Sabrina to the floor, covering their bodies with their much larger, stronger ones.

There was a roaring in Sabrina's ears, like the surf during a hurricane. But it didn't stop her from hearing the sharp crack that splintered the air.

An instant later, Harlan Honeycutt crumpled to the floor, a spreading red stain blossoming in the center of his chest.

One shot. One kill.

64

The ambulance took a weeping Misty away. Sabrina hoped she would be all right, but suspected it would be a long time before she was back to the way she'd been before stumbling into Harlan's sick and deadly web.

Or maybe this would turn out to be a life-altering event for Misty. Perhaps, having survived an experience that so many others hadn't, she would realize she'd been granted a second chance at life.

As Sabrina herself had.

Although she'd protested, Titania had allowed Nate to take her to the clinic, where she'd been given some ice for her bruises, then sent home and told to rest. To which Nate had responded that he would be sure she stayed in bed.

Something she'd had no intention of arguing with.

"I can't believe I'd forgotten turning on my Black-Berry when I got edgy about the way Harlan was acting," Sabrina said after they'd taken John back home, where the team had gathered to plan the rescue mission.

They'd picked up the Viper and were on their way to Zach's rental house in the marsh. Although Sabrina still loved Swannsea, she wasn't quite prepared to return to it tonight, knowing that both her grandparents had been killed beneath its slate roof.

"It's probably a good thing the drugs he gave you made you forget." He laced the fingers of his right hand with her left. "If you'd thought of it after waking up in the cage, you might have shown a tell."

"A *tell*?"

"Yeah. The little signs people give that tell others what they're thinking. Like when you're playing poker and the guy across the table tugs his ear when he draws a bad card. Or taps his finger on his leg beneath the table if he's bluffing. That sort of thing."

"Oh." She thought about that for a moment. "So what are your tells?"

"I don't have any."

"I don't believe that."

"It's true. Which is why I almost always win."

"Except when your father takes you to the cleaners," she said.

"He told you about that, did he?"

"Not just me. I think everyone on the island knows who the big kahuna of poker is in the Tremayne family."

Zach shrugged. His lips curved. "He's not getting any younger. I figured his manhood might be in danger if he was publicly beat by his kid."

"Yeah. I noticed how old he looked the other day nailing those forms together. There were guys out there a third his age who were having trouble keeping up with him."

"It's a ruse. We all get together and do it for his ego."

"Right," she scoffed.

"He loved her," he said suddenly. "My father, your grandmother."

"I think I always sensed it. There was something special between the two of them. He'll miss her."

"Yeah, and he'll regret that he didn't figure out what was happening and save her. But he'll deal with that. Because he's a survivor. And that's what survivors do."

"I guess we both know something about that."

"I guess we do," Zach agreed.

"It's amazing that Harlan got away with all those murders for so many years." She shook her head, still stunned by the idea of the family's own Ted Bundy living among them. "Do you think all the stress of having the golf course built by his burial grounds and Lillian's illness was what had him spinning out of control?"

"Who knows?" Zach shrugged. "The guy was a nutcase for a long time. Makes sense that he would eventually unravel." He glanced up at the rearview mirror. "Shit."

"What?"

"You're going to think I'm crazy."

"Let's see. My grandfather's spent the past fourteen years buried in my grandmother's garden. My grandmother was killed by her insane cousin, who murdered not only his wife but apparently scores of other people that the police will probably start digging up any day—"

"Which will probably send Sumner's golf community property values into the crapper."

"Proving that there's always a silver lining," she added. "I myself have been drugged and kidnapped, forced to write a Unabomber-type manifesto, and have all these parts of my memory that seem to have disappeared, like soap bubbles. So, given all that, who am I to call anyone crazy?"

"Okay, maybe a better word is 'paranoid.' "

"Have I mentioned that I don't think I'll ever look at a fish delivery truck the same way again?"

"No, but that makes sense. Because you've got a reason. I could swear that every time I go out, someone follows me."

"Undoubtedly one of those infamous SEAL groupies," she quipped. When he didn't immediately respond, she looked over at his grimly set face. "Oh, wow. You're serious, aren't you?"

"Yeah. I am."

"Well, why don't you pull over? Not everything has to be planned to the nth degree. If the guy following you pulls over too, you can ask him, or her, what the hell's going on."

He glanced over at her. "That's not such a bad idea."

"Thank you."

He twisted the wheel, scattering gravel as he pulled onto the narrow shoulder.

"You might have thought about slowing down first."

"What fun would that be?" He leaned over and brushed a kiss across her lips.

A pickup truck pulled up behind them. And stopped. But did not cut the lights.

"Stay put."

"You're still wearing your gun," she said. Although she'd been really glad he'd brought it to Whispering Pines, it still made her nervous.

"That's the point," he said. "I'm going to leave the car running. If anything bad goes down, you get the hell out of here."

"Like if you're in trouble I'm going to leave you out here in the middle of the night in the marsh? Think again, Tremayne."

"I'm serious, Sabrina."

"Yeah. I can see that from the way your jaw juts out. Which is, by the way, I believe, a *tell*. Besides, if I let anything happen to you, who's going to father my children?"

"Children?"

"Your father and I had a little chat while you and Nate were talking to the state guys who showed up after you called in the shooting. He thinks we both missed out, being only children. So he's suggesting at least two. I thought three is a nice round number. Well, maybe not exactly round. But it *is* prime."

She glanced past him out the window. "Oh, look. It's the bulldozer guy."

"Who?"

"The man who's been driving the bulldozer digging up the garden. The one who found my grandfather. Which I suppose I should thank him for, because, as upsetting as it admittedly was, in the long run—"

"Fuck!"

"What's the matter?"

"Do you know what his name is?"

"Of course not. I haven't said more than ten words at a time to him. You know—good morning, nice day, great job. Does it make you feel powerful to drive such a great big machine? That sort of thing. Why?"

"Although he goes by Gunney, which is short for 'gunnery sergeant' in the Marines—"

"Which explains the cap. The USMC cap," she said at his look.

"Yeah. But I've taken over writing the payroll checks the last few weeks, and that guy's real name is R. L. Cunningham."

"So?" Comprehension, when it dawned, was stunning. "Oh, my God. It couldn't be . . ."

"Richard Cunningham? I'll let you know."

He opened the door, flooding the interior of the car with light for a moment. Allowing her to see both the hardness and the dread in his blue-gray eyes.

She watched the two men walking toward each other, like they were reenacting *High Noon* or something.

And remembering all the weapons the former military men who'd shown up to rescue her had been carrying, she had not a single doubt that R. L. Cunningham was armed with more than a cap pistol.

She cut the engine. Both men turned toward the light as she opened her passenger door and came around the wide red front of the car.

"I thought I told you to stay put," Zach said.

"You did. And I told you I wanted children."

She held out a hand. "Hello. I've watched you work. You're so amazing at what you do. I'd be afraid to even climb up that high."

She gave him the same smile she'd used to break the news to Brad and Angelina that their three-bedroom suite wasn't going to be available quite yet because the pop star currently in the room with members of her en-

tourage had read her horoscope that morning and taken
the warning about not making any sudden lifestyle
moves way seriously.

"You're the Marine's father. Richie."

His eyes narrowed, going from her to Zach and back
to her again. "Yeah, how did you know?"

"Well, the name, for one thing. And from what Zach
has told me about your son, there's a very strong family
resemblance." She reached out and touched a hand to
his arm. "I'm very sorry for your loss."

"Uh, thanks."

"No. Thank you. And your son. For your service."

She turned toward Zach, who had remained silent,
apparently willing to play this out. She did notice, however, that his hand stayed close to the holster he was
wearing on the back of his jeans.

"I imagine Mr. Cunningham has come here to hear
about his son," she said to Zach. "About how brave he
was on that mountain. And how he took out those tangos and saved so many lives."

"He told you about that?" Gunney asked sharply.
"About the battle?"

"A bit. Not all the details, of course, because I'm not
sure I'd fully appreciate them, being a civilian and all.
But he certainly told me about how brave Richie was."

Her smile was soft, sincere, and warmed her eyes.
"Although . . . I hope you won't be offended, but he
called him Opie."

To Sabrina's dismay, the big tough Marine's eyes
turned bright with suspicious moisture.

Oh, great. Make him cry, idiot.

"His mother and I called him that," he revealed.

"I didn't know," she said simply. "I'm also sorry you
lost your wife so tragically. And so young. I know the
pain of losing family members, Mr. Cunningham, having
lost both my parents and more recently my grandmother.
I also know, as I'm sure you do, that the pain never
goes away. But you do get so you can live with it."

She thought of Lucie's dream of her walking down the stairs in her wedding gown and felt her own eyes grow moist as it struck home that her grandmother wouldn't be here to see her come down those stairs to a waiting Zach.

"I'm sorry." She brushed at a tear with the back of a finger. "I guess I'm a little emotional. I've had a rather difficult day." Week. Month.

She turned to Zach. "Why don't you invite Mr. Cunningham to go out on your boat, Zach? I'll pack a lunch, and you can tell him about his son." She looked up at the older man. "I've recently discovered, thanks to you and your bulldozer, that knowing the truth, however difficult it might be, is vastly better than not knowing. And wondering."

The two men looked at each other.

"There's not going to be any work done on the site until SLED takes that tape down," Zach said. "I haven't been out on her since I got back. I'd be glad to have some company."

Gunney took a deep breath. Dragged his broad, scarred hand down his weathered face. "Yeah. Sounds okay to me."

"I'll meet you at the pier at noon."

"I'll be there." He shoved his hands in his back pockets and looked back and forth between Zach and Sabrina. "Would you mind, ma'am, if I have a word with Mr. Tremayne?"

Sabrina hesitated.

"I promise I won't shoot him."

She nodded, her expression as serious as his. "I'd appreciate that, Sergeant. Given that I have plans for him."

Both men watched her walk back to the car, climb in and shut the door, casting the interior back into darkness.

"I came here to the island to kill you," Gunney said.

"Yeah," Zach said. "I figured that out."

"Then I figured maybe I'd kill *her*. So you'd know

what it felt like to lose someone you loved more than your own life."

Zach shook his head. "Never happen. No way would I have let you touch a hair on her head."

"Yeah. I got that tonight. Good job taking that Honeycutt guy out. Put a nutcase like him into the system, and you never know what's going to happen. Maybe he escapes. Maybe he cops an insanity plea. Maybe he gets put in some hospital for the criminally insane and one day, twenty years from now, he's back on the streets. Threatening your wife. And kids."

"We're definitely on the same page there," Zach said.

"So." The Marine blew out a long, slow breath. "I guess I'll see you tomorrow."

"Noon," Zach agreed.

He was halfway to the car when Gunney called his name. "Yeah?"

"Better hang on to her. Because, although I don't know how you did it, being as ugly as you are, and all, and a fucking frogman to boot—but you caught yourself a keeper."

"Roger that," Zach said with feeling.

"So?" Sabrina asked as they sat in the car on the side of the road and watched the truck's taillights disappear into the night. "Can you tell me what he said?"

"He thinks I'm ugly."

"Well. They say beauty's in the eye of the beholder."

"And he's not real impressed with SEALs."

"I've heard there's a great deal of competition among the various branches of the service. So that's probably a positive thing. Makes everyone play their best game."

"There is that. He also thinks I ought to keep you."

"A brilliant man."

"You won't get any argument from me on that." He dragged a hand down his face. Cursed. "When I realized that monster had you, thought about what he might do to you, that he might even *kill* you, I was more terrified than I'd ever been in my life."

"I wasn't."

He shot her a disbelieving look.

"I wasn't," she insisted. "Oh, I was shocked. And horribly upset. But I knew that somehow you'd rescue me."

He shook his head in a blend of disbelief and admiration. "Do you have any idea how much I love you?"

"I do. Which is handy, since I love you that much back."

"I'd planned to do this right. Get all dressed up and take you out to some fancy dinner over in Somersett, ply you with imported wine, get down on one knee, dazzle you with a diamond—"

"You dazzled me years ago, Zach. I certainly don't need a fancy dinner, or wine, or even a diamond."

"Are you saying you'll marry me?"

"I think that's an excellent idea, since we're going to be having those children. And a dog. A big furry one that sheds all over the furniture and that'll chew up my expensive Italian shoes and dig holes in the garden. I was never allowed to have one when I was growing up, and I always swore if I ever settled down anywhere, I'd get one."

"Whatever you want. It's yours."

"Well, then, that's easy." She leaned over, framed his face between her palms and kissed him. "I want you.'

"Hoo-yah."

"I take it that's another SEAL affirmative?"

He grinned as he twisted the key in the ignition. "I'll demonstrate exactly how affirmative when we get home."

Home. Was there any more beautiful word in the English language? It didn't matter where they lived, she realized. Swann Island or Timbuktu. So long as they were together, they were home.

She laughed as he floored the accelerator, pushing her back against the leather seat.

"Roger that."

Turn the page for a sneak peek at

Crossfire

The next exciting book in
JoAnn Ross's High Risk series

Coming from Signet in September 2008.

Somersett, South Carolina

"Do you really have to leave so soon?"

"Now, darlin'." Brigadier General John Jacob paused while tying his spit-polished shoes to nuzzle the neck of the lusciously naked blonde lying in the middle of the rumpled sheets. "You know I do."

"Just a few more minutes?" She arched her back like a sleek Siamese, displaying the voluptuous breasts, which, although not natural, were still damn fine.

He was tempted. What male wouldn't be? A former Miss Watermelon Belle, Meredith Hawthorne was one helluva good lay. But he'd begun to suspect that she had set her sights on marrying up.

Her husband—who hadn't even attended one of the service academies—had only made captain before joining the faculty of the Admiral Somersett Military Academy. While he himself was not only a retired brigadier general but had graduated from West Point, as had all the males in his family, going back to the Revolution.

He was also, if Meredith was to believed—and it stroked his ego to accept her word—a better lover. But, dammit, he'd been honest about his intentions from the start. They were both married. Neither was looking for commitment. Both had reasons to keep their affair discreet.

As the highly visible commandant of a very successful

athletic department (which brought in beaucoup bucks from ASMA alumni), he was on the fast track to be commander of the school whose roots had first been established in the Lowcountry to supply the government with a citizen corps of cadets during the War of 1812.

His wife, the daughter of a former chairman of the Joint Chiefs, whom he'd married solely for her social and Pentagon connections, had served him well. Loyalty prevented him from putting her out to pasture just because some blond beauty queen gave the best blow jobs in the South.

"Your husband's going to be home at eighteen hundred hours," he reminded her.

He should know, given that he'd been the one to send Captain Hawthorne to Savannah on a recruiting trip. Both VMI and the Citadel had their eye on a seven-foot high school basketball center, but Jacob had every intention of winning the phenom for ASMA.

One more trip to the Final Four and he figured that plush commander's office with its stunning view of the Somersett River bridge, and the harbor beyond, would be his.

"I know." She sighed prettily, drawing his attention back to her breasts. "It's just that every time I'm with him, I wish I was with you." She touched a hand to his face. On a distant level, he admired the way she allowed the single tear to trail down her cheek. "In fact, just the other night, when he was upstairs, playing war games on that damn computer, I was thinking that maybe I should just tell—"

"Don't." He grasped her wrist. Tight enough to make her flinch. "You're not going to tell your husband anything. Because if you do, I'll make sure he's shipped out of here so fast that pretty blond head of yours will spin. And given that you dropped out of college when you nabbed yourself an officer and a gentleman, it's not as if you have a lot of career skills."

His face was inches from hers. His other hand was

tangled in her long hair, holding her gaze to his. "Unless you decide to take that pretty cock-sucking mouth of yours out on the pro circuit."

She frowned. Her eyes swam. This time the tears were real. "That's nasty."

"That's what we're about." His tone was hard. He could have been raking a cadet over the coals for an honor code infraction. "We get together twice a week to do the nasty. I get my rocks off, you get a man who, instead of treating you like glass, knows you like rough sex and likes giving it to you the way you want it."

"That's it?"

Hell. Realizing that this could get out of hand, he backtracked. "No." This time it was he who touched a hand to her unhappy face. "You're right. It was cruel and uncalled for. You know you mean more to me than that."

He stroked her cheek. "But we've got to be careful. If your husband gets so much as an inkling of what's going on, I could kiss my future good-bye."

"That's the most important thing, isn't it?" She sniffled, but from the tilt of her chin, he could sense she was regaining the spirit that came so naturally to stunningly beautiful women. Women accustomed to the attention of men. "You becoming commander of ASMA."

"It's important." He was not above lying. When necessary. But this was the absolute truth. "But you need to keep your eye on the big picture."

"Which is?"

"I'm going to need a proper hostess once I move into the commander's house."

Sky blue eyes narrowed. "I assume that would be your wife."

"You'd assume wrong." He stroked her arm and felt her stance soften. "You know that Eleanor and I haven't been living as man and wife for some time."

"That's what you told me."

He could also tell she hadn't entirely bought the story.

He didn't blame her, but again, it was the truth. His bride had let him know early in their marriage that she found sex messy and distasteful. So long as he behaved discreetly, and never slept with any of her friends, she'd been more than willing to allow him his affairs.

"Our marriage has always been"—he paused for effect—"complicated. But it's become more and more difficult for us to live under the same roof. So we have an agreement that as soon as I become commander, we'll divorce. At which time Eleanor will receive a substantial financial settlement."

From the way her smooth brow furrowed, he could tell she was sensing the lie. "Why would she give up the opportunity to play lady of the manor?"

"Simple. Because she's never enjoyed the role of an officer's wife."

"You could certainly have fooled me."

"She's a good actress." And a spectacular hostess. Having always believed in giving credit where credit was due, he allowed that Eleanor Longworth Jacob's inborn Southern graciousness was part of the reason for his success. "But she's growing weary of the part."

His lover's hair had tumbled over her shoulder. He smoothed it back, skimmed his hand over her breast, and felt her heart pick up its beat. "Besides, there's another reason she wants to be free as much as I do."

"What's that?" Her flesh was warming. Tempting him even as he played her.

"She's in love."

"You're kidding."

"On the contrary. And there's more." Like putty in his hands, her mouth softened beneath his as he pressed a line of kisses from one side of her lips to the other. "Her lover just happens to be a woman."

Her head snapped back. "Your wife is a lesbian?"

"It seems so."

"When did you find this out?"

"I've always suspected. But that's all it was. A feeling. She confirmed it last month."

"Wow." He could see the wheels turning as she absorbed the lie. "Talk about 'Don't ask, don't tell.' "

She tilted that busy little head and studied him. Despite her Barbie doll body and sugary Southern belle charms, Meredith Hawthorne was a cold, calculating female. It was one of the things he honestly admired about her.

"If that got out, it could really screw up your chances for making commander."

"Exactly." He kissed her longer. Deeper. Leaning her back against the pillows. "Which is why I'm counting on you to keep my secret."

He skimmed his lips down her rosy torso. He didn't really have the time for this, but neither could he risk her deciding to come clean with the cuckolded captain. "For just a little longer. Until we can be together."

Slender thighs opened. "In the commander's house," she said.

"Absolutely," he agreed robustly as he clamped his mouth over her and closed the deal.

Five minutes later, twenty minutes before Captain Hawthorne was due back from Savannah, Jacob, with his future firmly back on track, left the house that was six blocks from the ASMA riverfront campus.

It was a pretty neighborhood. Brick sidewalks were shaded by leafy green trees lined up like soldiers in front of tidy nineteen-thirties bungalows; the Stars and Stripes flew crisply from every porch; lawns were neatly trimmed, gardens darkly mulched.

It was dog days in the Lowcountry, the air so scorchingly hot it rippled along the ground as he strode with military bearing to the black Cadillac parked in the Hawthornes' driveway.

A sound like a tree branch cracking overhead shattered the summer silence.

Although he'd spent his entire life around weapons, Brigadier General (Ret.) John Jacob never felt the shot that penetrated his skull.

He was dead before he hit the bricks, crimson blood oozing from the hole left by the copper penny–colored rifle slug.

One shot. One kill.